ASSASSIN STRIKE

Knowing they had been discovered, the five men who were following Shunlar and Dolan rushed at their prey, drawing steel as they did. Shunlar and Dolan stood back to back, turning, watching the five who circled them.

Shunlar pushed her cloak from her head and dropped the illusion covering her, standing to her full height. Dolan knew what had happened by the way the two men who advanced on him froze and seemed to squint into the darkness behind him.

One of the three men who faced Shunlar lunged at her from the left, slamming his sword down with a forceful two-handed blow. She fended it off with an upward left-handed block and, as he felt the reverberation of the meeting metal clang through his arms, her right hand loosed the wrist dagger which found its target in the throat of the man farthest to her right.

Immediately the man in the middle swung his sword, which narrowly missed Shunlar's right shoulder as she turned aside. Bending her right elbow and bringing her hands together around the pommel of the sword, she brought the blade across in a wide arc. But her attacker ducked as her blade swung murderously through empty space where his head had just been. Moving so fast, the man lost his footing in the ice beneath the snow, and he went down on one knee. As he caught his balance, his head came up, a fatal mistake. The last thing he saw was her sword swinging in a return arc toward his neck.

Other Books in
THE SHUNLAR CHRONICLES *by*
Carol Heller

THE GATES OF VENSUNOR

THE SANDS OF KALAVEN

A NOVEL OF SHUNLAR

CAROL HELLER

AVON BOOKS, INC.
1350 Avenue of the Americas
New York, New York 10019

Copyright © 1998 by Carol Heller
Published by arrangement with the author
Visit our website at http://www.AvonBooks.com/Eos
Library of Congress Catalog Card Number: 97-94886
ISBN: 0-380-79080-7

First Avon Eos Printing: July 1998

AVON EOS TRADEMARK REG. U.S. PAT. OFF. AND IN OTHER COUNTRIES, MARCA REGISTRADA, HECHO EN U.S.A.

Printed in the U.S.A.

WCD 10 9 8 7 6 5 4 3 2 1

To Stuart

my darling husband
who years ago said to me,
"Why don't you sit down and write it?"

PROLOGUE

LONG AGO THERE LIVED A MERCENARY NAMED Shunlar whose skill at tracking placed her much in demand. While on a mission to find a stranger in the city of Vensunor, Shunlar was held captive by the dreaded Lord Creedath, who was conspiring to take over the city of Vensunor. For, it turns out, Shunlar possessed powers of which even she was not aware. And, as became clear, it was up to her to learn the truth of her mysterious heritage, meet her birth mother, and find—only to lose—her first real love.

Due to Creedath's greed, he died when the Lifestone of his ancestor exploded in his hands. Everyone rejoiced as Vensunor was released from the yoke of Creedath's tyranny. However, when the Lifestone shattered, Shunlar was standing near her foster-mother, Cloonth, and a sliver of the crystal became embedded in each of their arms.

Afterward, Shunlar and Ranth decided they want to learn more about the parents they never knew. She will go to the Valley of Great Trees and learn about her people. He will return to the Desert of Kalaven and learn about his. They agreed to separate and meet in one year in Vensunor.

1

ONE

MUMBLES OF HALF-SPOKEN WORDS WOKE HIM JUST as the first light of morning was beginning to give outline to the shape of the room. Instinctively Ranth turned his head away and raised his arm, just in time to block a very solid blow from the active—yet still sleeping—woman at his side. Keeping a firm grip on her wrist, he ever-so-gently approached the edges of her mind with a delicate touch, waking her.

My Lady, he whispered to her mind-to-mind. *It is but a dream. You are safe. Now wake up before you do me some permanent damage.* His voice had a touch of humor to it, but was nonetheless very serious.

Shunlar's arm muscles softened. When she opened her eyes, an embarrassed gasp escaped her lips. "Did I blacken another eye, or were you fast enough to stop my punch this time?"

Only then did he release his grip from her wrist, after which her hand moved across his face. In the darkness, she knew when she touched the bruise by the way he sucked in his breath, but he didn't stop her fingers from their exploring.

"Ranth, forgive me for making such a mess of your eye." The concern in her voice said what her words did not.

Ever since the death of Lord Creedath the nightmares had come. Each night they seemed to grow more terrifyingly vivid—and this was only the third night. Shunlar realized in the early morning chill that she was, once again, drenched in sweat from the terrors she had just woken up from. She rolled

2

closer to Ranth. Wrapped in a tight embrace against his chest, she let the tears come while Ranth rocked her and stroked her hair. After a time the tears subsided and they made love as dawn sent soft rays of sun into the room.

The room they shared was in the wing of the Temple of Vensunor where couples resided. Spending the last three nights in this part of the Temple had seemed to strengthen their desire for each other, not that they needed any help. Time was a most precious commodity to them now. In but four more days they would embark on separate journeys: she to the Valley of Great Trees and he to the Desert of Kalaven, home of the Feralmon. The thought of parting made them seek each other's company every waking minute. Torn between feelings of desire for each other and feelings of curiosity about the parents they had just met, a compromise had been reached, more or less. Since Shunlar and Ranth would soon be parting, they were left alone.

Several minutes after their heartbeats returned to normal they stretched, yawned, and rose from the bed, pulling their clothes on side-by-side. Exhaling a breath through her teeth, Shunlar announced, ''I must speak to Alglooth and Cloonth about the dreams. They're increasing in length as well as in detail, but as soon as I'm awake, I can't remember anything. Only the feeling that something is wrong stays with me for hours.''

The tone of her voice grabbed Ranth's attention, making him realize the dreams must be more disturbing than she had been able to explain to him. He knew that it wasn't easy for Shunlar to admit she needed help from anyone. He had been unable to see her dreams when she attempted to show him the pictures by mind-touch, no matter how hard he tried. They both thought this was odd, but had dismissed it. Besides, when Ranth saw how relieved Shunlar was to be awake and no longer caught up in the dream, he hadn't pressed her for more information.

Ranth nodded his silent agreement and squeezed her hand as they walked together to the baths. It seemed they wanted to touch every inch of the other so they could commit to memory even the slightest bends, curves, or scars. With Shunlar's hand-to-hand combat experience, Ranth had much more of the latter to memorize than she did.

Together in the water, he tried to rub away the crease between her brows so many times that it annoyed her until finally she slapped his hand away. She could feel the tension stiffening her spine and shoulders. His retaliation was to splash her face and laugh at the way she scowled.

She stared at him with water dripping from her chin as an apology formed itself in her mind. *There is no reason for you to be angry with Ranth*, she lectured herself. *He is trying to help.* Breathing a deep sigh, she reached out for his hand. As they touched Ranth met her thoughts and accepted her apology. The effect on Shunlar was instantaneous. She calmed down, sinking deeper into the water. He could feel her troubled state of mind and touched no further, just maintaining an easy presence at the edge of her mental barrier, closing her off from his thoughts for the moment also.

Yes, he agreed, *we must speak to Alglooth and Cloonth soon.* Then he remembered the truth. They were leaving in four short days and Alglooth, Cloonth, and Bimily were already gone. Now he had a crease forming between his eyebrows. As a wet, tentative finger began to rub away at the crease, he looked up into Shunlar's smiling face.

In the process of covering up their thoughts from one another, Shunlar suddenly felt strangely alone. Realizing this, she quietly asked Ranth, "Is there a reason for your scowl, or are you mocking me?"

"Worry. All I'm up to is worry. I know we have our separate lives to return to and people that care about us, but I cannot help thinking that our parting should not happen right now. I keep having this feeling that you will need me soon and I'll be on the other side of the world, unable to come to you." He kept his eyes down, seeming to study his hands under the water as he spoke.

"Ranth, do you remember how disturbed I told you I was the first night we spent under this roof together? It was never my intention that we remain here. I want you to come with me. It is important that we leave today. Away from the Temple and Vensunor and the noise of all the other minds, I believe I will be able to think more clearly. You can still join your father on his journey and I'll go on mine to meet the rest of my people, but we can't shelter under this roof another minute. If we do, I fear for my sanity.'' A shudder ran up her spine, causing ripples to move across the surface of the calm pool as she began to tremble.

The shrill, frantic tone of her voice was so very unlike Shunlar that it caused Ranth to snap his head up and stare at her for several seconds. Then he embraced her and held her until the shaking stopped. Once she recovered, a calm came over her, as well as an unusual, faraway look to her eyes. Then she felt again that burning itch across the back of her forearm. Without thinking she scratched at the spot that hurt when she did so.

"We have no need to stay here, Shunlar. Certainly our families will understand our need to be off together, alone. They may even be relieved to have us gone from their sight. How long can you be in the presence of two young lovers and not be affected?'' he joked, trying to get her to laugh. When she didn't, he continued.

"But how can we speak to Alglooth or Cloonth now? They're many days ride from us and you need some answers very soon. Perhaps we should speak with my father or your mother or uncle about the dreams. I worry that they may be doing you some harm. You know that I felt the fear wash over you just now, don't you? What caused you to shake like that? Tell me, please.''

He was becoming more concerned and would not stop questioning her until she gave him an answer. Whatever had happened to her while she was a captive within the dungeon of Lord Creedath was causing this, he was sure. When Ranth had questioned her for details about it, she had refused to discuss it.

Only from the mouths of Alglooth and Bimily did he receive any information about what had happened to Shunlar under Creedath's severe questioning. The truth was, Creedath had very nearly killed her with the forcefulness of his untrained telepathic scan. So deeply had Shunlar hidden within the recesses of her mind—while maintaining the illusion that she was an old man as a disguise—that she had not been able to find her way back to reality. If Shunlar had been alone afterward, she would have died. As it was, her awareness wandered on a plane between death and sleep for an entire night and part of the next day, eluding her father, Alglooth, as he searched for her.

"Shunlar, I know this has something to do with your interrogation by Creedath," Ranth whispered.

"No. I refuse to remember anything that has to do with that man, curse him and the sow that bore him. It is over and I need more than anything to wipe the memory from my mind."

Ranth continued to hold her and refused to let her get away with no for an answer again. He kept on in a most gentle way and finally convinced her to answer a few questions. Soon, Shunlar began talking.

They were in deep rapport when Marleah came into the baths. She noticed them on the far side of the hot water pool and immediately misinterpreted what they were doing. Having never been deeply in love, Marleah just shrugged and smiled and let them have their privacy. *They look so serious,* she thought to herself. There seemed to be nothing unusual about the way Shunlar and Ranth left the baths a short time later, so engrossed in their private conversation that they never saw her.

After collecting their few belongings from the room they shared, Shunlar and Ranth went off to find breakfast in the dining hall. Entering the room, Ranth saw Benyar sitting at a table with Gwernz and Delcia. They waved for him and Shunlar to sit with them.

"Am I correct to assume you are both leaving us?" asked Delcia with a curious smile.

Ranth blushed and Shunlar spoke up when she realized he could not. "Your hospitality is most kind and we thank you, but I need the quiet of my forest to gather my thoughts and recover from the . . . last few weeks." Shunlar now blushed when she realized that she had stumbled over her words.

Gwernz knew what she meant about needing the solace of the trees. He sent a silent, thankful prayer to them for their protection and deliverance. He cast a warm smile at his niece, nodding his head. "I understand," was his only reply.

"Father, by your leave, I will go with Shunlar." Ranth

bowed his head to Benyar and without waiting for an answer, continued. "And be assured that I will be here on time to begin our journey to Kalaven."

"Actually, we will hardly know you are gone, we have seen so little of you these last three days." Benyar's black eyes glinted mischievously.

Ranth turned to speak to Delcia next. "Coming back to the serenity of this, the only home I have ever known, has done much to restore my health. By your leave, also, I will accompany Shunlar."

"Of course, my son," Benyar and Delcia answered together, then laughed. It helped brighten the mood of everyone at the table.

Even Shunlar seemed to be in much better spirits when Marleah arrived for breakfast. She sat next to her daughter and put an arm around her shoulder, careful not to open herself up to anything other than physical contact. Marleah was, after all, a master at shielding her thoughts from others. She surprised herself at how much she enjoyed being around this daughter she knew so little about.

"How wonderful to see you all smiling. Can I be let in on the secret?"

"Marleah . . . mother," Shunlar answered, not being entirely used to calling her that yet. "Ranth and I have decided to leave today for my cottage on the outskirts of the city. I need to be in familiar surroundings, away from so many minds. Since you must pass by that way on your return to the Valley of Great Trees, I will give you and Uncle instructions on how to find your way there, and I will join you then."

Shunlar found it hard to ask for her mother's permission, but the surprised look on Marleah's face compelled her to do so. "Does that meet with your approval?"

"I understand your need to be away from people . . . together," was all Marleah answered. Then she bent around Shunlar to get a better look at Ranth and winked.

"If you intend to do more sparring, be sure to brush up on your blocking technique." More laughter followed and Ranth blushed, self-consciously touching his bruised eye.

Relieved to be nearly on her way, Shunlar found she was very hungry. She practically inhaled a large bowl of hot porridge with butter and honey, then reached for the platter of cheese and apples. Ranth seemed to be famished as well, and together they finished their meal in pleasant conversation with their family and friends seated around them.

As Shunlar and Ranth rose to leave the table, Morgentur entered the room. From his purposeful look it was apparent that he knew what had transpired just moments before. Solemnly, he approached the group to stand next to Delcia. They joined hands; Delcia's face held a look of inquiry that was soon replaced by a look of understanding. Turning to the group at the table, they announced in unison: "We ask you, Shunlar and Ranth, to join us at the Cauldron of the Great Mother. A message awaits you within that sacred presence. Come with us now, young ones."

Delcia and Morgentur, the spiritual leaders of the Temple of Vensunor, held out their hands to Shunlar and Ranth. They rose and bowed to the Venerable Couple, accepting their offer. The four of them made their way from the dining hall to that part of the Temple that housed the sanctuary of the Cauldron. As it had happened so many times before, when Delcia and Morgentur reached the ornately carved doors, robed acolytes who stood guard at the chamber of the Cauldron of the Great Mother bowed and pulled the doors open. The couple entered with Ranth close behind, leaving Shunlar standing, awestruck at what she saw.

Before her awaited a triangularly shaped room. The marble floor was a deep red color, with thin veins of silver and gold sparsely interspersed throughout. From the center of the ceiling hung the enormous pale green Cauldron that was nearly transparent. Directly beneath it, the polished marble floor appeared to have a large crack-like opening, from which a thin wisp of white vapor was beginning to spiral, rising toward the Cauldron.

Delcia and Morgentur, halfway to the oracle, turned and beckoned for Shunlar and Ranth to enter and stand beside them. Ranth offered Shunlar his hand, which she reached for without looking, her eyes fixed on the sacred Cauldron. The doors closed behind them as they stepped closer and the flames of the oil lamps danced in the currents of moving air. The two younger people joined their hosts and together they walked across the room to stand in the center, encircling the oracle.

"We greet Thee and honor Thy word, oh Great Mother of us all. Grant us the wisdom of Your words today." The ritual greeting, spoken by Delcia and Morgentur, in the language known as Old Tongue, was understood by the two younger people, who waited with their heads bowed respectfully.

As the curls of mist that rose from the crack in the floor became thicker, they wrapped around the Cauldron itself, which began to glow. Branches of mist reached out from the sacred vessel to slowly coil around the four who encircled it. The glowing Cauldron seemed to begin to boil as runes and ancient symbols appeared on the sides in flashes of light and then were gone.

"For you who journey afar, it is time to partake of the oracle which awaits your questions. Which of you will be first?" Delcia's delicate voice asked.

Ranth bowed from the waist and said, "If it please, I will."

"Form a question in your mind, if you have not already done so, and you will know by the signs when to draw forth your answer."

Thinking that he would ask about Shunlar's troubling nightmares, when Ranth looked inward he was surprised to find that his thoughts were drawn to the journey he would soon be undertaking to meet his mother and the rest of his people. He started as the Cauldron made a bubbling sound. Thin strands of vapor curled up and runes flashed on its sides. Taking his cue from Delcia and Morgentur, he reached into the sacred vessel and removed the glyph for Mountain Cat. A second draw produced Hunter, a third the rune for Saw, and the fourth was Single Eagle. After drawing the fourth tablet, the mists and lights subsided and Ranth moved back a few steps.

Now it was Shunlar's turn, and she paused and quieted her thoughts to find her question. In doing so she was startled when the face of Creedath appeared, smiling at her in a sinister way. Though she knew the man was dead, she began to sweat, and her breath quickened with fear. She bowed from the waist when she saw the Cauldron acting as it had done for Ranth, bright symbols appearing and fading on the sides, mist growing thicker and wrapping itself around her middle as if to draw her close enough to put her hand into the vessel. She stepped closer and did so, drawing out the tablet for Horse and Rider, then second choosing Female Warrior. Her third choice was the Female Dragon, and last she drew Mountain. Abruptly the Cauldron quieted. When Shunlar stepped back, the last final wisps of vapor faded, as did the lights.

As Delcia and Morgentur prepared to begin the ritual of thanks and closing, they observed the color of the Cauldron darkening, becoming nearly black. Suddenly a thick, black mist began to spill over the lip. Before the mist could escape the container, however, Delcia and Morgentur locked arms around it, very nearly knocking Shunlar and Ranth down they moved so fast. A high-pitched keening sound rose from the opening in the floor, nearly drowning out their voices. Within minutes the floor began to quake and the sacred Cauldron, suspended by its three golden chains, began to swing as if it were trying to break out of the circle created by the arms of Delcia and Morgentur. Standing their ground, their voices became more insistent until finally, the sound stopped, the black mists turned back to their normal white color, the vessel regained its shade of pale, opaque green, and the floor, thankfully, stopped moving.

All of them were shaken and for a few moments did not move, as if waiting for the ground beneath their feet to begin trembling again. When sufficient time had passed, Delcia and Morgentur slowly unlocked arms and spoke the ritual words of thanks to end their session with the Cauldron of the Great Mother. When they finished they joined Shunlar and Ranth, who were standing off to the side clinging to one another.

"Respected Teachers, never have I witnessed anything like this in my past meetings with the sacred oracle. Perhaps it was the nature of our questions?" asked Ranth.

"We have no explanation for what occurred here today. It is a puzzle that we will attempt to resolve another time. For now we can only review what has happened and answer any questions you may have about the meaning of the answers to your questions," answered Morgentur. "Come, let us record what you have withdrawn, then we can sit for a time and reflect upon their meaning. I know you are both anxious to leave and we will not keep you too much longer.''

Ranth and Shunlar followed them to a table in one corner
of the room where the tablets they had picked could be written into the Temple's permanent record and, hopefully, explained. It never occurred to either Shunlar or Ranth that one
or both of them might have been the cause of mysterious
black mists spilling forth or the room shaking.

Delcia and Morgentur knew better. They suspected it had
to do with Shunlar, because, after all, the change had happened after she had chosen the runes. The why of it was a
much bigger puzzle, the answer to which they hoped to discover soon. In the meantime, they pretended that everything
was fine and did not allow the disturbance to affect their feelings of love for the two young people before them. They
freely offered interpretation and advice to the best of their
ability and wished the young couple a safe journey.

Hours later, after the farewells were behind them, Shunlar
and Ranth made their way to her cottage hidden in the woods
on the outskirts of Vensunor. Weary from lack of proper
sleep, Shunlar was happy to let Ranth take care of the horses
once they had arrived, and was even more thankful that she
had allowed the cooks of the Temple to pack them an abundance of food. All she wanted now was sleep, and later, a
meal that took no preparation. Overjoyed to be in familiar
surroundings, she slept at last, until she was awakened at dusk
by Ranth's familiar touch. Her smile told him all he needed
to know. She had rested and was returning to herself. His
heart beat contentedly as he gently kissed her cheek.

Two

BIMILY SAID HER GOOD-BYES TO EVERYONE THE morning after Creedath's demise, anxious to be away. There were now four people who knew of her shape-changing abilities, and she had come close to telling Benyar. Before she did that, it was best to go. At the outskirts of Vensunor she quickly found the cover of trees. When she was sure no one was near who could see her, the air around Bimily sparkled with a pale blue shimmer. Where a lovely copper-haired woman had once stood, there now stood a large black eagle. She lifted herself off the ground and shot upward toward the stars at a dizzying speed, ecstatic to be airborne once again, the wind currents adding to her speed.

Bimily flew for hours, going north toward the mountains where she knew her mate waited. It had been nearly a month since she had seen him and the air was pierced by the sound of her calling out to him as she flew. Finally, one of her calls was answered and the larger male joined her in her flight. He appeared happy to see her and Bimily reached out with her awareness to the male's mind, projecting the feeling of hunger. He immediately banked off toward the sea and she followed, content to be in his company once again.

The fall weather was colder this far north, near the sea, a constant source of food. Today was no exception. As Bimily looked down she saw several fishing boats on the water, all but one heading back to land with the day's catch. It was early morning and the boats had been out all night.

She had taken her eyes off her mate, but his call pulled her attention back to him. As she turned back to the direction of his voice, another call, this time a frantic one, rent the air. Bimily dove toward him without thinking. At the last minute she saw that he had somehow gotten tangled in the enormous net that was being slowly hauled onto the last boat. She dove repeatedly, tearing with her talons at the netting which was twisted around his neck and one leg.

When his head was free, Bimily used her beak to attack the netting that tangled around his leg. His wings hit her head several times in his frenzied struggle to free himself. Focusing all of her attention on her mate, she forgot about the men aboard the boat. Until, that is, an arrow pierced the male eagle's chest, quickly followed by another through his neck.

Too late, Bimily spread her wings to fly away and she was struck in the leg. She screamed in pain, then rage, as she flew out of range of their arrows. From above she circled and watched as they hauled the giant net across the deck of the vessel. She saw them disentangle her mate's limp body and hold up their trophy. She screamed again and flew away to find the nest. When she landed, she bit off the head of the arrow that protruded from her leg before she changed back into her human form. Heartbroken and bleeding, she cried as she pulled the arrow from the calf of her right leg.

The wound was deep and she had to tie a piece of cloth above it to stop the bleeding. Exhausted, she fell asleep, only to awake several hours later and remember what had happened. She was alone for the first time in years. Because eagles mated for life, and Bimily had no desire to be alone, her life as an eagle was over and she must choose another animal shape. Hungry and wounded, she could starve, unable to hunt for food in her condition, a prospect that didn't appeal to her. Her only recourse was to leave this place and the memories behind as soon as possible.

However, Bimily knew that to shape-shift when wounded was very dangerous and should only be done if one's life depended on it. If the pain were great enough to take away her concentration, the shape of the animal would not hold, and she would return to human form. Not a good thing to do, especially if you were in the body of a bird flying miles above the earth. There was also the possibility that the wounded

animal's awareness might take over her consciousness, causing Bimily to temporarily forget who she was, especially if
the animal whose shape she had taken on was not particularly
intelligent.

Sundown was hours away, so Bimily decided to remain in
the nest and sleep until then, and make her decision at dusk.
She would most likely try to make it to Stiga to ask for
Cloonth and Alglooth's help. It was going to a be difficult
journey.

It was dark when she woke and she was hungry. When she
moved her leg, Bimily remembered again everything that had
happened. Hot, bitter tears of loss streamed down her cheeks
as she tried to block out the pain and return to her eagle form.
A flicker of blue light outlined her body as her first attempt
failed. Her second attempt worked for a brief moment and
the eagle reappeared, only to shrink to a much smaller form
as a stab of pain shot through her leg. She should never have
put any weight on it. She looked down at herself and discovered she was now a small, black bird. She called out and a
sweet, mournful song trilled on the air.

So, she thought to herself, *a black songbird is it? Well, at
least I'm not a godforsaken carrion eater. Let's see if I can
find myself something to eat and then be on my way.*

She would have known better had she been in full control
of herself, but Bimily had no choice. An entire day had gone
by and she needed food. Bimily the small, black bird swooped
down and began to peck away hungrily at the seeds scattered
on the ground. She wasn't a very smart little bird, not like an
eagle, and she hopped pitifully on one leg. She never saw
who captured her or how it was done. When she woke the
next morning, Bimily was still a small bird. Her leg had been
bandaged and she was in a cage. She had a fever and only
wanted water. It had been provided. Once she satisfied her
thirst, she ruffled her feathers and put her small head under
one wing, too sick to care or think about escape, too sick to
realize she wasn't really a small, black bird.

ᏗᏎᎬᎬ

THE NEED TO HIDE FROM HUMANS HAD BECOME AN obsession with Cloonth. She also desperately wanted to be alone—alone, hidden deep beneath the ground. She and her mate Alglooth had returned to Stiga, the long-dead city that had been their home for centuries, but being here had not felt right either. She was growing acutely aware that the human form of her beloved, Alglooth, was beginning to frighten her more each day as her pregnancy advanced. The changes to her physical appearance were what had begun to bother her most, however. She was not more than a month with child but already her belly was swollen and protruding beneath her clothes.

The evening they left the Temple of Vensunor, she had felt as if her skin was so dry it might crack. Already the scales on her upper body had lost their sheen and her wings were becoming dull. This, only Alglooth had been allowed to observe in the privacy of their bedchamber. Their leave-taking seemed normal enough, a few tears for Shunlar, with a promise to meet her again soon. Only Bimily looked at her curiously, but once their good-byes were said, Bimily returned to the conversation she had been engaged in. Everyone was still so elated at the death of Creedath that a mood of festival prevailed, and Cloonth and Alglooth's decision not to spend even one night under the Temple's roof went unremarked. No one suspected Cloonth's fear.

The strain of flying had taxed Cloonth's endurance so much that she had to ask for help the last half of the journey. Her first pregnancy had not been like this at all. No, she had had more energy than ever before in her life, and not for one day had she experienced such foreboding. And there was this strange rash on her left forearm that hurt when she scratched at it. It was becoming more pronounced and the bumps were turning an ugly shade of yellow.

They landed in the light of midmorning, her panting and pale, her very concerned mate holding her up. One or two steps were all she managed before Alglooth scooped her up in his arms and carried her to bed where she slept away the day. In the evening when he brought her some broth, the look on his face told her more physical changes had taken place, and rapidly.

With a wavering hand Cloonth pointed to the mirror, which Alglooth reluctantly brought to her. Nothing could have prepared her for her reflection. She was no longer the pale, small-boned beauty with high cheekbones and delicate white curls framing her face. No, quite the opposite. Her color was now a light brown and her face was taking on a definite animal look. Her small nose was growing into a snout, and her jaw had elongated to accommodate a tremendous set of teeth. Her hair was now massed mostly on the top of her skull, just covering a ridge that started at the crown of her head in the form of round nubs, and seemed to be growing all the way down her spine. She ran her fingers over her back and blinked at Alglooth, who held the mirror for her with a steady hand.

When she opened her mouth to speak, a long stream of flames cracked the mirror in his hand. He never flinched but bent to kiss her cheek and then knelt down to pick up the pieces of broken mirror from the floor.

A sound unlike anything he had ever heard touched his ears while his mind felt the familiar touch of his mate. She screamed in horror at what she was becoming and begged to be taken to a place deep in the mountain. He looked up from his work and saw her enormous eyes spilling over with tears. The words—if you could call them that—coming from her mouth were unintelligible, but the message to his mind was clear. He nodded his assent. "Yes, my beloved, we will leave this hour. I understand your needs now more than ever. We will find the cave of our mother and there in the room where we first breathed life into our own mouths, you will feel safe when you give birth. And I will be at your side, never fear.''

Her reply came as a total assault to his senses. His body began burning inside and out, causing sweat to run from all his pores at once. The mind-touch of Cloonth overwhelmed him with instant forced rapport. He seemed to be within Cloonth's mind, seeing what her eyes were seeing. With her eyes he saw himself looking at her and the look of shock on his face. It was translated instantly to his body by a feeling of cowering and an overwhelming desire to hide. Sudden terror for his life and hers, as well as visions older than time flooded his mind. There were memories of men stalking and killing with swords and spears. Then he heard over and over in his head Cloonth's voice as it pleaded with him, *Hide me and save our children. Hide me and save our children. Hide me and save our children.* Over and over the chant continued.

With the greatest of effort Alglooth tried to pull his mind free from his mate's. Tears welled in his eyes as he looked upon Cloonth lying on her side trembling in fear, no longer able to control her thoughts or emotions. Taking great care not to frighten her, Alglooth managed at last to extricate his mind from the grip she had on his. In the next instant he blinked and realized he was on his knees in the middle of the room gasping for breath. Somehow, he managed to construct around her the illusion that she was in a cave deep beneath the mountains. Gradually, her trembling stopped.

Heaving a great sigh of relief, Alglooth sat on the floor collecting his thoughts, planning the next move. He could tell by watching Cloonth's breath rising and falling that the only answer was to hide her, as she had pleaded with him to do. But where? He knew he had just moments ago promised to take her to the cave where they had been born, but could she really want that? He remembered finding the place when they were young, but they had only stumbled upon it while they were exploring. The bones of their mother, or what they thought to be her, occupied a great portion of the cavern. They had left her remains untouched, hurrying out before they had time to look around.

Is the cave damp or dry? Will she need a bed to lie upon? How long will she be there? Once we reach the depths, will she permit me to stay, or will I frighten her as well? He could answer none of his questions, nor could he expect a response from Cloonth. He rubbed his face, trying to clear his head, when he heard a strange clicking noise. Focusing on her peacefully sleeping form, he watched as the scales on her arm dropped off and formed a pile on the floor. The skin beneath the scales was slick, moist, and somewhat orange in color. As he continued to watch, the skin slowly dried, hardened, and became a shiny shade of darker brown. She continued to metamorphose before his eyes.

Hours later Alglooth was still sitting on the floor, watching, trying to make some sense out of what was happening. The only recognizable parts left of his beloved mate were the iridescent green and gold wings, which though much duller were now twice as large as before, and the small patch of white curls that clung to the top of her head in a three inch wide strip, and continued down to the middle of her neck. Her belly was enormous and seemed to be growing as he watched. Nothing else about her resembled a woman. And she continued growing. She had almost doubled in size and he could tell she wasn't finished yet.

He must risk a mind-touch now, before she changed completely and didn't know him. *What if she doesn't recognize me now?* he thought to himself. Alglooth rose and slowly approached her sleeping form. A deep rumble came from her throat as he stopped in midstep and took one step backward.

It might already be too late, he said only to himself. *No, she is merely sleeping a deep, restful sleep at last.*

It seemed to take hours, but at last he mustered his courage and sent a small tendril of thought to her mind. The presence it touched seemed more accepting and gracious, but now there was a depth to it that could best be described as very crafty.

"My beloved, it is Alglooth, come to see what I can do to make you more comfortable. I apologize for waking you, but you must eat something dear one, for we have a short journey to make."

The thought of food sparked a deep yearning in Cloonth, something older than time. "Food, yes, ummm-meat." And her jaws began to work back and forth, but she did not open her eyes. That took effort and she was not prepared to see anything more. Fear washed over her as she asked again, "Bring me meat, will you?"

Very hesitantly he asked, "Shall I bring raw or cooked meat?"

She yawned and sent out a stream of fire nearly five feet long that threatened to set the room ablaze as she answered. "You sound so frightened, my love. I remember you and won't do you any harm, nor myself for that matter. Just . . . no more mirrors, please. And hurry with the food, lots of food. Cooked, of course, tsk, tsk." After more nuzzling into the pillows that were dwarfed by her size, she was once again asleep.

He left then to hunt, relieved that she had responded to him so positively, and pleased with himself that the cave surrounding her made her feel secure at last, even if it wasn't real. Alglooth took to the sky instantly and found a lone deer, killing it swiftly and mercifully. A very hot, concentrated blast of fire startled it and brought it down as its heart stopped. Alglooth removed the hide and viscera, and he blasted it again with a fiery breath, cooking the meat and curing the hide at the same time. Once done, he wrapped the meat in the hide and took flight.

He began to reach out to Cloonth with his awareness, but stopped suddenly just as he was about to land. Hovering above the steps of their dwelling, he blinked several times in disbelief, then closely studied the heat trace of what appeared to be a very large being who had passed through the doorway. The marble steps were not damaged at all, but the wooden doorway was in sorry shape. She must have kept right on growing and have had to break out of the room.

Alglooth turned so fast that the venison he had draped over his shoulder swung out in a wide arc and threw him off balance. He righted himself and flew after Cloonth's vastly different, much larger heat trace path. He knew instinct had taken over, yet he trusted her last words to him, that she did, in fact, remember who he was. That thought urged him on faster as he followed her to the western side of the mountain. There, slightly off to the middle, was the opening she had flown into. He followed, still carrying the food.

At the mouth of the cave, he landed and listened for any

sounds of her. Her heat path glowed brightly ahead of him in the darkness. As Alglooth entered the cave, he began to form an announcement of his arrival in his mind. Something warned him not to startle her now. Just as he rounded a bend, her awareness settled over him smoothly, enveloping him in a blanket of desire. But it was the desire to please her and nothing more. A feverish feeling to do her bidding overcame him as he hurried down into the depths of the mountain, tunneling deeper at each turn. It got warmer the further down he went. A soft golden glow filled the air; the heat nearly suffocated him, as at last he entered the chamber.

Her voice echoed in his head, *Food, my beloved. Food, please,* with the barest of whispers.

Alglooth knew Cloonth's condition was weak from the erratic way her control of the compulsion on his mind slipped away and grabbed hold again. Something that felt like an apology formed itself with her next breath, but as he stepped into the light of the chamber she drew up to her full height and gasped. *What are you? Who are you? You're so small! Where is Alglooth, what have you done to him? Tell me now or I will kill you!* Her tone was desperate and the threat very real.

Alglooth threw the food onto the floor of the cave and stood his ground as he looked up at what his mate had become. She had grown at least fifteen feet tall and her coloring was darker than before. Gone were the delicate pale skin and slender bones. She was a dark brown and golden color, with wings to match. No longer did white curls cascade down her back. Now, starting at the top of her head, a giant ridge of spikes ran down the length of her spine. Her long, slender hands had become huge paws with five-inch claws at the end of each finger.

Cloonth, my Cloonth, it is truly me, Alglooth. Here, feel for me deep within yourself, he offered as he sent a stronger mind-to-mind connection toward her. *I understand that this must be a shock to you, beloved, but you are the one who has been doing the growing and changing, not me. As I promised, here is food.* He pointed down at the venison carcass he had brought and realized that to her, this was not going to be a meal, but merely a snack.

"Oh, I have been doing some growing, haven't I?" was her thunderous reply. Too late he covered his ears as the volume of her unintelligible words echoed off the walls of the cave. She spoke a language he had never before heard. Instinctively he knew it was the tongue of dragons.

Very delicately she reached for the deer carcass under the hide, uncovered it with one flick of her enormous, claw-bedecked fingers, and picked the entire thing up with one hand. She hungrily bit off the legs, mashing the meat with her mighty jaws, the juices dripping from her chin. With small tendrils of smoke rising from her nostrils, she finished it off, bones and all.

Ah, so delicious. Tasted of berries and it has made me hungry for more. Can you manage another three or four, my dear? she asked, this time remembering to communicate with him mind-to-mind.

Alglooth only stared at her with his jaw hanging slack. When he did not answer, she reached toward him with one long claw that shut his mouth for him. Touching him physically, she controlled herself long enough to show him how she could "make" him bring her more food. Cloonth let him know that a small part of her had no wish to force her will on him, but that part of her awareness was diminishing more and more rapidly with every second. A compulsion had seized her and in a very precise way she let him know that he would continue to bring food to her. He could only agree, and did so knowing that what was happening to her was well beyond either of their abilities to comprehend or control.

Though he was trapped by her, Alglooth knew she was the being he loved and her physical form was in no way frightening to him. It just took a lot of getting used to. No, something about her was actually drawing him nearer. He reached up to remove her claw from beneath his chin. It had broken the skin and he felt a slow trickle of blood run down his throat. He held onto her finger and stepped forward, unafraid. He needed to be with her as much as she depended on him now solely for her survival. One of their bodies might be different now, more different than either of them could ever have fathomed, but their bond of love remained. He tried to put his arms around her, succeeding only in spreading them wide across her belly. She very carefully—very delicately, so as not to crush him—wrapped hers around him and they stayed this way for a long time, feeling the lives that stirred within her belly.

"They clamor for food and sap my strength. Please go again and return soon, my dearest." This time her voice was a hoarse whisper and she sounded bone-weary.

Alglooth left the cave with a heavy heart, downcast, knowing that this change was exacting such a toll on her. Only after he surfaced from the entrance to the tunnel and he was in flight did he dare ask himself the question that troubled him. *Will she return to her former self once she has given birth, or will I have a dragon for a mate the rest of my days?*

So troubled was he that it was days before he noticed the messenger dove that had arrived, perched alongside the others with a note attached to its thin ankle. He had been so busy supplying Cloonth with a constant source of food that he hadn't attended to any of the normal aspects of life.

He opened the note and read it, a growing frown covering his face. It was from Shunlar and it told of her dreams and the difficulty she was having trying to sleep each night. She asked his help in figuring out the reason for them. She awaited his reply at her home in the woods, where she would be for only the next four days.

So, my daughter needs me. My mate needs me. What of my needs? Do my needs mean anything? Alglooth was near breaking down from fatigue. He hunted all night and most of the day. Cloonth's belly continued to grow while he grew thinner by the hour. All she did was demand more meat. Shunlar would just have to wait.

He sent a reply attached to another dove's ankle, one that disclosed nothing about the circumstances of his and Cloonth's life at the moment, but only the fact that her pregnancy and the coming children took all of his attention at this time. There was no way he could come to her because it meant he would have to leave Cloonth and he could not do that. It hurt him deeply to reply in this way, but he could only deny his firstborn's call for help. He suggested she look to her mother's people and to Ranth. With tears in his eyes he watched the dove fly away with its message as he took flight to resume his hunting.

Four

TOMORROW WAS THE DAY THEY WERE TO PART AND there was still no sign of an answer from her father or Cloonth. Shunlar was deep in her own troubling thoughts as she absently picked up her belongings and stuffed them into her saddlebags. She had to do something, anything, to keep herself busy and occupy her mind. She didn't want to go on thinking about the dreams. The first night she and Ranth had spent here in her cottage, she had not been plagued by the dreams. She was so elated the next morning that Ranth could hardly believe she was the same woman. But when the second night approached a sense of foreboding came with it. Once she slipped into sleep, the terror returned.

Ranth finally left the bed and tried to sleep on the floor, it being safer than dodging blows from her flailing arms and legs all night. The skin around his left eye was finally returning to its normal shade. But he didn't sleep either. He spent most of the night watching her toss and turn and fight her imaginary attacker.

The most worrisome part of it all was that he could not see into her dream. When he tried to look at it by reaching out to her mind with his, an unusually forceful barrier pushed his touch away. Nothing he did seemed to be able to change or influence the dream. Shunlar was so deeply asleep that he could not rouse her all night. The same thing had happened the previous nights as well. While at the Temple, Shunlar had thought to blame the nightmares on being in such close prox-

23

imity to all the others who also were housed under that roof.
Ranth knew now that that was not true.

The only consistent thing was the way Shunlar scratched
at her right forearm. Yesterday he had put an ointment on the
strange rash. When Shunlar thrashed about the most, she also
rubbed and scratched at her arm. When he examined the spot,
he could only see the chafed skin that was beginning to bruise
from her constant abrading.

Tonight, they had decided to stay awake all night. A good
strong wind was blowing and threatening to bring rain. Shunlar had banked the fire to keep the room warm and set about
laying in an ample supply of wood. Ranth had decided he
wanted fresh meat for dinner, and she expected him at any
moment. With a sigh Shunlar decided to check the doves once
more for a message. As she left the cottage she sensed Ranth
approaching and sent out a soft mind-touch to him. He answered and hurried his pace, promising her a rare feast tonight.

Her heart leapt when she checked the doves and saw the
newcomer sitting on its perch. Quickly she removed the message from the bird's ankle, and ran back to the cottage to read
it, out of the rain that had begun to pelt the ground with huge
drops.

"Hurry Ranth," she called out loud, laughing as he stumbled in through the doorway. Shunlar slammed the door behind him and as he began to unload his bags, she remembered
the message from Algiooth.

"I found," he paused for breath, "a wonderful meadow
filled with greens and mushrooms. And see, there is even
dessert! There was an old hollowed out honey tree. Doesn't
this look delicious?" He offered her a large chunk of honeycomb wrapped in a piece of oiled leather with one hand,
while he continued to talk, mostly to himself, with his head
partially inside his bulging carrying pouch. He was still busy
pulling food from the pouch, talking to himself, when he realized Shunlar was not taking the honeycomb from his hand.
She was sitting on the end of the bed reading the message
with a shocked look on her face.

"They cannot help me. In fact, they recommend I speak to
Marleah or Gwernz." She tried to cover up her disappoint-

ment and added quickly. "It's getting ready for the children. Has them working so hard, I imagine." Shunlar looked up at him asking, "Ranth, what will I do now? I don't know Marleah or Gwernz well enough to trust them with something like this. I don't know if they will understand what this is about. They may not believe me."

Ranth listened to her, shaking his head as he wiped the honey from his fingers with a wet cloth. "Shunlar, I don't mean to make light of this, but after they spend one night sleeping near you, as they will on your journey to the Valley, they will have no choice but to notice something is very wrong. Trust me, they will believe you."

Wiping the last sticky bits of honeycomb from his hands, he put the cloth down and came to sit next to her on the bed. Shunlar was trembling and had a wild look in her eyes. Putting his hands on her shoulders, holding her at arm's length, he shook her. She continued to stare into space.

"Speak to me. What's happening, Shunlar?" After several minutes of silence Ranth let go of her shoulders and left her side to clean the birds he had killed for their supper. She continued to sit where he had left her and stare at the message in her hands, saying nothing. Outside the rain began to hammer on the roof.

"Shunlar, the fire needs to be built if we are to eat tonight. Can you hear me?" he asked softly, breaking the silence.

Finally, she got up to tend the fire, brushing the fingers of her left hand across his back as she passed by him. His scream of pain made her whirl around and pull her dagger from the sheath at her wrist. Ready for an attacker, she looked for one and saw nothing.

"What is it?" she demanded of him.

Ranth remained where he had fallen to his knees, panting hard. He was reliving a scene in the market, so long ago, watching as his beloved teacher, Master Chago, took an arrow to the heart. He could see himself being rendered unconscious by Creedath and taken captive. Shunlar's touch across his back had been like the rake of hot coals, similar to what he had felt on that day. How was it possible? He glowered at her as if she were a fearsome creature while at the back of his mind he could hear someone's strange laughter. Then, as fast as it had started, it stopped. Before him Shunlar remained standing with her dagger pointed at his chest.

Ranth licked his lips and in a slow quiet voice began telling her the story of how he had become the unwilling servant of Lord Creedath, the man whom they had helped destroy. Through it all, he remained kneeling. She listened intently as he told of trying to trick the feared man that day in the market by pretending to be feebleminded. When it didn't work, the soldiers accompanying Creedath had attacked and killed his mentor and friend before his eyes, while he writhed on the ground in pain, unable to assist, trapped by Creedath's demon-like mind control.

He told Shunlar how his attempt to hide all of his knowledge and Temple training in the hope of remaining unnoticed had been to no avail. There came a day when he had been appointed to the house staff, given new, expensively cut clothing and privileges, while the soldiers of the house guard snickered behind his back. He found out later what he was really being trained for when one night Creedath had ordered him to spend the night with a visitor from another city, a man. His voice became louder as he described how the hatred built up in him and how helpless he had felt. The man he had been given to for a bedmate, however, had turned out to be his father, who had been searching for him since he had been abducted as an infant.

"Ranth, I am so sorry. But why did you scream when I passed behind you? All I did was touch your back, like this." Shunlar reached down to where he continued to kneel on the floor and very gently moved her hand across the same spot on his back. Nothing happened.

"Try it with your other hand," suggested Ranth, sweat forming on his brow at the thought of the pain he was certain he would soon be enduring.

Again, nothing happened.

"I must understand this," Ranth said through clenched teeth. "There are too many questions and strange occurrences for it to be merely imagination. The pain sparked a very real memory for me just now and I want to know why!" He shouted, angry and positive it had something to do with the late Lord Creedath.

Ranth rose to his feet and looked at the carcasses of the fowl he had been cleaning. Suddenly he wasn't very hungry. He craved a drink to settle his nerves. As if she had read his mind, Shunlar reached for two goblets and a jug of brandy. He could only nod his thanks as he sat down heavily in the chair next to hers, while she poured. He blew several feathers from his fingers, remnants of the birds he had been cleaning, and reached for the brandy she offered, perversely enjoying the way it burned his throat on the way down.

"Now that we are alone and I have told you a part of my story, I ask that you answer my question, the one that you have avoided since we left Creedath's palace. What happened to you while he questioned you?" Ranth's voice was a whisper and could barely be heard above the thrumming of the rain on the roof.

"I told you I don't want to remember," she answered through clenched teeth.

"But you must! Can't you see this is part of what's wrong? The pain I felt, the pain you are feeling, your fear. I can't reach your mind with mine when you are asleep and in the grip of your dreams. I can't even waken you! Did you know that? That is a sign to me that something is very wrong. Soon I'll be gone and who will you trust to speak of these things? If you keep it all inside, it will poison you. Talk to me, Shunlar. Tell me what Creedath did to you." There were tears streaming down her cheeks as he implored her.

She swallowed all that remained in her goblet and poured both of them more brandy. There was a look to her eye that he did not altogether enjoy, but he pressed her further.

"Tell me what happened."

Shunlar was very tempted to say no to him. *Who does he think he is, demanding I talk about something I have no wish to remember?* The look on his face told her he meant to continue pushing her until she told him the story. What if he was right? Could doing so stop the pain they had both been experiencing? She decided she must face the terror and put it behind her.

Shunlar took a deep breath and began, in a halting voice, retelling the events of that night in Creedath's dungeon. The plan, which had been agreed to by all of them—Cloonth,

Alglooth, Bimily, and Ranth—was that Shunlar would cast
an illusion over herself so as to look like a grizzled old man.
She and the others, minus Ranth, became captives of Creedath
so that they could rescue the other young women and men
who were being held in the round dungeon. Their imprisonment was assured once Shunlar, illusion covered as she was,
flaunted the bulging purse of Lieutenant Meecha, the leader
of the band of soldiers and mercenaries who had been sent
on a mission to find her, Ranth, and his father, Benyar.

"It was easy for me to maintain the form of the old man
with all the help I received from Cloonth and Alglooth, even
though it did put a strain on me. By the time we arrived in
the dungeon, I felt confident that no one could break down
my defenses. That was, until I was to meet Creedath face-to-
face. He was much stronger than any of us had anticipated
and it took nearly all of my reserves to keep him at bay and
prevent him from penetrating my mind. From the moment he
entered the cell, he kept at all of us; he seemed to grow
stronger the longer he held us within his grasp. There were
moments when it felt like great surges of liquid fire were
running through my body and even with the combined assistance of Cloonth and Alglooth, I began to falter. My only
escape was to pull my awareness further away from my body,
but by doing so I nearly died." Here Shunlar stopped to calm
down. Her heart was racing and her eyes were wild.

Ranth poured her another brandy, which she sipped this
time instead of gulping down.

"I don't remember much after that except that I had this
sense of running away from someone. Panic took over and
the instinct to survive was so strong that I just kept running.
I don't even remember much about the place I was in except
that I seemed to be in a great fog. Finally—after hours of
trying, I am told—my father, Alglooth, came close enough
for me to see him and he reached out to me with his hand.
The moment I touched him, I remember being wrapped within
his arms and carried to a place of safety.

"When I woke, sometime later, all I could see were their
eyes looking at me with such remorse. I felt ashamed . . . felt
that I had let them down." The panic started to rise in her
voice once more.

Ranth slowly shook his head from side to side. "No, you didn't let them down. Can't you see they were overjoyed that you were alive? Those three people are devoted to you. Bimily has no better friend than you, does she? And Cloonth and Alglooth are your parents, are they not?"

Shunlar mulled over his words for several moments, staring off into the fire as she did. "Perhaps you are right again," she answered at last. "Now that I have relived that night of terror, I do feel a bit lighter. And we all did manage to play a part in the demise of that monster, Creedath." Absently she began to scratch at the spot on her arm again. "What in the name of the three moons could have bitten me so that I continue to scratch like a dog with fleas?" She laughed out loud at herself, finally. Some of her humor was returning and it made Ranth smile, a smile that reached his eyes.

"Gods, I haven't heard that laugh for too long. I was beginning to wonder if I ever would again. But, tell me, has your appetite returned, as mine has? The birds can be roasting on the spit soon."

"Ah, your honeyed tongue is again distracting me. Come closer and I'll show you how my good mood has changed my appetite," she responded, laughing once more.

"Insatiable wench," he retaliated in a husky voice.

Tomorrow they would be parting, and they knew it would be months, perhaps years, until they held each other again. They were determined to make the minutes last as long as possible.

Five

THERE WAS A SHARP BITE TO THE EARLY MORNING
air. Winter was closing in and they must be on their
way to the Valley of Great Trees soon or be caught
in Vensunor until spring. Already the cold from last night's
storm had turned the puddles in the road to ice. The air was
heavy with mist as well as the breath of four people and their
mounts who waited patiently for another to join them. They
heard the horses before they were able to see the two riders
approaching through the fog.

It was a tearful parting for Shunlar and Ranth. Riding side-
by-side, they held hands tightly until they reached the road
where Marleah, Gwernz, Ranla, and Loff waited. Silently
their hands parted. Turning his mount toward Vensunor and
the road where his father, Benyar, awaited his arrival, with a
last wave of his arm and one look over his shoulder, Ranth
urged his horse into a gallop. Shunlar stood in her saddle, her
arm raised, until he was gone from sight. Bringing her arm
down slowly, she wiped her cheeks with the back of her hand,
then, with a straight spine, turned to greet the four riders who
waited for her.

"We bid you a good morning, niece." It was Gwernz who
spoke first.

"And to you." She nodded to him and the others. "Shall
we begin our journey then?" They nodded assent and turned
their mounts away from Ranth, toward the mountains.

Taking the lead, for she was familiar with this part of the
road, Shunlar led them over a narrow, circuitous route that

wound through old-growth forest. For most of the morning Shunlar rode in silence. Every so often her hand reached to touch the gold medallion that hung on a gold chain around her neck—a parting gift from Ranth. It was the same one Benyar had given his son when they met and, as his father had said to him, Ranth told her the medallion would give her safe passage to the Desert of Kalaven.

They stopped once for the midday meal, making only a small fire for tea. When at last the party of five came to the forest's edge, a cold, damp wind greeted them, blowing into their faces as they left the shelter of the trees, the promise of rain on its breath. One by one, each member of the party wrapped a cloak a little tighter around his or her neck, pulled up a hood, or adjusted some article of clothing, in an effort to block the wind and imminent rain.

Several hours later, after all of them were drenched and shivering, the wind driving sheets of water against them, Shunlar saw a stand of trees with what looked like a traveler's lodge in the midst of it. She pointed to it and attempted to make mind contact with Marleah, but the effort only made her wince and rub her temple. Instead she gave her horse its head and it trotted straight for the shelter, the others following her lead.

The shelter was barely large enough for all five riders, but the horses crammed themselves in under the small roof to get out of the stinging rainstorm. One by one the riders ducked their heads as they entered the low doorway. Once inside, they dismounted, pulling their soaked gear off the backs of the horses. Shunlar heaved her bags, much heavier now that they were wet, against the stone wall. Her hands free to unclasp her dripping cloak, she shook the excess water from the well-oiled wool, then draped it back over her shoulders.

Turning around, Shunlar began to look their surroundings over carefully. The lodge didn't leak too much; only in the left rear corner could she see water dripping, the sound drowned out by the downpour that continued to pummel the roof. The front wall was constructed of flat stones piled carefully one atop the other, unlike the other three log walls. The floor here was dry—at least they would not be soaked through while they slept—but there was no evidence of a safe place to build a fire.

In the dim light she noticed a door off to one side of the wall. Carefully, Shunlar unsheathed her sword. As she did so, Marleah joined her. The two women nodded to one another and Marleah cautiously approached the door, lifted the latch, and pushed it open. Instead of leading to the outside, there was a small chamber that contained only the welcome smell of smoke, which promised a warm, dry night. They wouldn't have to spend the night cramped together with the horses.

"Ah, the people hereabouts know how to treat travelers well," said Marleah, a tone of satisfaction in her voice that she hoped would cheer up her daughter. All day Marleah had watched Shunlar as she withdrew more and more into her private thoughts. This daughter that she didn't know at all, was she a person of good spirits or one prone to moodiness? Marleah would get to know her more in the months to come; for now she could only guess at the young woman's nature. But it was only natural for Shunlar to be a little unhappy, what with parting from Ranth, and then this wretched storm.

"We could all benefit from a warm fire and a change to dry clothes. Gwernz, can you set a spark to some logs in here while I hunt up the kettle to make some tea? I feel a chill down to my bones." Marleah sheathed her sword, rubbing her arms to warm them.

As his eyes adjusted to the dim light, Gwernz stood at the doorway holding his dripping saddlebags that hopefully, if they hadn't soaked through, contained a dry change of clothing. He was delighted to find logs piled high near a short, pot-bellied stone fireplace. Carefully he set a few logs into the hearth. Reaching up his sleeve, he pulled out a small wand and began to whisper softly. A spark ignited at the end of the wand that Gwernz touched to the logs, setting them aflame.

As light and heat began to take the chill from the small room, Shunlar settled near the fire to warm herself. She became lost in her thoughts as tears overflowed her eyes and ran down her cheeks. She clutched the medallion that hung around her neck. There was an ache in her chest and a deep feeling of loss like nothing she had ever felt before. She longed to reach out to Ranth with a mind-touch, but knew he was too far away.

Marleah, busy searching for the tea in her saddlebags, observed her daughter's misery. Finding the tea, she added a precise amount to the water, put the kettle over the fire, and sat next to Shunlar. Steam rose from their wet clothing in the welcome warmth of the fire. Saying not a word, Marleah very tenderly put her hand on Shunlar's shoulder and they sat quietly, watching the logs burn.

The silence was broken by the door banging open loudly as Loff and Ranla entered. Dripping and shaking, they laughed despite the fact that they were so cold their teeth chattered as they dropped their wet bags on the dirt floor of the little room.

"There are pegs on the wall to hang your wet cloaks. If the wood holds out we will have a warm evening and dry clothing to begin our journey with tomorrow." Marleah gave instructions and was up taking care of Ranla, settling her down near the fire. "Tea will be ready soon. I have a special blend that will warm you all the way to your wet toes."

"Speaking of which, Ranla, your boots were not properly oiled. I can see the way the leather is stained and absorbing the water. Off with them and let me dry you out and properly seal them so no more water can . . ." her voice trailed off.

Shunlar watched as her mother took over caring for the young woman who Loff, her half-brother, was so obviously in love with. Ranla may have been an accomplished housekeeper in Vensunor, but she knew little of life on the trail. Shunlar wiggled her dry toes in her boots; she would never venture out on a journey on horseback without proper waterproofing.

She and Ranth had agreed to this parting. It had sounded like a great adventure: each of them would go to the land of their birth and find out who their people were. Well, at the time it had sounded like a good idea, but not now. Who knew she would become so attached to Ranth in so short a time? They hadn't even known each other for a month. She missed him desperately.

The spot on her arm itched suddenly and she scratched at it, swearing under her breath. A stab of pain like liquid fire shot through it up to her shoulder and she gasped, clenching her arm and shuddering.

Observing Shunlar from the corner of her eye, Marleah pretended she was still absorbed in getting Ranla into dry clothes as she cautiously studied her daughter. Shunlar seemed to be in better spirits; likely the shudder was only her body adjusting to the warmth. Likely. Marleah desperately wanted this journey to be an easy one for all of them. Together at last, after many more years than she wanted to count, Marleah sent off a silent prayer of thanks to the Great Trees. *Mighty Trees, my daughter is coming home to your midst. Let this be a safe journey for us all.*

Huddled together in the warmth, the small party shared a simple supper of bread, cheese, dried meat, fruit, and tea. Loff unstopped a small jug of brandy which they passed around, happy to warm themselves with it. At last they found a place to uncurl their bedrolls and were soon lulled to sleep by the sound of rain rattling on the roof.

In the middle of the night Shunlar had another dream. This time she didn't thrash about or strike out at anyone, she just let out a blood chilling scream that woke everyone up. One of the horses began to kick at the stable wall in fright.

Gwernz went to her side, backlit by the glowing embers of the fire. Marleah kept her distance, choosing instead to build up the fire and warm them up a bit more.

In the corner Ranla and Loff sat together whispering, Loff's arm about her shoulders. Within a few minutes, Marleah motioned for them to lie down and go back to sleep.

"I know you had a bad dream, Shunlar. Perhaps if you tell me about it, I can help," her uncle gently whispered in her ear.

Shunlar was sitting up on her bedroll, cradling her arm, just barely willing to tolerate her uncle's touch, unable to answer him. She knew when he finally withdrew and returned to his bedroll next to Marleah, by the way her arm stopped its steady throbbing. After a time she lay back down and fell into a deep, dreamless sleep.

Side-by-side in their bedrolls, Marleah reached for Gwernz's hand. They entwined fingers; touching physically enabled them to easily slip into the other's thoughts.

"Brother, I am very troubled by the way she is acting. Were you able to reach her or manage to get any response from her?"

"No, Marleah. I fear something is very wrong, but I cannot figure out what it could be. Usually I am able to project my wishes to the edges of another's mind and that person will respond by accepting my touch or turning it away. Shunlar responded in neither way. It was as though her mind was not there, but was still engaged in her dream. We must consult with Arlass when we return. She will have an answer, I am sure."

"Gwernz, this is so painful for me to watch. She acts, as you said, as if she is within a dream, and not only when she sleeps, but sometimes when she is awake. Even before Ranth and she parted, she was plagued by dreams. Remember the black eye she gave him? Did either of them ever come to you for help or guidance? I never did take the time to question Benyar about whether Ranth had mentioned anything to him about her strange behavior."

"No, sister, nothing was ever asked of me, nor did I take the time to question Benyar. I confess I was too engrossed with studying what I could of the mysteries of the Cauldron."

They remained silent for a minute, continuing to hold onto each other's hand, as if for strength. Finally, with a sigh, Marleah gave his fingers a quick squeeze and let go of his hand. After a while she settled into sleep.

Gwernz lay awake, mulling questions over in his mind until he became too exhausted to think. He carefully checked on the hex signs he had set around the perimeter of their shelter for protection. Once he was sure everything was firmly in place and they were all secure within the safety of the web he had woven, he too slept soundly.

In the morning, Shunlar rose first to put another log on the dying embers. The rain had stopped and it looked as if the sun would be warming them for at least the morning. Stoking up the fire, she brought in the kettle brimming full of rainwater. As she knelt, attaching the kettle to the chain to suspend it over the fire, she noticed that Marleah was watching her.

"Good morning, daughter. I trust you slept well and are rested?"

Shunlar took several breaths before answering. "I wish I could report that sleep comforted me through the night, but I can't. It seems that I have many questions and have no one else to turn to. As we travel today, will you ride with me so that we can talk?"

"Yes, of course. I was hoping you would ask me," was Marleah's quiet reply.

"Excellent! Now, uncle, brother, Ranla. Wake!" Shunlar called out in a loud, happy voice. "It is nearly full light and we must eat and be on the road. I'll be back after I've relieved myself of last night's tea." With that Shunlar slapped her knees, stood and headed for the door.

Gwernz yawned and stretched, then chuckled to himself, *"Yes, she certainly is her mother's daughter."*

Within the hour the party was on the road. The air was clear and cool and smelled fresh from the previous night's storm. Shunlar and Marleah rode several paces behind the others, engaged in an intense conversation. Every so often Gwernz would turn to check on them, satisfied that he might soon have some answers about Shunlar's strange dreams.

Only when they had stopped at midday for a meal and to rest the horses did the two women join their three companions. As they dismounted, Gwernz noted the strain on Marleah's face, while Shunlar maintained a look that was unreadable.

"Uncle, I must ask your advice, as mother has no answers to this mystery. She asked me to show you what seems to be a strange bite that I have on my forearm." Holding her right arm up for Gwernz to examine, he could see that the skin was bruised from her constant scratching.

He looked it over thoroughly. His brow knit together, but he had no idea about what kind of a bite it might be, nor was he helpful when it came to the dreams that terrorized her nightly. Continuing on their way, they rode together so that Gwernz could ask more questions in his attempt to help Shunlar understand what was happening to her. After several hours, Gwernz admitted that he could not help her. Shunlar thanked him, but was clearly dismayed, and spurred her horse forward to ride alone.

"Brother, she is frightened and confused," said Marleah as she rode up alongside Gwernz.

"I'm at a complete loss and only hope that Arlass and the Great Trees will be a comfort to her once we are safely home." He looked grim and offered no more in the way of an answer.

Due to the weather, their going was slower than they all hoped it would be. One more day they were forced to cut short their travel and find shelter because the rain had become so unrelenting. Wet, cold, and saddle-sore by now, they all were short tempered.

All except for Loff. He was, by this time, head over heels in love with Ranla and she was not exactly discouraging his advances. She felt uncomfortable, however, with any display of affection in front of the others, especially Marleah. During the day Loff was filled with hope that by nightfall she would change her mind, but by the end of the day his mood soured. Here it was, the fourth night, and he was still sleeping alone. He began to think that Ranla would put off his advances forever and his sighing was getting on everyone's nerves.

As twilight approached, Shunlar rode ahead of the small party to scout for a place to spend the night. Marleah rode next to Gwernz, bringing up the rear several paces behind Loff and Ranla. They kept a discreet distance between themselves and the young couple who were engaged in yet another heated discussion.

"No, Loff, absolutely not tonight or any other while we sleep so close to your mother and your uncle," Ranla vowed.

"But, Ranla, mother will not even notice. Our customs are different in the Valley. If two people are drawn to each other, as we are, then it is understood, um ... how it is between them." Loff's stumbling explanation only made matters worse. Ranla was certain by now that he had little knowledge where women were concerned. His attempts to convince her otherwise only did more damage.

Once more, Loff exhaled a loud, resigned sigh. Hearing it made Marleah and Gwernz wince.

"Brother, I feel a man's touch is needed here. My son will

resent my offering any advice about his situation with Ranla.
Do speak to him for I swear by the moons, we will all be
making that same unbearable sighing noise before long.''

Gwernz grinned. He suppressed the urge to laugh out loud,
afraid that Loff would figure out in a minute the reason for
his laughter. They would all, most likely, be terribly embarrassed. Gwernz cleared his throat and asked quietly ''Offer
my advice? What would you have me say, sister? Won't any
words from me be taken as interference?''

''Whatever will work will suffice. Suggest they sleep apart
from us. Help him find another campsite, if necessary. Come
now,'' Marleah gave him a sly grin, ''surely you have noticed
that Loff has been unsuccessful in his advances. I believe it
is the woman's natural shyness and nothing more that keeps
her saying no.''

''Look at them,'' Marleah gestured with her chin. ''They
need privacy. They crave it. Talk to my son, or I swear, I
will.''

''Marleah, for sanity's sake, I will speak to the lad while
we gather firewood tonight. I promise.''

Just as they finished their conversation, Shunlar returned,
waving them off to the right, a sign that a campsite had been
found. They followed Shunlar's tracks to a campsite that,
from the looks of it, had been used before by travelers. Enormous overhanging rock formations formed a natural cave that
would shelter them if it should rain. They were close to a
river, and it was cold and damp within the cave, but a fire
would soon warm the stone. A well-used fire pit was already
in place; ringed with stones, the ashes of former fires were
partially covered by sand.

As they examined their night's lodgings, Gwernz decided
to do a little exploring. He soon discovered another grouping
of boulders just a little farther from the river. He inspected
the area and determined that this would be where Loff and
Ranla would spend the night, away from the rest of the party.
Satisfied, he returned to the campsite and discreetly sent a
quick mind-to-mind message to Marleah, who nodded to him,
thankful for his find.

Soon everyone was busy unloading supplies and removing
saddles from their tired, patient mounts. Afterward they care-

fully checked each animal for soundness of leg and hoof, something even Ranla had learned to do out of necessity, for to be short even one horse in this country would put them at such a slow pace they would surely see snow before reaching home. There were grasses growing nearby, something Shunlar made sure to find as she searched for the campsite. One by one they turned the horses loose to drink and graze.

Gwernz checked each horse in turn, but his inspection was internal. Only when he was satisfied that each one was fine did he surround the campsite with an invisible barrier that would prevent each horse from straying.

"Ready to collect firewood, Loff?" Gwernz asked.

"One moment, uncle." Loff quickly kissed Ranla's cheek, causing her to blush as he left her to join Gwernz.

Shunlar was oblivious to the exchange, deep in her own thoughts about Ranth as she unpacked provisions for the night's meal. Marleah pretended not to notice.

As the two men walked away to begin gathering wood, Gwernz led Loff to the small campsite he had found earlier, mulling over how to begin his discussion with Loff. Hearing yet another loud sigh from his nephew convinced him it was the right thing to do and hesitation was quickly left behind.

"Loff, let me suggest something, if I may," he asked hopefully. "It appears to me that you and Ranla need privacy. Perhaps this campsite offers the perfect solution."

Loff considered his uncle's words as he took in the surrounding area, a smile spreading across his face. "It would seem to be the perfect solution. After all, the cave will be cramped if we were all to sleep in it. And Shunlar is keeping us awake most nights." His tone turned solemn.

"Do you and mother have any idea what it is that troubles her each night? I see no remembrance in her eyes the next morning, or remorse for our lost sleep for that matter. Ranla and I prefer not to ask her any questions. She does seem to be able to handle a sword very well, after all."

"She has spoken to your mother and me, and all I am at liberty to tell you is they will take the matter up with Arlass when we return. For now, it would be best to take Ranla aside and get some rest." A wink from his uncle told Loff the rest of what he meant to say.

"Nephew," added Gwernz. "Shall we keep this conversation between the two of us men?"

"Yes, of course. I will suggest to Ranla that we will sleep much more soundly tonight if we are away from Shunlar. Perhaps for the rest of the journey that would be wise too." He began to gather wood faster, his mood immensely improved.

Together they collected two large bundles of firewood, one of which Loff left at the small campsite on the other side of the boulders. After their meal was finished, while Ranla, Shunlar, and Marleah went down to the river to bathe, Loff set up a small nest. He laid his bedroll out flat and put Ranla's on top, making one bed. Lighting the fire, Loff sat back, awaiting her return.

He could hear their approach before he saw them in the failing light. Marleah and Shunlar bid him a good night as Ranla came to sit next to him, an unusual look on her face. "Loff, do you have some reason for setting up this camp away from the rest of us?"

"I had hoped you would share this fire with me tonight. My thought was that we would sleep more soundly away from Shunlar and her nightmares." He held his breath as he saw that Ranla had noticed her bedroll and the way it had been arranged.

"Oh. That was your thought, was it?" Ranla answered, finally succumbing to Loff's gentle insisting.

"Well," she hedged, "her dreams are getting louder and no one is getting much sleep." As Ranla slowly reached for Loff's hand, they embraced. Alone for the first time in days they sat and watched the fire, listening to the sound of the river in the distance. Ranla's head rested on Loff's shoulder and she was aware of how in the last few minutes his heart was pounding and his breath was coming faster.

Barely able to keep his voice from trembling, Loff whispered, "Lie next to me or I fear my heart will burst soon from wanting you."

She hesitated at first, then began to help him off with his shirt. Undressed, they slipped between the blankets. As they kissed, a blaze of light appeared behind Loff's closed eyelids. Startled, he opened his eyes wide and pulled away, the light disappearing as suddenly as it happened, leaving him with white specks swirling in his field of vision.

"What is it? Why do you pull away? Isn't this what you wanted?" asked Ranla, very confused.

"Nothing is wrong, at least I don't think so. It was something I imagined. I'm sorry if I frightened you." He began to kiss her again and the same thing happened but this time Loff did not open his eyes. Instead, he kept them closed and reached toward Ranla with his mind as well as his body. The next thing he knew, Loff could hear her voice.

Yes, kiss me softly, not hard. My throat ... kiss my throat ...

Though neither of them was skilled at lovemaking, Loff's newly discovered ability to read her thoughts when he was touching her allowed him to fulfill her desires.

Each time he heard her voice whispering her unspoken wish within his head, he followed her instructions. Astonished and extremely pleased, Ranla realized that she had fallen in love with him. They seemed to melt into one another, slowly, tenderly, lost in the moment.

Six

ON THE MORNING OF THE FIFTH DAY, THE CITY OF Stiga was at last within sight. Shunlar realized when she saw Stiga looming in the distance that she was very anxious to find Cloonth and Alglooth. Her conversations with Marleah and Gwernz had left her with unanswered questions; more than ever she needed insight about her dreams. Also, she was puzzled by the fact that she couldn't see anyone's heat trace any longer, something she was sure her father, Alglooth, would have an answer for.

They traveled for half the day before they were close enough to enter the city. The gates of Stiga were as Gwernz and Marleah remembered them—charred remains of massive timbers, strewn where they had fallen many centuries ago. There also remained the flocks of birds living within the eaves of the crumbling houses who took flight at the sound of the horses' hooves, nearly covering the sky. As the birds passed overhead, tatters of once-thick draperies fluttered from the windows of Stiga's deserted buildings.

Shunlar had not been in Stiga since she was a child, yet she remembered the way well. She and Gwernz led the others to the dwelling that had been the home she shared with Cloonth and Alglooth. Dismounting, they hurried to the door, only to stop in bewilderment. The doorway was in shambles. Something very large had recently forced its way through, from the inside. Once more Shunlar felt frustration building within herself. Her ability to see the heat trace, something that she took for granted, was gone, and with it a part of her

42

seemed missing. Although she carefully hid her concern behind a strong mind-shield, Shunlar was close to a state of panic.

"There is no animal alive that could have made such a mess of this doorway," said Gwernz in a quiet voice. "If you will all remain still for a moment, I will attempt to find out what or who passed through here."

Gwernz slowed his breathing and within seconds placed himself in a trance that enabled him to see the faint form of the large, terrified beast that had crashed through the doorway. When he returned from the trance state, he gave everyone a chance to see the vision by touching the floor directly in front of the doorway with the tip of his wand. For several seconds they were able to see what Gwernz had seen: a dragon.

Astonished, Shunlar gasped when she saw the patch of white hair atop the dragon's head, refusing to believe what her eyes told her to be true. As she stared at the cracked timbers of the doorway, her arm began to throb, a pain so intense that she immediately passed out.

Assuming that the shock of seeing the beast had caused her to lose consciousness, no one knew or suspected that a small shard of the Lifestone of Banant, the evil wizard who had ruled Stiga and ultimately brought it to ruin, was embedded in her forearm. When Creedath immolated, the large amber-colored Lifestone of his ancestor, Banant, had exploded into thousands of tiny pieces. One needle-thin sliver flew into the air, pierced the skin of Shunlar's forearm, and became deeply embedded there; another had found its way into Cloonth's arm.

Being in such close proximity to the Temple of Stiga and the very chamber that had been the stronghold of Banant's nefarious sorcery had given strength to the shard. Banant of Stiga had been a ruthless tyrant who bent his knee to neither deity nor oracle. The wand that Gwernz had used was an ancient piece of magic fashioned from a small limb of one of the sacred trees from the Valley of Great Trees. The wand activated the venomous power of the Lifestone and what spilled from it into Shunlar's body made her fall very ill with fever. They had no choice but to remain in Stiga waiting for her to recover, sheltering in the only quarters suitable, those that had recently been inhabited by Cloonth and Alglooth.

Gwernz and Loff set to work at once repairing the door, so they could close off the chill night air. Marleah and Ranla cared for Shunlar, desperately trying to bring down her fever. As their supplies dwindled fast, each day there was still no sight of the half-dragon, half-human couple. To compound their problems, as Marleah nursed her daughter, she too began coming down with the mysterious fever.

Ignoring the risk to herself, Ranla continued to nurse both women. Her supply of herbs proved invaluable to them when she came up with an elixir that began to strengthen and heal Marleah, then Shunlar. As a precaution, Ranla had insisted that Loff and Gwernz drink the herbs too. And it worked because she and the men never got sick.

Finally, Shunlar's fever broke. It was about two hours before dawn, and though exhausted, Marleah sat at her bedside. When her eyes opened and she saw the anxious look on her mother's face, Shunlar knew something was very wrong. "Tell me, how many days?" she asked in a whisper.

Offering her water, Marleah answered, "Four days, daughter, and I myself have been ill. If it were not for Ranla, we might all have come down with this mysterious ailment. Drink now." Marleah propped her up as Shunlar reached for the cup with a trembling hand.

"Rest now, daughter. Sleep and gather strength for we must continue our journey." As soon as she finished speaking, Shunlar fell back into a deep sleep.

Later that morning, when Shunlar awoke, her head was much clearer. She told her mother, "We must leave now, today, while I feel stronger. Something about this place has made us both ill. Don't ask me to explain how I know, I just know it. Can you ask Gwernz to come see me? Please," she asked.

Marleah nodded and several minutes later she returned with Gwernz. "I see you are awake. Feeling better?" His smile warmed her as no else's had been able to since she and Ranth had parted company.

"Yes, much better, thank you. I must tell you, I dreamed very disturbing things while in the fever's grip. One thing kept recurring. I saw myself being led away by my arm by a man whose features were almost identical to Creedath. This is curious, because never yet have I been able to remember what it is I have dreamed about, although I know my dreams have been disturbing others much more than me. You both know what I mean.'' Shunlar looked at Gwernz and Marleah and they both nodded gravely.

"Each time I was led to a chamber and then left in the dark. You, Gwernz, rescued me every time, taking me to sit within a large grove of trees. It is the most safe and peaceful I have felt in weeks, and I take it as a sign to leave here as soon as we can. I am able to ride and we need to leave this place, now.''

"We can be ready within the hour. But tell me, have you given up hope of finding Alglooth and Cloonth?'' Gwernz asked.

"For now, yes. I feel that our lives depend on leaving here. If my father and foster-mother were here and wanted to be found, we would have found them. As it is, I can only assume that something is keeping them away. Perhaps it is the spirit of the man I saw in my dream.'' Her words made her shudder.

Had Shunlar been well and her heat trace ability intact, she would have been able to find the entrance to the cave that Alglooth had come and gone from, several times, in his constant search for food. But the shard embedded deep in her forearm prevented her special gift of heat-trace sight from working. And Alglooth, under the compulsion placed on him by Cloonth, was so occupied hunting for food far from the walls of Stiga that he never saw them.

Undetectable at first, the most unusual physical changes began to occur to Shunlar. While she was sick with fever, her skin became dry and in a few places it began to crack. Ranla's ointment seemed to do the trick at first, but then Shunlar's entire body began to crack and peel. Everyone assumed she was fighting off the residual effects of the strange malady that had her so wracked with fever.

It was midmorning and they readied to leave Stiga. As Shunlar rose to dress, she swore loudly. Her breeches were several inches too short. Nearby, packing her saddlebags, ready to help her daughter if she should need her, Marleah called loudly for Gwernz.

"Brother, what strange wizardry has happened? Shunlar appears to be taller than she was four days ago. How can this be?" she asked, her voice angry.

"Calm yourself, Marleah. Anger will do nothing to help us solve this mystery," he answered as he carefully checked his niece over. He realized as he stood face-to-face with Shunlar, that she had grown several inches and they were nearly the same height. He was truly puzzled.

"Shunlar, can you tell me anything about the last few days? The fever could not have caused this, I am sure. Think, is there any other detail from your dreams that could explain this change in you?" he asked, very concerned.

"I remember nothing more of my dreams than I have told you, except that they are a constant terror and I loathe the coming of night. The only thing different that I have done . . ." her voice trailed off. Considerably stronger than before, she shoved Gwernz out of her way, knocking the wind out of him, grabbing her sword as she ran from the room.

She's going after Ranla. Go quickly and stop this, Marleah, Gwernz's insistent voice rang in her head as he struggled to regain his breath.

In the next room Ranla sat at a table, sorting and repacking her supply of herbs. Shunlar stormed through the doorway, grabbed Ranla by her hair and hauled her up out of the chair, placing the sword under her chin.

"I demand to know what sort of witch's brew you have made me drink that could make me grow taller."

Terrorized, Ranla gasped. "Surely you cannot believe that I would do anything to harm you, Shunlar. Please believe me that I only gave you herbs to dispel your fever. Your mother was given the same. She and you recovered together."

Because Shunlar had grabbed her from behind, Ranla could not see the physical changes in Shunlar, but Loff, who stood on the other side of the room, was staring, wide-eyed.

"You lying sow! Only a spell or some strange concoction could do this to me!" The last words from Shunlar's mouth produced a small puff of smoke, followed by a spark. Seeing this, she roughly released Ranla with a shove that sent the smaller woman flying across the room, where she collided with Loff. Both of them held onto one another, staring in disbelief at Shunlar as Marleah burst into the room.

"Shunlar, child, Ranla is not to blame for this . . . whatever this is that is happening to you. Look at me, at all of us. We drank Ranla's herbs. Have we changed at all?" Marleah pleaded to her.

Only after Shunlar had looked her mother up and down, did she begin to consider her words. "What is happening to me? First the dreams, now this!" She held her arms out for all to see. There were small, iridescent scales growing on her once-smooth skin, scattered from her shoulders to her elbows.

"I am becoming like Alglooth," she whispered with another puff of smoke. Then she ran from the room, nearly knocking Gwernz down once more as he entered.

Marleah was about to follow her, but Gwernz held his hand up to stop her, saying, "Let her be. She has many things to sort out. Pack everything and be prepared to leave as soon as she returns. There is a strange feeling building up in this place for me and I long to be back in our Valley to seek the council of Arlass and the Great Trees."

Outside it was beginning to rain again, but due to the altitude of Stiga, the temperature was dropping rapidly and the smell of snow was in the air. Within an hour it began snowing.

Hours later, with wet, heavy flakes falling, Shunlar finally reappeared. She had again grown a few inches taller, but the biggest difference was her hair. At first everyone thought it was just covered with snow. But when they took a second look, they saw that her hair was turning white. Afraid that her temper might flare up again, Loff and Ranla just turned away while Marleah and Gwernz tried to figure out how to tell her that yet another physical change had taken place.

"Ranla," Shunlar began, "I apologize for my behavior this morning. I was frightened and confused and gave in to my passions. I would do you no harm, truly."

"I accept your apology," Ranla answered, not turning to face her.

"What?" Shunlar demanded to know, smoke spewing from her nose and mouth. "What is it now? Am I becoming so repulsive to look upon that you shun me with your eyes?''

Marleah tenderly put her hands on Shunlar's shoulders. When it was apparent that touching her was causing no retaliation, Marleah said, "Come and see why Ranla is avoiding looking at you." And she walked her daughter to stand before a large mirror hanging on the wall.

For long minutes Shunlar stared at her reflection, touching her cheeks and hair as she inspected herself. Her face was growing more slender, as was the rest of her. She even suspected that soon she might sprout wings because of the way her shoulder blades itched. A quietness settled over her, as if she had accepted her fate. After all, the two fire-beings that raised her were beautiful, were they not? Hadn't she always had a secret desire to look like them?

When she turned back to the four people in the room, she simply said, "It is time to leave here." This time there was a confident tone to her voice and no smoke escaped her mouth or nostrils.

The next morning as they lay sleeping under the trees, exhausted from yet another night of interrupted sleep, Marleah and Gwernz were woken by the sound of someone retching miserably. When several minutes later they hear the sound of feet running off to the other side of them, followed by heaving, they silently sent off a prayer to the Great Trees.

Marleah reached out to touch her brother's hand. She sent a thought directly to his mind that was colored with happiness. *They both carry a child.*

"Yes," he answered out loud. His mood, however, was grim.

SEVEN

THE MORNING OF THEIR LAST DAY OF TRAVEL brought relief to everyone. Each day it had been more difficult than the last to continue. They were all weary of sleeping on the ground and the weather had not cooperated, although as they descended the last mountain range, the wind had died down and the air had turned pleasantly warmer.

Loff had developed a cold that none of Ranla's herbal remedies could cure; Shunlar was becoming more surly with each passing hour; Gwernz had taken to spending long periods in silence; and Marleah's back ached. For the better part of each day they rode in silence, stopping only for rest or a meal, pushing on until the pass into the valley could be seen.

As they encountered the first sentries and entered the Valley of Great Trees, the ram's horn sounded to let everyone know they had at last returned. The torches were lit, and several of Loff's friends soon joined them, bringing chilled wineskins to welcome him and his party home.

Their arrival was cause for days of celebration. Venerable Arlass, the spiritual leader of the Valley, was first to greet them at the door of the communal house. Though she had been very weak when Gwernz and Marleah left nearly a month ago, Arlass seemed to have recovered much of her vitality and received the entire party with open arms. Being the end of harvest season, most everyone was on hand to welcome them, as they gathered at the evening meal for a night of eating, drinking, and entertainment. After introductions were made they gave thanks for their abundance and the feast commenced.

Since no one had ever seen Shunlar before, they accepted her height and white hair to be the natural inheritance of her father, a fact that was partially true. She caused quite a stir among the men. Fascinated by her beauty, several men offered to give Shunlar personal tours of the Valley once they were introduced, making their intentions quite clear as only one from the Valley would do. Surrounded by a group who kept her occupied for the better part of the evening, Shunlar seemed to be in her element, using her limited ability to speak the language to her advantage. Though it had nearly been an afterthought, Shunlar and Ranla had been given concentrated lessons, which made fluency in the tongue quite impossible.

Loff had stayed at Ranla's side throughout the evening, making it clear to any who were unsure that he and Ranla were a couple. After all, he needed to translate for her.

Sitting several paces away, slowly savoring a brandy, Marleah kept a watchful eye on her family. She realized Gwernz was right, when he had chided her about desiring a large family. Her daughter had been returned to her, and her son also. Loff was obviously in love with Ranla, and soon there were going to be grandchildren. She smiled to herself. It felt good to be home.

Hours later the travel weary group followed Marleah as she led the way to the family home.

"We bid you a good sleep, Ranla and Loff," Marleah said as she kissed them on the cheek.

"Yes. Good sleep now that our journey has ended," Gwernz added, yawning.

Ranla had lost her shyness, and with her arm around Loff's waist, she walked down the hallway with him to his room. Until other arrangements could be made for them to set up their own household, they would stay with Marleah and Gwernz.

"Daughter, come with me," beckoned Marleah. "I don't expect you to remember, but this was your room when you were an infant." Her mother took her to a small room that was sparsely furnished with a single bed and a child-sized chest for clothing. Several pegs on the wall were placed at a child's height.

"My parents and I couldn't bear to change anything in this room, in the hope that you would return to us one day. Loff was given his own room and no one has used this one since you were taken from us." Marleah had tears in her eyes, and her voice choked on the last words.

"Mother, I have returned, but I doubt this room will be large enough for me. Already I have grown taller than you. Who knows how much more I will grow. Soon the bed will be too short for my legs, as perhaps it already is." She lay down and her feet hung past the edge of the bed.

Ever resourceful, Marleah pushed the trunk to the end of the small bed, opened it and brought out a pillow and several blankets. "This should do the trick for the time being. At least for tonight," she said as she padded the trunk with the extra pillow and blanket.

"Perhaps your child will make use of this room," Marleah added, smiling, remembering she was going to be a grand-mother.

"Perhaps it will," agreed Shunlar, yawning.

"Rest, sleep now. You are home, my daughter, after so many years." Marleah covered Shunlar, kissed her cheek, and left the room.

Once the door closed, Shunlar fell into a deep sleep. For the time being, at least, she had no dreams.

In the morning when she woke, before she opened her eyes she knew more changes had taken place. In the early morning light, she inspected herself. Her hands were longer and more slender. She threw aside the blankets and saw that shiny scales were growing on her thighs. "Ach, my feet are longer too. And I just broke in those new boots." Shunlar swore under her breath.

The aroma of freshly baked bread invaded her nostrils. Nausea overwhelmed her, and soon she was retching into the chamber pot. Just as she lay back on the bed, there was a knock at the door. "Come," she called in a hoarse voice. Marleah entered with a hot towel and some tea.

"Shunlar, this should put a stop to the nausea. If you can

keep it down, that is,'' said Marleah quietly. In the next room the sound of Ranla vomiting could be heard.

"Mother!" Loff called for her loudly.

"Duty calls," was all her mother said as she left Shunlar's side.

When Shunlar joined them for breakfast, she noticed immediately how much paler Ranla appeared. Though she was fair-skinned and blonde, her coloring was lighter this morning. Loff appeared concerned. Gwernz looked unhappy. Marleah was the only one who seemed to be content. With her family sitting at her table, she was nearly purring.

Everyone stopped eating, however, as Shunlar padded into the room in her bare feet. She looked different again. It was obvious that she had grown more. Her breeches were an inch or two shorter, as were her tunic's sleeves. And, she was ravenous.

"Is there no meat?" she asked, a small curl of smoke escaping her nostrils as she sat at the table. Ranla covered her mouth with her hand, choking as she swallowed hard several times.

"I thought that you might only be able to keep porridge down, but there is some smoked venison," answered Marleah as she rose from the table and returned with a large joint of meat on a platter and a carving knife. She placed it before Shunlar.

As Shunlar sliced off a portion and began eating, Ranla left the table in a hurry, running for the bedroom. Even though she had closed the door, the sound of her being sick carried down the hall.

"Mother, is there nothing that can be done?" asked Loff. "I . . . I feel so helpless."

"My son, her body must adjust to the changes that are taking place. Some women have the morning sickness worse than others. But I will ask the midwife for advice," she answered.

"You must speak with the midwife soon," added Gwernz. "There is another matter I would take up with Ranla." His tone was suddenly more serious as he studied his nephew from across the table. "Loff, you do realize, it is not your child that Ranla carries."

Several seconds passed before Loff answered. "Yes, I know that. But, the child will be raised as my own. Ranla and I have spoken of it already."

"That remains to be seen. We shall discuss this today, for to wait longer will only cause more pain." Gwernz rose from the table. "I do this because I know whose child she carries and the danger it presents to everyone. Please tell her that I would like to speak to her this afternoon. This morning I will consult with Arlass and the Great Trees."

Loff left the table reluctantly, to deliver his uncle's message.

Only Shunlar and Marleah were left at the breakfast table. Marleah paced while she watched her daughter devour the entire platter of meat that had been set before her. Between bites, smoke curled from Shunlar's nostrils. She swore that Shunlar had grown a bit more by the time she finished.

"Before Gwernz returns from his visit with Arlass, can you tell me where I might find boots that will fit me again, or clothes for that matter? Before this day is over, I might need new ones, so"—Shunlar sighed—"the larger the better." She laughed at her predicament and it did clear the air somewhat. Marleah seemed to calm down and stopped her pacing.

With food in her belly, Shunlar felt better able to face the world outside the door. She and Marleah walked to the other side of the Valley to the house of Calem and Darta. They were but two of the people who sewed and fashioned clothing here. Their cottage had been turned into a spacious workroom that was filled with every shade and texture of cloth, leather, and thread. Since everyone who lived in the Valley shared their talents and wealth, it was not necessary for Shunlar to purchase anything.

Since the breeches and shirt Shunlar was wearing were merely too small and not worn, they were added to the stockpile of clothing. Fashioned by the tailors of Vensunor, there were subtle differences in the placement of buttons or laces from the Valley clothing. These would be carefully scrutinized by Darta and Calem and would soon be seen on several new designs.

Choosing leather breeches and a vest, Shunlar asked Darta if he could make her a copy of her vest with the secret dagger sheaths in the seams. His eyes brightened when he saw the hidden pockets and he agreed, saying her vest would be ready within two days, sheaths and all. By the time they left, Darta was already busy showing Calem how to implement the design changes to several others.

Wearing clothing that fit her for the first time in a week, Shunlar had a confident bounce to her step. She had gotten a pair of soft boots that wrapped themselves around her legs to mid-calf. They were dyed a dark brown and had silver buttons around which the laces wound. She even found herself waving back at several of the men who called to her and Marleah.

"Daughter, have you given any thought to what you might like to do while you live with us? You must have noticed that everyone has a profession," Marleah added. "If you could choose a way to spend your time productively, what would you do?"

She hadn't expected to be put on the spot so soon. Shunlar knew she would have to earn her keep in some way, but she was a sword-for-hire and in this peaceful valley it didn't look as though anyone here would call upon her for that skill in the too distant future.

"Is that how I am to learn about life in this Valley, working at 'something productive'?" she answered sarcastically, feeling rather full of herself.

"It is the only way I know how," Marleah answered very honestly. There was an edge of temper showing in her mother's voice. Shunlar eyed the woman walking beside her, after she waved at yet another young man.

"How does a young person begin here? One who knows no skill and who wishes to learn one."

"By spending days as a guard, learning to converse with the Great Trees and listening to his or her heart. Instruct us in your fighting art. Though there is no immediate need, everyone who hears that you will be teaching will come to learn. Especially some of the young men." Shunlar smiled and shook her head at her mother as they continued walking home.

The hours seemed to pass slowly. Marleah paced as she waited for Gwernz to return from his meeting with Arlass. It seemed nothing could calm her down except to be constantly in motion while she waited.

Finally Gwernz returned and his look was dark. "It is as I feared," he said to Marleah, "and worse."

"No," she whispered in denial.

"Calm yourself. We will all need your strength soon." Gwernz patted her shoulder and then slowly walked down the hall and knocked on the door. Ranla's eyes were swollen and red from crying, but she invited him in.

Immediately Gwernz was aware of Ranla's confusion and sorrow. He embraced her gently, giving what comfort he could, but only as long as he did not try to touch the essence of the life within her. Each time he reached toward the small spark of life, feelings of such venomous anger, much greater than the minute essence should have been able to produce, lashed out from it. It was strong, and gave promise of growing.

Ranla, Gwernz spoke to her mind-to-mind as he held her, *you know who fathered this child.*

Hearing his voice in her head, Ranla jumped and broke out of his embrace, pushing him away from her. "Don't ever speak to me in that way again," she whispered in horror. "That is how Lord Creedath spoke to me when he wanted to control me and I could do nothing to prevent it." Ranla was shaking.

"Ranla, please hear what I have to say. I have no wish to control you, nor do I intend to. You must believe me. Forgive me for frightening you by speaking directly to you as I just did, but in your heart you must know that only great pain will come from this child, for you and anyone it touches," offered Gwernz.

"How can you know? While it is true that the father was an insensitive beast of a man, he's dead. I am the mother and I will influence this child." Her tone was confident until she looked at the great sorrow in Gwernz's eyes. "None of the evil will pass on to it, surely," Ranla pleaded. A tone of disbelief had crept into her voice.

"Ranla, I wish with all my heart that I could agree with you. But the life growing in you is a direct descendant of Banant of Stiga. His blood flows in the veins of the child and

already may be beyond your influence. But, see for yourself.''
Gwernz held out his hand to Ranla. ''Take my hand and you
will be able to see and feel the essence of the being inside
you. Tell me after you do this, what you want to do. No one
will force you to do anything, I vow solemnly.''

''No. This I will not do. You will influence me and my
mind cannot be turned against the child.'' Ranla's trembling
hands covered her belly and when she looked at Gwernz a
flicker of orange light appeared in her eyes for an instant and
then vanished. Seeing this, he knew it was already too late.
Gwernz bowed to Ranla and excused himself.

Solemn and more shaken than he wanted to admit, Gwernz
returned to Marleah, who waited, still pacing back and forth
before the kitchen hearth. He reached for her hand, and once
in direct contact with her mind, Gwernz opened his memory
of the conversation that had just taken place with Ranla. Marleah also knew when she saw the light in Ranla's eyes that
the child had already taken over and would do whatever it
took to ensure its survival.

''Surely something can be done to convince the girl that
she is in grave danger. And what about my son? Will it harm
him as well?'' Marleah was becoming quite frantic. Gwernz
had to settle her down.

''Please hold onto some sense of calm so we can find a
solution. I believe that while Loff is by her side, loving her
as he does, no harm will come to him. But I would never say
that is the truth. We must consult Arlass and the Great Trees
again for counsel on this matter and soon. There is no way
to tell how far-reaching the influence of the child will be.

''But now I must also speak with your daughter. I have
found out why she is plagued by strange nightmares. You
must promise me that you will be strong, sister. We have
many difficult days ahead of us and I will need your strength
if we are to succeed.''

At the mention of her daughter, Marleah's head snapped
up. ''What have you learned about her? Tell me there is not
more bad news, brother.'' Now there was panic in Marleah's
voice.

''Where is she, Marleah?'' His voice had become gentler
and that gave Marleah hope.

At the mention of her name, Shunlar appeared. "Yes, uncle, I am curious. What has your oracle to say about me?"

"So, you were listening," he answered her quietly with a shake of his head.

A flash of color brightened Shunlar's cheeks before she answered. "I couldn't help but overhear. The walls are thin and Ranla's voice carried. She sounded quite hysterical, in fact."

Gwernz gently placed his hand on Shunlar's shoulder and immediately pulled it away with a jerk, sucking his breath in as he did. Her shoulder felt as though it were on fire.

Though she was startled by Gwernz's sudden movement, she had felt nothing. But, curiously, in that instant she had been able to see beneath the surface of the skin of her arm. And, there appeared to be something embedded in her forearm, between her bones. When she searched Gwernz's eyes she knew that he had also seen it. Puzzled, Shunlar waited for an explanation from him.

"You were able to see it in your arm just now as I touched you, were you not?" he asked, waiting for her to answer. Shunlar nodded yes and Gwernz continued. "I have learned that it is a piece of the Lifestone of Banant of Stiga."

In disbelief, Shunlar's jaw came open and she shook her head "no" slowly.

"That is what I was told by Arlass. When Creedath died and the Lifestone exploded, a sliver flew through the air and entered your arm. This is what is causing your strange dreams and likely, the metamorphosis. Being in Stiga, in the very room where the Lifestone lay for centuries before I found it, has somehow accelerated your physical changes. Perhaps because you are pregnant, or perhaps it is just because you are the child of Alglooth. That part is unclear. Tonight we will take counsel of the Great Trees."

"The only thing I wish to know now is how it can be removed." Facing her uncle, Shunlar trembled as a wisp of smoke escaped her lips.

Later that evening Shunlar, Gwernz, and Marleah met with Arlass to confer with the Great Trees and ask their help in removing the sliver of crystal from Shunlar's arm. After they were all seated around the small fire within the Circle of Great Trees, Gwernz drank the cup Arlass offered him.

Sitting before her uncle, Shunlar spoke the ritual words in Old Tongue that would enable him to answer her. "Please my whims, I request a formal asking this night. My name is Shunlar, daughter of Marleah and Alglooth, and I have returned of my own accord to the place of my birth. Will you grant me audience?"

Shortly, Gwernz began to speak. "Ask and I will answer, guided by the Great Trees who will speak through me." His eyes, though open, focused on nothing, and his skin began radiating a golden glow. His voice had a throaty, dry quality to it.

"Tell me about this thing in my arm. Can it be removed?"

"It has begun melding with your bone," the Trees answered through their mouthpiece, Gwernz. "No, it cannot be removed."

Shunlar's face didn't flinch. She seemed to accept the truth. Taking a deep breath, she asked, "Is this thing alive?"

"No. It is a sliver of the Lifestone of Banant of Stiga. Although it has strong powers, it is only a piece of crystal," answered Gwernz.

"Do you mean to tell me that it will stay with me forever?" she asked, a spark escaping her lips.

"Yes. It is even now becoming a part of you."

"But I have no desire for it to remain with me. It has caused me to look like another person. Soon, I may even sprout wings and fly. And the dreams. What about them?"

"Once the shard has become part of your bone and once you give birth, you will physically return to the way you looked before you were with child. Only then will the dreams stop.

"Being in Stiga, in such close proximity to Banant's dwelling and the chamber where the Lifestone was discovered by Gwernz amplified the powers of the sliver enough to produce these side effects in you. You will discover, when you return to looking like your normal self, that you will have the abilities to cast an illusion and to take on the body of half-human and half-dragon. And yes, you will fly."

Sitting opposite her uncle, Shunlar's face was frozen in

shock. Her breath came fast as beads of sweat formed across her brow. In her confusion she forgot to ask about whether or not her heat trace ability would return.

"Do you wish to know the sex of the child you carry?" Gwernz asked, breaking the silence.

"Yes," Shunlar answered quietly.

"You will birth a son. More than that I am forbidden to say."

Shunlar thanked him and at last managed a smile. *A son*, she mused to herself. *May he possess a strong sword arm.*

"He will," came the reply from Gwernz.

Eight

IT HAD BEEN A WEEK SINCE RANTH AND BENYAR left the people and city of Vensunor behind. As they traveled, Benyar taught Ranth the tongue of the Feralmon. It was not exactly an easy language to master, what with the shushes and rolling R sounds, but Ranth eagerly learned and continued to ask questions about the origins of many of the words.

As they neared the Desert of Kalaven, the home of their ancestors, the towns became sparse, and the population dwindled. This day's journey had brought them to a small oasis city enclosed within a compound, called Beratom, which in the local dialect meant "sour water." There was one small inn for travelers, with a tavern that served food as well as drink. The stable was off to one side and was empty, like the inn.

It was nearly dark when they arrived and both were weary of traveling and sleeping on the ground. They hoped the beds here would be at least softer than the ground and free of vermin. They saw to their horses themselves, for to trust any other with them would be foolish; in this part of the world a sound mount was the difference between life and certain death. After their animals had been rubbed down and fed, Benyar made sure to tip the young stable boy generously. Ranth watched the boy's eyes grow wide as he accepted the coin, and he bowed many times, grinning an open-mouthed grin that showed his new, budding, front teeth under his top lip.

"There will be another for you if you see to it that they

60

are both well cared for," promised Benyar as they walked away.

They were the only visitors so far on this night and had their pick of the rooms, although there was no difference between them.

"Allow me to bargain for the rooms, father," suggested Ranth. "After all, I must begin to speak my birth tongue sometime. If I am able to negotiate well enough, our rooms might be free tonight!"

"May I suggest our finest room. It has the comfort of a fireplace and it faces the oasis," tried the innkeeper with a hopeful tone to his voice.

If they said yes, he charged a higher fee to the unsuspecting guest, a local custom. But Benyar and Ranth were not fooled. After all, both of them were able to read the thoughts that the innkeeper seemed to be broadcasting.

"Which way will the wind be blowing tonight?" asked Ranth confidently, speaking with only a slight accent.

"Why do you ask, young sir?" replied the innkeeper, licking his lips uneasily, trying to place Ranth's accent.

"May *I* suggest the fine room upwind of the stable, for even though the breeze is not brisk, we will not find it agreeable to smell the horses all night long," answered Ranth with a straight face.

"Indeed, young sir, that would be a wise choice," nodded the man, less hopefully, but agreeable nevertheless. "If you wish to bathe, I will have hot water brought to your room. That will, of course, cost extra."

"Of course it will. We both wish to bathe before our meal. Bring two tubs and hot water, lots of it, and soap," ordered Ranth. His tone had just the right amount of command to it, no more, no less. The innkeeper bowed as he accepted the coins for the room and bath, scurrying off to do his guest's bidding.

Benyar smiled his approval as they walked to their room. "You did well, but we must work on your accent. If not for that, our baths would not have cost such a price."

An hour later, both men were soaking in deep, round, wooden tubs by the light of the fire. In the privacy of their room, as they washed, Ranth noticed something peculiar about his father's body. A curious pattern of scars covered his torso and the tops of his arms and legs, stopping above the elbows and knees. Benyar had chosen not to hide his true appearance from his son any longer.

"Father, do my eyes trick me?" was all Ranth could think to ask.

"Your eyes are fine, my son. It is the custom of our people to be marked like this from an early age. We men do this to one another in the midst of a ritual dance. To truly be a Feralmon, you must also be marked."

Ranth bit off a protest but the disbelief showed plainly on his face. *How barbaric!* he thought to himself, but instead asked aloud: "Will this happen to me?"

"In time, you will not think the custom so barbaric," his father answered curtly. "Dress now and let us have our meal together. As we eat I will continue your education on the customs of our people." Benyar's tone had the bite of annoyance to it. He got out of the tub and dried himself off, dressing in silence as Ranth did the same.

In the tavern, they chose a table that allowed them a full view of the room and its only door. As they waited for their meal, Ranth began his apology. "Father, I regret that you were able to hear my thoughts so easily while in the room. I can only offer in the way of an explanation that my surprise at hearing about the custom of marking one's body made me forget myself. I assure you, it will not happen again."

"Apology accepted. If I seemed angry, it was more at myself than at you. As my son, your actions will reflect directly upon myself, your mother, and our house. Because you are not schooled in our customs, there will be leniency, but, only to a point. A large part of your education will happen, I fear, when I am not around. But, you must not fail to remember your promise. Above all else, shield your thoughts from others. Since so many of us are capable of mind speaking, it is considered to be the most rude and highly unforgivable action another can do among us."

"I understand," Ranth replied quietly.

Their food was served then, breaking their uneasy silence. Since it was their first hot meal in many days, both were delighted with the platter of sliced, roasted mutton the innkeeper placed before them, accompanied by a basket of flat fry-bread with mashed garlic and what appeared to be red peppers. Benyar spread the red mixture generously over a piece of the bread and rolled it around a piece of the mutton. Ranth followed his example.

Within seconds, Ranth was sorry he had. Sweat began pouring from his face and he felt that his tongue and throat had been seared. As he reached for his wine, holding his breath, the innkeeper returned and plunked a large bowl of buttermilk down before him. He shook his head sadly, "tsk, tsk," as he walked away. Benyar watched his son and took another bite, not a drop of perspiration to be seen on his face, but an amused look in his eyes.

As Ranth gulped the buttermilk, a group of mercenaries entered the tavern. They wore dusty, travel-stained riding leathers and among them was Lieutenant Meecha, the man who had been sent by Creedath to hunt for Shunlar and Ranth and bring them back to Vensunor. Ranth recognized him instantly, but it was with mixed emotions.

While Ranth had been a servant under Creedath's roof, Lieutenant Meecha had been his teacher in the sparring yard, specializing in sword technique. At the time, Meecha had taken a great liking to his young student. He could see the promise of a fine swordsman in him. Being a professional soldier, Meecha had had no choice in the matter of being sent out on patrol to capture Ranth and the woman. His explicit instructions had been to not bother returning until he had. It was his job, after all, and Ranth, his former student, had been responsible for the death of three guards, he reasoned with himself. Ranth had, it seemed, killed those men when he freed the woman from Creedath's prison.

In the last month, Meecha's life had taken a great turn. He thought his life and career were secure once he and the band of soldiers and mercenaries had captured Ranth and the woman. But when both of them had mysteriously escaped from under their noses, taking all the horses with them, they not only robbed him of his ride out of the desert, and his money, but his position as a soldier as well. Now Meecha, too, was an outcast, a mercenary, like the men and women with whom he traveled. And from the looks of him and his companions, times were very lean.

Hiding his face over the bowl of buttermilk, Ranth whispered, ''Father, one of the men who has just entered with that group was my teacher for many years. He was Creedath's lieutenant and I fear he may recognize me . . . or you,'' he quickly added. ''Be prepared for a fight.''

Benyar's reply was to appear to pay sudden attention to his food. In actuality he was covering the corner of the tavern where he and Ranth sat with what appeared to be a veil of darkness. As he continued eating his dinner, he gazed lazily across the room, methodically checking each person. When he recognized Meecha, he reached for his drink and took a long swallow of the wine.

Remember the toning sound I taught you the night we rescued Shunlar? Begin making it now and direct it toward that group. Benyar's instructions were sent to Ranth mind-to-mind.

Nonchalantly they sat finishing their meal, subvocalizing the tone, directing the sound at the group who had just entered the inn. The men and women took a table on the far side of the room. Quietly talking among themselves, Ranth noticed several of them yawning. They seemed not to notice him or Benyar. Soon they too were eating a meal and talking in hushed voices.

My son, echoed Benyar's familiar voice within his head, *continue making the tone as a cover against possible detection while I send a mind probe to see what information I can learn from their thoughts or conversation.*

Ranth nodded and complied with the instructions. He would have liked more than anything to greet his old friend and teacher, but remembered how he and Shunlar had been savagely beaten and taken prisoner by Meecha's dinner companions. As the minutes went by Ranth grew impatient. At last, Benyar smiled at him, a look that Ranth had begun to recognize as appreciation for a job well done.

''A direct approach is best. Come, let us order them another pitcher, this time something a step above the sour ale that they can afford. I believe the man will surprise you, my son.''

Benyar raised his arm for the innkeeper. The robust-looking, balding man with a slight limp arrived and Benyar placed his order, giving the man payment plus a generous tip.

Ranth and Benyar waited for their gift to arrive. When the innkeeper set the pitcher upon the table, several of the mercenaries protested because they hadn't ordered it and they couldn't pay for it. Once they learned it was a gift, one of the women poured herself a goblet and took a hearty swallow. Her expression required no further words of encouragement. Soon they all lifted their goblets high in a toast of thanks. That was the signal Benyar and Ranth had been waiting for. They rose to cross the room.

As they approached Meecha, recognition crossed his face. The table once more fell silent as he stood to greet the two men. The rest of his companions at the table stood with him, but Meecha was the first to bow. Ranth was delighted, and after bowing lower than Meecha—as a sign of respect to his former teacher—he looked up to see an expression that he didn't recognize.

Ranth and his father, for no one could dispute that fact seeing them together, were dressed in perfectly fitted traveling leathers, of a quality that bespoke money. No longer was he clothed in the uniform of Creedath's house guard. Furthermore, something about the carriage of the father set off a spark in Meecha's memory.

"Sit with us," Meecha offered, "if you will," suddenly aware of the forlorn state of his clothes and those of his companions. "Ah . . . that is if you have the time. I'm sure you must have business elsewhere. We all thank you for the generous gift of the wine." And he bowed again, along with the rest of his group.

To see his former teacher in this sorry condition touched Ranth deeply. He knew that Meecha had only been doing his duty to Creedath, his former master, the man who made him fear for his life.

"Sir, allow me to introduce my father, Benyar sul Jemapree. Father, this is Lieutenant Meecha. He was a fine swordmaster to me for years."

Both men bowed curtly to one another, each quickly assessing the other with swift, detail-devouring eye movements.

"My son has told me how you befriended him and later

captured him. I believe what he has to tell you will be of great importance to you." Benyar's eyes told more than his words. There was a wariness to them that Ranth had never seen before and likely hoped not to see again anytime soon.

"Lieutenant Meecha, Lord Creedath is dead. Whatever his last orders to you were, they no longer have any hold on you. What has passed between us is over and I bear no ill will against you."

"Ah, dead you say? I am then doubly cursed because my fate is sealed with a dead man. What is there for me to return to now? My life in Vensunor is over. It has been taken from me by his death. What future could there be for a man who failed his last mission?" Meecha seemed despondent. In fact, he looked to be thoroughly crushed by the news. His companions seemed to be pulling away from close proximity to him, as if they knew his mood would be foul.

"But you did not fail," protested Ranth. "You are still on the mission, duty bound to complete it, and have received the news that your former master is dead. His house will soon be headed by another and I am sure your position will be available upon your return. In fact, I can assure your future will hold promise, if you will allow me to do you a kindness." Ranth was animated and happier than Benyar had seen him in several days.

He ordered paper from the innkeeper and sat down to write a letter to Delcia and Morgentur, requesting they write a letter of recommendation for Lieutenant Meecha. When he finished he handed the paper to Meecha along with the purse he carried.

"Please accept this purse as a token of respect and as a replacement. You see, I know who stole yours along with the contents of several other purses as well. In fact, if you care to hear the story, I would be happy to tell it."

He waited for assent from Meecha and when he had given it, Ranth began his tale of how they escaped from the desert, ending—hours and several pitchers later—with the demise of Creedath.

When he and Benyar finally headed for their room, his father put an affectionate arm around his shoulders. "My son, you will truly be a fine leader one day, respected by all and loved by many.''

They rose to leave before dawn, Ranth feeling quite hung over from the previous night's wine. The young man was pleased when Meecha, alone, came to say farewell to him. They bowed, clasped arms, but said nothing. Making physical contact with Meecha allowed Ranth to hear and somewhat feel the other man's thoughts. Meecha radiated gratefulness. He would return to Vensunor and begin again, perhaps even open a school for those wishing to be taught the sword. With his experience and attitude, many things were possible. Hope filled the man.

NINE

BLISTERING HEAT TOOK AWAY ALL TRACES OF MOIS-
ture, threatening to dry out his eyes. "Keep yourself
covered, my son. It is the only way to retain water."

They had been riding for endless days, or so it seemed to
Ranth. Now as they rode, looking for a small scrap of shade
in which to pause and rest the horses, Ranth was thankful for
the protection the long riding cloak gave.

Benyar had outfitted Ranth in clothing at the beginning of
the journey that, at first, he thought to be very strange. After
several days of wearing the clothes, he saw their value. Made
of soft leather and bleached the color of sand, the pants were
cut to fit him perfectly, as were the riding boots. The shirt,
which laced up the sides and fastened in the front with buttons, had epauletlike cap sleeves to protect his shoulders. It
was the same light color, but the leather was much stiffer. In
fact, it was part shield, fashioned from two thicknesses of
leather, between which was a thin layer of metal mesh. Over
that he wore a loose fitting, long-sleeved cloak, belted at his
waist. Upon the belt hung an elaborately tooled scabbard. To
further protect him from the sun and sandstorms, the hood of
the cloak could be pulled up, and he was given a mask to
keep the sand out of his nose and mouth.

As they approached the mountains that days ago had been
so far in the distance, the desert changed; more rocky out-
croppings began to appear. Their weary horses plodded upward in the sand that was now mostly small rocky chips and
pebbles. As they reached the crest of yet another small hill,

a blast of wind threatened to blow their cloaks back down the path they had just finished climbing.

To Ranth's surprise, they were at the top of a very tall peak. He looked down onto a vast plain that appeared, from this vantage point, to be a teeming city, part of which was carved into the rock of the surrounding mountain. The eyes that had been on them this last part of their journey began to show themselves at last. Several figures dressed in leather, dyed to match the muted shades of the rocks they hid within, could be seen leaving their hiding places, climbing down to meet them.

Riding to a spot out of the wind, Benyar dismounted and gestured to Ranth to do the same. He knelt on the ground and then bent forward, touching his forehead to the earth. Sitting back on his haunches, Benyar took a handful of the rocky sand and sprinkled some of it into the air so that it fell on himself and Ranth. Then he touched his forehead with it, removed his mask, and put a pinch of sand on his tongue, beckoning for his son to do the same.

Ranth felt a calmness settle over him as he performed this strange ritual. All around him he was aware of the silent figures drawing nearer, still watching him and his father warily. When Benyar unsheathed his dagger, Ranth followed suit. But he was surprised when Benyar made a small cut across the back of his hand, then held his hand away from his body allowing the blood to drip freely into the dirt. Ranth knew he must do the same thing and he slowly drew his dagger across the back of his hand, watching the blood swell then run off and drip dark stains onto the sand in front of him.

"My son, you are home. Your blood is now mingled with the blood and earth of your forebears, as is fitting. One day you will protect this land in my place, but for now you have returned to sit at my side and learn the customs of our people."

As Benyar spoke, the dozen or so guardians who were gathering around them had slowly realized who these two strangers were. One by one, they knelt before the two newcomers. The wind had quieted as the last slight form knelt and bent forward, touching forehead to the ground. Again

Benyar spoke, but this time his quiet voice had such commanding presence that it startled Ranth.

"I have searched for years for the man who sits beside me. He was stolen from my wife's arms as a babe and by a miracle has been found. Our people will again be proud and strong. Send a messenger to the High Priestess that Benyar sul Jemapree and his son, Ranth sul Zeraya, have returned."

One of the guardians was on his feet and running as soon as the echo of the words had stopped bouncing from the surrounding stone. Ranth suddenly seemed transported to another time. Benyar had risen and was standing next to Ranth, who remained kneeling, waiting for his next instructions. After several moments he turned his head slowly and looked at his father, careful not to make eye contact. Benyar stood with his hand held out to him, as if he meant to help him rise. Aware that the back of his hand was still bleeding from the ritual bloodletting of moments ago, Ranth reached his hand up to his father. Benyar firmly grasped Ranth's hand, touching the cut, which instantly closed and healed, leaving no scar. Then Benyar bid Ranth stand beside him.

None of the guards had spoken yet, nor had they gotten to their feet. They remained on their knees with their heads bowed, waiting for a signal to rise. Turning his attention back to the entourage kneeling before him, Benyar sent a mind touch to them, instructing them to rise. They stood as one unit with the merest whisper of leather. One man came forward and, bowing from the waist, held out his right hand, palm up, in what Ranth guessed must be a form of permission to speak. Instead, Benyar answered by placing the pommel of his dagger in the outstretched palm and the man went down on his knees again, as did all the others. Clutching the dagger to his chest, he touched the back of his left fist to his forehead in a salute that each of the others mimicked.

"Rise now, you who have the honor of protecting our home. The time for celebrating has come. Ketherey sul Jemapree, meet again my son, your nephew, Ranth sul Zeraya." At this invitation to rise, once again the entire group solemnly brought their arms down to their sides and stood.

The man who had just been identified as Ranth's uncle, Ketherey, slowly unfastened one side of the mask that pro-

tected him from the all-pervading, ever-blowing sand, and
fixed a piercing gaze on Ranth. Just as he remembered to
keep his guard up, Ranth could feel an intense probing at the
edges of his mind that reminded him of his father's touch.
The eyes of his uncle softened a bit to a more kindly expression, but was this a man to be trusted? A shudder passed
through Ranth as Ketherey removed his mind-touch and
smiled at his nephew. He nodded a curt bow of acknowledg-
ment to Ranth and allowed his smile to grow as he did so. It
seemed Ranth had just passed the first of many tests that he
would be subjected to in the coming days.

Ketherey turned away from Ranth to embrace Benyar. The
two brothers tried unsuccessfully to control their emotions.
They clutched each other hard and finally, pounding one another on the back, they both began to howl. The group of
guardians took up the sound and soon all were hooting and
howling and slapping each other on the back. Unaccustomed
to this type of behavior from his father—or from anyone, for
that matter—Ranth stared with a bewildered look on his face
until Benyar put his arm around his shoulder and encouraged
him to join in on the chorus.

Several young men who had removed themselves to the
back of the group stood, watching. They didn't join in on the
howling, but stayed off by themselves, milling around, kicking at rocks absently. One among them, who watched with
eyes like a wild animal, seemed to be a little older than the
others; their body language told that they deferred to him. He
kept up a glare so forceful that Ranth felt it and turned to
return the stare, curious. Their eyes met and Ranth knew he
faced an enemy. The young man, as he would soon learn,
was his cousin, Korab, himself only a year younger than
Ranth. For reasons he could only guess, Korab was furious
at the news that Benyar had returned with his only son and
heir.

The years Benyar had been absent while searching for
Ranth had given Korab a sense of false security and the con-
fidence that he would one day rule the Feralmon. His mother,
Fanon, and father, Ketherey, had been named regent and First
Protector while Benyar was away. Together with the High

Priestess, Honia sul Urla, they had been doing just fine without Benyar and Zeraya.

Korab was quite persuasive when his needs must be fulfilled, and he had done everything in his power to ensure that a young priestess, Septia sul Prakur, assist him in learning the arcane teachings that were forbidden to one of his age and rank. She agreed with Korab that he must do everything he could to ensure that he remain the successor, especially when he promised her she would rule as his consort. This meant, of course, that Septia would ultimately have the power, the Feralmon being a matriarchy, a fact that Korab did not seem to fully realize.

Korab was not positive but he believed that if he and Benyar were to have a contest of wills, he would be the victor. And he was not far from wrong. Already Korab had surpassed his father, by studying the Temple texts, a secret that he guarded well. No, only he and the woman knew—for now— what knowledge he possessed.

Unknown to even Septia, Korab had sent assassins after Benyar, none of whom had been successful. This setback, the return of Benyar and Ranth, would not deter him from his plans. Korab had a definite vision of what his future held, and it did not include the scene that was unfolding before him. In an effort to hide the many secrets firmly within the recesses of his mind, Korab closed off his thoughts behind a secure barrier. He knew well the stories of Benyar's powers, and it would not do to have his uncle suspect that he was anything but overjoyed at his return.

As the group began to quiet down and make their way into the city of the Feralmon, Korab quickly changed his demeanor, smiled, and nodded to the small group of young men who surrounded him. Like practiced puppets, they all returned his smile as they joined the others.

Ketherey, who had finally remembered himself, looked around for his son and called him to his side. "Ranth, I wish you to meet my son, Korab sul Fanon. He is of an age with you and it is my wish that you become friends. There is much you must learn about your people and our customs and I hope that Korab will begin to teach you."

A dark look crossed Korab's face that he quickly hid from

his father and Benyar, but Ranth was not fooled. He had seen behind the façade as he watched his cousin on the far side and he chose to play the game. Ranth projected a person with a foolish mind to his cousin, and when Korab saw it, he was delighted.

Ranth smiled broadly and bowed to Korab. "Cousin, I am most honored and anxious to speak with you. I have many questions, as your father has mentioned. Tell me, what does one do to amuse oneself at the end of a long ride? I am weary from the saddle and would not refuse a cool drink if it were offered."

Korab seemed anxious to please as he pretended to take Ranth under his protection. He returned the bow and offered refreshment.

TEN

BLENDING ONCE MORE INTO THE ROCKS, THE RE-
maining guards resumed their posts, while Ketherey
and six others escorted Benyar and Ranth into the
city of the Feralmon, Kalaven, named after the desert. Ketherey and Benyar began a quiet discussion as they walked
through the stone portal of the city. Since Benyar wished
absolute privacy, he covered himself and his brother with a
spell that prevented any ears from hearing them.

Banners in the colors and designs of the various Feralmon
clans hung from poles, snapping sharply in the afternoon
breeze. The city teemed with people, who took little or no
notice of the party entering into their midst. Once they had
passed, however, eyes watched them openly. Ranth caught
the looks of those who stared at his back, causing some red
faces to quickly avert their eyes and go on about their business. He continued to play the part of an awestruck outsider
as he walked beside Korab. However, he never let his guard
down. Call it instinct; somehow he knew not to trust his
newly met cousin. And Korab also continued to play his
game, tolerant to a fault as he answered the many questions
Ranth asked. For any who watched, the two young men were
striking up a friendship.

"Brother, my first duty is to speak with Honia sul Urla,"
Benyar told Ketherey as they walked. "But I have no wish
to insult her, and one whiff of me in my travel leathers surely
would. I must bathe and change into proper attire to be presented to her. For the sake of time I wish to do that at the

74

public baths. I trust your messenger has already reached the Temple and Honorable Honia will be waiting.''

"Benyar, we are on the very street that will pass the baths, or have you forgotten in the years that you have been away? How many have passed this time, brother?" Ketherey asked.

"Since last I have walked in the midst of my people, four long years, and no I have not forgotten. I am grateful for your letters, but feel saddened that I have been away so long. How is it with our people?" Specifically saying "our people" indicated how much he trusted his brother. Ketherey and his wife, Fanon, had ruled with a fair and just hand all the years that Benyar had searched for Ranth.

"Our people," answered Ketherey with an easy smile, "are faring well as can be expected. Raids have continued near the border, but let us discuss this another time. Now you must prepare to meet with Honia." An anxious tone crept into Ketherey's voice as he asked, "Tell me good news, brother. Has luck smiled upon us and returned Zeraya's Lifestone?"

"Yes, Ketherey. For now tell only Fanon that Zeraya's Lifestone has been restored to me. We will need your help and hers for many months yet, possibly years. But soon, Zeraya will walk among us again." Benyar's eyes had tears in them that he made no attempt to hide.

Ketherey put his hand on his brother's shoulder, giving it a quick squeeze. "Come, let us hurry. While you make yourself presentable I will bring Fanon so that she may hear the news from your own lips. Believe me when I say that I am unable to express my joy at your return and that we will be at your side for as long as you need us. I speak for Fanon and myself when I say that both of us will be more than happy to leave the task of governing and decision-making to Zeraya and you." The brothers smiled a knowing smile at each other.

"But, if you are as overburdened with work as you say, how is it that I found you at the entrance to the city today?" Benyar asked.

"Fanon had decided it would be better to have me away from her today than suffer my mood. I had no idea being arbiter for so many petty disputes would consume so much of the day. I tell you, Benyar, it will give me great pleasure to relinquish my title and all the duties that go with it to its rightful bearer.'' The brothers laughed as they made their way to the public baths.

At the entrance to the baths Benyar and Ranth removed their saddlebags from their tired mounts and turned them over to their escorts. ''See that they are given special attention, for they have carried us far and well,'' instructed Ranth as he handed the reins to an outstretched hand. Only after he gave his horse one last pat on the neck did he notice that the person leading it away was slight of form and a woman. It appeared for a moment that he might have committed a social disgrace. Benyar had warned him that it was not permitted to speak to a member of the opposite sex if one were unmarried. How did that apply to him, he wondered? ''Father?'' he asked when he noticed all eyes were on him.

Benyar merely smiled and nodded. ''My son, bring your clothes. We must be clean when we meet with Honia and your mother.'' Ranth nodded and followed Benyar into the baths.

Ketherey called Korab aside. ''My son, accompany me so that together we can tell your mother that Benyar has returned.''

''No, Father,'' Korab declined. ''I feel my place is at my post with my oath-brothers.'' Abruptly he turned to join the group. Dismissing them so that they could return to their guard posts, Ketherey watched his son walk away, mixed emotions playing over his face. Finally he turned in the direction of the palace.

Lowering themselves into the tub of steaming water, both men sighed as the knots in their tired, aching, muscles began to unravel. ''I apologize if it was wrong to instruct the woman about caring for the horses, but I spoke before I saw it was a woman.'' His voice, though quiet, echoed off the walls of the chamber.

''My son, you were not judged today, nor will you be for many months, but there will come a time when you will be expected to conduct yourself with great concern for what your actions could do to the reputation of our house and clan. As far as telling one of our warriors how to care for a valuable animal, she will probably endure some ridicule for several days, but everyone knows you are not familiar with our ways. Besides, she is an adult and a married woman, else she would not be guarding the entrance to our city.

"For now, do all you can to remember what I have taught you. There is so much more that I did not have time to tell. Some of the lessons you will learn will seem harsh to you, but times are not easy in the Desert of Kalaven. My brother has informed me that raiders yet strike at some of our northern borders and it may lead to war soon. He and Fanon have not moved in that direction because they waited for me to return. No one wants to be remembered for a war," he said lowering his head. "Yet that is how Zeraya and I shall be remembered." With those words Benyar stopped talking. His look was one of remorse, and Ranth did not ask any further questions.

When attendants came in with clean robes, Benyar waved them away in annoyance. They bowed and left at once. Ranth did not relish spending much time with his father while he was in such a mood, and he found himself avoiding the older man's eyes.

"Ranth, I am not myself. Forgive me if I seem preoccupied, but I am anxious to see your mother and restore her life to her."

They dressed in silence, side by side, as they had every morning while traveling. That part of the journey was over and now for Ranth an unimaginable one was beginning. Everything was new to him. Every custom was different. His hands trembled with expectation as he belted his sword to his waist.

The attendants had brought a tray of fruit and cheese and a large pitcher of water for them, but Benyar had only water to drink. Ranth was hungry and knew his father to be, but he too drank only water.

No sooner had he set the empty cup down than Ketherey arrived with Fanon and an escort of men and women to see him to his audience with the High Priestess, Honia sul Urla. She had been the person solely responsible for caring for Zeraya all the years since her injury. Honia was well practiced at her craft of herbs and spells. It had been Honia's decision to put Zeraya into the sleep state. Under Honia's watchful eyes Zeraya had not only healed from the injury that she suffered from a blow to her head, but she had not aged one day.

"My Lord Benyar, welcome home," was the heartfelt welcome from Fanon. She and Benyar embraced as kin, kissing on each cheek. But Benyar whispered something in her ear before he released her from his embrace. Her smile brightened her face and soon tears overflowed her eyes.

"It is true?" she asked in a hushed voice. He nodded in the affirmative.

"Fanon sul Eliya, meet my son, your nephew, Ranth sul Zeraya," He smiled as he introduced Ranth to Fanon.

Delighted, Fanon hugged Ranth tightly saying, "So long ago I held an infant . . . now look at the grown man you are. Welcome to your home, Ranth sul Zeraya. Forgive a happy woman her tears," she said wiping her cheeks. "Go now. Your mother awaits."

The city was buzzing with the news of Benyar's return. As he, Ranth, Ketherey, Fanon, and their escort wound their way through the streets to the Temple, the men, women, and children they passed bowed low after them. Soon people began to follow at a respectful distance, gathering in the square, speaking in hushed tones as they anticipated news of Zeraya.

"Ranth, my son," Benyar whispered. "One day these people will be your subjects. They do you great honor today and it pleases me. However, I must tell you that I will meet with Honia and your mother alone. Since she will yet be in stasis, this might be a great shock to her, if she were to see you, a grown man, when she first awakens. I will tell her of you and when she regains her strength, then you and she will be reunited. Please understand this is not an easy thing for me to ask you, but for your mother's sake, I must."

"Certainly, Father. I will do as you ask and wait until my mother is stronger. Perhaps by that time I will be able to speak to her properly, in more than a few halting phrases and words." Although Ranth agreed, he was disappointed, something he did not even attempt to hide from his father when Benyar affectionately patted his shoulder.

In the distance, Ranth could see that the gates in the wall

surrounding the courtyard of the Temple were open and an escort of young women, most of whom were future priestesses, waited silently inside. Lining both sides of the walkway, they were dressed in ankle-length robes and barefoot. Covering them from head to toe was a thin, golden, sand-colored veil that glittered in the late afternoon sun. As Benyar, Ranth, and their small entourage entered into their midst, each woman bowed as she was passed.

Benyar and Ranth came first, followed by Fanon and Ketherey. In twos they walked the length of the courtyard between the lines of young women, then they began to climb the polished marble stairs that brought them to the doors of the Temple. Three times the height of a man in width and twice that in length, the doors were crafted of wood and polished, hammered copper, and they shone brightly. The building seemed to be fashioned out of pale white and pink marble that had great streaks of gray running throughout. Columns lined the top stair and supported a roof that seemed to come out of the side of the mountain itself. In fact, the entrance had been built over the mouth of the natural cave that had become the Temple years ago when the young Zeraya had found it.

Off to the left side was a spacious atrium where several benches were provided for people to sit and remove their shoes, for to enter in other than bare feet would be considered shameful and rude. A fountain offered the possibility of washing one's feet if necessary.

The entranceway was covered by thin, gauzy curtains; Ranth was only partially able to see into the sanctuary where Benyar would enter. On either side of the curtains waited attendants who would show Benyar the way, their heads respectfully bowed to all who had entered the atrium.

Ketherey bowed before his brother. As a further sign of respect, he knelt to remove Benyar's boots. When Benyar protested, Ketherey would hear none of it.

"Brother, allow me to do you this honor, as is my right. Can you not see that my heart rejoices at your return?" Ketherey's smile could be very persuasive, and it worked its magic once again. Benyar bowed to him in thanks, then sat down so that his brother could remove his boots. Then they embraced once more, parted, and Benyar entered the Temple.

The symbols of his people were all around him. Great tiled murals in stones of bright colors enlivened the walls he passed. The ceiling, decorated with gold leaf, portrayed the path of the sun as it crossed the sky. The center of the floor, where one was not permitted to step, was painted with images of the three moons: Daleth, Malenti, and Andeela. Benyar's heart pounded with anticipation as he neared the room where his wife had lain, unmoving, for twenty years.

At the entrance to Zeraya's chamber waited Honia sul Urla. She knelt before Benyar—a great honor to him—and he bowed low to her.

"Please my whims, but rise, Honia. You do me more honor than I deserve. It has taken too many long years. Tell me, truthfully if you can, will the healing be complete?" Benyar asked in Old Tongue, taking her hand to help her rise. The older woman stood in one fluid motion.

"My lord, Zeraya sul Jemapree awaits you and her Lifestone. I have no doubts that she will recover fully. In fact, it has been seen that she and you will beget other children," was her reply. This time she smiled.

Hurrying to Zeraya's side, clutching her precious Lifestone in his hands, Benyar gently placed it upon her chest. She began to breathe, haltingly at first. After some time passed, she turned her head and opened her eyes. As her breathing became deeper, she coughed, and a bowl of water was brought to her by an attending priestess. The young woman carefully administered small spoonfuls of water into Zeraya's mouth.

Minutes went by and finally Zeraya tried to speak, but her vocal cords had been still so many years that she could only manage a rasping noise.

Benyar, my husband, what has happened to me? Why am I here in the Temple? The sound of her voice ringing within his head once again was too much for him. He went down on his knees beside her bed, covering his face with one hand while he clutched her other hand tightly.

Zeraya, to hear your voice after nothing but silence from you. . . . I feared I would never hear it again, and now that I do, I cannot find words. He answered her in the same way.

Something about the way Benyar was acting frightened

Zeraya. Her feeling of fear transferred to him immediately and he quickly stood to look into her eyes, trying to calm her.

"Where is my child, husband?" she demanded, suddenly regaining her voice. Benyar bowed his head and his gesture was similar to the way the men at the entrance to the city greeted him and Ranth. He touched his forehead with the back of his hand but this time his fist covered his eyes. He did not want Zeraya to see his tears.

"I will bring him, soon. Please believe me that our son is alive and well. No harm has come to him. But you must rest now for you have suffered injury at the hands of my enemies." As he lowered his arm he could see the terror in her eyes.

"Why do you cry, beloved? Am I badly injured? What happened to our son?" Zeraya demanded frantically.

Using every ounce of control he had, Benyar answered her. "Your injury healed many years ago. You have been kept alive by the High Priestess, Honia sul Urla, something that was necessary because your Lifestone was taken from you at the time of the raid. But at that time, my enemies took our son."

At those words Zeraya flinched and began to cry. Benyar touched her face and continued. "He has been found, my heart. I have spent years returning home and leaving again and again to search for him. I tell you now that I have found him, and by a miracle your Lifestone has been returned to me also. If not for that, you would not be hearing my words now."

Benyar paused, wishing his next words could somehow be avoided. "But, you must be strong, my beloved, for you have been in your sleep for so long, that our son is a grown man. In fact, he is now older than you."

Zeraya took the news that she had been nearly dead so long very badly. But her will to live was strong. She knew that she must prepare herself by gathering her strength before seeing her son. Being apart from her Lifestone for so many years had very nearly caused her death. It would take many months for her to recover, but recover she would, she resolved. And she and Benyar would have more children, she vowed. After all, her body was still eighteen years old.

When Benyar left her side hours later, he seemed content, knowing that her strength was being restored. The room glowed with a strong pink light from the Lifestone that rested upon Zeraya's chest as she slept, breathing evenly.

The shock of seeing her son so soon, even though that was what Zeraya wanted, could kill her, and Honia told Benyar that in no uncertain terms. He must concede to Honia's pronouncement that Ranth wait until his mother was stronger before he could be brought to her and it was left to Benyar to tell his son the news.

By now, most of the inhabitants of the city had gathered and were crammed into the courtyard and the square beyond. Ketherey and Fanon had remained, with several of his oath-brothers, and also Ranth, who was anxious for news of his mother. When Benyar arrived at last, all rose and bowed to him.

Benyar addressed the crowd assembled before him. "As I look upon you, I see many faces of old friends and I thank you for waiting. Zeraya sul Jemapree will make a full recovery and soon be walking amongst you again." He gestured for Ranth to join him and he placed his hand on his shoulder, continuing, "Our son, Ranth sul Zeraya, has also been restored to us." A cheer rose from the crowd and they all bowed together to Benyar, their lord, consort of the ruler of the Feralmon and his son.

"Now is the time of initiations. Go and pray well for us," Benyar finished. The people turned and began to leave, excited and happy.

Honia, who had escorted Benyar to the outer doors of the Temple, looked upon Ranth for several long moments after they had been properly introduced. Ranth returned her bow by going down on one knee before her. She smiled and touched his head, blessing him in Old Tongue, contacting his mind directly by her touch.

Child of Zeraya, Ranth sul Zeraya, welcome back to your home. May you prosper all your days.

Honia sul Urla, I thank you for your welcome and your

blessing. May you prosper all your days, he answered her, careful not to look at her until he was permitted to. She tapped his shoulder lightly and looked deeply into his eyes when he raised his head. Ranth did not flinch at her intense mind probe, and maintained the strong, carefully constructed barrier around himself that years of living under Creedath's roof had made such a part of everyday survival.

Indicating that Ranth should rise, Honia turned to Benyar and whispered something to him. Then, bowing low, she returned to attend Zeraya. It was not until she was halfway through the Temple that she realized Ranth had spoken the proper response in the Old Tongue! She was intrigued and made a promise to herself to seek this young man out as soon as possible and find out who had educated him. But now she cleared her mind of other thoughts. Zeraya was breathing again and she must concentrate all of her energies on the recovering woman, now more than ever before.

Ranth accepted the news that his mother must be stronger in order to receive him as well as he could, given the situation. He hid his true feelings well in front of the others, something that did not go unnoticed. "Father, tell my honored mother when next you see her that I am most anxious for her recovery and our meeting. I will await her summons."

Then, unexpectedly, Benyar gave Ranth over to Ketherey's safekeeping, saying, "Brother, will you take my son and treat him as your own? I had not anticipated that we should be apart, but there is no other choice. I must be with my wife now. Honia has asked and I cannot refuse."

"Aye, my lord. Your son will be as mine, and will be taught many things tonight. Has he been prepared?" asked Ketherey.

"Ranth knows little of our customs, but I trust in his instincts to do what is right and necessary." Benyar lowered his voice then and added, "You will see that he has no clan markings and that must be changed before he can be presented to his mother." They exchanged a long, meaningful look, and then bowed to one another.

As Benyar returned to the doorway of the Temple, Ketherey cast an unusual glance at Ranth, seeming to scrutinize

him hair by hair. He and the rest of their small party left for
their evening meal as soon as Benyar was gone from their
sight. Ranth began to have a very uneasy feeling in the pit of
his stomach as he walked with them.

ELEVEN

RANTH AND BENYAR HAD ARRIVED AT THE MONTH of the full moons. This was a time of initiation among the Feralmon, when the men and women reverted to an ancient custom of living apart. It had long been the traditional way for men and women to conduct their secret rituals in separate quarters. Each clan had its own tent, enormous affairs that could hold thirty people comfortably, and everyone would leave their permanent homes to live in their clan's pavilion for the duration of the season.

Once the children were weaned, the girls learned from their mothers and the boys from their fathers, at the ceremonial times of year. When children reached the age of puberty, however, speaking to the opposite sex was only permitted in the company of adults. Punishments were severe if this law was broken—though not as harsh as several centuries previously—and few, if any, dared to break it.

His first night in the men's pavilion Ranth discovered that his status within this society was that of a child, because he had never been initiated and no one knew if he could even defend himself properly. Rite of passage involved going into the desert and killing a sand cat, or one of the equally poisonous large snakes or lizards with little other than a knife, bow and arrow, or spear. Benyar had told him of this custom, but Ranth didn't fully begin to comprehend how much fulfilling the obligation of first hunt meant to these people until he was left in the care of the two male relatives that were strangers to him. Though everyone was civil, Ranth could feel a sense of something close to apology—mixed with embarrassment from his uncle, Ketherey. Korab, his cousin, emanated anger and, not very well hidden, a deep hatred.

Ranth had to work hard to conceal his true feelings. Once again it seemed fate had cast him into a situation with little or no preparation. As before, he remembered his early training within the confines of the Temple of the Cauldron in the city of Vensunor. He remembered the face of his teacher, mentor, and friend, Master Chago, heard again the revered old man's words and they comforted him. Memories of reading and studying the ancient texts, meditating, and the sound of the evening bells chiming helped him to project an outward calm. He was treated like a guest and made comfortable. Some of the younger adolescents attended to him; some asked questions and were polite, but no one sat with him when he ate.

In this particular clan there were about twenty adults, five adolescents, and ten children. In the late evening, hours after the meal was finished, everyone, including Ranth, gathered to sit in a circle in the middle of the tent. The ground in the centermost part of the pavilion was bare sand, unlike the rest of the tent floor, which was covered with thickly woven carpets. Ketherey had chosen to sit at Ranth's right side. One of his oath-brothers, a slender man by the name of Bellat sul Cameera, whose merry, penetrating eyes missed nothing, sat at Ranth's left.

In the center, directly beneath the smoke vent, a fire had been laid and two of the younger boys proudly approached Ketherey. He lit the torches they carried from a smoldering charcoal; they in turn, all bright and smiling, set them to the wood. The lanterns hanging on the walls were snuffed out and the fire became the only source of light.

Ketherey began by unstopping a wineskin, tilting his head back, and pouring a long stream into his open mouth. Swallowing, he offered the skin to Ranth at his left, saying, "Ranth sul Zeraya, we make you welcome to our house. We make you welcome to our clan. We make you welcome among us, your brothers. Drink and become one of us."

Ranth accepted the wineskin with a low bow to his uncle. "You do me great honor, Ketherey sul Jemapree," he an-

swered, then tilted his head back as Ketherey had done. The
liquid was sweet with a very bitter aftertaste. It had an immediate numbing effect on his mouth and throat. Since the
flow came faster than he had expected, Ranth swallowed
much more of the fiery liquid than he had intended. He controlled his urge to choke as, bowing and swallowing, he
passed the wineskin on to Bellat on his left, who accepted the
pouch from Ranth with a wide, knowing grin, drank, and
passed it on.

After each man had taken a drink, he began to clap a simple
rhythm that became more complex each time another joined
in. The young boys who weren't asleep sat next to their fathers and tried to imitate them. Several of the men had drums,
some had small percussive instruments, others had polished
wooden sticks. As the rhythms reached a crescendo they suddenly stopped.

As if on cue, two men stood and shed their robes. Clad in
only loincloths, they entered the circle. The rhythms began
again. Ranth was fascinated to see that they, like Benyar, were
scarred over most of their bodies in patterns that began on
their torso and extended across their arms and legs, stopping
at the elbows and knees. This was one big difference that
Ranth immediately saw would set him apart. He remembered
his father telling him how the marks were acquired during a
"ritual dance." This, he surmised, must be that dance.

Only the youngest boys stared openly at Ranth, noticing
his inability to clap the rhythms. A few older boys shyly cast
sidelong glances from the corner of their eyes. Another pair
of men joined the two in the middle of the circle. Together
they began to perform a strange yet fascinatingly beautiful
succession of movements that became faster and more deadly
as the tempo increased.

Watching intently, Ranth tried to compare the moves with
those he had learned at the Temple, or his combat training in
Creedath's yard, but there seemed to be few similarities. The
men flew through the air, leaping and landing on hands or
feet, that turned into a roll, that turned into a perfectly exe-
cuted kick or sweep of the legs. They tumbled by or landed
on their hands in a cartwheel, constantly in motion, some
more graceful than others. Ranth continued to study each pair

and soon could see several patterns, but he did not fully comprehend how they were done.

Most all of the men and some of the younger boys had risen and taken their place within the circle. Even the youngest had some small scar on his back or chest or belly. Ranth had noticed that one or two of the youngest who were closest to him seemed to be bleeding, from very precise points that matched on their front and back, but the light was very dim, he told himself, and everyone was sweating profusely. As each youngster returned to where he was sitting, a man on either side of him took something from a small pouch and applied it to those specific areas of their bodies.

He began to feel uncomfortable and very unsure of himself when he noticed that his cousin, Korab, had been staring at him from where he sat, about six places away to his left. Korab rose, shed his robe and walked to stand before Ranth who recognized this as an invitation to "dance." Feeling strangely compelled to accept, Ranth realized he felt giddy as he floated to his feet without knowing how after the last two men had seated themselves.

Ranth felt heat rising to his face as he removed his robes, carefully mimicking his cousin's moves. Many of the men openly sucked their breath in and stared at his bare, unmarked body. In only a loincloth, he joined Korab on the sand. They began to circle each other. Ranth matched his cousin in size; in fact they looked remarkably alike, except for the sneer on Korab's face. He openly showed his distaste for the smooth, unblemished body of his cousin.

The first strike was Korab's, and it stung Ranth's belly. When he looked down at his belly in disbelief, he saw a small trickle of blood. Only then did he realize what was about to happen to him.

"Defenseless. Soft. Outsider." Ranth could hear those words being whispered about him. He closed off his mind to all of them and set his jaw, determined not to allow Korab to cut him any more.

Korab tried another strike but Ranth blocked it and instead managed to place the heel of his foot in Korab's belly. It took the wind out of Korab and he staggered. Fury washed over Korab's face as he recovered his breath and straightened. In two swift moves he was nearly on top of Ranth. He kicked out with one foot, whirled around, and swept Ranth off his feet before Ranth could retaliate. Another sting to his belly, this time on the opposite side, let Ranth know what happened. Whether the men had knives embedded in their fingertips or toes or a small blade concealed, he couldn't tell, but Ranth decided he must either submit to being cut or knock his opponent out. He chose the latter as he slowly stood to face Korab.

As Korab leaped at Ranth to deliver another blow, Ranth dropped to his left knee and punched upward with his right fist. Too late, Korab tried changing his tactic in midair, but Ranth's fist neatly connected with his jaw from underneath. The blow sent Korab up into the air; before he landed on his back in the sand, he was unconscious. The rhythms stopped immediately and several of the men were on their feet as weapons appeared from nowhere.

Ketherey was at his son's side checking him for signs of life. When he was satisfied that Korab was still breathing his grim features rested on Ranth.

"Leave this to me," was all he said. The group of men and boys sat down slowly, reluctantly and Ranth alone was left standing to face his uncle.

"Your father has entrusted me with your education. This is your first lesson." The back of his hand flashed up so fast that Ranth did not see it coming. It struck his face and left a welt. Ranth tasted blood but did not flinch or blink. He opened his mouth to speak and was again rewarded with a slap, this time from the other hand.

Closing his mouth, Ranth steeled himself for another blow that did not come. Instead, silently, one by one, the rest of the circle stood. Each male clapping a complex rhythm, each one humming a sound that soon had his head buzzing just as much as the slaps had. Ranth stood there deciding whether or not to accept whatever punishment was coming to him. There appeared to be no choice. Confused, he tried another approach. He tried to touch his uncle's thoughts to read them. All he wanted to do was understand. His attempt failed. The sound each man made, together with the rhythms of the clapping, made it impossible for Ranth to use his mind-touch.

The group moved around him and each took his turn with a blow. Ranth found that he couldn't lift his arms to defend himself. He only had the ability to stand and take what came. Even Korab had awakened and his strike, when it landed, reverberated all the way through Ranth. Most of the young boys had a light touch that left a sting afterwards. Some of the older men moved so swiftly that they were a momentary blur in his eyes, striking and gone before he could blink. Their whisper-like touch left behind a sharp sting as the only evidence that contact had been made.

Soon consciousness left Ranth. After he fell someone brought a rope that they tied to his wrists. He was hung, arms spread wide, suspended in the midst of the clan so that the dance could continue around him.

Because Korab had hoped that Benyar would never return, he had his own idea of how he wanted Ranth to get through this initiation. Several of the young men were secretly happy to see Ranth knock Korab out, but fear kept them from trading loyalties or speaking up. They knew Korab planned to provoke Ranth so that he would retaliate with a blow that would knock Korab unconscious. To knock out one's opponent was forbidden, if the blow came from one who was lower in position within the men's society. Positioning was everything within the ranks of the Feralmon. Because of his mistaken action, Ranth had to endure the most brutal of their initiations.

As soon as Korab awoke he had signaled one of his oath-brothers, to call men from the other pavilions to enter into their midst. Ketherey observed the look of smug satisfaction on Korab's face, but did not stop his son. *Was this planned?*, he wondered. He would deal with that later. For now the momentum of the ritual had picked up and he could not stop it, not even if it meant sacrificing Ranth's life.

Surely Benyar had mentioned something of this to his son. The young man had reacted properly after the second resounding slap. Could he be at a total loss about how to conduct himself now, as he had seemed to be moments before when he had knocked Korab out? Ketherey secretly allowed himself to feel admiration toward Ranth for that move. He liked the clean execution of the blow and felt Korab had deserved it. Surely Ranth had known that to knock one's op-

ponent out during an initiation was forbidden to the one being
tested. He must have forgotten. At least he had shown all of
them that he could fight.

Hours later Ranth awoke, as someone was cutting his arms
free. He forced his legs to hold his weight and bring his body
to a standing position. As he focused his eyes, he recognized
his father, who now reached out to him tenderly. Ranth had
to bite his lip to keep from making a sound as the blood
returned to his hands. He was able to move them a little,
finally, and as Benyar offered his shoulder to lean on, Ranth
felt a great sorrowful apology rise up from Benyar as he
helped him to his sleeping mat.

Confused, aching, and more frightened than he had ever
been in his life, he trembled as his father lowered him to the
mat. Benyar had a bowl of hot, herb-scented water nearby.
He wet a soft cloth in it and began to carefully wash his son's
many cuts and bruises. The heat and the herbs took away
most of the sting. Afterward, Benyar took out a pouch and
began to rub an ointment into each small cut, physical touch
allowing them to communicate freely mind-to-mind.

Will this mark me as it does all the others?

Yes, my son. Be still so that I can tend to your wounds.

*NO! I will not be like them. What did I do to deserve being
beaten so savagely? You told me I would learn the customs
and be in the keeping of your brother. Is this how you were
taught? Did you know I would be beaten and cut?* Ranth was
so panicked he nearly vomited.

*Remain calm, my son. Now is not the time for explanations.
Now is the time to heal. I will remove all of your pain with
my touch, but choose wisely, for unless you are marked as
one of us, you cannot remain. And if you choose to let these
wounds heal without marking them with color, what happened
here tonight will only be repeated.* The sorrowful tone never
left Benyar's voice.

Tears were coursing down his cheeks as he applied the
pigment to Ranth's many small wounds. The pattern of them
would be seen in the light of day. Ranth was unaware of how
long it took for his father to anoint his body, and he offered
no resistance. His consciousness and his pain had been taken
from him by Benyar.

The ritual was meant not only to be a test of Ranth's courage but of his patience as well. If he had tried to lash out or stop Ketherey after the first insulting slap, they all would have attacked him at once. Ranth was a stranger in their midst and he was treated severely by them. He did not know that each of them had been tested in similar ways by their elders and peers.

Because Ranth was Benyar's son, not only the men of his clan had come to have their turn at him, but from all the others. Each house had left its particular mark as part of the pattern that would mark Ranth's body. Had he been raised among them, this part of his initiation, the scarification, would have happened to him from the time he was a small boy and continued at each level of his training. As it was, being the outsider he was, and because he had rendered Korab unconscious, they chose this night to do it all at once.

It stemmed not from malice, but from a sense of protectiveness. The men of his pavilion truly believed they were doing him a very large favor. To be unmarked in their society was a source of great shame and a cause for ridicule. His acceptance of Ketherey's invitation to "join them" in the clan had been a sign of consent for the ritual to begin. And Benyar had not explained too many details to Ranth, for he knew what must happen to his son before he met his mother.

But something had gone wrong and Benyar wanted to know what or whom had instigated such a severe initiation. The next day, Benyar knew, Ranth must conduct himself before all the men in a way that showed there were no ill feelings. If Ranth acted improperly toward any or all whom he must someday rule, Benyar was certain there would be trouble. He had been gone so long and spent so much time searching for his son that he had forgotten to tell him many things about life among the Feralmon. That mistake would not occur again, he vowed. Sitting cross legged next to Ranth, Benyar placed one hand on his son's forehead and the other on the middle of his chest. He remained that way until the sun was rising.

The tread of many footsteps approaching their sleeping mat made Ranth stir at last and when he opened his eyes, it was to look into the concerned face of his father. Benyar removed

his hands from his son and Ranth slowly sat up. His body
shuddered suddenly when his gaze turned away from Benyar
and landed on the men of their clan who had gathered around,
and were now sitting, waiting for him to awaken. Ranth was
wearing only his loincloth. He reached for his long robe that
lay folded nearby, and pulled it over his head.

When he was dressed, Ranth turned to face the group,
knelt, and tucked his legs beneath him, something that took
an enormous amount of effort. He knew these next moments
were very important. In front of everyone assembled sat
Korab, with his father, Ketherey, at his side. Ranth put all of
his attention fully on his cousin and bent forward, touching
his forehead to the carpet.

A flash of rage crossed Korab's face. Although he immediately attempted to cover his feelings up, it wasn't fast
enough to escape the watchful eyes of Benyar. He knew at
once that Korab had instigated the initiation rites of last night
and felt as though he had just suffered a wound from the act.
This young man could never be trusted and Ranth must be
made to know that, if he had not already figured it out.

Minutes passed. Sweat was beginning to trickle down
Ranth's face and Benyar could tell that his son was having
great difficulty enduring the position he waited in. Even Ketherey was casting nervous sidelong glances at Korab. After
what seemed like an interminably long time had passed,
Korab spoke.

"Rise and speak," Korab's carefully controlled voice gave
permission.

Ranth pushed himself up into a sitting position, taking great
gulps of air as he did so. Everyone was aware of how much
his strength had been sapped the night before. He quieted his
breathing before he spoke. With a whispered voice, careful
to keep the gaze of his eyes on the pattern just inches from
Korab's knees, he spoke.

"I ask forgiveness for my actions and any injury that I
may have inflicted upon your person last night. The fact that
I am ignorant of your customs gives me no excuse. You took
me in among you, as one of you. You gave me water and
food and shelter and I acted in a foolish manner. Let there
not be bad blood between us, as we are of the same blood. I

wish there only to be peace and brotherhood between us. There is much I must learn and would do so at your side, if you permit it. I await your answer and will submit to your judgment.''

A stunned silence filled the space. Only Ranth's breathing seemed to be audible and he waited with his hands on his knees, palms facing toward Korab. Some of the older men nodded their silent approval. It seemed that at least they were willing to accept Ranth's words.

"What answer do you give my son, Korab?" After more than enough time had passed, Benyar's voice broke the silence, the timbre of it indicating his disapproval for the obvious wait that was being inflicted upon Ranth. The air in the room suddenly became thick with tension as Benyar came to his feet.

"The damage was not to my physical self, but to my honor," Korab hissed at Ranth through clenched teeth. "You are an outlander. How could you know of things like honor or blood? No, I will not permit you to learn from me. Seek another who would permit a clanless dog following two steps at his side like a sick shadow."

"*Korab!*" The sound of Ketherey's voice cut like a knife, and some of the younger boys jumped. He was furious. "On your face before your lord." Korab obeyed instantly and Ketherey knelt beside him, both men pressing their foreheads to the carpet.

Benyar came and stood over Korab, clenching and unclenching his fists as he stared at the young man's back.

"Arise, brother," Benyar ordered Ketherey, who instantly returned to a sitting position. Everyone else remained stonestill as Benyar spoke to Ketherey.

"This one," Benyar pointed an accusing finger at Korab, "needs to learn some compassion. To judge another so harshly is cruel. Have the young been taught to treat others in such heartless ways in my absence?" Calling Korab "this one," indicated that he was in very grave trouble.

"No, my lord," Ketherey answered, using the honorific to address his brother. This demonstrated to all the severity of the situation unfolding before them. Though Benyar had been gone many years, he still held the highest rank among the

Feralmon. For Korab to behave in this way meant that he was challenging Benyar's return and the taking of his rightful place. The older men who were allied by blood oath to Ketherey understood this at once and bent forward, pressing their foreheads to the dirt. Several seconds later, the younger ones allied to Korab did likewise.

Ketherey was furious with his son. Because of this foolish young whelp's arrogant comments, Ketherey himself was at risk of losing his place within the men's society, not to mention what might happen to his son. Benyar was lord here and his word was law. If he wished, he could have Korab banished, crippled, or even killed.

With all of the men bent fully to the ground, some of the youngest boys who were sitting in the back of the pavilion looked around them, bewildered by the goings on of the adults. They were hungry for breakfast, and one small voice began to show his fright by wailing loudly. He was silenced quickly by an older boy, who took his hand and sat him upon his lap. The youngster sucked his thumb and wiped his tears away.

Choosing not to notice the interruption, Benyar took a deep breath to assume some control over his emotions. He wanted to punish Korab with physical violence, but would not permit himself to do so. Instead he returned to stand beside Ranth, who had remained sitting with his hands still held toward Korab, palms up.

"Rise and put your hands beneath your robe, my son," Benyar instructed, as he hid his own hands from sight.

"Ketherey sul Jemapree, open your eyes to me. Men that are oathbound to him, do the same." Benyar's voice had taken on a soft tone. More than half the men in the room obeyed, sat back on their haunches, and turned their eyes to him.

"The remainder of you, rise also." He still refrained from calling his nephew by his name. Instead he fixed his stare on Korab.

"You have greatly angered me this day." Benyar pointed at Korab. "A simple *no* would have sufficed, yet you dared to speak in such a manner. For that insolence you must be punished."

Ketherey was holding his breath as he waited for sentence to be announced, his face suddenly gone pale. Would Benyar harm his son?

"You are silenced. There is no one to whom you may speak and none may speak to you until the time has passed that I deem it otherwise. You may remain among us, but only so long as you are careful not to cross my path or that of my son. Go quickly while my fury is controlled, for to look upon you angers me and I may yet strike out at you if you remain longer." Benyar struggled to regain his composure as he watched Korab stand, turn, and swagger from the pavilion, the set of his shoulders attempting bravado.

But before he left their sight, Benyar called out to him. "Stop." Korab froze where he stood, expecting some worse punishment. Only words were spoken to his back. "Those of you who are sworn to him may leave with him if you wish, but be warned, to do so means you will share his fate." None moved from their positions as Korab waited for at least one or two of his closest oath-brothers to join him.

After several minutes had passed, Benyar spoke in a quieter, more controlled voice, "Go. Leave us." Korab walked through the doorway, some of the defiance gone from his demeanor.

Returning his attention to the men assembled before him, Benyar let the rest of his anger cool. He was tired from having spent the night beside his son, healing him and also instructing him on how to conduct himself in front of the clan this morning. Obviously it had all been worth the effort, as Ranth had once again proven himself to be a worthy and very capable student. He allowed a sense of pride and respect for the son he had searched for all the years of his exile to wash over him and when he spoke again, the love he felt for his son was apparent in his voice.

"Ranth, look at these faces before you. Know who your teachers are."

At those instructions, Ranth looked up and locked eyes with each man in the room who faced him, beginning with his uncle.

When Ranth had finished, he eloquently said, "I am greatly honored," bowing low to them.

"Arise now, my son, and show yourself to us so we may know you for the man you have become." Benyar's voice nearly broke with emotion.

Ranth stood and stepped out of his robe, as his father instructed him to do so that all could see his body. The green clay mixed with the ointment, plus the healing that Benyar had performed on his son, made the design of the markings shine like beads upon his body. The length and breadth of him was marked, from neck to elbows to knees, in an intricate pattern that wove each clan's markings together, but his arms looked as though they were covered with the scales of a dragon.

TWELVE

RANTH SPENT THE NEXT WEEK RECUPERATING FROM the shock of his strange initiation into the men's society of the Feralmon. His father returned from the Temple each day for at least an hour or two to check on him, but left Ranth to fend for himself the rest of the time.

On the morning of the third day, Ranth gathered up his courage and asked Ketherey if he would consider showing him some of the finer points of the "dance." His uncle was, of course, delighted that Ranth had come to him and he began to show him how to execute some of the turns, kicks, and sweeps that were done with the feet. Since most of Ranth's muscles were stiff from the ordeal of his initiation, he became winded sooner than he expected, but he pushed himself. He discovered that he wanted his uncle's approval, something the older man sensed.

"Nephew, were you to overtax yourself and become ill, my honor would be questioned. Tonight I will ask you to join me in the circle. Perhaps it would be best if you rested now." Ranth could only nod his head in agreement, bent half over as he was, with his hands on his knees, inhaling in great gasps.

"These are for you," Ketherey whispered as he handed Ranth a small pouch. Opening it, Ranth discovered two tiny blades that were attached to thin cords. With a puzzled look on his face, he waited for his uncle to explain.

"Has my brother neglected to tell you about these also?" Ketherey asked in disbelief.

"Uncle, my father taught me the language as we rode, some of the rules of Feralmon, and how to survive in the desert. Never did he mention such as these to me." There was a bite of exasperation in Ranth's voice.

"I apologize if I have offended you or my brother. He did explain much to you, but, not to tell you of the foot blades . . ." his voice trailed off. "Here, let me show you how to wear them." And Ketherey carefully tied one small blade between Ranth's first and second toes.

"It will take some time getting used to them. Use them cautiously, or not at all at first. See those two young ones practicing?" Ketherey pointed out two small boys kicking at a board. Ranth nodded. "Join them. They will teach you how to make the mark of our clan."

Ranth did as he was told. Soon he was laughing with the two boys, cutting small lines into the board with his toes. By the end of the week he could manage a fairly good mark with both feet, although the two younger boys were faster and more precise. He was in the midst of enjoying his practice when Benyar arrived and called to him.

"My son, your mother awaits. Come with me to the baths so you can cleanse yourself and change into proper clothing before you meet with her. For this first time, however, I must ask you to be prepared for a short visit, for I fear her strength will not hold out for very long. But you should know that she is most anxious to hold you close again after so many years."

As they entered the baths together, Ranth could tell his father was anxious about his first meeting with Zeraya. This time Benyar did not shoo the attendants away, but allowed them to soap and rinse him and Ranth, treating them like the high-blooded men they were.

Only after they were left alone to soak in the hot water did Ranth ask, "Father, did you hide me from the eyes of these men the first day we came here because you were ashamed of me?"

"It was not shame that compelled me but caution. I knew what thoughts would go through their minds and I chose not to deal with it at the time. No, my son, I was not and never have been ashamed of you. The shame has been mine. I will still have many more things to answer for, things that I have not taught you, proper actions, proper customs. But first and foremost, I must answer to my wife for permitting my enemies to abduct you." Benyar's voice had taken on an apologetic tone.

"Yes, I fear it was my fault. A man whose father's father's father was killed in a raid by one of my ancestors was responsible for that, I am sure. I didn't allow myself to believe that his vindictiveness would reach my wife or my child, but it did. When Zeraya finds out the truth of the matter, I am afraid she will ask for retribution. And, being at fault, I cannot refuse her."

Ranth was silent after that. He had many questions but couldn't think of how to ask them. When the attendants returned to help them dress, Ranth was somewhat thankful for their intrusion. The very duties the men performed were what he had been learning to do only months ago as a captive under Creedath's roof. As he walked to the Temple with his father, Ranth couldn't help but reflect on how his life had changed. The memories were bittersweet, but as his thoughts focused on Shunlar, his mood turned from hatred of the man who had imprisoned him to longing for the woman whom he had given his heart to.

Benyar broke his reverie when they arrived at the Temple. "We are expected," Benyar whispered. The doors stood open and lamps were lit inside. Ranth and Benyar removed their shoes and entered unescorted. The walls were covered with scenes of life among the Feralmon.

"Another time I will explain to you what the murals represent. Some of the men and women pictured here are your ancestors. For now, walk only where my feet tread and prepare yourself to meet your mother." Benyar lowered his head and walked ahead of Ranth, leading him to Zeraya.

Zeraya sul Karnavt sat waiting with the High Priestess and several younger priestesses, who were her attendants. It was in this room that she had spent the last twenty years in a state of suspended life.

It was difficult for Ranth to believe that this woman was his mother. She was very pale for one of these dark people, but Ranth was instantly taken by her beauty. Barely five feet tall, she waited regally in her chair for Ranth to approach. He noticed that her hair fell in long, loose curls that trailed behind her along the floor. Her dark eyes looked him over inch by inch, from top to bottom and back again, widening with each sweep. And she was so young, another detail that Benyar had not mentioned to him. During all the years of waiting for her Lifestone to be restored to her, Zeraya had not aged one day. She remained eighteen, younger by two years than the son who now stood before her.

Ranth slowly went down to his knees and bowed before her. He had had no instruction from Benyar, so he improvised. He heard a small voice say, "Rise and come near, my son." He did as he was asked, though cautiously.

Keeping his eyes cast down, Ranth came closer to the chair. Zeraya motioned for him to kneel down and when he did, she tenderly traced his face with shaking fingers. Placing her hand under his chin she tilted his face up so she could look into his eyes. She held her arms out to him then and he let himself be encircled in them. The touch sparked deep, forgotten memories in Ranth. He knew this woman and he felt himself soften and return her embrace. Zeraya placed her head upon his chest, and Ranth held her as she sobbed.

Zeraya was overwhelmed when she saw Ranth, as Honia had guessed she would be. He resembled his father so much. She cried through most of the meeting, and Ranth was not sure if from joy or grief. Only Benyar could console her.

Headstrong as always, Zeraya had insisted on sitting in a chair to meet her son, something that cost her dearly. When exhaustion took its toll on her, much sooner than everyone expected, Ranth was informed that he must leave. A young woman who had watched him from the other side of the room came forward and bowed to him. Benyar told him to follow her, but cautioned him against speaking to her, promising to join him soon.

In silence, walking behind the priestess who spoke not a word to him nor dared to make eye contact with him, Ranth was taken to quarters in the palace. At the door the young woman bowed low to him. He returned her bow and she departed. The room was spacious and comfortable, but Ranth did not understand these were his new quarters. Instead, he thought they were his father's rooms, so he sat in a chair awaiting Benyar's arrival. Hours later Ranth was woken by Benyar gently shaking his shoulder.

"My son, there was no need to wait in this chair for me. Why didn't you lie on your bed?"

"My bed? Father, I thought these were your quarters. I will go back to the men's pavilion now if you tell me the way," Ranth answered quietly.

"No, these are your rooms, Ranth. This is now your home. My rooms and your mother's are close by. Besides, the pavilion is used regularly only during our rituals. I'm afraid that's another thing I forgot to explain." Benyar bowed his head, sorrow and exhaustion apparently taking their toll on him. "Can you find it in your heart to forgive me, my son?"

For the first time since he met his father, Ranth began to understand some of the burdens the man had lived with for the last twenty years. Remembering their brief conversation before the interview with his mother, Ranth tentatively placed his hand on his father's shoulder. Before Benyar could fully cover up his feelings, Ranth felt the loneliness and frustration that went to the core of his father. But there were no traces of self-pity. Benyar was a man of strong conviction and will. He was determined that Zeraya live and become stronger than before. For the briefest of seconds Ranth was shown the deep and tender love Benyar had for Zeraya, just as his awareness was gently pushed elsewhere.

"Understand, my son, that I must concentrate all of my healing powers and time on your mother now. Soon she will gather strength and begin to heal without my help. Then I will have time for you and will continue with your education. For now, have patience and remember that I will not permit any harm to come to you."

Ranth removed his hand suddenly, closing off his thoughts to Benyar. His father, however, knew how Ranth felt.

"The injuries that happened to you at the hands of Korab could not have been foreseen by me, or by my brother, Ketherey, for that matter. If I had been present, you would not have been treated as you were. You would have been marked as you have been, though not in one evening. It would have taken place over the course of the week."

Ranth nodded his acceptance of Benyar's explanation, then asked, "Is there anything else I must know that you have not remembered to tell me?"

"Only this. Ketherey has vowed to guard your life until a time when we both concur that you have mastered the art of fighting as well with your feet as your hands. Since Korab will be the chief suspect should any harm come to you, we believe you are safe for the time being. But never let your guard down, understand?"

"Yes, father."

"This is the price one pays for being in a position of power—to be always ready for challenge. And to be always surrounded by bodyguards."

Ranth looked shocked. "Do you tell me that I am guarded? By whom? I have seen no one."

"Reach out with your mind to the other side of that door," Benyar ordered, pointing.

Ranth did as he was told, sending a thin tendril of his awareness out to search. To his dismay he discovered there were two men who stood guard in the shadows. He stopped abruptly and pulled his mind-touch back.

"Be mindful to shield your thoughts at all times, even your dreams. Have you ever learned to shield dreams?" Benyar asked.

"No. I never knew it was possible. Will you show me now?"

"Of course; I must. It is my duty to you."

Though bone-weary, Benyar quickly began an explanation of the technique, as he showed Ranth how to construct a cover that would prevent anyone from seeing into his dreams. The lesson over, both men yawned and bid each other a good-night.

As his father left the room, two servants entered and offered to help Ranth undress, something he was not prepared for. He dismissed them, though not before one of the men handed him a sleeping shirt.

Checking that the dream shield was firmly in place, Ranth fell asleep and began a disturbing dream about Shunlar and their escape into the desert. In the dream she was bleeding heavily, even though her wounds were tightly bound. He tried to reach her, but a sandstorm sprang up out of nowhere and they lost each other. Frantic, he called her name repeatedly and finally woke in a cold sweat, very troubled. For a long time he lay on the bed, realizing how alone and miserable he was.

Thirteen

It had been four weeks since Ranla and Loff had moved into their own home. The cottage was small and sparsely furnished, nothing like the palace of the late Lord Creedath, where she had been the house-keeper. The simplicity of it was exactly to her liking. Outside, in the surrounding yard, were beds of herbs and flowers and though no one had lived here for most of the season, many of the plants had continued to grow. This garden had been the deciding factor when it came to choosing where they would live. Seeing the plants that needed tending sparked renewed interest in Ranla. She decided to salvage what she could of the herbs and began working each day.

Many of the herbs she found she knew uses for. Others she had no idea whatsoever; still she cultivated and watered, bringing the garden back to order, preparing the soil for winter. Since it was so late in the season, most of the herbs and flowers were ready to harvest. Those she could save she bunched up and hung from the rafters inside the house. Others she could only harvest the seeds of, and those she carefully bundled and marked with names she knew, or else she marked them with descriptions of the leaves and flowers.

The crisp, fall weather had the promise of frost on its breath and the days were sunny, having a different color to the light than summer. Being outside in the fresh air, able to work with the plants and put her hands into the dirt, gave Ranla more pleasure than she could remember having in years. The garden seemed to have an almost magical effect on her health.

Color returned to her cheeks, and her eyes seemed an even deeper shade of blue than Loff remembered. Each evening when Loff returned home from his work in the fields, she would be radiant, telling him of her discoveries.

Though outwardly she appeared healthy, Ranla remained deeply troubled. The constant mental control, the humiliation, and the violation Creedath had inflicted on her year after year was something she could not forget. She had thought the memories safely tucked away in the depth of her mind, buried. But each night when they lay down to sleep, Loff would open his mind to her so that he could read her thoughts. Though it was gently done, many times it had the strange effect on Ranla of pulling a troubling memory back into focus about her days in Vensunor, and she would have to force it away.

One night, as she was drifting off to sleep and Loff was reading her thoughts as usual, he saw something he was never meant to. She dreamed of the horrible experience of being raped by Creedath. He felt as if it were his own hands, not Ranla's, being controlled and undressing himself. He witnessed and felt the horrible violation of her mind as well as her body, not able to stop the memory or close himself off to her.

Ranla woke suddenly, crying out, but not before Loff saw and felt everything she had suffered at Creedath's hands. He held her and tried to close off his mind to her as she cried.

"What is it, my sweet one?" he asked, knowing all too well what troubled her. Soon, Loff was crying too. With a great effort he managed to close his mind off at last, but not before Ranla felt it. She jumped and pushed him away, the tears suddenly gone, replaced by distrust. She got up and went to sit before the fire, adding another log.

Tension hovered in the air as they sat watching the flames. Ranla had decided to tell Loff that she knew he had been reading her thoughts. She wasn't angry, but she was also not pleased.

"Loff, you must know how content I have been these last weeks." She waited for some kind of reply from him, but he just continued to stare into the fire, holding his breath.

Loff had been fighting a battle within himself every night

as he lay beside her. He knew that Ranla was carrying Creedath's child, but did not know any of the details of how she
became pregnant until now. Being the young, patient man he
was, he had hesitated to even so much as kiss her hand, content just to be sleeping close to her each night. Now, as he
waited for her to speak, he was certain she was going to tell
him that she wanted to live alone. He waited for the inevitable
to happen and when it did not, he tried to open his mind to
her so that he could hear the whisperings of her mind. But
he heard nothing. Surprised, he turned and looked at her. His
eyes took in her beauty. Her hair had a golden sheen to it
that picked up the lights from the fire. Her mouth . . . he
wanted with all his heart to kiss her mouth.

Suddenly he realized that Ranla was leaning toward him,
as if in response to his thoughts. Could it be? He swallowed
as she leaned even closer and very gently kissed him. His
head was swimming with words and ideas, all of them not
his, he realized. *Ranla, can you hear my thoughts?* he asked
as they continued their embrace.

Yes, Loff, as well as you hear mine, apparently. When he
jumped and pulled back from her, she laughed. "Did you
think I would never figure out how you have been able to
anticipate my every need, my every want? Yet, I am not angry. You have been waiting so patiently for me to be able to
do more than sleep beside you each night. Soon, I fear, you
will grow tired of waiting."

She finally said it, Loff thought to himself. The worst was
coming true before his eyes.

"How long have you been able to hear my thoughts?" she
asked him.

"Since first we kissed and held each other that night by
the river," he answered somewhat sheepishly. "I intended to
tell you. One day," he added.

Suddenly she wasn't quite so curious as angry. "Intended
to tell me, one day! Loff, what if there are things from my
memory that you have no right to know? Things that were so
horrible that even I don't want to remember? And that perhaps if you knew, you would no longer care for me."

"Nothing could make me stop caring for you or loving
you, Ranla. Please believe me. I know it was wrong of me

to hide my ability to read your thoughts, but it seemed such an easy thing to do. Besides, I was able to please you the way you wanted me to. You're not the first woman I have been with, but you are the first that I have wanted with such desperation. I will wait as long as it takes, I swear. Even if you want me to go away and leave you alone for a time, I will do it. I will wait for you to decide. After all, it's your decision, considering all that has happened to you . . .'' Loff's words trailed off. Ranla gave him such a piercing look he had to avert his eyes.

"What do you mean, 'after all that has happened to you'? What do you know?'' she demanded. Though Ranla had hidden the memory of the rape deep within her mind, refusing to even think about it, she knew Loff had seen it in her thoughts. Many years ago she had learned how to hide a thought behind another so securely that not even Creedath could find it. It was pure survival instinct that had taught her how, and she did it very well, but Loff had been able to see beyond whatever barrier she had fashioned.

"Tonight, while I held you, I saw how he controlled you . . . how he. . . . Ranla, I'm so sorry.'' Loff covered his face with his hands.

"Stop!'' she said icily. "I don't want your pity.''

"But Ranla, it's not pity I feel. I truly love you. If I had been there I would have done anything to stop what happened to you.''

"You couldn't have done a thing. Don't you understand? You were there, lying drugged in your room, a prisoner like the others and myself. You were right about one thing, though,'' her voice sounded strangely flat. "I want to be left alone now. Just go.''

Loff's heart nearly stopped beating. The world was becoming dark and he thought for a moment he might black out. After several minutes had gone by he quietly acquiesced. "Whatever you wish, Ranla.'' Then he dressed and left.

Ranla continued to sit before the fire until the logs burned to red coals. Finally, near morning she stiffly got out of the chair and went to bed, covering herself with the blanket as she lay down. She cried until she slept.

The next day Loff spoke little to his companions as they

worked in the field. When one young friend tried to get him to talk, by attempting a joke about the virtues of women, Loff made a threatening gesture at him with the scythe, thought better of it, and walked away from the group to work alone. No one bothered him after that.

At noon, when the threshers stopped for their midday meal, Loff took his threshing tool to the shed and went directly to the baths. After washing all traces of the field off, he went home to Ranla, ready to beg forgiveness if necessary—ready to do whatever it took to win back her affection. Finding her gone, he decided to seek solace in the Grove of Great Trees.

Ranla was lost deep in thought as she gathered herbs in her basket. Today she had decided to leave the yard and go in search of some of the fever and cold remedies she knew she might find in the forest, growing in the shade of certain trees. One type of moss was good for soothing a sore throat when boiled into a tea. She was happy to find it, for in her store of herbs, it was completely depleted. She intended to gather what she could today and take note of any others she saw along the way in case she couldn't fit them all into her basket.

Ranla was so engrossed in her work that she forgot to pay attention to where she meandered as she picked her herbs. One minute she knew where she was, the next she seemed to be lost, surrounded by a circle of trees of such enormous height and girth that for a moment she held her breath. A comforting, peaceful feeling surrounded her, and for several moments she forgot everything that had been troubling her. No breeze stirred a branch nor touched a strand of her hair as she stood, closing her eyes, turning slowly in a circle, relishing the quiet while a soft warmth enveloped her.

When she opened her eyes, several paces away a soundless wind appeared to pick leaves and bits of foliage into the air, swirling them in a miniature whirlwind that came closer, to twirl directly before her in a column, collapsing all of a sudden at her feet. She looked around to see who or what could have made this happen and, convinced that she was alone, bent down to examine the contents of the pile. Moments later, soft footsteps approaching from behind made her turn and see Arlass coming to greet her, a kindly smile on her face.

However, as soon as Arlass stepped closer, she stiffened.

"Do you know what you look upon, child?" she asked Ranla.

Confused, Ranla stood and bowed to her, remembering that the older woman was the spiritual leader of the Valley. "Yes, Arlass, I remember your kind welcome to me when I arrived here."

"I did not ask whom, but what," answered Arlass with a gentler tone. "The collection before you, did you find them there when you entered the Sacred Grove?"

"Oh," she said, startled, "forgive me. I had no idea I had trespassed into the Sacred Grove. I'll leave at once. I meant no disrespect," she bowed hastily picking up her basket of herbs.

"Child. Ranla, is it not? Please don't misinterpret my meaning. It is never forbidden to enter the Grove of Great Trees. In fact, it is encouraged. But to find one who has no knowledge of our ways, here, with these before her, then I must ask why, but more for your protection than to chastise."

Surprised, Ranla said, "Oh," once more, adding, "I was walking, gathering herbs for winter storage and I found myself here, though I am unable to explain how. I closed my eyes for a moment and when I opened them, these leaves and sprigs spun from over there"—she pointed—"The next thing I knew, they spun to a stop directly in front of me, and all of these landed here as you see them on the ground. That is all, I swear." Ranla was frightened that she had done something very wrong.

But Arlass patted her arm softly. "Now, now. Fear not. It would appear that you have been given a remedy for someone, perhaps even yourself. Only you will know for whom when the time comes. Come, I will explain the mystery to you. But first, allow me to help you gather them and place them in a proper container." To Ranla's amazement, Arlass unloosed the cords of a small pouch from her belt and together she and Ranla filled it with the mixture. When all the pieces were put away, Arlass pulled the cords of the pouch to close it and handed it to Ranla.

"You have been recognized for the healer you are. I suspected there was a depth to you that would show itself once you had settled into life among us, and I am rarely wrong in my suspicions. Will you humor an old woman's whims and have a cup of tea with me? You seem troubled and perhaps there may be something I can do to help you release this great burden you carry.''

Hearing her words, Ranla began to cry. She and Arlass walked from the Grove together, Arlass gently consoling her with tender words.

From the shadows Loff had seen and heard all that had been said between the two women. He bowed his head and whispered a fervent prayer to the Great Trees that Arlass could indeed help Ranla release her burden. Then he turned back the way he had come. He had an apology to deliver to a friend in the fields.

FOURTEEN

THE SMELL OF SNOW WAS HEAVY IN THE AIR WHEN Gwernz began to have the recurring dream of Klarissa, a woman from the far city of Tonnerling, near the sea. Her father, Vinnyius, had found Gwernz and for fifteen years kept him as a captive servant and, eventually, an apprentice.

The name Tonnerling meant *People of the Water Caves* in Old Tongue, and they made their living from the sea. The first settlers there lived in the natural caves of the mountains that bordered the sea. The mountains sometimes shook and sent rivers of lava from their depths. The people worshipped the stone of the mountain, and their most sacred places were in the caves that burrowed into the belly of the mountain. Large animals were sacrificed to the gods of the mountain in hopes that the sacrifices would appease them and stop the mountains from shaking and spewing forth lava. Whether it worked or not no one knew for sure, but one day the volcano quieted and ceased its flow. As the years passed and the population grew, the Cave People replaced their principal dwelling places within the caves with houses built from stone blocks that they had carved out of the rock.

Klarissa was the eldest daughter of Vinnyius. Because of a deformity of her leg she was unwed, while all of her sisters were married. Her leg had been broken in a fall when she was a child and the bones had knit improperly. She walked with a limp and no man would have her, even though she was lovely. Klarissa ran her widowed father's household, a

task she did exceedingly well. An educated female was rare
in Tonnerling society, but being a strong-natured young
woman, she had convinced her father that she had to know
how to read and write in order to record the household expenses and run the household properly. And Vinnyius had
succumbed to his daughter's charms and agreed.

Gwernz had been carefully guarded, and his excursions into
the midst of the population were always supervised. He never
went anywhere alone in fifteen years. This would have driven
the average man mad, but Gwernz was not an average man.
He had the ability to close off the presence of another fully
from his mind, no matter how physically close that person
was to him.

But, at night, in the home of her father, Klarissa would
come to speak with Gwernz. At first she came because he
was such an oddity. She would ask questions about his family
and home. He always told her the most beautiful stories and
made her laugh. She was younger than him by eleven years,
which at the time of his capture, made her sixteen. They became friends, and it wasn't until years had passed and he saw
her three younger sisters married off one by one that Gwernz
began to understand she would never be married, something
he was secretly thankful for. Before long he realized he was
in love with her.

At first, she thought of him as a brother. But little by little,
she too, knew the truth. She had been coming to visit him in
his room where he was locked away every night. There was
a chair just inside the door where she customarily sat, at first.
For propriety's sake, the door was left open and they kept a
respectful distance, he on one side of the room, she on the
other, for the first few years. As she grew to trust him more,
she would bring her knitting or embroidery and sit in the
room with him with the door closed. Gwernz had pointed out
that should they be overheard, her reputation would be in
jeopardy, but she scoffed at that.

"Already no man will look upon me because I am educated
and probably a good deal smarter than they," she retorted,
never mentioning the limp.

And he never took the liberty to try to question her resolve.
It would have been easy to read her thoughts, but Gwernz

never tried. He had fallen in love, and he couldn't bear finding out the truth of how she looked at him. When he finally declared his affection, she turned pale, got up, and left the room, not returning for two nights. It was then that she realized how much she missed him.

When on the third night Klarissa reappeared, Gwernz was overjoyed. But he controlled himself.

"Klarissa, I overstepped the limits of our friendship and ask you to accept my apology," he began.

She entered the room, closed the door, and blew out the candles. In the dark she found him where he stood and she allowed him to enclose her in his arms and kiss her. It was the first time she had been embraced by other than a kinsman. Thus their nightly meetings turned into lovers' trysts. Sometimes she brought her knitting or embroidery as before, but many times she did not. It was because of his love for Klarissa that Gwernz never tried to escape his imprisonment.

As the years went by, he was moved to larger, more spacious quarters. After that, once more he was moved, this time to quarters that had a secret, adjoining door to Klarissa's suite, hidden in the back of the wardrobe. No one noticed or paid attention. It was as if their love was a secret because it was so taboo. Only in her brother, Dolan, did she confide. Never did she speak of her affection for Gwernz to her father, or to her sisters when they visited at the holidays with their families. Gwernz seemed absorbed into the family, but mostly as a treasured pet.

When Vinnyius found out that his daughter and the man whom he secretly thought of as a son were and had been in love for years, he had Gwernz brought to him. At first he was furious, but he also realized that Klarissa had no other chance for happiness and he urged Gwernz to leave, to escape, and to return as an ambassador from the Valley of Great Trees. Only that way would he allow his daughter to marry and leave his household. The stigma of marrying her to a prisoner was unacceptable. Gwernz must return to claim his bride as an honorable man.

But as preparations were being made for Gwernz to leave, Vinnyius died, thus freeing Gwernz of his servitude. He asked Klarissa to come with him but she would not. Being the respectful daughter that she was, she would adhere to the proper period of mourning. She didn't fear for her safety or her position, foolishly. In Tonnerling society a woman had no rights or position unless she was married or the eldest daughter, as she was, who cared for the family estate in the event of her mother's death. Even being the eldest brought her only partial right of inheritance, and that only through her husband, if she had one. With no husband, the eldest brother inherited everything, and Klarissa had one brother.

With her father dead, the entire estate went to Dolan, her younger brother, including responsibility for her, single woman that she was. Klarissa, though left with nothing, felt content to wait for Gwernz to return and propose marriage. Until then, she mourned her father and took care of the household for Dolan as she had done so competently for so many years for her father. And then the final blow. She was told that in his will, her father had arranged a marriage for her, to make sure she was cared for as a proper father would. The ceremony would take place after a suitable period of mourning had passed. She began to send for Gwernz with her dreams, as he had taught her.

It had been three months now since Gwernz had returned to the Valley of Great Trees from his journey to Vensunor. Nearly five months had passed since he had left his captivity behind in Tonnerling. His thoughts were never far from Klarissa, and he dreamed of her often, but he had yet to tell anyone of her.

One night his dream of Klarissa was so vivid he knew that it was not merely a dream, but a message from her. She begged Gwernz to come for her because, as she explained, she would be forced into marriage at the end of winter unless he returned with a suitable offer of trade and a show of wealth or power. The prospective bridegroom was anxious to add Klarissa's sizable dowry to his wealth.

Gwernz slept little the rest of the night and in the morning he announced to Marleah and Shunlar that he had something he wished to discuss with them. Finally after much clearing of his throat and several starts, Gwernz began. "In Tonnerling there is a woman, whose name is Klarissa."

"I knew it," Marleah muttered under her breath.

"Yes, I have been in love with her for quite some time, sister. She has been sending me messages through her dreams, as I taught her to do. If I am not there by winter's end she will be forced to marry another. I must return to Tonnerling now and make my intentions known to her family."

"And what intentions would those be, brother?" snapped Marleah.

"Why marriage, of course. I will bring her here to our valley. You will like her, Marleah. In fact, what attracted me to her was her strength of character and will. She reminds me of you in many ways." Gwernz smiled as he spoke, watching Marleah's mood being turned by his charm.

"Ach, flatterer. You think you know me so well that a few soft-spoken words thrown about will have me sending you on your way. Brother, you have just returned home and winter is nearly upon us."

"Truthfully, Marleah, I cannot wait any longer. These months without her have been terribly lonely ones for me. If it were not for the special instructions I have been receiving from Arlass and our traveling to Vensunor to search for Loff, I might have been gone long before this. While Arlass is yet strong and able to perform the duties of spiritual leader, I must go. Once she is gone and I take her place, I will not be permitted to undertake such a journey. Do you understand?" He watched her face as the words sunk in.

"Aye. You will be leaving soon, possibly tomorrow. Once your mind is made up, there is no force on this earth that can change it." Marleah smiled at her brother, shaking her head. "And who will you take with you? I would gladly accompany you, if you want me."

"My thought was to ask Shunlar. What say you, niece? Have you ever wondered what the great city of Tonnerling was like?" Now Gwernz tried to work his charm on her.

"Why choose me, uncle? Surely Loff or mother can accompany you on this bride-quest." She answered more sarcastically than usual, smoke and a few sparks spewing from her nostrils as they sat before the fire.

Lately, people had begun to politely excuse themselves from her company. She had continued to grow, much to her and everyone's amazement. In three months' time, Shunlar had grown taller than her uncle and most of the men of the Valley. Her height gave her an androgynous look, especially when her hair was pulled back in a warrior braid. Her upper arms and legs were now covered with a fine layer of soft scales, and she was grateful that the colder weather made it convenient for her to cover her arms with a long-sleeved tunic.

"Because, niece, I have decided to take advantage of your new form. Since I must arrive to claim Klarissa with a show of wealth or power, guess which one I choose?" He chuckled aloud when he saw the expression on her face.

"You are becoming more dragon-like every day, and will most likely frighten off anyone who might try to harm us. All you need do is conjure up a bit of anger and cough a stream of sparks into the air." Again he laughed.

Shunlar was not amused. She focused her hardest glare on Gwernz, looking him over inch by inch, but when she reached toward him with a mind probe, she saw what he imagined— people cowering before her as she protected Gwernz with bursts of flame.

"And niece, you will be pleased to know that the Tonnerlingans speak several dialects, something that I was surprised to discover in the years I spent there. It is because they are traders, of course, which means you won't have to learn another language. In fact, many things about these people will surprise you."

"Please my whims, uncle, but tell me that they are fluent in the Old Tongue," she answered scornfully, spitting a few sparks across the room.

"Now that is the one tongue I never heard in the fifteen years I was held captive. Perhaps none of them could converse in it, but most probably it was because I was never privy to conversations with anyone who knew it." For several minutes he stared at the fire, lost in his thoughts. When he looked up at last, it was to see Marleah and Shunlar impatiently waiting for him to continue.

"Gwernz," began Marleah tentatively. "You must know how surprised and shocked I am to hear you speak of this woman, Klarissa. Why have you not mentioned a word of her before now? Are you sure you can trust her and that this isn't some sort of trap? I can't say that I'm happy with the idea of you and Shunlar leaving now. After all, it will be snowing soon and we have just recently returned home. Can you do anything at all to reassure me this isn't dangerous?" Marleah's voice had risen in concern as she paced.

"I suppose I was waiting for the right time, but I was unsure of what to say. Klarissa is a very headstrong woman and when we parted, we had decided that I would return in the spring to marry her. I suppose I have come to rely on myself for so long that I never realized how important it would be for you to know about her. Forgive me for being insensitive." Gwernz stopped before continuing, a look of great sadness coming over him.

"It was not easy for me to be away from everyone and everything I had ever known. The loss of our parents while I was held captive was particularly hard. In the years I spent in Tonnerling, no one befriended me save Vinnyius and Klarissa. You must believe me when I say I have no wish to shut you out; I just no longer remembered how to include you."

Marleah encouraged Gwernz to tell her and Shunlar what his life had been like in Tonnerling. Marleah listened in silence, occasionally wiping away the tears that ran down her cheeks in a constant stream. Shunlar also listened closely, but found she didn't have any tears to shed. When he finished he embraced Marleah and she went off to bed, leaving her daughter and brother alone to make preparations for their journey.

Early the next morning as the sun was rising they said their good-byes. Marleah watched them ride away with six pack animals stringing along behind them, loaded down with hides. Finely tanned leather was a highly prized commodity in Tonnerling, as it was impossible to raise livestock on the mountainside.

Once they rode beyond the sentinels at the edge of the Valley, Gwernz covered himself, Shunlar, and the animals with a ward that protected them. One day's ride north of the Valley, their pace slowed, what with so many pack animals and the difficult terrain. Snow had begun falling, and though most of the passes remained open, soon they would be filled with drifts.

"Uncle, you and I must be particularly lost of our wits to be journeying so far from our hearthside in this cold," she said to him over her shoulder. It was their fourth day out, and they were gradually making headway through snow that was up to the horses' chests in many places.

"If I had warned you, would you have come?" he asked. Only silence and a sense of brooding could be felt emanating from her back.

Shunlar had taken to keeping her thoughts to herself and avoiding conversation; she hadn't turned out to be the glib traveling companion Gwernz had hoped for. She knew she was just a bit over three months pregnant, and the sliver of the Lifestone embedded in her arm was changing her physical appearance drastically. She was taller than him by about one hand and was far more beautiful than any woman he had seen, except for Cloonth, her foster-mother.

One morning when they arose, Shunlar felt a terrible itching on her shoulders. When Gwernz looked at her back, he saw nubs of wings growing. Shunlar was rapidly becoming more like Alglooth and Cloonth.

"This will take some getting used to, I think," Shunlar decided soberly.

"Which part of it? The fact that you will have wings and your appearance is changing again, or the fact that you will be able to fly?" Gwernz asked.

"All of it. I find these days that I am adjusting continually. First, after Creedath was killed, the nightmares began and I had to learn to live with a gnawing fear that robbed me of sleep each night. I parted from Ranth, the first man to make me realize that living my life alone was not enough any longer.

"Then, I began growing, as well as adding scales to my arms and legs and torso. Breathing fire came next. On the journey with you to the Valley of Great Trees, I learned that I was going to have a child. Next, I discovered, with your help, that there was a piece of the Lifestone of a generations-dead, evil wizard embedded in my arm that may not ever be able to be removed, and most probably is the cause of my physical changes.

"Now, it seems, I shall be able to join Bimily soaring in

the sky. In three short months my life seems to have become a ballad written by some gods-be-cursed, dragonweed-addicted minstrel.''

Gwernz looked at her and saw there was a twinkle of mischief in her eye. ''Your humor, niece, will probably be what will save you from yourself.''

''Aye. Humor.'' She nodded agreement and shook her head.

FIFTEEN

THEIR ENTRANCE INTO TONNERLING WAS EASIER than Gwernz had expected. Once near the gates, Shunlar's senses came alert, and she waited for the hairs at the nape of her neck to give her warning of possible danger. When nothing happened she cursed quietly under her breath. It had been weeks since she had needed to rely on this built-in sense. Like the disappearance of her ability to see the heat trace left by another on the air, it seemed her warning system had stopped functioning also.

Panic rose in her and she fought it. She remembered why Gwernz had brought her along, to guard him and assist him in bringing Klarissa out if there was protest from anyone about her leaving. The gate guards made a quick pretense of checking them and their pack animals, anxious to be back inside their guardhouse around the charcoal heater. Once past the gates, she casually held the pommel of her sword as they rode through the city streets.

It had been only a short time since Shunlar had been in a large city. She remembered the numbers of people who inhabited Vensunor and how the crowds in the market would sometimes seem to press against her. Now, because of the many changes she was experiencing within her physical body, the sight of groups of people made her more uncomfortable than she remembered. Panic threatened to overcome her again, but this time she concentrated on protecting Gwernz from any possible attack and it subsided.

As he had predicted, however, when people noticed her,

121

their first impulse was to avert their eyes and then quickly look again, as if to make sure they really saw what they did. She even watched several women shield their children's eyes from her. Though her winter cloak hid her form, she was still very recognizable as a woman. In this part of the world, a proper woman wore skirts, not breeches as she did. And the more wealthy her husband, the more strands of pearls would be wrapped around her neck or wrists, or coiled into her hair, or looped into earrings. Shunlar wore only gold circles in her ears and the gold chain and medallion Ranth had given her, well hidden under her tunic. Her white hair was simply braided, warrior fashion, with a braid that started at the crown of her head and continued down her back, bound by a leather cord. That and the sword on her belt marked her as an outsider.

Gwernz shrugged. "There seems to be little to protect me from here except women and children. No one knows yet who we are or what we come for. People of this city, if memory serves me correctly, wait and watch before they strike. We are safe enough now. Besides, I will construct a shield around us that nothing except the strongest wizardry can penetrate. Only Vinnyius had that power, and he is dead."

Shunlar shivered for a moment as his touch moved across her. The black gelding she rode shied, and she calmed him. After one or two snorts, he regained his stride and they rode to the gate of Gwernz's old master's house, a route Gwernz knew well.

Once inside the courtyard of the household, Dolan, who was master now, was summoned. He arrived to meet his guests with his sister Klarissa by his side. It was obvious to all by the flush of her cheeks that she was overcome with excitement at the arrival of Gwernz. They greeted their visitors, while servants were summoned to take over the care of the horses and pack animals. Two menservants removed the saddlebags and bedrolls, then waited patiently for the party to move inside as snow fell in increasingly thick flakes.

Gwernz bowed formally to Dolan, an appropriate greeting to the master of the house. Only seventeen, Dolan was bright and eager to learn anything he could about the unusual woman standing before him. Barely taller than Shunlar, Dolan had deep blue eyes and a dazzling smile. His thick, straight, blond hair had been cropped short, signifying that he was in mourning.

"Greetings, Dolan. And my lady Klarissa. Allow me to introduce you both to my niece, Shunlar." Klarissa and Dolan bowed to Shunlar, whose cloak's hood still covered her head. She pushed it back and Dolan's eyes widened. He was instantly entranced.

"I have come with items to trade, but first and foremost, with a proposal of marriage for your sister, Klarissa," Gwernz added with a smile. "That is, of course, if she will have me."

Klarissa's answer was to bow, deeply, once more to Gwernz. "I will most happily accept."

Dolan nodded in agreement. From the moment he had seen her face, his eyes had been locked on Shunlar. He stood before her, bowed, and gestured gracefully with his hand. "You are most welcome to my house. It is good to see you again, Gwernz, under such different circumstances. I know my sister is much relieved that you have returned. Please come out of the cold and have some refreshment to warm you. Then we will see to settling you into comfortable quarters. Will this be a long stay?" But Dolan wasn't asking Gwernz the question. He was speaking to Shunlar, offering his arm to her as if she were some great lady.

Unaccustomed to such courtesies, she looked sideways to Gwernz for a hint of what she should do, but he was holding Klarissa's hand and gazing so deeply into her eyes that he hadn't heard the question. *Yes*, she decided, it was very good that they had come.

"Master Dolan, I cannot answer for my uncle, but left to me, we should leave within the week, weather permitting." Feeling awkward, she placed one hand on the pommel of her sword and the fingertips of the other lightly on the arm of Dolan's jacket and let him lead her proudly into the warmth of the hold.

The main hall of the hold was much more spacious than the entire cottage she had been living in these last weeks. The stone walls were fashioned from huge square blocks, that for the most part were covered with thick tapestries depicting scenes of fishermen hauling gigantic nets aboard ships, filled to bursting with fish and other sea creatures. While not in the grand style of Vensunor, the stone houses of Tonnerling were large and comfortable.

Dried rushes and aromatic herbs had been strewn across the stone floors. Nearest the fire, where chairs were arranged, lay thick, woven wool carpets. A warm fire blazed in the hearth, and Shunlar immediately felt a sense of well-being as she accepted a cup of hot, unusually scented wine. Out of habit, she waited for her host to drink first. Only after he sipped did she take a taste. Klarissa and Gwernz entered the room and they sat for a time, warming themselves with the hot wine, answering questions about their journey. Soon they were led from the hall to comfortable quarters.

Shunlar's room had a low ceiling, with rounded corners where the walls met it, giving it a warm, cave-like feeling. Her belongings had been placed on a long, low chest with many drawers, under a hanging tapestry that depicted a dragon soaring above the cloud-covered mountains. Before the fire sat a tub of hot, steaming water fragrant with the aroma of lavender and pine, and soon she was soaking in it. Six days had come and gone and she had not had a proper bath. Later came a polite knock on the door, and a quiet-voiced servant summoned her to the evening meal.

Well rested, smelling of the herb-scented water, dressed in clean clothing, Shunlar radiated a kind of womanhood that Dolan had never dreamed existed. No woman he knew would wear breeches as a man. Proper women wore skirts. He was enchanted.

The weather would not permit them to leave Tonnerling. The snows came harder that night and continued until dawn of the following day, and every day for five days. By week's end the entire household was wakened just before morning light by a rumble that shook the foundations and seemed to continue forever. Shunlar came racing from her room, only to crash headfirst into an older servant who was hurrying down the hall.

"A thousand pardons, lady," he mumbled as he bowed, holding his head.

"What is that shaking?" she demanded, rubbing her forehead.

Just as he was ready with an answer, the bells of the city began to toll. "There has been an avalanche, as the bells tell us by their pattern of ringing. If you listen, lady, you will hear how the three and two rings repeat over and over. That tells us the passes will be closed to all until the spring thaw and digging can begin. If that is all, I will be going now." He bowed and waited for her dismissal.

"Yes. And thank you," she answered awkwardly. Shunlar was not used to dealing with servants. Rubbing her head, she went in search of Gwernz to tell him the bad news, if he wasn't already aware of it. It looked as though they would be spending all winter under Dolan's roof.

Klarissa and Gwernz were married in a private family ceremony at the beginning of their second week in Tonnerling, much to the dismay of her promised bridegroom, a sour, elderly man named Cedaric. Although he knew that Klarissa greatly abhorred the idea of marriage to him, Cedaric wanted her dowry, a considerable sum that Vinnyius had set aside for his favorite daughter. But Gwernz had taken away his prospect of a very wealthy, comfortable old age, and Cedaric decided to make life uncomfortable for him. He started several rumors among the local merchants about "the foreigner" in their midst. Under the pretense of protection, he placed spies around the house to watch and report on the comings and goings of Gwernz.

Knowing that once she was another man's wife Cedaric couldn't do a thing to pursue her, Klarissa had been making arrangements for her marriage the moment she'd started to send for Gwernz in her dreams. All the banquet arrangements were taken care of down to the last detail. Even the bridegroom's clothing had been sewn, awaiting only a final fitting. She enlisted an old family friend, Da Winfreyd, the priest who had officiated at her three sisters' weddings, to marry them.

He was positively the most ancient man Shunlar had ever seen. What little hair he had left grew in long white wispy strands that puffed out from his head in every angle. His beard was nearly as thin and billowed at the slightest stir of the air. Leaning heavily on a tall staff for support, his step was slow and careful, yet he was not hunched over in the least. Though he had long ago retired and spent his days in prayer and seclusion, he had not forgotten his promise to come when Klarissa called. He had known of her love for Gwernz and secretly prayed for the former captive's return every day.

Klarissa's sisters, however, were not pleased with her choice for husband. They thought it disreputable and told her so. All three of them refused to come to see their oldest sister wed, saying they would not permit their children to be witness to the ceremony as their situation in society would forever be tainted.

"Prella, Dorissa, and Matelyn have all sent letters declining our invitation, and it's just as well they're not coming," Klarissa told Gwernz, Shunlar, and Dolan at dinner the night before the ceremony. "They would be so dour and petulant it would ruin my wedding. And, besides, none of the servants would be able to join in on the fun!"

"You're inviting the servants!?" Dolan choked on his wine.

"Certainly I'm inviting them. Aside from father, mother, or you, they're the only real family that ever cared for me. Once my three dear sisters were told that I would most probably never catch a man's eye, they stayed away from me as if I had the plague. It was only a broken leg, not a deformed one!" Gwernz sat with his eyes wide as his bride-to-be admitted her anger.

Dolan blinked in amazement. "I'd say you've made the best match of the three of them, sister." Then he confided to them quietly, "If the truth be told, Prella's husband, Darred, is too often in his cups. Dorissa's husband, Praetor, is interested more in his mistress than in Dorissa. And Matelyn's husband, Adrel, is so often seen in the company of his steward, it's nothing short of a miracle that they have one child at all!"

"Dolan," Klarissa scolded. "That's vile gossip. Where would you have heard such things?"

"Why, from the lips of the very men I speak of when we meet in the tavern. Many's the night that I've had to walk Darred home, and with not much prodding he's spilled out his anguish to me about how he's married to a shrew. A 'bilious woman' is what he calls Prella. She does go on about his drinking, you know, which leads to more when he can't take her prattling.

Klarissa was speechless as Dolan continued.

"Praetor told me about his mistress years ago. And many's the night I've watched Adrel and his man holding arms about each other all evening, though they've not seen me," Dolan added.

"Oh, I see," Klarissa answered quietly, taking all the information in. She looked anxiously at Gwernz and Shunlar, then said apologetically, "Please excuse us. I didn't mean for all the family secrets to be laid on the table, but it seems you have learned all of it at once."

"There is no reason to apologize, Klarissa. Every family has secrets. If it would make you feel better, we can tell you something about ours. I do, however, ask that we do this in private. This is something the servants need not know, yet. It will become apparent to them soon, however. Am I not correct, niece?" Gwernz asked Shunlar.

"Yes. It's time they were told." Shunlar nodded and smiled crookedly.

Dolan dismissed the servants.

Gwernz began with his story of being accepted by the Great Trees as the next leader of the Valley. "The Trees showed me the story of Porthelae and Banant of Stiga and how Banant had cast a spell that turned Porthelae into a dragon. The female dragon, the last of her kind, felt the power of the spell and the two dragons flew into the air and mated. Porthelae knew what had happened to him as soon as he and the female dragon touched, but he could do nothing to break the spell. He dashed himself onto the rocks and his mangled body was found by those who had been sent to search for him.

"Two children, male and female, were found after their dragon mother had died, and they were raised by the inhabitants of Stiga. Years later Cloonth, the female, had a child by Alglooth, the male, but the child died. He left their home in a terrible rage, seeking revenge on any full human he could find. But, the wizard wars had left behind no one. Those that could escape had done so, and he only found the bodies of the dead.

"Alglooth flew from Stiga and found himself in the Valley

of Great Trees where at the Darkest of the Moons Festival, nearly two years before, he had mated with my sister, Marleah. She had a child from that union and had taken it with her on this particular day. My sister had put her child in a cradle in a tree and gone off a short way to make the rounds at her guard post. Alglooth found the child, which was his also, and stole her so that his mate, Cloonth, would not waste away from grieving the death of her child.''

Klarissa and Dolan looked from Gwernz to Shunlar and back again.

"What are you telling us?" asked Dolan with a puzzled look.

"That my mother is Marleah and my father is Alglooth and the blood of dragons runs in my veins." Shunlar stood away from the table and removed the long-sleeved tunic. The sleeveless undervest revealed her throat, some of her chest and her arms. The new growth of scales picked up the light of the candles and made them glisten and wink as if hundreds of tiny gems were embedded in her skin. She locked eyes with Dolan, and it kindled such desire in him that he shuddered. Then she exhaled a breath of smoke and sparks that flew across the room.

Klarissa jumped and Dolan nearly moaned with passion; he was hopelessly in love.

"We believe that Shunlar is continuing to change before our eyes because a sliver of the Lifestone of Banant became embedded in her forearm. How that happened is another story. For now, we know that she will be taller, but, that is all we know," concluded Gwernz.

"You forgot to mention the wings, uncle." She turned around so they could see her back and the small nubs, somewhat larger now, unfolded from beneath her tunic and she flapped them slowly.

Now Dolan did faint. When he awoke later he was in his bed and he thought he had been dreaming of an angel with the face of Shunlar, hovering over him. Opening his eyes, he saw that she sat nearby watching as one of the servants applied a cold compress to a bump on his head.

*   *   *

Dolan was very happy for his sister. He joyously presented the bride to Gwernz before they stepped under the archway of pine and holly branches to say their vows. In front of Shunlar and Dolan and all of the household servants, with Da Winfreyd presiding, the two promised their fervent love and devotion to one another.

Their wedding feast was sumptuous, and even Cook sat proudly at table to eat her own food. With the young master and mistress and her new husband smiling down on her from their table on the dais, Cook blubbered happy tears through the entire meal. Many kegs of wine and ale were tapped, and goblets were lifted and drained in heartfelt toasts. Once the formal feasting had ended, the tables were pushed back and Klarissa and Gwernz led them in dancing.

For some reason, the louder the laughter rang around her, the more sullen Shunlar became. As she drained yet another goblet of wine, she felt someone standing before her. When she looked up, Da Winfreyd was looking at her with his clouded eyes and near-toothless smile. No one was quite sure if he still was able to see.

"My child, why are you not dancing? This is a time to be merry, to celebrate the union of two people who are well-matched." Da Winfreyd held out his hand to her.

Not knowing why she did, Shunlar reached for his offered hand and was surprised by the strength of his grip. Suddenly she found herself with him in another place, the sound of the wedding party around her strangely muffled as if in another room. Da Winfreyd was greatly changed. He was much younger looking, his eyes were a bright blue-violet, and there were no gaps in his smile. Around him glowed a faint blue-violet light and when he spoke, it was in Old Tongue.

"Please my whims, but you are a surprise!" his husky voice exclaimed.

"And you, sir," she answered in the same language. "Please tell me why you have brought me here and what you need to tell me in such secret words."

"First, I would have you tell me who you are for I have seen the likes of you before, though it has been so long ago I, by rights, should be dead." There seemed to be a hint of fear in his voice.

"What can you mean? You've seen me and know I am Gwernz's niece."

"Look for yourself then." Da Winfreyd waved his staff and a mirror appeared before her. The figure in it looked like Cloonth, but with straight, white, hair. The woman before her was taller by at least two heads and her wings were fully developed. Shunlar laughed and touched her face and then reached for her reflection. She flapped her wings and effortlessly rose several inches off the ground. "By the three moons, is this what I will eventually look like?" she asked him.

"My child, I have no answer for you. You appear only as my eyes see you on this plane, and even I cannot be sure why. Long ago, when I was a boy, there were two people who looked like you. Tell me, do you know of whom I speak?" His eyes looked so hopeful that Shunlar felt strongly compelled to tell him everything she knew. Instead, she held back, shaking her head in denial.

It took a substantial amount of effort for her to pull her hand from his grip. When she did, she found herself seated next to him in an outer hallway, far away from the wedding festivities. "How did we get here, old man?" she asked not holding back any of her anger. "I like it very little when I find myself in situations not of my choosing. Perhaps we will continue our conversation another time, when my head is not swimming from wine." She got up and abruptly left him sitting alone on the stone bench, his head bowed.

"So close, so close," he mumbled to himself. Soon Da Winfreyd pushed himself onto unsteady legs to amble down the hallway in the direction of his quarters. "In the morning, I will ask Klarissa about her," he promised himself. But alas, his age had affected his memory and in the morning he had completely forgotten the encounter with Shunlar.

Sixteen

Shunlar's appearance did much to inflame outmoded ideas and misgivings about women and their place in Tonnerling society. Very aware of how she was perceived, Shunlar was at first delighted that she was the cause of so much gossip.

Suspecting that Shunlar had some degree of skill with the sword, Dolan asked one morning if she would show him some of her fighting art. She agreed only after she discovered that he had been taught by some of the best swordmasters in the city. Always willing to add something new, something that might give her an edge in a fight, she agreed to give Dolan lessons on the condition that he would also teach her. They began to meet each morning for a practice session in Dolan's fighting hall or, if weather permitted, outside in the courtyard. But most days the snow was too constant.

On their first morning session, Shunlar asked Dolan to show her what he knew so she could determine his level of competency. She was very happy to see that he was beyond mere beginner level, and soon they were exchanging blows, laughing and enjoying themselves tremendously. Dolan and she were well matched in height and arm length. Though she was much faster, he was younger and more reckless, deliberately taking chances, not caring if he bruised.

At first they sparred with wooden swords. After a week Shunlar determined that Dolan could defend himself well enough, and they switched to real weapons. She found a practice sword that seemed well balanced to her hand, even though Tonnerling swords were more slender and longer than she was used to. Because her strange metamorphosis had made her taller and added inches to her arms, her own sword felt strangely short in her hand and she realized unhappily that she would soon need a new weapon, one balanced to her longer reach.

Shunlar had taken to wearing a long-sleeved tunic rather than the sleeveless one she was much more accustomed to. She felt Dolan might fall over himself if she were to expose her arms and their covering of scales that increased daily. She was still growing taller; her breeches were creeping up her legs.

On one morning, two weeks and a day since Shunlar and Gwernz had arrived in Tonnerling, Dolan offered her the gift of a sword and was delighted when she accepted. The night before he had attempted to give her a long strand of pearls, which she graciously refused. She had been told by Gwernz that accepting such a gift could be taken as a sign that she was interested in Dolan as a lover or suitor.

But accepting a sword was another matter altogether. Shunlar agreed to meet Dolan after their practice session to visit the swordmaker. The man was astonished when he learned that a woman was calling with Dolan to purchase one of his weapons, but once he had spoken to her, he agreed to make her a sword.

Afterward her young host took great delight in taking Shunlar on her first excursion into the city. First Dolan showed her the docks and warehouse district, where he proudly pointed out the two ships that were now his, part of his inheritance; there were three others that would be back in the spring. Vinnyius had been a wealthy merchant with a good head for trade, and Dolan seemed to have inherited that trait from what Shunlar could tell by listening to a brief description of the merchandise he would trade the following season.

Then they were off to the marketplace and, after a brief tour, it was the lunch hour, and the taverns were where Shunlar's interests beckoned. Never in his wildest dreams had it occurred to him that a woman would want to be seen in a public place with a man who was not her husband, and drinking! He took great pleasure in creating a somewhat scandalous display, introducing her to many of his friends. Some of the older men politely bowed and introduced themselves, others nervously excused themselves and left soon after introductions were made. Those closest to Dolan's age seemed the most likely to stay and engage in conversation. Shunlar observed and remembered the faces, names, and expressions, knowing it was more than her physical appearance that was sending so many of them scuttling from the tavern.

Because Dolan was young, he cared little for what his peers or his elders would have to say about him. For now, Dolan was having the time of his life. Besides, he was wealthy; a certain amount of scandal would make him more interesting to the ladies, he surmised. Being the only son, his father had spoiled him, and with Vinnyius dead, the young man had no one to guide him away from the mistakes he was unwittingly making. Innocent though his infatuation with Shunlar might be, many of the wealthy, older merchants would not allow their daughters to marry someone whose reputation was in any way sullied. Marriage to any of the young women of his social standing was the farthest thing from Dolan's mind, however.

Shunlar wished to remain as anonymous as possible. Their forays into the night life of Tonnerling—what little existed in winter—were kept to a minimum. One evening in five they ventured out, and this evening found them in a comfortable corner of the Spinyfish Tavern. They'd come to drink here four times in the four-plus weeks that Shunlar and Gwernz had been snowed in. It was smaller and less grand than the other drinking establishments that Dolan preferred, but Shunlar had refused to go elsewhere. Besides, the innkeeper here was the first one who didn't treat her as if she were a pariah.

She ordered a bottle of the desert-made cactus alcohol that was labeled, *Desert Myst*, and poured a generous goblet for Dolan and herself. After several swallows she noticed three men sitting off in a dark corner, in deep discussion with a flamboyantly dressed fourth man. She recognized the three as Feralmon, from the style of their clothing and the dark color of their skin. Dwellers in Tonnerling were not that dark, but had a more ruddy complexion, fair hair, and tended to be taller.

Shunlar wondered why they were in Tonnerling, so far from Kalaven Desert. "Have you seen those men before?" she asked Dolan, pointing discreetly in their direction with her chin.

"Yes," he replied. "I have seen them here several nights, always in that corner, always in deep discussion with the same man. The one in the bright clothing is captain of a ship. But I could not say who the others are, or where they might be from. They are traders, and we here in Tonnerling have many long established trade agreements with people from many cities. Perhaps, like you and Gwernz, they are here until the passes are open." He grinned at her across his cup, the drink making him bolder than usual.

Ach, boys, she said to herself, exasperated nearly beyond her limits. If this had been another time and place, Shunlar might have returned the flirtatious behavior; he was an extremely attractive young man. As it was, she seemed not to mind the attention, but Dolan's immaturity was unappealing and beginning to annoy her. She was not beyond asking favors, however, knowing full well that any request from her would be fulfilled with gusto by Dolan.

"Don't you agree that it is late in the season for traders? Who would risk a cargo in the passes with all this snow? Besides, there seem to be only three of them. What could three men bring that was so important this late in the season?" she asked.

Dolan looked pensive for several moments. "You do have a point. Tonight I will follow them and listen in on their conversation, if you like."

"Can you do that undetected?"

"Yes I can. In fact, I have many talents, some of which I would be pleased to show you."

She eyed him suspiciously for several seconds. The feelings he emanated were complex. There was definitely sexual desire, but something much deeper was hidden beneath that. In order for her to discover what he hid, Shunlar would have to touch his mind and she would not do it without his permission. She smiled and said, "Shall we meet later in my room so you can tell me what you have learned?'' He nodded with wide eyes.

"Dolan, do you trust me?" she asked suddenly.

"Yes," he answered. Dolan had not spent much time in the company of women, especially one so exotic as Shunlar. He was completely infatuated with her. "I would trust you with my very soul," he told her breathlessly.

"I don't want your soul, but what I do ask of you, you may find, unusual."

Dolan was beside himself with excitement. "Anything that you ask of me, I will do." His eyes were liquid pools of blue.

"Don't misunderstand," she snapped, her anger showing. She had taken up the habit of carrying a pipe on public excursions; as smoke curled from her nostrils, Dolan trembled with anticipation.

"What I need is information and to have it I will need to touch your mind with mine. That is what I ask. Will you allow it?"

"Yes," he answered, while a tremor passed through his torso.

"But I caution you," she added. "There may be other things that I might be able to see. If you have secrets that you don't wish to expose, do what you can to bury them well. Understand?"

He nodded yes, but more thoughtfully than before.

Much later that evening Dolan returned, bursting with information. He went directly to Shunlar's room, knocked quietly at her door, and she gave him entry.

"They are assassins!" he began in a hushed tone. "They represent a faction of the Feralmon who are not traders in goods but in human lives. Someone by the name of Korab sul Fanon is offering two coffers of gold to whomever can deliver the head of a man whose name is Benyar sul Jemapree."

Shock drained the color from Shunlar's face. Why would they travel so far to find an assassin to perform this deed? Why not look within their own people, or to someone in Vensunor?

"Lady Shunlar, are you all right? Will you faint?" Dolan

asked, very solicitously. He was definitely fraying her nerves with this behavior.

"No. I will not faint," she snapped at him angrily, sparks jumping out of her mouth. "But, are you sure you heard it correctly?"

"I heard correctly," Dolan answered her stiffly, after several seconds of strained silence filled the room. He shifted his weight to his front foot and when he next spoke, his bearing was that of a person used to giving orders and being obeyed implicitly.

"You have overstepped the bounds of my hospitality by questioning the authenticity of my report to you. Though I agreed to your request earlier, I regret I cannot allow you to reach into my mind and look for further information. What I have told you tonight is very serious and took some effort to obtain. Do not expect that I am someone who can be ordered about at your whim. I bid you goodnight." He gave her the slightest bow possible, turned, and left the room, seething with anger.

Shunlar hardly cared that he was angry; she was barely aware of him, lost in thought, trying to formulate a way to warn Benyar—until she heard her door slam. Jumping at the sound, she knew she would have to make amends later.

She wanted to tell Gwernz immediately what she had just learned from Dolan, but the hour was so late. *What can he do about it tonight?* she asked herself. She thought of Ranth and feelings of loss and remorse flooded her. What was she doing here with her uncle when she could be with Ranth, possibly protecting him and his father? Why had she agreed to part from him? Her mood was strange and soon she found herself crying. Later when she fell asleep, she dreamed of Dolan screaming at her in a horrible rage.

The next morning Dolan did not meet her for sword practice, though she waited for him for nearly an hour. Finally realizing he was not coming, Shunlar left the sparring hall in search of breakfast and Gwernz. She was still formulating how she would ask him to join her at the tavern that evening to wait for the men, but her mentioning the possibility that Benyar's life was in danger was all Gwernz needed to hear. He agreed to a late night excursion.

When they arrived at the Spinyfish Tavern, Dolan was there with a group of his friends. From the looks of him, he had been drinking heavily. He was polite, but didn't ask them to join his group, and Shunlar guessed why. She smiled, raised her cup to him, and watched the other young men around him smile and make secret remarks behind their hands. Dolan looked in her direction but did not return her salutation.

"Careful, Shunlar," advised Gwernz when she explained to him what had occurred the night before. "Are you so bored that you make enemies while we wait for the snows to stop? We have at most another two months to spend here, and I would do that with peace within the household."

"I suppose you are right. I should apologize to Dolan. After all, he did do me a good service. Not that kind!" she protested when Gwernz raised his eyebrows. "Whatever you might think of me, I do have limits to what I will do for information."

For many hours Shunlar and Gwernz sat talking quietly as they waited for the men to show up at the tavern. As Shunlar was about to give up and go looking elsewhere, through the door walked the three men, soon followed by the man Dolan had described as a ship's captain.

None of the young men in Dolan's group paid any attention to them, except Dolan himself. He watched over the top of his goblet and shifted his eyes nervously between Shunlar and the men as he did.

The air seemed to become very close as Shunlar sent a mind probe into their midst. Gwernz sat protectively close to her, his hand on her arm so that he could hear and see what she did. She was able to understand all of their words, because Gwernz translated any she did not know. She saw Benyar and Ranth in their minds, as well as a young man who resembled Ranth so remarkably that he might be a brother. Try as she might, Shunlar was unable to stop her emotions from taking over; several seconds after the sight of Ranth, she began to cry, pulling her mind-touch away from the men who sat on the other side of the room.

As Gwernz comforted her, she stopped crying, and calmed herself so she could focus on what information she had just learned. But as she looked across the room at Dolan, she was startled by the way he glared at her.

"Shunlar," Gwernz interrupted. "We should go now."

Their walk back through the streets was quiet, neither wanting to discuss anything they had learned until they were sure no one followed them or would attempt to listen to their conversation. Once safely behind the closed doors of the house, Klarissa joined them and they told her what they had learned.

"One thing we know for certain," mused Gwernz. "Those men are as stranded in Tonnerling as we are for the winter. The only chance we have of a courier getting a warning to Benyar will be if we can leave before they do. Once back in the Valley of Great Trees, we will send a courier with a coded message through our friends in Vensunor, Delcia and Morgentur. They, I am certain, will be helpful in contacting Benyar and Ranth, since they are closer than we to Kalaven Desert. For now, we must remain as inconspicuous as possible and hope that spring will arrive early.

"And, niece, see what you can do to make peace with Dolan," Gwernz added.

"What's this?" asked Klarissa, suddenly interested.

"I'm afraid I've offended your brother, Klarissa," Shunlar admitted. "I asked him to find out what he could about the men and their dealings with the ship captain. When he came to my room last night, I made the mistake of questioning the authenticity of what he told me and he became very angry."

"Shunlar, I must tell you something that you may not be aware of. Dolan believes he is in love with you. He has told me that. I cautioned him against it, but he was always my father's pampered son and can be very strong-willed. He was also my father's apprentice and knows how to manipulate and pull ideas and more from a man's tongue without him knowing how or why it was done. More than that I cannot reveal. Let me talk to him and explain . . ."

"No, mistress. The fault is entirely mine and I intend to make things right as soon as he returns tonight. I will wait for him here, with your permission." Although she didn't need to be formal, Shunlar bowed to Klarissa and waited for an answer.

"As you wish," Klarissa replied, bowing back. "Husband,

it is very late and I am ready for bed. Perhaps it would be less embarrassing for Shunlar and Dolan if we are not here to greet him when he returns. It sounds as if he will be in no mood for an audience. Will you join me and get some rest?"

"Of course, wife," Gwernz answered her. "I agree we should not interfere with Shunlar's apology. Do you wish for some salt to help with the taste of the crow, niece?" His eyes twinkled mischievously.

Shunlar replied wryly, "If salt is what the voice of experience recommends, uncle, then salt it is."

"Ah, you mock me. Let us leave her alone, Klarissa, before I say something else I will regret." But he was smiling and both women once more bid each other a fond goodnight, embracing as they did.

Shunlar sat in a large, cushioned chair with her feet propped up before the fire, waiting. She was nodding off to sleep when the doors banged open noisily and Dolan staggered in with the help of two of his friends. They dumped him into the chair next to Shunlar, looking suddenly anxious and out of place once they noticed her. Her quiet stare was all they needed. Both men left without waiting to be introduced, bowing nervously as they backed out of the room, themselves in little better shape than Dolan.

Shunlar watched them go. When she turned her eyes back to Dolan, his red-rimmed eyes gave her a piercing look that she could not read, but it made her shudder.

She spoke softly. "I hope I do not offend you with my presence, but I wanted to apologize to you before the night was over. It is plain that I have angered you and I ask for-giveness for my thoughtless behavior." There was no way she could read him. His face remained a sullen, drunken mask.

Getting up from her chair, Shunlar knelt beside Dolan, careful not to touch his hand that dangled over the arm of the chair. "Because I am a guest here, and I acted so foolishly, I can only prevail on the goodness of your heart to allow me to stay under your roof. If you wish, I will leave . . ."

He cut her off, slurring his words, "How d' you know 'bout my heart. You don' haff one." His voice quavered as he spoke.

Before he said anything he would regret, Shunlar raised her hand and interrupted him. "Please hear what I have to say. The man whose life is in danger, Benyar, has a son named Ranth. The son is a man I have come to love. I had not told you this, but I carry his child. Mistakenly, I took your good nature and intentions toward me as one would from a brother. Had I paid more attention, I would have seen more, but I regret I did not, as I was pledged to another." It was a small lie, but it seemed to penetrate his drunken state.

Suddenly wide-eyed, Dolan tried to straighten himself in his chair as Shunlar added, "Will you forgive my unkind words of last night? I do need a friend and would count you as one, if that is your wish."

"Yes," he answered, his head bowed. Then he said, "Call a servan' an' leave. I'm gonna' be sick. Don' want you ta' see that," his slurring was worsening.

"Dolan, my friend, I've seen sickness brought on by drink and worse over the years. Many times I've held a head or a friend has held mine. Come, I'll help you to your room and leave you or stay, whatever you wish. You don't really want the servants to see you in this state, what with the way their tongues wag. After all, we're friends."

"Don' hafta' be so gods awful cheerful," was all he said as she helped him stand and half carried him to his rooms, hiccuping as he went.

"Let me tell you about a night in Vensunor not so long ago. I was with two friends, Jaleel and Bannin, and the Feralmon cactus alcohol was particularly good that night. We drank two bottles and because we had several more stories to tell and our money was running low, we ordered a pitcher or two of ale. Bad judgment on our part. The three of us spent the night in the stables because the innkeeper threw us out. She knew what was about to happen to us. We took turns holding each other's heads and the next day . . ." Her voice trailed off as they stumbled along down the corridor.

SEVENTEEN

THREE MONTHS WINTERING IN TONNERLING HAD turned into four, what with all the snow, and after four long months in the city by the sea, Shunlar was more than anxious to leave. Dolan and she had formed an easy alliance; he stopped treating her like a potential mate and more like a friend; she stopped treating him like a student and more like a comrade in arms.

But, as she continued to grow taller, she knew their excursions into the night life of Tonnerling would soon cease. Though she had the ability to cloak herself with illusion and appear shorter, the effort tired her easily. Gwernz surmised it was because of her pregnancy.

On the evening which, as luck would have it, turned out to be their last outing, Shunlar and Dolan were making slow progress as they walked to the Spinyfish Tavern. They hadn't ventured from the household for five days and the snow—which had been falling since dawn in flakes larger than an eye—was up to their knees. All day it had continued this way, blowing in swirls and billows, drifting against buildings, making any excursion outdoors a miserable experience. By nightfall the wind had finally stopped, and the impossibly large snowflakes floated lazily down to cover everything with a thick mantle of white.

Many of the residents hadn't bothered to light the lanterns at their gates or set torches out as they customarily did each evening. Why bother when so few would be leaving the warmth of their fires? The occasional burning torch didn't do much to light their way as they walked through the falling snow, and sounds carried in a strangely muffled way. At first only Shunlar was aware of the echoing crunch of footsteps in the snow behind them. She whispered to Dolan to change the cadence of his steps to match hers and when he did, they both heard the others.

Dolan grabbed Shunlar by her cloak and pulled her into an alleyway, only to discover it had no outlet. From a window two stories up, a lantern partially illuminated the alleyway. Before they could find a doorway to hide themselves in, the crunch of several pair of feet behind them made them turn, draw their swords, and take a low defensive stance.

Knowing they had been discovered, the five men who were following Shunlar and Dolan had decided to make their move. They rushed at their prey, drawing steel as they did to encircle the couple. Shunlar and Dolan stood back to back, turning, watching the five who circled them.

She pushed her cloak from her head and dropped the illusion covering her, standing to her full height. Dolan knew what had happened by the way the two men who advanced on him froze and seemed to squint into the darkness behind him. He grinned, as only a young man would in the face of danger.

One of the three men who faced Shunlar lunged at her from the left, slamming his sword down with a forceful two-handed blow. She fended it off with an upward, left-handed block and as he felt the reverberation of the meeting metal clang through his arms, her right hand loosed the wrist dagger, which found its target in the throat of the man farthest to her right.

Immediately the man in the middle swung his sword, which narrowly missed her right shoulder as she turned aside. Bending her right elbow and bringing her hands together around the pommel of the sword, she brought the blade across in a wide arc, screaming, "Dolan, duck!" But her attacker also ducked as her blade swung murderously through empty space where his head had just been. Moving so fast, the man lost his footing in the ice beneath the snow, and he went down on one knee. As he caught his balance, his head came up, a fatal mistake. The last thing he saw was her sword swinging in a return arc toward his neck.

The two other men were more than Dolan could handle alone. Shunlar turned, located Dolan in the dim light. Hesitating only the briefest of seconds, she thrust her sword between the ribs of the man who had nearly overwhelmed her young companion. She knew Dolan was wounded by the way he breathed, but not where or how badly. Still, he managed to fend off his last attacker.

When the last attacker saw his fourth mate fall, he made a pretense of a lunge and practically fell onto Dolan's sword. Seeing how the last man died meant only one thing: the men were paid assassins, something Dolan, inexperienced as he was in matters such as these, could not know. The silent way they had all died told her that also.

As Shunlar offered Dolan her shoulder, city guards came running, carrying torches that hissed as the snowflakes fell into the flames, throwing an eerie light over the bodies and the dark, fast-spreading stains beneath them. The unmistakable sound of swords clashing had summoned them surer than any outcry. The captain of the guards rushed forward, demanding to know what had happened. In the torchlight the carnage was apparent. Shunlar had already covered her height with illusion and was holding Dolan upright, he being near to fainting or retching. She sincerely hoped he did neither.

"Captain," Dolan managed to say once he caught his breath. "We were on our way to a tavern when we were attacked by these men. I have no knowledge who they might be or why we were their target." He faltered and nearly passed out as his knees buckled and all of his body weight fell against Shunlar.

"You, Malik, and Andren," the captain called two guards forward. "Assist this man. I would speak with his *companion*," he said, emphasizing the last word.

Shunlar reluctantly gave Dolan over to the two guards. When she raised her head to the captain, his look was malicious. "What do you wish to know, sir?" she asked carefully.

He grabbed a torch from one of his men's hands and held it near her face. Only after several seconds did he pass it back, his demeanor somewhat changed. "If I hadn't seen you with my own eyes, I never would have believed it. What kind of woman are you who carries a sword and dresses like a man?''

She did not answer immediately, thankful that the damp cold was giving everyone's breath a frothy billow. She held her tongue and calmed herself as best she could, knowing that sparks would spring from her lips if she allowed herself to become angry.

"Captain, what kind of woman I am seems not to be a question to ask at this moment. Who paid assassins and who sent them after us is foremost on my mind, but I would not tell you how to go about your business.''

"You say these men were assassins. How do you know that?''

"By the way they fought and the way they died. Master Dolan is wounded and I would see him safely home now, by your leave.'' Shunlar carefully bowed to him, but he did not return the courtesy.

He ordered his men to take Dolan to his home, and watched her go with a grim look. After they had left his sight, he bent over the first man and searched the body himself. Startled by what he found, he ordered his men to uncover the upper arms of all the dead. Each had a flying fish tattooed on both arms. When he saw their markings he turned to stare in the direction that Shunlar had gone.

Returning home with a wounded Dolan was not how Shunlar had anticipated ending the evening. His right forearm had taken a long gash and he had lost a fair amount of blood, but Shunlar saw to it that the bleeding stopped as soon as she sent the two guards on their way. The wound was washed and bandaged by Klarissa with the help of a servant, as Gwernz and Shunlar watched. Only when Dolan had taken several sips of a strong herbal tea laced heavily with brandy and laid his head back on the pillow to sleep did Shunlar leave his chambers, satisfied that he was safe.

Gwernz and Klarissa waited for her in the main hall, expressions of worry clouding their faces.

"Shunlar, what happened?'' Klarissa asked, troubled.

"I don't know. We knew only seconds before the attack came that we were being followed, but we never found out who they were or who sent them after us. I am certain, however, that the men were hired to find and kill one or both of us.''

Klarissa's face went white and she stood up suddenly. ''How do you know they were hired?'' she demanded.

''It is my business to know such things, after all, I myself have been hired as a tracker. But I have never accepted a job as an assassin.''

Klarissa nearly fainted at her words. Putting a hand to her head, she sank into a chair, and then looked up at Gwernz questioningly. ''My husband, you knew this about your niece's profession? Have you both put my brother in jeopardy of his life?'' Now anger clouded her judgment. ''The evening excursions into Tonnerling will stop tonight. Dolan is only seventeen and I demand that you and he no longer leave this house without a proper guard or in each other's company. Furthermore . . .'' But she was abruptly cut off.

''You will not order me about,'' came the carefully calculated words from Shunlar's lips, followed by a cloud of smoke and sparks. It stopped the other woman immediately. Shunlar continued, ''Believe me when I tell you I have no wish to endanger your brother. My life is not now my own either. Do you forget that I am with child? How stupid do you think me to put this life''—she cupped her belly with her hands—''in danger. No, we will not go into the city any more. It is foolish to do so and I will not be thought of as foolish. Now if you will forgive my rudeness, I will check on Dolan once more before I retire.'' She turned on her heel and strode from the room, a stream of smoke marking her passage down the hall.

Not until she had laid upon her bed did Shunlar admit how shaken she had been by the incident. *No*, she told herself and the child as she covered her belly with her arms, *I will never let harm come to you, little one*. She felt close to tears when a knock sounded softly on her door.

It was Dolan; he looked pale but was smiling. ''Are you all right?'' he asked, concerned but not overly solicitous.

Her answer was to hold her arms open to him. Without hesitating, he hurried to her side, encircling her in his arms. She fell asleep so soundly that she never knew when he left. Her strength had been sorely sapped, and Dolan alone had recognized it. He very gently had helped her sleep by touching her and heavily planting the suggestion that she rest.

Hours had gone by, and Dolan's arm was sore and stiff. The wound had not shed any blood since the moment Shunlar had touched it, but damage had been done. When he left Shunlar's room for his own bed, he realized that this was the only intimacy he would have with her. Curiously, he felt only relief now that he knew she would be leaving soon.

In his own quarters, Dolan unwrapped his arm to inspect the wound. He was surprised when he saw a dark bruise with a scab that had formed over a long slice in his arm. When he touched it, the scab fell away, uncovering only a thin pink scar.

Within two weeks they would be leaving Tonnerling, and Shunlar felt like she was being released from prison. Because they wanted to leave as soon as possible, Dolan made arrangements for them to travel with the first group of traders. Once the spring melt had begun, teams of men rode out from the city daily to check on the passes. Finally, the first pass was opened and within one week the others followed, though not fast enough for Shunlar. Some of the passes had to be cleared of rocks and trees that obstructed the road, leftover debris from avalanches.

Leaving Tonnerling behind was the most difficult for Klarissa. For months she had worked hard to secure a mentor for her brother, choosing a man who had been a friend of their father, hoping that Dolan would find one of his daughters attractive. A marriage would cement the relationship, and of course she reminded Dolan of that. Only after he agreed to consider it did she begin to plan her departure. Secretly she had the seamstress sew her leather riding breeches so that she could ride astride comfortably. She knew it would be scandalous for her to be seen wearing them while within the walls of the city, so she planned to wear a full skirt over them that had the dual purpose of hiding her saddle—a man's—until they were far enough away. Then Klarissa intended to dispense with wearing the skirt altogether.

Shunlar admired Klarissa's practicality. Klarissa's belongings took up only two of the pack horses. The other two animals carried just enough items for trade to make them look genuinely like the rest of the caravan they traveled with.

The morning of their departure finally arrived, and Dolan and Shunlar took a long time to say good-bye. Parting was more difficult than she had imagined it would be. "Practice every day with your sparring partner," she reminded him firmly. "Remember your dagger can mean the difference between your life or your opponent's."

Dolan was grinning at her and she stopped talking. "You have told me that two hundred times in the last week. I won't forget. Now, if you will be quiet for a moment, I have a farewell present I hope you will accept." He handed her a wooden box which she opened slowly.

Wrapped in individual cloths were a set of three matched daggers, each one smaller than the last. The blades gleamed in the light, soft ripples showing deep in the metal telling that their maker had taken hours folding and pounding again and again. Perfectly balanced for throwing, the hilts were polished smooth, and inlaid with copper, bronze, and silver in the shape of a dragon.

"Since you now have my sister to watch over, as well as her husband, I felt these would be an appropriate parting gift. They were made by the same swordmaker who fashioned your sword, Master Clain, and are a gift from both of us. He asks only that you remember him and return to us one day to tell him how his weapons have served you."

Tears welled up in Shunlar's eyes as she picked up each dagger and flipped it end over end. When she was satisfied that they were the most exquisite blades she had ever held, she carefully wiped each one clean of fingerprints before wrapping it and setting it back in the box.

"A promise to you and Master Clain then. I will gladly return one day with stories of how his fine blades have served me. Prosper, friend Dolan. Enjoy what life offers you and always watch your back." She hugged him and kissed him on both cheeks, making him blush.

Then they rode out of the courtyard with all the servants waving good-bye in the early morning light, most of them sniffling into kerchiefs as their mistress rode away. Dolan waved, then stood silently as the gates closed behind them, not in the least ashamed of the tears he cried that day.

EIGHTEEN

THE RETURN OF GWERNZ, KLARISSA, AND SHUNLAR to the Valley of Great Trees was again cause for a great celebration. Arlass let it be known that she was especially heartened by Gwernz's return, for it meant that she could at last step down and let Gwernz take his rightful place as spiritual leader of the Valley. Klarissa and Gwernz were welcomed by family and friends, and they began to settle into life together. They would live with Marleah until a home could be built for them.

Loff was now living with Marleah. Because he and Ranla had not come to any agreement in their relationship, Ranla and Loff had lived apart for the entire winter. Gwernz was deeply troubled by the news, and vowed to do what he could to help.

Ranla had sought the council of Arlass and spent most days and nights in her company. Since the day Ranla had stumbled into the circle of Great Trees and they had given her the gift of the herbs, they had not been willing to communicate anything to Arlass about Ranla, a fact that Arlass was beginning to worry about. Had she somehow lost favor with the Great Trees, she wondered to herself alone? Each time Arlass attempted to tap into their wisdom, they had refused to answer her. She was aware of strange whisperings in the distance, but in no way could she hear or report what had always been their clear communication. Arlass realized after several attempts that it only happened when Ranla was present, yet another reason for her to be happy about the return of her successor. She had great confidence that Gwernz would find the answer for her.

This was the fifth month of Ranla's pregnancy and it seemed that neither food nor herbs could put any weight on her. All Ranla seemed to be was belly. The rest of her had become pale and painfully thin. Her hair had lost its sheen in just the last month, and her eyes had circles beneath them that seemed to darken each day. Arlass was worried. She questioned the midwife and had her examine Ranla, but she could find nothing wrong with her except that she was pregnant.

It had been about one week since anyone but Arlass had last seen Ranla. Invited to the homecoming celebration for Gwernz, Klarissa, and Shunlar, Ranla had arrived late and left soon after she had offered her congratulations to Gwernz and Klarissa, making sure to miss Loff altogether. Shunlar noticed the change in Ranla immediately, and commented on it to Marleah once Ranla had left.

"Mother, something is dreadfully wrong with her. I was repulsed by her appearance and my child became very active as well. What is she doing all alone in that cottage of hers?" she asked, trying not to spew smoke and ash into anyone's face. It was obvious that Shunlar had become agitated; several people moved out of close proximity to her. During the winter months Shunlar had spent in Tonnerling, not only had she grown taller, she had grown wings, though no one in the Valley had seen them yet. Her emotions were harder to control than ever, but she did try to contain her everpresent fiery discharge.

"Shunlar, perhaps you can find out. Arlass and she have been spending most days together, and now I fear she, too, may have come down with this strange ailment. You did notice how thin Arlass has become?" asked Marleah.

"Yes I did, but I thought it impolite to ask after her health. You say she and Ranla have been spending a lot of time together? That could explain it," she mused.

"Explain what? What are you talking about?" Marleah demanded.

"Mother, we must discuss this in private." Marleah nodded and they left the celebration, several people watching them go. Once outside they waited until they were sure no one was close by before they spoke.

"Now, daughter, what is it that you are able to see that we who have been watching so closely have missed?" Marleah asked.

"What little I can tell you is based on my reaction and my unborn child's, though not much else. It felt to me as if this babe was trying to scramble away from Ranla, so active did he become. It can only mean that the child she carries is somehow doing something. Can it be that the life-force is being drained from both Ranla and Arlass by the child?"

Marleah quickly decided, "We can't wait for Gwernz or tomorrow. Come, we must do a formal asking of the Great Trees now."

The two women ran toward the sacred grove. As they approached, they noticed a light coming from the grove that grew stronger the closer they got. Reaching the outer circle of trees, both felt a heavy, painful pressure in their ears. Shunlar yawned and held her hands over her ears.

Gesturing to Marleah, Shunlar stepped back several feet and the pressure lessened. With her mother beside her she whispered, "It was as though I had lost my hearing. Did the same thing happen to you?" Marleah nodded as she rubbed at the side of her neck. "Do you recall this ever happening before?"

Marleah answered, "There is no predicting what the Great Trees will do, but I cannot say I have ever heard of such a thing occurring. Also, the light there is very unusual." She looked worried as she peered toward the light that continued to illuminate the Grove with its unsettling glow.

"Someone is within the Grove now, asking guidance from the Great Trees, but I was not able to see who. Something is making me feel very uneasy about the asking that is taking place. We must be very careful. This could be dangerous. Since we won't be able to hear one another, stay close as we approach the circle. I doubt that weapons will make a difference, but protect yourself if you must." Shunlar nodded to her mother, and they moved forward again toward the lighted grove.

As the air became heavier, breathing grew harder. The

pressure on their ears increased; each step was more difficult than the one before. As they neared, Shunlar thought she could make out a person lying in the midst of the circle of Great Trees. Finally, shaking and holding onto one another for support, Shunlar and Marleah reached the soft grass of the inner circle. Only from here was it possible to see that it was Ranla lying on the ground, curled into a fetal position, with her arms wrapped around her belly. Her belly was the source of the potent light, and as soon as they had stumbled into its glow, it began to fade. Once the light was gone, the pressure of the air changed, and their ears popped.

Both women struggled to regain balance, their muscles trembling as they stood up straight and fought to remain standing. Then they heard the sound of Ranla's ragged breathing.

"Poor child, she is being drained of her life's essence as sure as I stand here." Marleah and Shunlar went to her side and tried to rouse her. Finally, Ranla stirred.

"Please help me," she begged, clutching Shunlar's arm in desperation. She gasped as a spasm washed through her, making her nearly pass out again. When the pain stopped, and Ranla opened her eyes, a strange orange glow blinked in their depths for an instant. Then it, too, was gone. Suddenly, as if nothing had happened, Ranla pulled her hand away and bounced to her feet in one fast motion. She bowed to both women and walked away from the grove without saying another word.

Stunned, Marleah and Shunlar could only watch her walk away, forgetting altogether their reason for coming to the Great Trees. Overcome with exhaustion, it took them nearly an hour to get up and walk back home, holding each other as they went. Shunlar's arm ached and itched at the same time, all the way home. Both went to their separate beds, forgetting they had gone to the Great Trees for a formal asking.

But the next morning, Marleah knew something was terribly wrong. She felt as if she had drunk an entire keg of bad wine. Her head pounded and when she looked at herself in the mirror, there were dark circles under her eyes. Though she would have rather stayed in bed, the smell of fresh bread pulled her from her room. When she entered the kitchen, Loff, Gwernz, and Klarissa turned and stared at her with the most curious looks on their faces.

"What is it?" Marleah demanded, wincing at the sound of her own voice.

"Sister, sit down and let me take a close look at you," Gwernz ordered. She did as he asked, somewhat puzzled. Not until she looked down at her hands did she understand why. Her hands, arms, face, and throat all looked burned, as if she had been in the sun too long.

"Shunlar. Go to her and see if she is harmed. I will explain later. Please go!" Gwernz hurried down the hall to his niece's room. He knocked and opened the door without waiting to be admitted.

Shunlar still slept, but she, too, had the strange burn markings on her face and arms. Gwernz gently touched her shoulder to waken her. She groaned, reaching for her temples.

"By all the cursed sows in Vensunor, who drugged my wine?" she complained to no one in particular. Then her eyes opened wide and she saw her uncle standing over her. "I drank no wine last night. What happened to me?"

"Tell me what you remember," Gwernz said comfortingly as he sat on the bed next to her.

"The Grove of Great Trees. There was a weird light and such damnable pressure on our ears as we walked into the center. Then the light was gone and Ranla was lying there. When we tried to help her, she pushed us away and left. Then, we came back here and went to bed."

"What compelled you to go there?" he asked.

"I . . . I can't remember."

"Would you permit me to look directly into your thoughts to see if I can find out?"

"If you must. But be brief, my head is pounding."

Gwernz touched her hand and tried to slide into rapport with her thoughts, but he couldn't.

"What are you waiting for? Begin," Shunlar said, agitated.

"But I did begin. It seems I can't reach your mind this morning. Is anything else different with you?" Gwernz asked.

Shunlar looked frightened then. She tried to reach toward

her uncle and nothing happened. "No, this is gone too?" She cursed under her breath.

"Calm yourself. I'm sure there is an explanation. I need to know what happened last night. Come and I'll see if I can touch Marleah's thoughts."

Shunlar rose from the bed and pulled her breeches on under her sleep shirt, lacing them as she padded barefoot behind Gwernz.

"It seems another fine puzzle has presented itself this morning. Marleah, I need to look at your thoughts to find out what happened to both of you last night. As you can see, Shunlar is similarly afflicted."

Sitting beside Marleah, Gwernz touched her arm and quickly was in rapport with her thoughts. He saw Shunlar through Marleah's eyes as they walked into the Grove of Great Trees and felt everything that happened to them. He was astounded when he saw how many details Shunlar had left out when she had told him what had happened the night before. Especially intriguing was the light that shone from Ranla's unborn child. When Gwernz finished, he released her hand and returned to his own thoughts, his brow deeply furrowed.

"Do you remember your reason for going to seek the advice of the Great Trees last night?"

Marleah shook her head. "But I can't begin to describe how much pain I feel now that the memory has been revived. Can you do something about my head first?"

"Allow me," was all he said. He reached toward her temples with both hands and seemed to grab the pain from her tissues. Turning away from her, he blew a loud breath over his fingers. She smiled and sighed.

"Much better, thank you. Let me think. Ah, yes. We went to the Grove for a formal asking about Ranla and whatever it is she carries in her womb. Not only did her belly glow so brightly that it burned our skin, but we saw a strange orange light in her eyes. Then she got up and just walked away as if we weren't there. Seconds before that she was clinging to Shunlar's arm, begging for help."

"It seems that this child of Creedath's has grown strong and is sapping Ranla's life force. That it has managed to involve Arlass concerns me greatly. Could she be unaware because its power is deceptive and it presents itself to her as needy? That it was able to cloud your memories so well concerns me also,'' Gwernz said.

Shunlar spoke up. ''Uncle, another thing happened. When Ranla gripped my arm, the sliver of Banant's Lifestone responded. My arm throbbed as we made our way home. Something must be done now, before it grows stronger. We must go to Ranla today and somehow convince her to rid herself of the seed she carries, or surely she will die.'' Though she didn't say anything, Shunlar was worried that she had placed her own child at risk.

''I appealed to her once, before our journey to Tonnerling. I believe there is a way that I can show her just what it is that will be unleashed on the world when she births it, but I must do it alone. Stay here and rest until I call for you. And be assured, I will call for you.'' He kissed Shunlar gently on the forehead before leaving.

Gwernz didn't have to ask Loff twice to accompany him. On the way, he answered Loff's questions, filling in the details of what had happened to Marleah and Shunlar the previous night. It was with heavy hearts that both men approached Ranla's door.

The woman who answered the door looked far different from the Ranla they knew and loved. Gone was the sheen from her blonde hair, which now hung in dry, brittle, strings down her back. Her eyes were dull and sunken; her lips were parched and her hands shook. There was little weight to her once-robust figure; she was all belly. When she saw who it was, hope seemed to light up her face and she invited them into the house that felt stuffy and close. Ranla offered them some refreshment, and when both politely refused, she sat back in her chair, the strain of getting up and moving around showing.

''Ranla, I'm afraid I must be blunt,'' began Gwernz. ''We have come to speak to you about the child. You are not faring well and all of us who care for you are greatly concerned. Once, many months ago, I was foretold by the Great Trees that only misery would come from the offspring you carry. Now that I can see with my own eyes what harm it is inflicting on you I must be firm. You know what I speak of, don't you, child?''

Her eyes filled with tears, and as she spoke, Gwernz was sure it was only Ranla who communicated with him. "Many months ago you offered to show me this child. Can you do it now while it rests? You see, for several hours of the day it seems to be inactive. Only then can I fully engage in the world around me. The rest of the time I can't seem to remember what I do or how. Show me now. Quickly. While there is time.''

Ranla reached out her trembling hand and with what looked like a great effort, grabbed hold of Gwernz's hand. He spoke aloud to further dispel her fear, but his voice echoed within her head as well. "Ranla, I will approach you gently. First, imagine that you have a barrier that looks like this,'' and he formed a picture in her mind of a seamless, stone wall, several inches thick. "If the need arises, you must see yourself behind this wall, understand?''

Ranla nodded her head yes, eyes wide. She was able to see the wall and imagined herself able to jump behind it at the first sign of danger.

"Good. Now take a deep breath and close your eyes.''

Again, she did as she was instructed. Through a haze, she saw herself standing with Gwernz in a room much like the one they were in. When she looked at herself on this internal plane, however, she appeared healthy and robust, the way she had looked before her life had been threatened by this pregnancy. She could see a bright glow radiating from her belly, a glow that compelled her to look at it yet hurt her eyes when she did so. She couldn't take her eyes from it, and soon tears were streaming down her cheeks. Her head pounded. She tried to reach toward the light with soothing words and thoughts but was rewarded with more pain around her temples. Then she felt a sharp prickling feeling in her belly.

"Breathe again and calm yourself, Ranla,'' Gwernz's gentle voice echoed in her head.

When she did so, the pain retreated somewhat. Again she reached out to the life, only to be rewarded by sharp claws raking her arms.

Too late, Gwernz yelled, "Look out! Jump behind the wall."

Ranla did it, startled at how fast she saw herself move. On the other side of the wall, she examined her arms, which were bleeding from deep gashes that ran from elbow to wrist. Then her gaze fell on her belly, which flared with a bright orange light. What she heard next made her lose consciousness. A voice she thought she would never hear again was laughing wildly. *Creedath.*

When she awoke, hours later, Ranla found herself in bed with a hot towel on her forehead and several blankets piled on top of her shivering body. All she could remember was the horrible sound of laughter that she heard just before she blacked out. It brought with it images of Creedath and the afternoon he had so coldly and methodically controlled her and raped her. Ranla was terrified and afraid to open her eyes. She knew there was someone else in the room with her but not who, and she couldn't remember where she was. She inhaled sharply and forced her eyes open.

Loff sat next to the bed, wringing out a towel that was soaking in a hot herbal solution. When he saw her awaken, he smiled at her and gently replaced the towel on her forehead with a fresh hot one. Ranla moved her arms and winced. Pain shot down the length of them.

"Loff, what is wrong with my arms? I want to see them."

He carefully folded back the blankets to reveal bandages from her elbows to her wrists. In some places blood had seeped through. Ranla gagged and turned her head away, gasping. "Cover them."

"They will not heal while she carries the child," she heard Gwernz say, his sad voice sounding as if it came from across a great chasm.

He had been waiting for Ranla to awaken. "I have been conferring with the Great Trees. They told me that because you were attacked by it so savagely, your body will not heal properly." His voice echoed sorrowfully.

"Ranla, forgive me for endangering you so. Had I known that you would be so sorely used by the life growing in you, I would never have suggested that you try to make contact with it. Never did I expect so much power in a being so small.

I can, however, offer you protection. If you will allow me to do so, I can weave a spell that will keep you safe.''

"Yes. Do what you can, and hurry. Already my resolve is growing weaker and I can feel the life force of it taking over.'' She let out a scream as a pain that felt like a knife in her middle ripped through her abdomen.

"Tell Marleah to come with the midwife.'' Ranla ordered quickly, gasping as another spasm came. She was beginning labor. "Loff, go and bring Shunlar to me. I will need her strength as well.'' Her voice was shaking as Loff helped her into a comfortable position against the pillows. He left in a hurry to bring Marleah and Shunlar and the midwife as she had asked.

When all three women were gathered, Ranla asked Loff and Gwernz to leave the room. "Thank you, Gwernz, for the protection you have placed around me, but now I ask that you leave. This is a time when I want only the comfort of women around me.''

Loff gently kissed her cheek and Gwernz bowed to her as they left.

Ranla turned to Kinia, the midwife. In a quiet, controlled voice she said, "Bring me the herbs that are in that pouch.'' She pointed to a small bag that hung on the wall. Its contents were the pieces of twigs, leaves, and assorted bark that had been given to her the day she had stumbled alone into the circle of Great Trees. Arlass had told her she would be shown who they were for and their purpose. With certainty she knew now they were intended for her and always had been.

A tea was infused from the herbs, and Ranla seemed to relax after she had drunk a cup. Her mind became sharper than it had been in months, and she felt truly herself again. The birth contractions continued for hours and finally, exhausted, Ranla fell into a deep sleep.

Although everyone had expected it to be a long night, the child that Ranla carried was much stronger than they had anticipated. Toward morning Ranla was unconscious. Her color was wrong and her breath was coming in inconsistent short gasps. The circles beneath her eyes had become dark purple stains.

Marleah decided it was time to bring Loff and Gwernz back

into Ranla's room. Even though Ranla had asked the men to leave, all three women were exhausted from their long vigil and needed their strength.

As Gwernz and Loff entered, Shunlar approached Ranla's bedside, and reached toward Ranla's belly with her right hand. Suddenly Ranla's belly began to contract and move in a rolling motion. Ranla remained unconscious, though she groaned loudly. As Shunlar touched her belly, a strange orange-hued light appeared for just a second and traveled up her arm. Shunlar pulled her hand away, and the light disappeared so fast, she was not quite sure she had seen it.

Touching Ranla again, carefully, very tentatively, Shunlar began to send a small tendril of her mind's awareness inside Ranla's body. When she encountered the essence of the tiny being growing within the other woman, a feeling similar to recognition seemed to emanate from it into Shunlar, through her arm. That moment enabled her to see the shard of crystal embedded deeply between the two bones of her right arm. It glowed with a sickly orange brightness that matched the glow coming from Ranla's belly. Shunlar trembled. Strangely alert, her emotions suddenly felt raw and she sent a plume of smoke and sparks across the room.

Shunlar scanned herself to see if she was in any immediate danger before proceeding. The only thing she was certain of was that the spell of protection Gwernz had woven around Ranla was strong and still firmly in place. She nodded to her uncle, and he expanded the protective spell to envelop her.

Shunlar again reached out to touch on the awareness within the glow of light. It responded to her with amazing speed. She lightly touched only her index finger to Ranla's belly. As before, a spasm passed through Ranla's middle. Shunlar moved her finger slowly down Ranla's belly and the essence of the life followed it down and out the birth canal, the towels between Ranla's legs turning crimson in one large spasm. As soon as the child left Ranla's body, the essence dissolved, and the glowing light that Shunlar had watched abruptly blinked out of existence.

A tiny, lifeless babe lay unmoving, covered in blood. When Kinia lifted it, it remained still. She wrapped it in a blanket and took it away before Ranla woke. No one asked what sex it was. No one had wanted to find out.

Ranla awoke and screamed. At her side, Loff held her hand and tried to soothe her, reading her thoughts as he gently stroked her hand. Ranla began to toss and turn, in excruciating agony. She flailed her arms, causing her wounds to begin bleeding again. Before she did more damage to herself, Kinia managed to get her to swallow some of a potion that would stop the bleeding and dull her pain, allowing her to get some rest.

Loff began his bedside vigil once more, carefully applying hot compresses to Ranla's forehead. Soon her color did change. Her face no longer looked pale, but began to take on an ashen shade. Her breathing slowed until it was so shallow that it seemed she might not take another. Frightened, he called out to Marleah and the midwife.

Kinia bustled into the room, closely followed by Marleah. They both felt for Ranla's pulse and were aghast when they discovered how slow it was. She was dying. Suddenly Kinia thought to check to see if Ranla had stopped bleeding. She cried out when she pulled back the blankets and saw the sheets.

The herbs Kinia had given Ranla to help her blood coagulate weren't enough. Loff continued his bedside vigil, but Ranla did not have the strength to live. She had lost far too much blood, and giving birth prematurely had taken the small amount of vitality she had left. The child, the malevolent seed of the evil Lord Creedath, had tried to use it all, yet, it too, had lost its battle to survive.

As Ranla lay dying, Arlass entered the room. Her skin shone from within, and it was evident that she would be speaking with the voice of the Great Trees.

"My poor Ranla," Arlass began in the whispery voice of the Trees. "You have been sorely used by this monster Creedath and his seed. Do you remember the many women Creedath tried to father a child on? None of them or the children survived childbirth no matter how many doctors or healing women were present. You yourself attended at two such events, did you not?"

Ranla, barely conscious, could only nod yes, she was so weak. Arlass continued.

"In the past the other women died when Creedath was present. Being an untrained telepath, he never realized that by reaching toward the child he compelled it to be born before its time, bringing about the premature birth and death of each one.

"Ranla's child was no exception. Its desire was to join with the sliver of Lifestone that is embedded in Shunlar's arm. The compulsion was strong because the Lifestone's master, the evil sorcerer Banant, had taken the stone from another in death, and passing to him through the blood of a dying man, it became tainted. Unbeknownst to Banant, this taint was passed to his offspring through his blood.

"But it was that eagerness to be born too early that has saved us all from what might have been unleashed upon the world. Sleep now, child. Be peaceful. The Great Trees await you." Arlass then bent and kissed her forehead, greatly sorrowed, knowing that Ranla would not live.

"Loff," Ranla whispered, "come closer." She clutched his hand and sent a thought to him for she was too weak to speak further. *Thank you for your kindness and your love. I beg you to forgive me for not returning it to one who deserved it so.* Her eyes glazed over with one last spasm of pain as her breath left her body.

Loff sat for long minutes holding her cooling hand, refusing to believe that she was gone. Closing his eyes, he reached toward Ranla with his thoughts, trying to find her on the internal plane, but he could only catch a glimpse of a shadowy form in the corner of his eye that disappeared each time he tried to look at it directly. He called out to her continuously. Finally, exhausted and overcome with grief, he allowed Gwernz and Shunlar to lead him away from Ranla's body.

Ranla was cremated with her prematurely born infant and their ashes were scattered across the meadow where she had gone daily to gather her herbs. It would take Loff years to return to his quick-witted, jovial self. After her death, he returned to the house to sleep in the bed that he and Ranla had shared so briefly. But sleep eluded him, and several days later he moved back into the family home with his mother and sister. He spoke rarely, if at all, and most of his time was spent seeking the comfort and solace of the Great Trees.

Nineteen

TODAY ALGLOOTH DECIDED HE WAS GOING TO TRY something different. On one of his excursions into the ruins of Stiga, he had found an enormous kettle. He planned to drag it into the cave, set a fire beneath it, and make a large stew for Cloonth the Enormous, as he had taken to calling her these days. It kept his spirits up to be able to make a joke, however small, in such a desperate situation. He had found a source of water in the depths of the cave and had decided a change of menu would be good for both of them.

He'd been horrified by the way he looked and by his own actions these last months. How many had passed? He couldn't remember. One day while in the midst of bringing food to Cloonth, he discovered how much he had been controlled by the compulsion set on him by her. He had stopped to quench his thirst and got a good look at his reflection in the pool of water. It startled him at first, then it frightened him. His clothing and even his hair were spattered with blood and bits of dried entrails and gore. The look in his eyes was that of a hunted animal, much like the deer he continued to prey upon. He had dark circles under his eyes as well, and his wings were tattered at the edges. The pain he only felt now that he had stopped to rest and think.

Thinking, what a difference it would make. He hadn't been doing much of that at all. No, he had been driven by animal desire and fear for months and he knew it now, deeply. He bathed and then took the time to change into clean clothing.

For now, Cloonth must wait, he told himself. Yes, he was regaining his ability to think and plan. He remembered suddenly who he was and what he was capable of. There was no need to hunt down animals and kill them. No, he could touch their minds and herd them into the cave. Let Cloonth take care of the rest. He was slowly coming back to himself, feeling stronger now that he had been able to sunder her spell.

He planned culling some of the animals from a herd of cattle he had seen—when or where, he couldn't remember now, but no matter. The compulsion put on him was beginning to peel away, small layer by layer. He remembered mountain spotted sheep he had seen so far away. These he could also herd down into the cave. What part of him had Cloonth touched so deeply that he had been left a shell of his former self? Thoughts were sparking off inside his head and they rejuvenated him. Happily he turned to the task of finding the herds and bringing them in.

Cloonth stood at the back of the chamber and bellowed from a pain that she was certain was about to split her in two. Several large cracks appeared on the ceiling directly above her head with the next anguished cry, and small particles of rock and dust began dropping onto her shoulders and head. She stood clenching the larger boulders for support as her stomach began a roiling motion that increased with each minute. Her lizard-like body shuddered as a small split at the base of her tail cracked open and grew larger, a milky-white substance oozing from it.

Alglooth came running into the cave out of breath. He had felt the same spasm in his middle and knew what it meant. Hurriedly he spread sheepskins over the ground near Cloonth's tail. Just as he finished and was about to breathe a sigh of relief, he heard a strange stretching noise that seemed to be coming from the split in her tail.

The opening had grown wider, and from it a whitish, opaque, fluid-filled cylinder squeezed out. Inside there wriggled a small form whose features he could barely make out. As he focused his attention on the child that squirmed within, another cylinder slid out of Cloonth's tail. It was the same color and, like the first, contained an occupant. He got down

on his knees to get a closer look and saw that both small
cylinders were connected by an umbilicus.

All Alglooth could do was step back and allow nature to
do its work as another orb popped out of Cloonth's tail.
Cloonth was looking over her shoulder as yet another "pearl"
oozed out into the world.

With her soft underbelly sagging, spent from the energy of
the birth spasms, Cloonth carefully turned and lay on her side
gathering six orbs to her, as she crooned over her new brood.
With an enormous grunt the last of the cord came loose from
deep in her belly and was expelled. A small trickle of blood
came with it, followed by clear liquid.

She carefully lay the still connected cylinders back down
on the ground and beckoned for Alglooth to come near. "We
must help them out of their little eggs, my dearest." Her voice
was soft and sweet and there was no suggestion of compulsion or force in it. His beloved Cloonth had returned!

"How can I help? Tell me what must be done and I will
do it."

"See how the shells are beginning to harden? We must
pierce each one so that they can truly be born. Can you not
see that they are helpless?" Her voice was worried.

But the little ones were not helpless. Already Cloonth and
Alglooth could hear a tap-tapping sound coming from the
eggs. In seconds all of them began to move, vibrating, shaking, and bouncing up against one another until the hardened
shells cracked. One by one four eggs opened, emitting a thin
wisp of moisture that evaporated quickly and spilled out its
liquid. The two parents watched as first a small hand appeared, then a very human-looking infant tumbled out, righted
itself, and began to crawl around.

All of the children had a delicate covering of rainbow-
colored scales. Their hair was still wet, although it would be
light, very nearly white, the parents were sure. All of them
had light, amber-colored eyes.

But the last two orbs were not open yet. Inside each could
be seen a small, dark, body that wriggled and twisted and
bounced against a shell prison. The four babies, one male and
three female, crawled to these two eggs and began a high-
pitched croon until the shells began to fracture. As Cloonth

and Alglooth watched, first one head then another burst out, and tiny fists punched their way out. These last two were not at all like their other siblings. Both had the same wet and matted hair but their yellow eyes had a more reptilian look. Their bodies had a covering of dark scales, and when they cried out, sparks flew from little fang-filled mouths. Examining them, the parents discovered they were both male.

Cloonth at once scooped them up and held them to her bosom, instinctively licking them clean. They responded with small mewling sounds, their mouths searching for food. With almost one movement, the other four infants crawled to Cloonth, making the same sounds, all hungry. As Alglooth inspected them, he noticed that some of them had small tails, especially the two who had emerged last from their eggs. All had the small buds of wings that they stretched and flapped as they crawled across their mother's belly searching for food. Amazed, Cloonth saw that her belly had been transformed in the last hour during the birthing. Up and down her chest and belly now swelled breasts, some of which were dripping milk. Her eyes glazed over as the children each found a nipple and began feeding.

Leaning back against a large boulder, Alglooth watched for some time. When he saw that Cloonth seemed to be falling asleep, he allowed his eyes to close. Hours later, he was awakened by her voice in his head, sounding more gentle than it had in all the months of her pregnancy. *My dear one, the children are going to take many more hands than ours. Please my whims, but fly to the Valley of Great Trees for help. I am sure Shunlar, our first daughter, can talk some of them into helping us. What do you say to that?*

He was delighted. Not in all this time had Cloonth spoken of anyone else, much less in Old Tongue. He knew his mate had truly come back to him now. His answer was instantaneous. *As you wish, my heart. I will go to make arrangements and return as soon as I can. Will you be able to manage while I am away?*

Manage? I suppose. Perhaps they will all sleep when they are full and I know I shall remain alert. The cave is secure and there is plenty of water, even if you were to be gone for several days. Please take your time. I know what a tremen-

dous burden I have placed on you these last months and I fully intend to repay you for all your hardships. She laughed softly then and shooed the father away, very gently this time.

When Cloonth was certain Alglooth was on his way out of the cave, she began to sniff hungrily about. Finding the egg shells and afterbirth she devoured all of it, then turned to look upon her brood. They lay together, all six of them, like a pile of puppies. Very gently she covered each one with a warm blanket of soft sheepskin. They stirred, and some burrowed deeper into the pile of warm skins. She knew they would not sleep like this for long, so to take advantage of the quiet Cloonth wrapped her still quite enormous body and tail about the nest of sleeping children and settled down to rest also. As her breath slowed and sleep washed over her, the air around her began to ripple curiously. Though no one was there to observe it, Cloonth's metamorphosis was already beginning.

Alglooth, filled with strength and a new sense of purpose, left immediately for the Valley of Great Trees. It was night, and no one could see him, so he decided to make several passes over the sentry posts, hoping that he might find Shunlar at one of them. Circling low, he searched for her with his heat trace sight until at last, he located her. She was seated on a wide limb of a particularly enormous oak. What he saw surprised him. Her heat trace, though recognizable, had changed.

Delighted to have found her after so many months, he sent out a mind-touch to her, but was not answered. Curious that she hadn't responded to him, he flew nearer to her and felt a difference in his daughter that was at once unusual yet familiar. Only when he saw her did Alglooth know what it was he had felt. Shunlar had somehow been transformed into a woman who looked remarkably like Cloonth. As he drew closer, Alglooth could see that she was also going to be a mother soon. Though surprised, he was happy to see her. He landed softly in front of her.

"Shunlar, how I have missed you these many months."

She was speechless at first, then found herself overwhelmed with emotion. They embraced, but her thoughts were very firmly closed off from him.

Alglooth blurted out, "Now that I have found you, let me tell you the news. Cloonth has given birth and you have three sisters and three brothers."

"Alglooth. Father . . . I never expected to see you here. But how did Cloonth have six children?"

"That I will explain, as I am sure you will explain to me the transformation you have undergone." Alglooth waited for her to speak.

But Shunlar was not ready to accept his sudden appearance graciously. She had felt abandoned by him these many months, and her temper took over as sparks and smoke spewed from her mouth and nose. Alglooth instantly recognized a mood was upon her and he held himself back for a moment, allowing her some time to react.

Finally, Shunlar said, "For months we searched for you. We were even in Stiga at the start of our journey to the Valley, and you and Cloonth were nowhere to be found. I want an explanation from you about where you disappeared to before you give me any more *good news.*" She bit the last words off sarcastically.

"My child, forgive me, but I had no say in the matter. If you will but give me time to explain, I will show you all that has transpired since we were last together."

"That is one of the things you cannot do, for it seems I have lost the ability to open my mind up to another and let my thoughts be touched in any way. And that is not all. My ability to see heat trace has left me and the warning signal at the nape of my neck no longer functions." When she had finished telling him how it was with her, she flew away from him, smoke trailing in the air after her.

Alglooth was worried. He hadn't expected her to react to him so hysterically, and never did he expect that she would just get up and leave. He followed her and landed shortly after she did at the door of Marleah's house—only to have Shunlar slam it soundly in his face. Alglooth entered quietly and followed her heat trace path down the hallway to the room she had entered. He sent a small tendril of mind-touch into the room, only to have it touch upon a strong wall of nothing. Having no other recourse, he opened the door and went in.

In a behavior totally unlike her, Shunlar was sitting on the bed crying. "Go away. Go back to where you came from and take your good news with you. I don't care how many children Cloonth has had, I want nothing to do with them. You left me to fend for myself. Didn't you wonder how I was or what I was doing here? Couldn't you have come or sent word somehow that you were both fine or missing me?"

"Daughter, I wanted to come, believe me. You have only to look at yourself and the transformation that has happened to you to begin to understand what Cloonth has gone through. It is a mystery to me how it happened. Can anyone explain it?" Alglooth asked.

"But, I thought you of all people would know!" Shunlar shouted. "This change has happened to me because a sliver of Banant's Lifestone embedded itself in my arm. The Great Trees told Gwernz that it could not be removed and that it had already begun to become part of my bones. And although I will return to looking the way I did before I became pregnant, I don't know if any of my abilities will ever return. Now do you understand the reason for my anger? I may never be the same again."

"Hush, child," he comforted her, holding her tightly against him as she sobbed. "I had no way to know this. Let me tell you how it has been for me these months and perhaps you will forgive me for neglecting you.

"I hesitate to tell you, for you may think ill of her, but I could not leave Cloonth. You see, she had become like our dragon mother in every way. As she grew, so did her powers, and she set a compulsion upon me that enabled her to control me completely. The snare that she used to bind the spell was my great love for her. Once she had reached her full size, her dragon nature took over and she hid herself at the bottom of the cave where we were born, terrified that someone might find her and kill her and the children before they could be born."

As Alglooth told his story, Shunlar remembered that the first thing they found when they arrived in Stiga was the destroyed doorway. Gwernz had touched his wand to it and they had all seen what appeared to be a great beast breaking through it. Only Shunlar had recognized the white hair on top of the beast's head; no one but Shunlar suspected it might be Cloonth.

"Cloonth's existence depended solely on me and my constant search for food for her and her ever-expanding belly. I knew there had to be a reasonable explanation as to why Cloonth would need to control me so completely. I thought her pregnancy alone had done it. After what you just told me I suspect that was not so." He sounded relieved. "So you see, daughter, I was powerless to come to you or even contact you, so ensnared was I by Cloonth's spell."

"But Shunlar, can you remember the exact words of the Great Trees? Think. If their message said you would return to the way you were, then all will be restored to you, even your special talent for seeing the heat trace." Now he had gotten her attention. Shunlar stopped crying and began to think over his words.

"Their message said that once the sliver of Lifestone had become one with my bone, and after I gave birth, I would return to my former human appearance. But I would keep the ability to cast an illusion or change my shape back to looking half-human and half-dragon, as I appear now, and I would still be able to fly."

"Then forget your fears, my beautiful one. Not only will you be restored to the way you were, but you will be given special talents for all your suffering." Alglooth almost got a smile from Shunlar with this comment.

But he was troubled by this new information from Shunlar. "Now I would like to speak with Arlass and Gwernz, for I wish to take counsel of the Great Trees to ask if Cloonth also has a sliver of this Lifestone somewhere in her. Will you take me to them?"

Alglooth held his hand out to Shunlar. Very tentatively she reached out and twined her fingers within her father's. Never before had she felt as much love for her father as she did in this moment, and she reached toward his mind with a mind-touch, forgetting that he would not be able to hear her.

But a curious thing happened. "Something has just brushed against my mind that reminded me of a small child I once taught." He asked, "Did you reach out toward me with a thought?"

"Yes! Do you mean you felt it? Not in months have I been able to touch anyone or receive any thoughts from another," she said, excited.

"You must be regaining your old abilities then. You will give birth soon, is that not so?"

She nodded, putting her arms around her belly.

"Then some of your talent is returning, as was promised to you. This is the best of signs. Come, let us find your mother and Gwernz and tell them all our good news." They left the room together in search of her family and Arlass.

Arlass and the Great Trees confirmed Alglooth's suspicions that a sliver had embedded itself in Cloonth's left arm. He remembered then the red and purple bruise that she had made, constantly scratching her arm, before her transformation into a fifteen-foot-tall dragon.

"But why would Cloonth's appearance be so changed?" Alglooth asked.

"Banant's Lifestone was filled with hatred for his mortal enemy, Porthelae. When Banant transformed him into a dragon, the spell was so powerful that the great beast who was your mother flew from her cave and they mated. We must be thankful that when the stone exploded, only a small sliver found its way into Cloonth's arm. If she or Shunlar had been closer, the result would have been fatal," Arlass answered in a hushed tone.

The Great Trees, speaking through Arlass, told him that this sliver, unlike Shunlar's, could be removed—in fact must be for Cloonth's well-being. The most welcome news, however, was that Cloonth would not remain in the shape of a dragon.

Later that evening it was decided that Shunlar alone would accompany Alglooth to Stiga to meet the children, and would help transport them to the Valley of Great Trees. Knowing how fearful Cloonth had been in the early stages of her pregnancy, Alglooth did not want to risk frightening her with any other visitors.

In the predawn hours, father and daughter left together. Marleah and Gwernz had woken up with them, to see them safely on their journey. Marleah watched as her daughter spread her wings and, catching an updraft, lifted off the ground to join her father in the air.

TWENTY

WHEN THEY ARRIVED AT THE CAVE NEAR STIGA, Alglooth decided it would be best if he went first and announced their presence. Cloonth was delighted to see them both and welcomed her oldest child with open arms, something that unnerved Shunlar at first. Even though she had been prepared by her father, she was shocked by Cloonth's appearance. But Alglooth was quick to point out that Cloonth had already begun to change. Several feet shorter, her skin was now a light shade of bronze, not the dark mud-brown she had been at the peak of her transformation. As the days went by, Cloonth changed more and more until she again looked like her former self and like Shunlar, something that delighted Cloonth.

Shunlar proved to be a great help to her father and foster-mother. The only thing she could not do was nurse. Because Cloonth's body returned to looking like a human's and not a dragon's, another source of milk had to be found for the children. The goats that Alglooth had herded into the cave for food became just that. Now that Cloonth no longer craved meat every day, most of the animals were set free, save for six that were kept for milking.

Within a month the babies were old enough to leave on their journey to the Valley. Shunlar again proved to be invaluable to them in her half-human, half-dragon form. They each carried two little ones as they flew, stopping frequently for Shunlar to rest, for she had the added weight of her unborn child and she was not accustomed to flying any great distance.

The inhabitants of the Valley of Great Trees had been waiting for their arrival. When the three of them were sighted flying overhead, all work stopped for the remainder of the day as people began to flock to Marleah's door.

Neither Cloonth nor Alglooth spoke of the physical changes she had undergone, even though they were aware of the question on everyone's mind: How could a woman of her size have given birth to so many?

One night, shortly after they had begun to settle into life in the Valley, Cloonth decided it was time to remove the shard of Banant's Lifestone that remained embedded in her arm. Cloonth and Alglooth hadn't traveled inside each other's skin for a long time, although they periodically had done so in the past to check each other out for any physical aberrations. Cloonth had not been amenable to his internal explorations once she became pregnant, and certainly not while she was in the physical shape of a dragon.

As Alglooth carefully checked her over inch by inch, he noticed a bright spot near the bone of her arm. As he approached it with caution, it suddenly flared up and sent a burst of light at him with such force that it pushed his awareness from her body and he was thrown across the room.

Astounded to see her mate lying unconscious on the floor, Cloonth ran to his side. When she had revived him, he described what he had seen under the surface of her skin. Curious to see for herself, she quickly linked minds with him and approached the spot tentatively with her awareness. A sweet, sickly odor touched her nose. As she got closer, the air swirled with bright, undulating images. As she watched, the images became an amber-colored flame that drew her awareness and held her there.

Only with Alglooth's help was she able to resist the spell it tried to set upon her. Fearful beyond words, Cloonth lay trembling in Alglooth's arms.

When she could speak, she asked, "How were you able to resist the pull of that thing while I could not?"

Alglooth held onto her tightly, soothing her with his hands. "The piece is beneath your skin and not mine. It was not as simple as you might think, my love. I have been trying for the better part of an hour to release you from its hold."

Upon hearing his words, she took a deep breath and announced her decision. "Though the hour is late, we must find Arlass and ask for her help tonight. I want no remnant of Banant buried under my skin, no matter how small. Come with me now. We will ask Shunlar to watch over the children."

They left quietly and set out for Arlass's cottage. As they approached, her slight form appeared at the door to greet them.

"I have been waiting for you, as you can see. My dreams were very troubling tonight. Tell me, have you come about the Lifestone?" Arlass asked.

Cloonth nodded her head as she and Alglooth entered the cottage. Arlass gently led her to the bed and asked her to lie upon it. "I will remove the piece as you have asked, though it may be difficult. Be assured that I will do everything in my power to make it painless."

"The pain is nothing. All I ask is that you take this piece from my arm as fast as possible. You see, I knew of Banant of Stiga. He was a vile creature, and knowing how he acquired this Lifestone makes it all the more important that it be removed immediately." Cloonth was trembling; sparks flew from her mouth as she spoke.

The water kettle hanging over the fire began to boil as she spoke. Arlass poured some hot water into a small bowl, mixed a powder into it, and set it aside to cool. Placing a larger bowl under Cloonth's arm, she poured the mixture over the part of her arm that looked bruised and swollen.

First a tingling sensation spread across Cloonth's forearm, then numbness. On a small table near the bedside was a lantern, and Arlass turned it up to its full brightness. Next she unrolled a cloth, revealing—among other things—a small obsidian blade and several pairs of metal tweezers in varying sizes.

After making sure that Cloonth's arm was numb, Arlass made a quick, clean incision. Guided by the Great Trees, her hands glowed with an inner light that seemed to dampen the brightness of the lantern. Blood trickled from the incision into the bowl. Putting her hands over the cut, Arlass spoke under her breath. Her hand glowed brighter for several seconds and the bleeding stopped. Taking her hands away, she opened the incision by gently pulling apart the skin of Cloonth's arm. Peering closely, she saw something glint in the light. Arlass grabbed the end of it with a tweezers and pulled it out in one slow movement to prevent it from breaking.

Arlass held up a needle-sized piece, about one inch long, to examine it in the lantern's light. The shard was red with Cloonth's blood. Arlass rinsed it in water and set it aside upon a piece of cloth to examine later. Turning her attention to her patient, she saw that Alglooth was gently wiping Cloonth's brow.

Cloonth lay quietly, catching her breath. She seemed much calmer than when she had first arrived on Arlass's doorstep. In a hushed voice she said, "When the piece was removed, I felt as though I had been released from a great hold that had been placed on me. So subtle was it, that I had no idea it was there until it was gone. Now that it is gone, I am aware of many things that I did, one which shames me beyond words. Can you ever forgive me for treating you so shamelessly, my beloved one? You nearly killed yourself doing my bidding, day after day."

"Quiet. All is forgotten. I knew when Shunlar told me about the piece of Lifestone in her arm that you too were afflicted by the same cruel bane. When taking counsel with the Great Trees, they confirmed my suspicions. I told you then and I say to you now, all is forgiven. Speak no more of it." Cloonth kissed the back of his hand ever so gently.

As Arlass bandaged Cloonth's arm, she spoke with the voice of the Trees, telling Cloonth that a scar would mark her arm—a scar that would never fully heal, but would remain sore and red. Arlass apologized, but concluded that it was because the Lifestone of Banant had been so tainted. Cloonth was not bothered by the information in the least. She felt better than she had in nearly a year and she embraced Arlass tightly, thanking her again. Then she and Alglooth returned to their home and the sleeping children.

When they had gone Arlass unwrapped the piece to examine it. Still in close rapport with the Great Trees, they instructed her to crush the piece into a fine powder and scatter it within the Grove of Great Trees so that it could do no more harm to anyone. She followed their instructions, carrying the small amount of powdered crystal that night to the circle. For several months after, a small part of the grass in the center of the circle looked as if it had been burned.

TWENTY-ONE

As THE WEEKS PASSED, ZERAYA BECAME STRONGER. Finally, Honia declared that she was fit enough to return to quarters in the palace. Moved from the Temple room where she had spent more than half of her years in a state of suspended life, Zeraya was settled into a spacious suite. Ketherey and Fanon still occupied the royal suites, in order for them to continue acting as co-regents for Benyar and Zeraya. Because Benyar did not wish to interrupt the flow of their lives more than he already had, he insisted that he and Zeraya occupy suites on the other side of the palace. Besides, he rationalized, that way they would be closer to Ranth's quarters.

The week of initiation long over, Ranth was finally settling into life in the palace where servants waited on him and provided for his every comfort. Each morning he spent an hour before breakfast with his uncle and father sparring in the courtyard near the stables. After bathing and breakfast he would be tutored on the history of the Feralmon by an old history master by the name of Tiban sul Falash.

One morning Ranth surprised the old man, however, when he told Tiban of the existence of Alglooth and Cloonth. Of course Tiban refused to believe Ranth. However, when Benyar arrived to see how his son's lessons were progressing, he confirmed Ranth's words. The old man was so shaken he had to excuse himself from their presence to consult with the other scholars.

The noon meal was generally spent in the pleasant company of Benyar and Zeraya. His mother had regained much of her strength, being constantly cared for by Benyar and several young priestesses, but she remained bedridden.

On some afternoons Ranth would sit in the great hall watching Fanon and Ketherey go about the business of hearing and settling disputes for the townspeople. Other days were spent listening to reports, and gathering information from the warriors who guarded the borders. There was speculation that war was imminent, something that left all of them feeling troubled and uncertain.

In the evening, at the dinner table with his parents, aunt, uncle, and cousins, Ranth learned some of the finer points of Feralmon etiquette, especially where young women were concerned. His two young female cousins, Tilenna and Cachou sul Fanon, giggled behind their hands each evening when he entered the room. Only in the company of the adults did they dare speak to Ranth or look at him directly. At other times during the day, when their paths happened to cross, they were the epitome of propriety. The only missing presence remained Korab. Two months ago the sentence of silencing had been lifted from him, yet he refrained from taking his rightful place at table and joining the family at the evening meal.

On this fine spring afternoon, Ranth and his parents were seated together at lunch in an outdoor courtyard, the weather being cool enough at this time of the year to do so. The subject changed abruptly when Zeraya announced, "Your father and I feel it is time you had a consort, a companion."

Ranth nearly choked on his food. He put down the piece of fruit he had been eating, suddenly not hungry anymore. "But I don't feel the need for a companion. My life is full, what with my studies, and weapons practice, and my daily meetings with Fanon and Ketherey. I am learning and doing all you ask of me, but in this I cannot agree."

"What do you mean, you 'cannot agree'? We are not asking you, after all. Honia sul Urla has consulted with the oracle by scrying at the full of the moon and the answer was: Ranth will marry." Zeraya's face was flushed in anger. She meant to be obeyed and she cast a look at Benyar for help.

Though he seemed reluctant to do so, Benyar added, "Ranth, it is not up to you, but to us to guide you in all things that concern your future here. That also includes the good of the people that your consort will one day rule, with you at her side as First Guardian.'' Caught between feelings for his wife and his son, Benyar clearly was siding with Zeraya.

His mother's temper seemed cooled somewhat by Benyar's support and she tried to appeal to Ranth. ''Marry so that our house has an heir. I will have my strength soon, and then will counsel you on how to rule. Until that time, marry. You spend too much time alone with your head buried in a book. A man of your age usually has other things on his mind besides study.''

Ranth couldn't find words. He sat between them looking to his father for some support. Hadn't Benyar promised him no more surprises? Though they hadn't spoken of it, Benyar knew of his love for Shunlar. Didn't he know that he still was in love with her?

Seeing how troubled he was, his parents dropped the subject, and exchanged a sad glance as Ranth excused himself from their company.

Several days later, again at the noon meal, Ranth was told by Zeraya that, ''A young priestess has been chosen.'' Oblivious to the look on his face, she continued, ''Tomorrow evening you will meet your intended bride and you will do whatever you can to make yourself ready to meet her. For the good of the people, you must marry. This is what your birthright is about, service to the people. It would be different if you were not our son, but you are and it is your duty to obey us in this decision.''

Ranth looked as if he had been slapped. ''Mother. Father. I agreed to return here to learn the ways of my people, something I am doing to the best of my ability. But you must understand that I have pledged myself to Shunlar and she to me. We have agreed to meet within a year and resume our lives. The thought never occurred to me that I would be expected to marry or rule someday in your place. I have no desire to rule, nor even the right. Is there no one else who can take my place?'' Ranth felt trapped.

Now it was Zeraya's turn to look dumbfounded. ''Who is this woman Shunlar, and why was I not told about your

pledge to her before?'' she demanded. It was Benyar she
asked, not Ranth, and her husband had no answer for her. He
cast a look at Ranth that was meant to stop him from answering, but before he could caution his son to choose his
words carefully, Ranth answered.

"She is the daughter of Marleah and Alglooth. If not for
her, it is very likely that my father would not have found me.
And it was her mother, Marleah, who returned your Lifestone
to him. While we are apart she is with her mother in the
Valley of Great Trees, learning about her mother's people,
much as I am doing here. Her father and foster-mother,
Cloonth, raised her.''

"You only knew Shunlar for a little more than a month,"
Benyar interrupted. "Don't tell me you expect her to remain
faithful to you. She is a mercenary, after all, and not of our
blood, not someone who has responsibilities to family and
clan.''

Benyar hesitated before asking, "Have you received a reply yet to any of the letters you've written to Shunlar in all
the months that you have been here?''

Ranth could only answer, "No, but I'm sure there is an
explanation.'' His lips were set in a tight line.

Benyar held up his hand and interrupted Ranth. "That is
enough. Your mother and I will discuss this privately until
you can learn proper respect. Go.''

"But, father,'' Ranth protested.

"Go. Now! And remain in your quarters until you are summoned!'' Benyar was furious. Zeraya was pale and shaking
as Benyar knelt at her side to comfort her.

Ranth left as fast as he could. But he had no intention of
complying with his parents' wishes. Ranth's heart was Shunlar's and he firmly believed he would be able to reason with
his parents and not be forced into an arranged marriage.

Of all the adjustments being made, Ranth's was turning out
to be the most difficult. His parents had not raised him, and
they had no idea how to cope with the fact that he was a
grown man with a mind of his own who knew nothing of
what was expected of him. He had grown up in another culture and nothing could have prepared him for this. Each day
brought a new surprise, a new way of handling a situation, a

new way of coping. But now he was being told that he must marry a woman that his parents had chosen for him, when he was already pledged to another. How could they expect him to forget that? If honor was so important, what about the honor of one's pledge to another? He had never suspected Benyar could be this much of a tyrant!

That night, Ranth ate alone in his quarters. He had not been sent for by Benyar or summoned by a servant to join his family at the evening meal. In fact, extra guards had been posted outside his door. Since there seemed to be nothing else to do but wait, he made the best of his evening, sitting in his courtyard until long after dark, trying to figure out the precise words that would convince his parents they must give him more time.

Ranth's jaw tightened when he remembered the way his father had banished him from his presence. He'd seen Benyar lose his temper once before, but his fury had been spewed at his cousin, Korab, for the brutality of Ranth's initiation. Today Benyar had turned that anger on him, and Ranth felt it was undeserved.

These two people he knew so little about, why should they rush him into a marriage? To suit themselves? He knew he must attempt to reach them again, even if it meant risking their anger.

The next morning there was a feeling of excitement in the air. Outside his door he could hear the sound of servants working, talking in hushed voices about the ''special banquet.'' True to their word, it seemed his parents were going ahead with his betrothal. He tried getting news when his breakfast was brought to him, and later his afternoon meal, but the servants were all tight-lipped. They just bowed and lowered their eyes when he asked them what all the commotion was about.

Sad and confused, Ranth spent the day trying to formulate a proper way to tell his parents that he was thankful they were concerned about his welfare, but he had no desire to marry at this time. Would an apology to them help to change their minds and grant him some influence concerning his future? He didn't know them well enough yet to be able to tell.

And he was surprised that Benyar and Zeraya had gotten so angry. Ranth could feel the frustration building in him. He felt like a prisoner. He waited all day for a summons from his father or mother and finally, near dusk, it came.

Someone banged loudly on his doors, and before he had time to stand, the doors were opened and a line of servants followed Benyar into Ranth's suite. Some carried clothing, others brought soaps, perfumes, and jewelry. Ranth, who had been reading near the window, stood at once and bowed to his father, who returned the gesture with only a curt nod of his head.

"My son, tonight is a very special one for our family and our clan. These servants will see that you are properly attired for the evening." Benyar turned and left before Ranth could utter a word.

Already another stream of men were entering the doors carrying a huge tub and buckets of steaming water. Two men began undressing him and Ranth held up his arms, allowing his anger to rise up and then melt away as he lowered himself into the hot, herb-scented water. Later, as four pairs of hands massaged precious oils into his skin, he banked his emotions into a quiet smolder. Just as the last servant finished lacing up his sandal, another knock came at the door. A servant announced that he was summoned to the banquet.

Ranth had been ordered to join them and he sat at the table trying his best to look calm. Only polite words of greeting had passed between him and his parents. Impeccably dressed in soft leather breeches and vest that were dyed gold and silver, the patterns of the scars on his arms glistened from the oil that had been massaged into his skin. His hair had been freshly braided with gold and silver beads woven into it in intricate patterns. Zeraya smiled approvingly to him as he sat, waiting. Ranth had to concentrate and force a feeling of composure over his real emotions.

He wanted more than anything to tell his parents that he felt as though he was being punished. His desire to be heard and understood by them was so great that he was even willing to risk another scene like yesterday's. Just as he gathered his courage to speak, however, Korab entered the room with his sisters, Tilenna and Cachou, one on each arm, and the moment was lost.

Korab bowed before Benyar and Zeraya first, taking great care to bow lower and longer than was necessary, making no eye contact. He then bowed to his parents, smiling shyly to them when he recognized the look of approval in their eyes. Finally he bowed courteously to Ranth, something that did not go unnoticed, before he turned away to take his seat. Benyar and Ketherey exchanged discreet nods. For the time being, Korab was acting in a mannerly fashion; it seemed he was playing by the rules.

Servants began filing quietly into the hall with tankards of wine, filling goblets as unobtrusively as possible. Ranth let his eyes wander around the room for the first time this evening. The walls, the ceilings, and the tables had been covered with thin draperies of gold and silver hue, into which jewels of every color of the rainbow were woven, picking up the light from hundreds of candles and oil lamps and sparkling around him. The tables had been placed in a square pattern with the four corners left open so that everyone entering would be able to properly greet their hosts and then be seated. Ranth realized as he looked at the members of his family who were seated around him that he was the only one dressed to match the decorations. Everyone else, including Korab, was wearing white.

At the main table sat Zeraya, Benyar, Fanon, and Ketherey. Seated at a long table to the right were aunts, uncles, oathbrothers, and warriors of high rank from their clans. At the table to the left sat Korab, his sisters Tilenna and Cachou, and several more cousins. The two places next to Ranth were empty, as was the fourth table, which faced the main banquet table and completed the square configuration.

Ranth licked his lips and swallowed. His mouth was dry, but he was determined to speak. He focused his attention on Benyar and cleared his throat. When his father turned to face him, Ranth quietly whispered, ''Please my whims, Father,'' in Old Tongue, but the sound of tiny bells chiming cut him off and the moment was lost as everyone's head turned in the direction of the sound.

A light evening breeze sent the aroma of incense wafting

into the room, closely followed by the High Priestess, Honia sul Urla, who led the bride-to-be, her parents, and an entourage of ladies-in-waiting. She was introduced to Ranth as Septia sul Prakur, and was seated next to him at the banquet table. Ranth quickly noticed that Septia was draped from head to toe in gold and silver, just as he was. Her entourage and Honia all wore white.

Septia's dark skin had been oiled much like Ranth's, but flecks of gold and silver had been rubbed into her as well. Even her hair sparkled with jewels and gold dust. Many tiny braids were interspersed in the mass of black curls that hung past her waist. Her lips had been tinted a dark berry color, and the lids above her hazel, almond-shaped eyes had been lightly shadowed with silver. Her sleeveless, many-layered, gold and silver diaphanous gown was not cut low, but was pulled very modestly across her throat, emphasizing her small breasts. Clasped at the shoulders and belted at the waist, the gown draped her body down to her ankles. Upon her feet were gold and silver leather sandals. Beneath the layers Ranth could see the outline of her slim, muscular body.

Septia was the young priestess who had watched Ranth secretly from the back of the room when he first met with his mother. Later it was Septia who was picked to lead him to his rooms in the palace that same night. She also had been the faithful nurse to her queen, Zeraya. It was not by accident or simple fate that she had been chosen to be Ranth's wife.

Her beauty, of course, was enhanced by casting an illusion over herself. Without the spell, she was still easy to look upon, but aided by it, she more than caught Ranth's eye. He found himself desiring her as he had not desired a woman since meeting Shunlar. His tongue tripped over words, making him blush when he spoke to her. When his cheeks grew hot, Septia's would also flush with color.

Between courses of food there was entertainment. First there were dancers, then jugglers, and even a man and woman who had trained a great cat to perform. Several times throughout the evening Ranth found himself staring at Septia, trying to interpret what he was reading in the faraway look in her eyes. Though he knew it was against every rule, he wanted desperately to touch her and see her thoughts. Once, when their fingers briefly made contact, they both jumped and he cleared his throat nervously. He had caught a glimpse of Septia's mind. Was she truly imagining kissing him so passionately?

Septia placed her attention suddenly on the plate of food before her. She cast a look around the room, then lowered her eyes. Everyone had seen her jump when Ranth's hand had brushed hers. Several people smiled knowingly. Approval seemed to shine from the smiles on Zeraya and Benyar's faces. Even Korab had been watching.

Again Septia ventured a glance in Korab's direction and when their eyes met, she lowered hers first demurely. Remembering herself and the promises she had made to Korab, Septia returned her attention to the man beside her. *She would marry Ranth. She would succeed. Nothing would stop her now that she was closer than ever to her goal.* She let her mind wander back to the past and to how she came to be sitting here at this banquet given in her honor, as another group of musicians began to perform for them.

Septia had always had plans. Born to parents who already had too many mouths to feed, Septia had been taken to the Temple early in her young life and given over to the life of a priestess. If one had no proud clan to be associated with, as was the case with Septia's parents, this was the best place for them to take her. Besides, ever since she had uttered her first words, all Septia had ever talked about was becoming a priestess. It was as if her life were preordained. The highest calling a woman could answer was that of priestess. Her parents knew she would bring them honor and eventually wealth—so the oracle had foretold—if she were taught the old rituals.

Honia had been the High Priestess when Septia was brought to the Temple. She took an instant liking to the child and Septia to her. Soon they were inseparable, and Honia knew that she had found her heir. Since the culture of the Feralmon relied heavily on the proper times to hunt, plant, harvest, marry, and even rest, Septia's place was assuredly going to be one of power, for the High Priestess's job was to interpret the oracle and give the orders. Septia's parents were raised to an important position overnight, when the oracle declared that one day Septia would be named heir to the throne of the Feralmon, and her child, a girl, would be named heir as well.

For many years now Septia had been certain that meant she and Korab were destined to be together. After all, the son of Zeraya and Benyar had been kidnapped and Zeraya lay near death with her Lifestone stolen. With Benyar gone on a quest for his son and his wife's Lifestone, his absence meant that someone had to rule in their place. It seemed unlikely that Benyar and Zeraya would ever take their rightful places. Searching for a missing child was one thing. Searching for the missing Lifestone was an even more impossible task.

As the line of succession usually passed through the female side in Feralmon society, Zeraya's sister, Zara sul Karnavt, should have been chosen as temporary regent, but she was too young and had no mate with whom to hold the throne at the time. Thus Benyar's brother, Ketherey, and his wife, Fanon, were declared consort and regent, until the time Zeraya and Benyar could return to their duties.

Septia was sure Benyar would never return; thus Korab would be named successor to his father and given the title of First Guardian. His wife, as she was confident she would be, would be ruler.

Had Honia been more observant and not quite so trusting of her young protégée, she would have watched over her shoulder more closely and found out about the secret liaison the young girl had made with Korab. More than that, she would have known about Septia's increasing desire for a Lifestone of her own. But Septia was very clever. She always got what she wanted from Honia, especially information.

Honia had explained that very little was known about Lifestones. Their origin was a complete mystery. As far as Honia knew, the Cave of Lifestones in the Temple was the only source of them. Furthermore, the Lifestones had not sent out a call to an individual since Zeraya and Benyar had received theirs. Honia herself did not possess one, but one could be prepared for a calling. She told Septia that there were secret texts that instructed one in the art of preparing oneself for a calling by a Lifestone, but that one must be a certain age and rank in order to study them.

"When you are older, my child, I will prepare you my-self," Honia had promised.

But that was not enough for Septia. She vowed that as soon as possible she would be partnered with a Lifestone. Septia found out where the library was hidden, and whenever she could get away she read the forbidden texts and learned more than was proper for her to know. A chapter in one of the books cautioned that she must be older by several years in order to handle the energies a Lifestone would push through her, yet she dared to risk trying now.

She shared her knowledge with Korab, trusting that the greed she saw in his eyes was real. It was then that Septia promised herself to Korab and Korab alone if he would help her prepare for a calling by a Lifestone. He agreed, on the stipulation that he also be prepared. She could not refuse him anything. She said yes to him and they sealed their profane pact with their bodies. Yes, for this she had finally succumbed to his constant pressuring, now that he had vowed to assist her in an enterprise that could result in their banishment—or worse, their deaths. They were treading on dangerous ground, going beyond the bounds of their positions in their society; and the danger had made Korab all the more desirable to her.

Septia's reverie of the past had been interrupted when Ranth touched her hand accidentally. She knew in an instant he had seen the images in her mind; however it was not Ranth she imagined herself embracing in a passionate kiss, but Korab. She had been remembering her vow to Korab and the way they had sealed it with her blood.

Ranth was quite a surprise to her. First, he looked a great deal like Korab. She had known this, but not being able to make eye contact in their other meeting had not prepared her for the similarities, though Ranth smiled more. Second, his mind was much stronger than she had anticipated. She could not afford to make mistakes like the one she had just made. Septia covered her thoughts very thoroughly behind a mask of innocence. When they touched again—and she would see that they did before they parted tonight—all he would be able to see would be a very nervous young woman.

Because of the custom that young singles could not speak to each other unless accompanied by proper escort, the evening was a long one. At no time was Ranth permitted to be alone with his soon-to-be bride. Nevertheless, he was quite taken by her beauty and the way she conducted herself while under such close scrutiny from everyone. By the end of the evening, Ranth's resolve seemed to be crumbling, something that Benyar and Zeraya noticed with delight. In fact, he seemed to be completely under Septia's spell.

With all eyes on Ranth and Septia at the betrothal banquet, no one paid close attention Korab as he talked to members of his family, drinking wine, toasting his cousin Ranth and his good fortune. Septia alone watched his eyes burn with hatred for Ranth and longing for her. She watched as Korab drank and became more sullen as the evening wore on.

Later, when she was in his arms, Septia would have to reassure him, as always, that she was his alone. The stakes were too high to turn back now. Already she was able to hear the whisper of the Lifestones, something she had not dared to tell Korab or Honia. They tantalized so strongly that sometimes at night she fell into a trance that sapped her strength for days.

Honia suspected nothing, thinking that the arduous schedule Septia kept herself to was the problem. She had cautioned her protégée more than once not to push herself so hard, and began keeping a closer watch over her. This only made Septia push harder. But what she applied herself to were the forbidden texts: learning how to manipulate others' minds, learning what drugs would render a person helpless, weaving spells and illusions around her and Korab so that they were never suspected of any wrongdoing.

It seemed to all be working so well. Here she sat, at her betrothal feast. Never mind that she was being betrothed to the wrong man; she would never let that set her back. Septia could tell by the way Ranth looked at her that the potion she had managed to drop into his wine was working. If she could only get close enough to Korab's goblet, she knew she could also subdue him—and it must be done soon, for Korab was on the verge of doing something foolish. Knowing he might drink too much, Septia had brought along a powder that would clear his head, unlike what she had given Ranth.

How Ranth seemed to moon over her. It was beginning to

turn Septia's stomach. But it frightened her to look at him at
the same time. Ranth was very handsome—he resembled
Korab so much, they could be brothers. His gestures were
completely different and he was much softer spoken, but his
face was very like his cousin's.

From the corner of her eye, Septia saw Korab rise from his
place at the table and approach them. All eyes were on him
as he raised his goblet to the couple of the evening. "I envy
you, cousin," he declared loudly. "I drink to your good fortune. And, with all that I have drunk tonight, by the moons,
your fortune will be vast! But, alas, I must leave this happy
gathering now before I am carried out." Suddenly he sounded
very sober. Placing his cup down, Korab bowed low before
everyone at the table, turned and left.

Septia knew then that it had all been an act. It was also an
insult that she hoped had gone unnoticed. Cautiously she
looked at Zeraya and Benyar. They were silent and their expressions unreadable. Fanon and Ketherey's weren't. Both
seemed worried and not pleased with their son's act of defiance. Only Ranth was oblivious to what had happened. He
gazed longingly at Septia until she finally smiled and hid a
yawn behind her hand.

That was Honia's cue. Rising, she bowed to everyone gathered. "The hour is late and I think it is time to thank our
hosts and retire. What say you, Septia, child?" Her voice
masked any emotion but the love she had for Septia.

"Yes, Honorable Honia, it is late." Septia rose and bowed
to Ranth and then his parents. "You have honored me greatly
and for that I am grateful. May your dreams be portents that
will light our paths." Bestowing on Ranth a beatific smile,
Septia left with her escort, brushing Ranth lightly on his
shoulder with her arm as she passed him. A shudder of desire
ran through him as he caught a glimpse of Septia's mind.

Within a month the announcement was made that Ranth
and Septia were to be married. A week before the ceremony,
Septia was moved into a sumptuous suite of rooms in the
wing of the palace opposite the side where Ranth resided.
The distance, guards, servants, and societal rules would keep
them properly apart until they were wed. Once they were

married, he would be settled into the quarters adjoining hers.

The day of the wedding arrived. As the wedding feast wore on and Septia grew tired, she slipped a drug into Ranth's wine and he became enraptured by her. Thinking it to be the heady sweetness of the perfume she wore that intoxicated him so, he decided he must have her. With his arm around her waist, Ranth attempted to leave the festivities with his bride. But the guests wouldn't allow them to sneak away. Much to Ranth's dismay, they were escorted to their nuptial bedchamber by an enthusiastic group of men, women, and musicians.

The custom called for the men to disrobe the groom and tuck him into the bed to await his bride. Once this was done, accompanied by much bawdy laughter and rude jokes about his anatomy, the women were called into the room. They escorted the bride, who was draped in a long, red veil that touched the floor. She was placed under the covers and the entire entourage left, taking all but one candle with them.

Ranth could scarcely wait for everyone to leave. His desire for her was overwhelming. He reached for her, nearly frantic with desire, pulling, tugging at the red veil that kept her from him. When at last the veil was removed, he caressed her shoulder gently and that touching enabled him to read her thoughts at last. As a gasp escaped his lips, Ranth saw Septia smile and return his kiss.

Covering her with kisses, Ranth's head was spinning and his hands trembled as they ripped away clothing. In the midst of his passion, for a brief moment thoughts of Shunlar entered his mind and shattered the illusion. Through a drug-induced haze Ranth saw that he was lying on the bed by himself. In the dim candlelight, he could see the silhouette of a woman and a man standing at the foot of the bed in a fervent embrace. Just when he was about to recognize them, the couple began to kiss passionately. Once again Ranth could feel his lips against Septia's, feel her chest pressed tightly to his, her arms enclosing him. He groaned and turned onto his side. When he awoke hours later, he was alone and the sheets were damp and torn.

No one suspected what Septia was doing. Because she was a Priestess of the Temple, and next in line of succession to be regent, she was given a great amount of freedom and respect. Each night she and Ranth had dinner with Zeraya and Benyar. Septia seemed the eager-to-please young wife. In reality, she used her knowledge of herbs to drug Ranth into thinking that they were passionate lovers every night. Most nights, he fell into a deep sleep as soon as he lay down and she invaded his thoughts with illusions of sex. On some nights, the illusion was stronger than others.

Septia's secret lover was Korab. On the nights that his duties allowed it, he boldly took his place at the table for the evening meal. Since Ketherey and Fanon remained the acting regents, Korab rightfully lived in the palace. He sat next to his sisters, at the same table that Septia and Ranth occupied, much to Benyar's dislike.

Benyar tried to tell himself that Korab was not a threat to his son, but not for one minute did he believe it. The living quarters that had been given to Ranth upon his return had been Korab's, after all. Surely the young man had some right to feel displaced or jealous that his lot in life had changed overnight. Now that Ranth was married, Korab occupied his old suite once more. That had been Benyar's suggestion to Fanon and Ketherey and they were relieved as well as grateful to see that their son was once more back in the good graces of Benyar.

We must see to finding Korab a wife. Soon, Benyar mused to himself, as he watched Korab from the corner of his eye.

Ranth didn't notice anything, so enraptured was he by Septia. They retired early each night and shortly after, so did Korab. But he didn't stay long in his rooms. Korab had found a very convenient way to enter Septia and Ranth's suite undetected, by placing men who were oath-bound to him to guard the couple's doors at night. Some nights he and Septia nearly pushed Ranth off the bed onto the floor, so bold had they become. The drugs with which Septia tainted Ranth's wine were so strong that he never awakened. Soon she was pregnant, but the child was Korab's.

Ranth believed, like everyone else, that the child was his. He was overjoyed with the news that Septia was pregnant. All of his waking hours were spent being taught the intricacies, customs, and rules of Feralmon society. He saw little of Benyar, who continued to spend most of his time with Zeraya—who was recovering more slowly than all had expected. When Ranth did see his father, it was usually at the evening meal, when Septia drugged his wine and Ranth became so enamored with her that it was useless to try and engage him in conversation. After finishing their meal they would just go off to bed like lusty young newlyweds. Ranth's life was akin to a perfect puzzle with all the parts neatly fitting into place. Nothing seemed amiss.

TWENTY-TWO

IT WAS THE MIDDLE OF SUMMER, THE FINAL MONTH of Shunlar's pregnancy, and although her middle was wider, her height took away much of the roundness of her belly. As her pregnancy advanced, she discovered that the mere presence of others around her made her jumpy and she did whatever she could to avoid people. More and more she sought the solitude of the trees; most of her days were spent alone at the Valley's perimeter.

Shunlar seemed content enough living with Marleah, but it had been difficult for Marleah to adjust to her daughter's larger stature and to Shunlar's being a full head taller than when she had left with Gwernz to go to Tonnerling four months ago. She not only looked like another person, her attitude had changed drastically also. She was surly most of the time, likely due to the sameness of her days, and the fact that there was still no word from Ranth. No one seemed inclined to get closer; Shunlar looked and acted dangerous.

The other inhabitants of the Valley had begun to treat her with a respect that bordered on awe. When she had first come to live among them, her exotic appearance prompted several men who dared to become suitors, but that had only lasted for a week or two. Shunlar made it clear that she would welcome no advances. Besides, which of them wanted a mate who could cough up sparks or start a fire in the hearth merely by blowing a stream of fire onto the logs? Only the bravest of heart dared even spar with her in the yard when she showed up to practice. None ever showed up at her door.

And then she was gone, off with Gwernz. Upon her return, at the beginning of spring, Shunlar was taller than Evon, the blacksmith, and her wings had grown to their fullest span. Though she had managed to cover herself with the illusion of being a smaller woman for safety's sake while in Tonnerling, once back in the Valley of Great Trees she was again free to look and act as she wanted. Since she had never gotten the opportunity to make friends with any of the women or men her age, she was more than a stranger in their midst; she was an oddity.

Because of her pregnancy and her half-human, half-dragon body, Shunlar was left alone by even Arlass. It seemed that the curiosity Shunlar had when she first agreed to return to the place of her birth had vanished. She showed not the least bit of interest in learning about the customs or history of the Valley. Nothing could persuade her to change her mind.

All Shunlar did now, day in and day out, was obsess about Ranth. She wondered what he could be learning about the Feralmon. What was his life like with them? Had he become so absorbed in his daily life that he had forgotten her and the promises they made when they parted? Eight months had passed thus far and still no word had come, not a whisper of an answer to her many letters.

She was positive he was still alive. Each passing day made her more determined that she would hear from him soon. Her last message had been sent from Vensunor via secret couriers. Surely they had succeeded in reaching Ranth, she told herself.

Upon Shunlar and Gwernz's return from Tonnerling, one of the first things he had done was send a message to Delcia and Morgentur in Vensunor. Gwernz asked if they had had any communication with Ranth or Benyar since their return to Kalaven. He explained that Shunlar had not heard from him, though she had sent several letters. It was Delcia and Morgentur who suggested they send secret couriers to try to reach Ranth, since they themselves had not been successful in reaching him through his dreams. Mysteriously, a woman had turned their thoughts away, saying she was a priestess who guarded the regent and her family. Then she abruptly cut off the communication and their further attempts had failed.

Shunlar was more than puzzled by all of this; she became maddened with the need to know. She had not heard from Bimily in all these months either. When she flew above the Valley for any length of time she would search for Bimily, but her heat trace ability was gone and she never saw the female eagle whose shape Bimily most frequently chose to live in.

And just when Shunlar was about to leave and go herself to Kalaven to search for Ranth, her father, Alglooth, had shown up telling her of her foster-mother, Cloonth, and their six little ones. Once more she became involved with others' needs, setting her needs aside, not because Cloonth and the children were more important, but because she didn't know what else to do. Shunlar had never been so ambivalent in her life.

Bringing Alglooth, Cloonth, and the children to live in the Valley, setting them up in a house, and finding nurses for them took the pressure off Shunlar to make a decision about whether or not to go after Ranth. Everything had happened so fast that before she knew it she was completely immersed in their lives. Until one day she began to notice her desire to shun everyone's presence, longing for the quiet of the trees.

This morning when Shunlar awoke, the first thing she noticed was how scents were heightened and seemed to nearly vibrate upon the air. Her own body smelled different to her, stronger and sweeter, and if she strained her nose, there was the faint aroma of milk. She was aware of how hot different parts of her felt—her belly and breasts particularly. They were heated and swollen and the child had been so active during the night that she had gotten little sleep.

Perhaps I'm just overly tired, she mused to herself.

Breakfast would probably be waiting for her, but this morning she had no desire for enormous quantities of roasted meat. Her appetite was gone; her desire to be alone was overwhelming. She said a polite good morning to Loff and Marleah before ducking through the doorway that had become so much shorter since she had first arrived. She stretched and breathed a long stream of fire into the air, stifling a scream that for some unknown reason tried to rip itself from her throat. Then she flew off to find a comfortable limb upon which to while away the hours of the day, alone.

It was a sultry summer day, and Shunlar lay on a large limb overlooking the Valley. In her boredom she had discovered she could blow smoke rings. Alone, high atop the tree in its uppermost branches, she practiced by herself, putting her hand through the circles, mesmerized with making bracelets of smoke.

Sometime in the middle of the afternoon, tired of laying about, Shunlar rose and stretched her wings, readying for flight, as was her usual habit. This time she felt a tiny "snap" in her groin and within seconds water gushed from between her legs, drenching her breeches and boots all the way down the insides of her legs. No contractions had begun, just a terrible ache spreading across her belly. Panicked by what she knew was about to happen, she spread her wings and unsteadily leapt off the limb to begin a slow flight back to the house. Once there she breathed a sigh of relief when she found Marleah and Loff were gone. As fast as she could she stuffed her bags with baby linens and blankets, food and water, and left again, anxious to be away.

Months earlier Shunlar had found a cave at the southern part of the valley and she flew there. She had already prepared it with a comfortable bed made from piles of animal hides atop pine needles, warm blankets, and an ample supply of water and firewood. Her nest secure, she closed off the entrance with the makeshift door of lashed-together branches. Once in place, she covered it with several blankets to shut out all the light. In total darkness at last, her labor began in earnest.

Her wet breeches were difficult to remove, taking more of her strength than she wanted to expend. In the midst of pulling them off, a sharp contraction took away her breath and left her gasping. Sweat began to exude from every pore in her body, and the next contraction brought her to her knees.

Her contractions came faster and harder, until at last she was able to grab hold of the child under his arms and pull him from her body. At the moment of her child's birth Shunlar screamed Ranth's name aloud with a breath of fire so strong it threatened to burn the bed she knelt upon. By the light of her flame she had seen the baby's tiny face and eyes

that looked at her, older than their years. In seconds her pain
was forgotten. She knew what to do and she took the dagger
in her hand and carefully cut the cord.

Next she lit the fire she had laid and hung the pot of water
over it. When it was warm Shunlar washed the baby by the
light of the fire, carefully inspecting every inch of him as she
did. He seemed perfect in every way. A boy, he resembled
Ranth more than her. He had his father's dark coloring and
curly black hair, with the exception of a white forelock. His
eyes were like his mother's eyes, green with gold specks. At
the nape of his neck was a small green birthmark, just like
the one at the nape of hers. Positive that he was sound, she
put him to her breast and fed him, astounded at how satisfying
an act it was.

In Kalaven, the desert city of the Feralmon, Ranth lay
sleeping with his wife, Septia. He sat upright suddenly, waking in a cold sweat from a strange dream. He heard Shunlar
screaming his name, calling out to him in pain, and he called
back to her loudly.

By this time Septia was also fully awake and she tried to
calm him down, placing her hands on his shoulders, urging
him to lie back upon the pillows. Just as Ranth pushed her
hands away, for the briefest of seconds he saw Shunlar's face
flash before him, but it had changed so. Though she looked
like Cloonth, Ranth recognized who she was. What astounded
him the most was the child Shunlar held.

Completely shaken, Ranth tried to tell Septia about how
vivid the dream was, but she insisted he lie back down. She
soothed him with words that worked another spell on him.
Within mere seconds he was back in a deep sleep. However,
Septia had seen into his mind when she touched him and
knew at once that this was no dream. Fortunately Septia had
not seen Shunlar's face. No, thankfully, Septia saw only a
woman bent over in the agony of childbirth.

This woman, Septia decided, was her enemy, as well as
the child. In the morning she convinced Ranth he had merely
had a bad dream as she slipped more of the potion she had
been administering to him into his morning tea. As the day
wore on, Ranth eventually forgot that he had seen Shunlar

giving birth, and although he continued to dream, Ranth remembered nothing.

After seeing to it that Ranth was under her control once more, Septia left his side to go in search of Korab. Still unusually agitated by what she had seen, Septia told Korab about Ranth's vision during the night. If Ranth had an heir and it was brought here, could it be a threat to her and her child?

Korab listened patiently, letting no emotions show on his face. Once Septia finished, he calmed her down, telling her he would never let anything threaten their child. With Septia reassured, they parted and Korab left in search of one of his oath-brothers. He told the man to discreetly begin inquiries about an assassin, but he did not tell Septia. There were many secrets between them, a fact that neither of them suspected.

TWENTY-THREE

THROUGH KORAB'S ELABORATE NETWORK OF SPIES, nothing came or went from Kalaven without his knowledge or interception. He was aware, from the letters he had read and subsequently destroyed, how eagerly Ranth had been waiting to hear from Shunlar and she from him. At first Shunlar and Ranth's letters had been outpourings from their hearts. Before four months had passed, Korab's interference was felt, and the tone of their letters changed. Each was beginning to believe that the other had forgotten their pledge.

This morning what Septia told him made Korab remember two letters from Shunlar to Ranth that had made it into his hands instead. He had not been prepared for the information that was revealed.

Opening Shunlar's first letter to Ranth he had read, "Once more I am back in the Valley of Great Trees. The winter in Tonnerling was long but not altogether unproductive. While there I happened upon some men in a tavern who were from your people. Listening in on their conversation I learned that someone by the name of Korab is offering a lot of gold to kill your father, but not why. Beware and be on guard, for if they attempt his life, they may well attempt to take yours."

Korab remembered how he had cursed under his breath as he crumpled the paper and threw it on the fire. A rictus of a smile slowly spread his mouth into an ugly sneer as he recalled the words of the second and subsequently last letter from Shunlar.

198

"I had hoped there would be a letter from you by now. I have sent you many letters thus far and not been answered. If no reply comes from you after this one I will finally believe that you have forgotten me.

"But, I have something that I must tell you. You and I will have a child, a son is what the Great Trees have told me, by the middle of summer. One day I will bring him to his father so that he can tell him in his own words why he did not answer his mother's letters."

Korab pounded his fist against his thigh. His brow was furrowed with a nasty scowl as he walked, deep in thought, remembering his meeting with Septia just now. So it was true. This woman Shunlar had given birth, as her letter had promised. Now she must die.

Korab petitioned Honia, the High Priestess, for permission to hunt, as was the custom. Once it was granted, Korab left Kalaven, accompanied by two of his most trusted oath-brothers, Tadim sul Kleea and Natha sul Ankar, with Honia's blessings and prayers for a successful hunt. No one knew that a secret meeting with another had also been arranged in the desert, far from any who might see them and suspect.

"Bring the man to me," ordered Korab as he rested his back against a boulder.

Tadim trotted away, returning shortly with another man close at his heels. The second oath-brother, Natha, had climbed to a higher vantage point to notify them should anyone approach. The newcomer remained standing as he bowed to Korab. His face was veiled as it would be if the wind were blowing sand, but he was covered to remain anonymous.

"Be seated. Have something to drink," offered Korab as the man settled into a cross-legged position before him. "I understand you are good at what you do. Your reward will be great and the sooner it is done, the happier I will be. To make me happy is a good thing, is it not, Tadim?" Tadim, who sat next to Korab, nodded his head and smiled a small uncomfortable smile.

"I don't want to know your name or your clan," Korab continued. "You will be paid generously when the job is finished. For your initial trouble and to cover any expenses, there is this." Korab gestured and a pouch of gold was tossed to the stranger by Tadim. Both men could tell by the way his eyes darted from the pouch to Korab that he was already ensnared.

"I have made inquiries and found out some information about you and the way you go about your work. The person I'm looking for must find a woman who goes by the name Shunlar and kill her, making it look like an accident. I believe you are that person." The man nodded in assent. "There is another matter that, once carried out, will make me very happy. She has an infant son. He is not to live either. Can you do this for me?"

The man looked down into the cup he held, not drinking. He, unlike Korab, was not young. The expression in his eyes was one of complete dejection and self-loathing and he slowly lifted his head meeting Korab's gaze directly, a thing he had not dared to do until now. It was a mistake.

"I am not a killer of children," he whispered, setting his cup down and beginning to rise. Korab's hand on his wrist stopped him from completely standing and he sat down again, staring at the hand that held him. After several seconds, Korab released his grip.

"Do think this over," slid from Korab's lips. Already he had begun to work on the other man's mind. The mercenary noticed the delicate mind-touch and, against his instincts, allowed himself to tolerate it. Something in his eyes changed and he became strangely subdued. He picked up his veil to take a thirsty gulp from his cup, letting a strange fuzziness envelop him completely.

Later, when the man had been dismissed, Korab called another forward from the shadows. This time it was a woman who arrived, so completely covered for anonymity that even her eyes were veiled. She moved across the sand with absolutely no sound, stopping to kneel directly before Korab, her hands hidden in the sleeves of her sand-colored robes.

"You heard everything I said to the other who came before you?"

She nodded her head slowly, once.

"He has agreed to remove this woman and her child, with some enhancement from me." His eyes studied the slight form of the woman kneeling before him to see if he could read her. She nodded once again, remaining silent.

He approved and continued, "You are to kill him after he has fulfilled his obligation to me, understand?"

She bowed her head twice, a sign that she accepted the job. Then she spoke—a quiet voice that held such power in reserve, it made Korab tremble with pleasure. "It will be my honor to rid you of this Shunlar and her son. I will not fail you, my lord." Bowing low, she touched her forehead to the ground before Korab.

To watch a woman he could not recognize perform this obeisance to him aroused Korab. Her quiet submission heightened his desire for her, but then he remembered the dangerous game he played. This woman who knelt before him was an assassin. To take the likes of her to his bed would be like sleeping with a poisonous lizard. That thought lit a fire in him. He smiled, but it was not a smile that instilled confidence. Tadim cleared his throat and Korab quickly remembered his purpose for bringing the woman here. He dropped the smile, thanked her curtly, and had Tadim finish their business.

As the woman walked away he gave her back a final glance. She stopped, turned, and bowed to him. Korab's mouth came open and he snapped it shut, clicking his teeth. An unmistakable heat was rising in his groin and he heard the sound of soft laughter near his ear. When he turned his head, no one was there. He formed a stronger shield around his thoughts and the sound vanished. When he turned to look at the woman again, she was gone. Only Tadim sat next to him, and his face was crimson.

What could he have been thinking to entertain such thoughts at a time like this? Korab had learned well how to overwhelm and manipulate another's mind. For him to become ensnared by someone else was unthinkable. There was no room for slips like the one he had nearly made.

"My brother Korab, did she seem to touch you anywhere?" Tadim asked in a breathy voice.

"Only with her thoughts. She was greatly distracting. And you?"

"Oh, yes, I feel the great need for a woman right now. I should have warned you, but I did not believe the stories.

Now I do. Forgive this oversight.'' Tadim bowed his head to
Korab, gripping the hilt of his oath-dagger. If Korab requested
it, his life would be forfeit.

''No, brother, you are more valuable to me alive than dead.
Just do not leave out such details again. She is good at what
she does. We may need to use her again someday and the
next time she comes before us, we will be prepared for her.''

Once more Korab became absorbed in his plans for Kalaven. More than anything, he wanted to rule Kalaven. He
would kill his own parents, if need be, to obtain his goal. His
desire had risen to a dangerous pitch, had become an obsession, since Ranth and Septia had been married.

However, the information contained in Shunlar's letter was
what pushed him to seek and hire the assassins. He never
dreamed the possibility existed that someone might discover
that he was behind a plot that included killing Benyar and
Ranth and beginning a war. His uncle Benyar believed that
the family's old enemy was behind the continuing border at-
tacks. But Benyar's old enemy had died twenty-some years
ago on the way back to Tonnerling with Zeraya's Lifestone.

In truth it was Korab. He smiled to himself, imagining the
looks of shock on the faces of his parents, his friends who
suspected nothing, the members of the clans—if they knew
the truth. Yes, he had promised the men of Tonnerling large
amounts of gold and plenty of women when they handed the
city over to him. Curiously, the one thing that seemed to seal
the bargain in the end was the mention of the Cave of Lifestones. Though Korab had not been there in person to see the
fervor in the man's eyes, his oath-brother had shown him the
scene when Korab touched his thoughts. Korab, of course,
had no intention of allowing them access to the Lifestones, a
fact he wisely did not disclose.

Since Korab had never seen Shunlar, he imagined her to
be soft and docile and perhaps from a wealthy family. Having
been raised in a society where the final word on all judgments
came from the highest ranking woman, Korab planned to re-
verse that custom, once he was ruler, using the mores of Tonnerling as his standard. He knew nothing of the customs of
Vensunor, or the Valley of Great Trees.

Returning from his reverie, Korab called Tadim and Natha

to him. "We must now concentrate on hunting and trust that the man and woman who have been loosed will perform the tasks they agreed to. As before, only the three of us know what transpired here today, and we will not speak of it again." His oath-brothers nodded their heads in agreement, then prepared themselves to hunt.

Twenty-Four

As Septia's pregnancy advanced, it occurred to her that playing the part of the sexy young wife would soon begin to look suspicious, given her condition. She could not continue administering the same drugs to Ranth. Besides, she was becoming bored with the game. She decided to alter the formula slightly, giving him one that had a subduing effect. He began to look pallid and was prone to sullen moods. Due to the drugs and the way Septia influenced his mind, he was powerless and suspected nothing.

But Benyar had noticed the change in his son and was worried. He decided to take Ranth away for several days into the desert on a hunt. The fresh air would do him some good, after all. Besides, Benyar remembered one of Ranth's initiation requirements, that of killing either a sandcat or the equally poisonous giant lizard, had yet to be fulfilled. Technically, no one was supposed to be with a young initiate on his first hunt, but because Ranth was no longer an adolescent and he was the heir, Benyar would go with him. No one would dare question Benyar's adherence to the rules.

The season was late fall; the morning was a bright one which held the promise of a hot day. Taking their leave of the city in midmorning, would bring attention to the fact that Ranth would be fulfilling his initiation hunt. No one would outwardly notice, as it would be considered highly rude for anyone to call attention to him. Only Zeraya and Septia came to see them off, their attendants left behind for the time being to allow privacy.

Zeraya had been carried outside in a special chair by bearers to say good-bye to her son and husband. She was recovering more slowly than anyone liked, but nothing, it seemed, could be done to hurry her healing. Her daughter-in-law administered to her daily, after all. What more could be done?

"Think of me," Septia whispered as she pressed a special wineskin into Ranth's hands and tenderly kissed him good-bye.

Septia offered Benyar a wineskin also, bowing low as a sign of great respect to her father-in-law.

"Daughter," he affectionately called her, "you will surely fall if you continue bowing in your condition. I appreciate the gesture, but think of yourself and the child."

Though there were three months remaining before she would give birth, Septia's belly was enormous and she stumbled, losing her balance when she straightened. Benyar beckoned several of her ladies to attend to her, but not before Ranth arrived at her side. He walked with her to the servants who fluttered around and whisked her away, back into the coolness of the palace.

Ranth was unable to see the tears that welled up in her eyes as she was assisted back inside. Lately Septia had been quick to cry, something that she never expected, especially when Ranth treated her gently. Although she denied it adamantly to Korab, she was quite taken by Ranth, and the continuing deception was a greater strain each day. Korab had been showing his true nature and become more surly, more intimidating each time they met. She had come to know him for the bully that he was.

"I fear he pampers her too much, my husband," confided Zeraya to Benyar as he bent to kiss his wife's pale cheek.

"My dear, this is nothing. Soon there will be an heir and if Ranth is anything like me, it will get even worse." They both laughed, a bittersweet sound, then embraced once more before Benyar reluctantly left her side to mount his horse. It had been one year since his return; in that time he and Zeraya had not spent one day apart.

Joining his father, Ranth mounted his horse and together they rode from the courtyard. Only Ketherey stood just inside the gates. He smiled proudly as they passed and he bowed to them as they rode by. Benyar sent a mind-touch to his brother, conveying his thanks along with a wish for Ranth's success. Ketherey concurred.

The two men, one nearly an exact copy of the other, rode through the city. One or two heads turned as they passed. Behind their backs, as custom demanded, everyone watched.

As they had not done for an entire year, Ranth and his father rode into the Desert of Kalaven, something that life at court had not allowed time for. Traveling for the most part in silence, Benyar occasionally pointed out a particular animal's track or a plant that was edible or medicinal. Because he and Ranth could also communicate by sending pictures directly to each other's minds, there seemed to be no need for words. Finally it was time to find a campsite. Both of them were weary from being in the saddle all day.

"My son, how is it that we have journeyed for an entire day and not a word has passed between us?"

"Father, for the first time in months I felt speaking wasn't necessary. My daily lessons and life with a woman have been demanding so much of my time, I had forgotten how much I needed silence. But you haven't spoken either."

"I have lived for weeks at a time with no words passing between me and another human. I too have forgotten how comforting solitude can be," answered Benyar. "For many weeks now your mother and I have noticed that something seems to be troubling you, and that is why I decided to take you away on this hunt. Besides, it is time you fulfilled your obligation of first hunt. Tell me, were our perceptions wrong?"

Ranth took several moments before answering. "There has been much to learn, to absorb, since I arrived here with you. You could say this is my third life. The second life, one that you rescued me from, for which I am profoundly grateful, was as a slave in Creedath's clutches. I would not have lived a long time there. My first life, however, still has a deep hold on me. When I was young, I was sure that I would become a scholar, like my friend and teacher, Master Chago. Seeing him die in my arms told me that part of my life was never to happen.

"Soon now I am to be a father. Another life is happening

to me before I am able to settle into this one. Yes, I have had much to contemplate of late. Have I been that distant?'' Ranth asked.

"You could say that you have been, ah . . . distracted. But what man wouldn't be with a young, beautiful wife? I must have seemed that way to my parents also. It was long ago.'' Benyar answered, wistfully.

"Tell me, my son, do you regret your marriage to Septia? I know how you resisted at first, and why. Do you ever think of the woman, Shunlar?''

"Father, thoughts of her are with me often, that I cannot deny. But I have had no word from her for a year. I can only conclude that you were right about her. She most likely has forgotten me.'' His voice trailed off as he gazed across the expanse of desert before him.

"But, we are here now. Together at last. And alone. The air seems nearly to be ringing without the chatter of women to fill it up!'' Benyar, said in an attempt to cheer his son.

Ranth smiled, nodded his head in agreement, then they began to set up their campsite. "Tomorrow we will start early. If memory serves me, I know a canyon where traces of sand-cat and lizard should be abundant,'' said Benyar, leaning back against a large boulder.

"Perhaps I will find tracks as I gather firewood. Rest while I do that. There is plenty of scrub and small dry bushes that will give us a fire.'' Benyar nodded his agreement and Ranth set off to gather the wood.

When he returned, he built a fire in the pit Benyar had prepared and they ate their evening meal of travel bread and dried meat. The air cooled quickly, once the sun went down, and they were both thankful for the warmth of the fire. While they ate, Ranth asked his father to tell him the story of how he courted Zeraya. "Did you know you loved her, or were you allowed that luxury?''

"I had noticed and chosen her before she noticed me. In fact, I took some pleasure in the fact that I could follow her and turn up wherever she happened to be, something that I'm sure her friends taunted her about. By making my presence so obvious, I made my intention known. That was how we courted long ago. And yes, we were allowed the luxury of choosing our own mate. If you had been brought up here among us, you would have been able to do so as well. Circumstances being as they were, we made a match for you, with the assistance of Honia and the oracle. Your mother and I are pleased to see that it is a good one.

"But after we married, Zeraya told me how it was from her side. If you would like, I can transmit directly to your mind the images of the day that your mother accepted me as her mate, as she showed them to me."

"Yes, I would like that," Ranth answered. They sat closer and as Benyar put his hand upon his son's shoulder, Ranth's awareness was flooded with that of the young girl, Zeraya.

A cat call echoed in peals of sound off the rocks of the canyon. She called out again louder this time, feeling brave because there was no one around that would hear her and tell her to hush. Her hair hung damp upon her neck where it had escaped the braids. She had been walking for a long time. Stopping for a brief rest, she lifted her hair off her neck to allow the sun and hot air to dry it. Then, leaping up, she bounded off with yet another cry, laughing at how the echoes made it sound like she were many children instead of one.

High atop one of the peaks a wild goat scrambled, causing stones, many of them large rocks, to cascade down and nearly spill on top of her. As she jumped aside Zeraya looked up to see the last flash of an indignant tail shake at her as the goat sailed over the top of the rocks and was gone from sight.

Remembering where she was, she sat and caught her breath. This was her first venture out alone. Her mother had cautioned her to be wary when she handed her the knife. Nearly fourteen summers old, she had felt so grown up belting it on at her waist. Soon she would make her way back to the camp bringing the unexpected armloads of firewood with her; wood that was difficult to find because these tall canyons gave up little to burn. The net pouch she had slung over her shoulders would usually be full with dung for the fire by now, but she had never liked the smell it gave off when it burned. She was determined to find firewood, and that's what compelled her to search this canyon.

Remembering that there could be danger about, Zeraya waited for any other signs of life to show themselves to her, as she had been taught. "This is not play and you are no longer a child," she told herself, sitting halfway down the eastern slope with the sun directly overhead.

Her water pouch was full and she realized she was thirsty, so she took a few careful mouthfuls and pushed the cork back in with the heel of her hand, securing it with the leather cord. Water was life out here and she knew not to waste it.

For the better part of an hour Zeraya sat with her back against a rock, only her eyes moving across the canyon. Her approach had been purposeful, to announce first of all that she entered and secondly, to frighten away anything that might harm her. The sound she had chosen to make was that of a large sandcat and it seemed to have done the trick. Nothing stirred.

Overhead she saw a tiny speck in the air. A large bird, probably an eagle, was circling. She observed it coming closer and could finally see it was in fact an eagle, a golden one. Another joined it and together they hunted over the canyon. One of them dived very suddenly and as suddenly was airborne again, this time clutching a large snake in its talons. The eagle's mate joined it and they flew away together. So still was she that the birds never saw her. But the sight of the huge snake made her shiver and for the first time today take the danger more seriously.

She sat watching the two specks disappear before deciding to move. Directly across the canyon from where she sat appeared to be the remains of a large bush that from the size of it would provide fuel for an entire evening. Deciding to go around the top of the canyon instead of down across the bottom and up, she picked out her route. That done, she began walking carefully, keeping the sun out of her eyes when she could, always checking for movement off to her sides, behind and in front of her. Halfway across she stopped. Something had caught her eye moving in the shade of the rocks very near the top. Slowly she sank to a crouch behind a large boulder.

For many long minutes, nothing moved. There was no wind to stir even the small dry flowers that grew in the shade of the boulders at her feet. Perhaps it is a bird or another goat, she told herself, not entirely believing her words. Patiently she remained frozen to the spot. Eventually her stillness paid off. The movement occurred again and she could just make out the body of a slender cat as it crouched along, its belly nearly dragging on the ground. By the dark spots alongside the spine she knew it to be a young animal, not quite fully grown. Even so, it was larger than Zeraya.

But, young or old, these cats possessed poisonous front claws. The younger they were, the less potent the poison, but if she were clawed, fever would set in and she would surely die out here before anyone could find her. She had specifically gone against her mother's instructions by coming to this canyon, it being in the opposite direction from where she was supposed to be gathering fuel. Zeraya felt trapped. At her back was escape, but no matter how fast she scrambled up and over the top, the cat would easily overtake her. It was twice as fast as she was, and where there was one young one, surely another was not far behind, along with its parents. These cats had the habit of mating and staying together to raise their cubs.

Certain that the young cat had seen her, she shivered as it slowly made its way to where she crouched. The closer it came, the louder was the pitiful mewling sound it made. This didn't seem to be the growl of a cat on the prowl. The young animal seemed to be as frightened as Zeraya, hunger and instinct driving it on.

Remembering the loud cat cry she had screamed as she came into the canyon, Zeraya thought to try it again. After all, maybe it would scare the cub off. She was already in danger of becoming this desert cat's dinner as it was. It knew where she hid and was coming closer to her every second. Maybe, just maybe, the Goddess would smile down and help rescue her. Maybe, this sound would frighten away her predator. Too many maybes.

She knew several of the cat sounds. Which one was likely to be the right one? In her fright, Zeraya's terrified mind went blank. "Oh Mother," she prayed, "help me to remember." She closed her eyes and tried to calm her breath, gulping and swallowing, nearly choking with fright.

She saw her mother's face before her, beautiful black almond-shaped eyes with the crinkles at the edges. Her per-

*fect mouth smiling, now opening to show teeth, now hissing
and forming the sound. Zeraya remembered.*

*She took a few deep breaths and made the hissing noise,
then at the back of her throat the hiss grew into a growl and
she allowed the noise to build. Again, but this time louder,
she screamed at the small cat who was more than halfway
closer than the last time Zeraya had looked.*

*It stopped in the midst of a step. Its ears went back and it
answered her with a similar growl and hiss, fangs and claws
bared.*

*Zeraya stood and on an impulse howled and came running
at the young cat. It jumped straight up in the air, twisted and
landed facing in the opposite direction, running before its feet
hit the ground. She watched it scramble over the top, dust
and rocks flying everywhere.*

*Only after the cat was gone did Zeraya stop running. Then
she laughed. It had worked. She remembered herself and bent
to touch the ground, sending a silent prayer of thanks to the
Mother of All.*

*Now only one thing remained to do and that was get to the
wood, load up her net bag, and be off in the direction of
camp. She looked up to realize that the sun was lower on the
horizon than she wanted it to be. Getting back before dark
was going to be hard, if not impossible. Her cheeks reddened
at the thought of how embarrassing it would be to have a
search party come looking for her. She set her jaw and began
to scramble toward the bush.*

*Once there she was pleased to see that it was larger than
she had thought. Maybe it would provide a fire for more than
one day. How pleased she was with herself as she loaded the
net. Not so pleased was she when she tried to pick it up onto
her back. Several larger pieces had to be left on the ground
but a thought came to her as she lightened her load.*

If I take enough back tonight, perhaps tomorrow father will
give me one of the pack animals so I can ride back for the
rest. Yes, I will be able to come back and bring my weight
and more in wood.

*Her thoughts helped to make the difficult climb easier as
she came over the ridge at last, panting under the weight of
the load she carried on her back. Standing at the top, bent*

*over, she was startled to see a lone rider off in the distance.
It was one of the young hunters and he had seen her. He
turned in her direction, urging his horse into a careful trot
across the rocky ground.*

*From the build of his slender shoulders and the lance he
carried, Zeraya could tell who it was before he had turned.
It was Benyar. He was a few years older than her and had
only been a hunter for the last two years, but he always
seemed to be around. At first it made her angry, him always
popping up when she was alone, watching, looking at her.
But lately, something about the way he looked at her made
her feel warm inside in a funny way. She felt a hot flush come
to her cheeks as she watched him ride to her, knowing he
would offer to carry her wood on his horse.*

*Suddenly she was furious. What right did he have to share
in her discovery of the wood? No one would believe that she
had found it herself, not if Benyar came riding into camp
with her wood piled on his horse. He would likely get all the
praise. Besides, she wasn't supposed to be here at all. Now
she might really get into trouble. She dumped the bundle
down and sat in front of it to prevent it from rolling down
the hill and tumbling out all over; it wasn't tightly enough
bound to stay together in this terrain.*

*As the horse and rider came closer she heard the faint sound
of rocks clattering behind her that instinctively made her pull
herself into a small ball. Very slowly she turned around, trying
to keep her body below the bundle of wood and out of sight. Another sound, the low moan of a cat at the hunt reached her
ears. That told her it would be over the ridge soon and she
pulled her knife from its sheath. The weight of it felt unusual,
but it balanced nicely and she gripped the hilt tightly with a
small amount of confidence. She knew how to skin animals and
cut meat, but using a knife to kill something this size was another matter.*

*Without a sound the cat's head cautiously peered around
the side of a large boulder. Seeing her, the cat froze. Zeraya
pulled her head back behind the shelter of the wood bundle
and began to tremble. This was not the cub she had seen, but
another, probably one of the parents. By the size of its head
this one had no spots, of that she was certain. This animal*

*was much larger than any she had ever seen and she pre-
pared herself to die, for surely she would.*

*Sitting with her back, neck, and shoulders pushing against
the bundle of wood, Zeraya clutched the knife's handle with
both hands. Her breath was shallow and her vision beginning
to go black from panic. Far in the distance the figure on
horseback seemed to be galloping toward her in slow motion.*

*Hours seemed to pass until finally the cat leaped into the
air over the wood and Zeraya. As its front paws came into
view over her head, Zeraya screamed and plunged the knife
into its chest, avoiding the front feet and the two-inch claws.
The knife went deep and she was dragged up from her sitting
position by the weight of the animal as it fell forward. Remembering to let go of the knife, Zeraya lunged to the side,
only to find that her legs were pinned beneath the animal's
torso. As the cat died, a trail of blue poison ebbed from the
extended front claws onto the rocks, mixing with the stream
of red blood. Zeraya could only lay there and stare as the
two vivid colors ran slowly down the rocky slope. She was
stuck and had no strength to pull herself out from beneath
the weight of the huge body that trapped her.*

*A familiar mewling sound could be heard accompanied by
the soft tread of paws that clinked small stones together as
two large sets of paws walked very near her face. She lay
breathing rapidly as two cats, young ones this time, came to
sniff at their dead parent. Another scream threatened to tear
itself from her throat as a third cat, the dead one's mate,
suddenly appeared, a low rumbling growl issuing from its
throat. Zeraya's vision went blank as she lost consciousness.*

*More stones clattered as the horse and rider raced uphill
toward the girl. A spear flew through the air and the second
large cat went down, dead as it hit the ground. The two
smaller cats scattered over the top of the ridge and from the
sounds they made, they wouldn't be back.*

*The horse stopped as its rider jumped from its back. The
young warrior ran to the very still form of the girl and began
to roll the beast off her legs. Jostled awake in this manner,
Zeraya managed to turn around and wrap her arms tightly
around his neck. Just as quickly, she unwrapped her arms,*

*gripped his shoulders instead, and pushed him an arm's
length away.*

What could she have been thinking? This was not permitted, touching him in this manner. She had talked of Benyar
many times with the other girls when they spoke of the future
and husbands. He was a man now, a hunter. He had killed
and proudly wore the skins to prove it. Her body shaking,
she pulled her hands away and stood apart from him, turning
her face away.

"Zeraya, I hear your thoughts and know why you tremble.
Look at me."

When she would not, he demanded in a louder voice,
"Look at me! You have become a hunter today. The cat, this
first one," *he pointed at the animal nearest her,* "has your
dagger in its heart. You will be a great hunter. No longer are
you a child, but a woman and such a woman as I would want
hunting by my side with me." *These last words he spoke
much softer, adding,* "If that woman would have me."

*Her trembling subsided as with an intake of breath she
turned to look at him. The sun was nearly setting below the
rim of the canyon behind her, and it cast a golden light upon
his dark face. Never had she seen him in such light and so
closely. Not since his initiation into manhood had they made
eye contact. It was not permitted between men and girls nor
women and boys who were not related by blood or marriage.
Small droplets of sweat shone on his brow and in his left
earlobe glinted a gold earring. His arms and shoulders were
slender, like his hips, but the promise of the man he would
become was apparent.*

*In answer she removed a leather necklace from which hung
a small piece of carved bone. She held it out and he bent
from the waist so she could put it over his head. When he
stood, he solemnly looked at the carving. It was a cat. He
gave her a small smile and touched the carving to his heart,
then his forehead, and lastly to his lips. She gave a shy smile
back and felt her cheeks flush with heat, but did not speak.*

*Together they shouldered the two sandcats and tied them
securely onto the back of the horse. They lashed the bundle
of wood onto its back also.*

Together they began the long walk home, on either side of

the horse, each leading it with one of the reins. From time to time he would reach up and touch the amulet that now hung from his neck. Every time he did, Zeraya would hold her head up just a little higher.

As they approached the camp, the evening fires blinking to them, she turned to look at him again, this time more boldly than before. Her status was changed from this moment on within the tribe. Forever after she would be looked upon as a woman, not a child. And as a hunter.

A crowd of people came running toward them; among them Zeraya recognized her parents and Benyar's. Soon a cry went up and they were swept away in a frenzy of embraces from their parents and wild cries from the other adults that came to welcome them both home. In the center of the camp, the noise finally subsided and in the quiet, both young people came under the eyes of all the assembled adults. More fires were lit and people began to take their places around Zeraya and Benyar, who stood side by side in silence.

Her mother embraced her once more, then her father. Both had examined her from head to toe when they saw the two cats across the back of the horse, but neither of them had questioned her. From the way she held herself erect and stood close to Benyar, they knew what had happened.

Several hands took the horse from them and began to untie the bundle of wood and the bodies of the two desert cats. These they lay down before the two young people who remained standing, waiting. The air was thick with anticipation. Someone should have spoken by now and offered them the welcome cup. In the quiet that followed, the scent of incense began to float upon the air and the solemn figures of the High Priestess and several of her attendants could be seen approaching.

She stopped at the edge of the gathering so the people could part to allow her to pass and she walked toward Zeraya and Benyar. When she stood before them, the two young people acknowledged her by bowing to her and kneeling. She touched them on their heads together and then bade them rise.

Very solemnly they looked at the Priestess and heard her announce, "This is the prophecy fulfilled. Here before me stand the pair that we have long awaited. No longer will the Feralmon of the Desert be nomads, but builders of great stone citadels. It is the hour of change and these two are the bringers of it.''

''Young woman, were both or either of these two killings made by you?''

Zeraya gave her answer in the loud, high-pitched voice of the girl that she still was. ''I pierced the heart of the animal that lies before me.''

''And who,'' *questioned the Priestess,* ''gave the other animal over to death?''

Benyar raised his spear, remaining silent.

''And who brings us the wood?''

Again Zeraya answered, ''I bring wood for our fires. I have also found more.''

As she spoke the words Zeraya remembered the prophecy that had filled her dreams ever since she could understand the words. The story of two young hunters who together brought their kills to the people with a bundle of firewood. Fire and food and skins to clothe. What every woman and man pledged to the people of the tribe in their initiation rites. Benyar knew this as well.

For the first time Benyar asked to speak by raising his spear and bowing to the Priestess. She acknowledged him with a nod of her head and he said, ''I ask permission to announce to my family that I have chosen this woman, young though she may be, to be my wife, when the time comes. She has accepted me by her gift. She has also honored our custom and spoken not a word to me alone.''

Murmurs could be heard going around the camp, and the Priestess clapped her hands for silence.

''Young woman, is this true? Have you gifted Benyar and held to custom?''

''Yes, I have accepted him with the token he wears around his neck, a cat carved from a piece of bone, made by my own hands.''

''Then it is done. We shall speak more of this later. For now I would speak alone to Zeraya. She will tell me where it is that our city will be built. When you see her again, she will truly be a woman. Come with me.''

The Priestess turned and Zeraya followed, eyes cast down at the ground. She was a woman in the eyes of her family, but not yet in the eyes of the rest of the tribe. For however long it took, she must study the sacred writings and become skillful with weapons. She was the chosen of the prophecy and all knew it was true. They bowed their heads in respect to her as she passed.

There was nothing she could say to anyone now until her time came upon her, but she was suddenly aware of how proud she was. Yes, she had brought firewood back to her people, as well as her first kill and her potential husband. Not only that, but everyone bowed their heads to her in great respect. The moment grabbed her and she began to feel tears coursing down her cheeks that suddenly burned hot. Behind her, she knew Benyar would remain, waiting patiently until she could come to him.

The story finished, Benyar removed his hand from his son's shoulder. "That is how your parents met and pledged themselves to each other. This is who we remain today: fulfillers of prophecy. And you, my son, will fulfill your destiny one day. But let us sleep now. Tomorrow we will need to be rested and sharp if we are to track and outwit the sandcat or lizard. Both are worthy opponents." Before sleeping, Benyar placed careful hex signs around them and the horses as an extra precaution.

The next morning they woke early and breakfasted together quietly as the sun sent rays of yellow and pink light across the desert. The morning air was cool but promised to change quickly as the sun began its climb and the early light turned brighter. They struck camp and began looking for signs of potential prey in the rocky terrain.

Hunting for the better part of the morning, they came upon the tracks of three horses. Benyar immediately sensed something was wrong. He and Ranth quickly dismounted as he checked the tracks, showing Ranth how to recognize whether they were left by friend or foe. Determining that the animals were not Feralmon by the shape of their horseshoes, Benyar suggested they remount. But as he was putting his foot into the stirrup, Benyar's horse shied, stamping his hooves and snorting nervously. Just as he got his leg over, the unmistakable sound of an arrow flying through the air could be heard.

"Ride," screamed Benyar. He and Ranth didn't need to urge their horses into a run, his scream had done that. It was seconds too late, however, for an arrow found its target and plunged into Benyar's right thigh.

Marking where the man was shooting from and before Benyar could stop him, Ranth turned his horse and rode down on him. Another arrow flew before he reached the attacker. It struck his shoulder but failed to penetrate his mail-enhanced, leather tunic. Ranth was nearly knocked from the saddle by the pain of the impact, the breath gone from him for the moment. Fighting to regain his breath as well as his balance, Ranth rode down on the man, who was desperately running for his horse.

Leaping from his horse onto the back of his attacker, they fell and tumbled together down a rocky hill. Shaken and bruised, they rolled apart, drawing their swords. The attacker, however, was no match for Ranth. With several sword thrusts, Ranth managed to disarm the man. Seeing his companions slinking to their horses, the assassin ran at Ranth's sword, choosing to end his life rather than be captured.

The other two men, having reached their mounts, scrambled away as Benyar, wounded though he was, loosed several arrows at them. One reached its target and the man slumped over, falling from his saddle, his horse chasing wildly after the third horse and rider, panicked by the smell of blood and the sounds of fighting.

Disgusted by the unnecessary death, Ranth pulled his sword from the dead man with such a scream of rage that it spooked his horse, which took off in the direction of Benyar and his stablemate. His adrenaline pumping, Ranth chased after it, calling out to Benyar, "Father, are you hurt badly?" When no reply came, he began to panic, putting speed to his steps.

Minutes later as Ranth scrambled uphill, he found Benyar leaning against a boulder, panting, very much alive, blood pouring from the wound in his leg.

"Ranth, I'm afraid your hunt must be postponed for a while longer. If this arrow was poisoned, we won't know for at least an hour." He swallowed hard, taking several more deep breaths. Sweat beaded on his brow and the hand that gripped his bow trembled. "Do you think you can remove it?" he asked through gritted teeth.

"Yes, I can. But first, let me look at the wound from the inside to see which will do more damage, pulling it out, or pushing it through." Kneeling next to his father, Ranth gently placed one hand on Benyar's leg, and then wrapped the fingers of his other hand around the protruding arrow. He closed his eyes, sending his awareness into the shaft, following it past the layer of skin into the muscle tissue of Benyar's thigh. As soon as his awareness went beneath the level of the skin, a searing pain shot through his own thigh, but Ranth did not lose his concentration. His breath caught in his throat. He saw how close the arrowhead came to the bone and was relieved that it hadn't appeared to have severed any major veins. The tip, unfortunately, was barbed. It would have to be pushed through the other side of his father's leg.

Benyar was immediately aware that Ranth could feel the wound as well as see it, because the level of his pain dropped as soon as Ranth touched his leg. It seemed to clear his head for several seconds, and he found himself intrigued to know that his son had this talent. He wanted to ask him where he had learned it, but before he could form the question, Ranth withdrew his touch and the pain brightened suddenly. For now, Benyar knew he would have to endure more.

"Do it quickly, what must be done," he told Ranth through white lips. The younger man nodded.

Ranth hurried to his father's horse, unfastened the bedroll, and unfurled it on the ground next to him. "Father, lie upon this." He offered Benyar his hand as he pulled him up onto his good leg. Getting up was far easier than getting down. Benyar held his breath as Ranth eased him onto his back. Gasping from the pain, Benyar lay trying to regain composure as Ranth cut open the leg of his breeches, exposing the wound.

Ranth licked his lips and rather than waste time thinking about what he was about to do, he unsheathed his sword and slammed the flat of it down on the arrow as hard as he could. The tip protruded through the other side of Benyar's thigh, but not far enough for him to get a good grip. Blood gushed.

He must do it again and he did. This time the arrow tip came out fully, and while Benyar managed to stifle another scream, Ranth broke away the feathered end of the shaft, grabbed the tip, and pulled the rest of the arrow through.

Benyar fell back, completely soaked with sweat. He managed an exhausted gesture of thanks, and then closed his eyes. Ranth went for his water pouch and spied the wineskin Septia had given both of them. He made Benyar take a long pull of the wine, then covered him with another blanket. Benyar was going into shock and beginning to shake violently. Quickly Ranth sat cross-legged next to his father and laid his hands on him.

Making contact, he spoke directly to Benyar's mind. *Breathe with me and I will take away some of your pain. I must tend to the wound now, before you become fevered. Work with me. Use your talents and your Lifestone, father.*

Soon, his father breathed evenly and deeply and his shaking had subsided. The Lifestone in the pouch around Benyar's neck glowed brightly through the leather. Ranth entered the area of the wound with a very delicate touch of mind probe. He worked quickly, reconnecting the tissues and the veins. The bleeding stopped as the wound closed and Benyar, exhausted by his ordeal, slept.

Pulling his awareness back into himself, Ranth realized he was spent, but he felt altered somehow, not merely tired. He felt as though he had just had several goblets of wine. His head was spinning. *It must be the effects of Septia's wine that I had father drink,* Ranth said to himself. He shook his head to clear it. Then he heard a strange noise. It came to him finally, *The horses are warning me of something or someone approaching!*

Ranth leapt to his feet, sword in hand. Several paces away lay his bow and quiver. He ran to them and nocked an arrow. A motion in the corner of his eye made him turn and loose it. The beast was struck in the eye as it charged, a hideous scream renting the air as it clawed at the arrow. From its open jaws spurted a spray of milky white liquid, falling short, thankfully, of Ranth, Benyar, and the horses. Everything it fell on hissed and sizzled for several seconds.

The dying lizard's outcry woke Benyar, who had reached

reflexively for his weapon. When he saw the arrow strike its mark, he lay back down, allowing himself the luxury of rest. "I thought you needed help, foolish old man that I am," was all he said, managing only a tired smile.

"Rest for a while longer, father. I will see to getting the lizard trussed up so we can return home and get you into a proper bed." Looking puzzled, he stood over the animal asking, "Do I remove the head?" Benyar laughed.

Late that evening Ranth and his wounded father returned to the city bringing with them the bodies of their attackers and the lizard. When the unknown men's bodies were examined, it was discovered that although they were dressed in desert fashion, their bodies were unmarked save for tattoos on both of their arms. The pattern, which was in the shape of a large fish, marked them to be from Tonnerling. Benyar and Ketherey were unable to determine if it was the mark of the same family that had blood feud with their ancestors, but it was enough. Benyar and his son had been attacked by assassins and very nearly killed. Thus the war began.

TWENTY-FIVE

HONIA SUL URLA THE HIGH PRIESTESS WAS AGAIN being called to scry. Lately she had felt an urge to do so daily, not merely at the festivals or full moon as was the custom. No, something kept pulling her to this, her most sacred task. Honia had dedicated her life to her people. She had never married, yet she felt more fulfilled now than she could have ever hoped to be. Her successor, Septia sul Prakur, after all would someday become ruler of the Feralmon, and High Priestess as well. There was no precedent for this, but Septia was a woman of many talents and great depth. Honia had no doubts she would succeed at both.

As Honia approached the elaborately carved wooden altar, her eyes seemed to lovingly caress the embroidered silk cloth that covered the wall behind the altar. The cloth depicted scenes of ceremonies in the Temple as well as scenes of the Feralmon hunting, dancing, and finding water, the most precious substance of all to these desert people.

Atop the altar waited the opaque oval of the deep blue glass bowl, four times as wide as it was deep. Standing before the altar, Honia began the prayer of invocation. She took hold of the pitcher of water, made of the same deep blue glass, and poured it into the bowl, completing her prayer. When the goddess was called forth, the person performing the calling ritual would look into the bowl, and each one was shown a different face.

Because Honia had no direct question to ask, she opened her mind to the oracle and watched as the water in the bowl calmed and at last stopped swirling. As it stilled she was shown scenes from the past, scenes that told how the Temple came to be found and built upon this site.

There in the water she saw the young Zeraya and Benyar walking together, exploring. Honia saw their excitement as they found the valley, and the cave at the far side that contained the spring that was to become the source of their water. She was shown how Zeraya and Benyar drank from the spring, saw it bubble up, and observed how the trickle became a flow that soon became a lake.

This very Temple had been carved from the cave. Stone-carvers working diligently every day transformed it into the many-chambered Temple in which Honia now stood. One day, early on, a worker had discovered a small chamber off to the side of the main hall, deep within the recesses of the Temple. It contained a cache of Lifestones that no one had suspected was there.

Soon Benyar and Zeraya were called, and each of them was claimed by a stone. The chamber of the Lifestones was left intact. Nothing was done to enhance the walls; the stones were not touched. They had a power that would not allow anyone into the chamber. Not since Zeraya and Benyar had been called had the Lifestones chosen a person to bond with.

Honia watched in fascination, transfixed on what the bowl had to show her. She could now see within the chamber of Lifestones. One stone flashed brightly, sending a call to someone whose name she could not quite hear. Straining mightily to hear whose name was being called, she saw Ranth's face and at last knew that it was his name the Lifestone was calling out.

Then the picture slowly faded and Honia was left alone with the knowledge that Ranth was following in his parents' wake. She knew it was just a matter of time now and Ranth would heed his call. Smiling to herself, Honia thanked fortune that Septia had married one such as Ranth. Surely the goddess had smiled upon her charge and she began saying prayers of thanks. Now was the time to wait, until Ranth showed up at the Temple doors to be united with his Lifestone.

*   *   *

Several nights ago the dreams had begun. Ranth would hear his name being called but would be unable to answer whoever was summoning him because in the dream he was mute. Each time he attempted to answer, no sound came from his mouth. For three nights the dream was the same.

On the fourth night he saw himself in a large room, dimly lit by fluttering, smoking torches. A breeze blew so hard that he was unable to make progress as he attempted to cross the floor. Each step forward became more and more difficult until he could no longer move. The voice called to him softly, urgently, but he was unable to get any closer to the door.

The next night not only was he mute, but he saw himself in his own rooms, the doors open, torches guttering wildly in the wind—and no one, not even the guards, was present. He lay upon his bed bound hand and foot, unable to move or call out as the voice continued to call his name, more urgently than before. Ranth began to long for whoever it was that called. When he awoke at dawn he was weeping.

Ranth could not understand why his dreams had suddenly become so vivid and disturbing. Why would he dream that a person called his name night after night? Never did he suspect that he was truly being summoned. So little was known about how a person was called by a Lifestone that no one had thought to explain it to him. Twenty years and more had passed since Benyar had been called, so he gave no thought to the fact that Ranth might be similarly touched. Once again Ranth was unprepared for what was about to happen.

Because of the potions his wife continued to slip into his wine each night, Ranth was unable to awaken. If he had, he would have known the voice calling his name was very real and not merely a dream. But the drugs prevented him from waking or hearing the call during the daylight hours. His senses had become so dulled by Septia's potions that he was only able to hear the call in his sleep.

It was beginning to take its toll on Ranth. He dreaded the thought of lying down to sleep, but because of what Septia administered to him nightly, he was back in his dream as soon as he put his head on the pillow. This was the sixth night and as before, he saw himself in a room that looked similar to his own, but was not. The light was wrong and the shapes of the furniture, doorways, and windows were off at unusual angles. He was again lying on his bed, though this time he wasn't bound with ropes but with plants that were growing, continuing to wind around his arms and legs, blooming as he watched.

The familiar voice from his dream began to speak to him this time, not just call out his name as before. It told him that he must not drink the cup that Septia set before him each evening. Ranth remained mute, as in all the other dreams, able only to nod his head yes. Once he had agreed, he watched as the bright red and golden poppies began to wither and dry. Only then was he able to wriggle out of the stems that had twined themselves about his wrists and ankles, flinging them to the floor. Free of his bindings, he lay back down upon his bed and slept, feeling a protective presence watching over him, confident he had made the correct decision.

The following evening, when Septia offered Ranth his cup, he felt slightly guilty but refused it, remembering the agreement he had made to the voice of his dream. Septia looked startled and encouraged him to drink it, saying it would help him sleep, but he again refused, kissed his wife goodnight, and left her suite.

Alone in his bed Ranth felt only anticipation as he fell asleep, not a bit unsettled as he had been for over a week, dreading a nightmare. Soon he fell into the same dream. He again saw himself in his room and could hear someone softly yet insistently calling out his name. This time, however, he was not bound. When he opened his mouth to ask a question, he was no longer mute.

"Who is it that calls me and from where?" he heard himself ask aloud.

His only answer was the voice that grew louder and more persistent than ever before. Sure of himself now, Ranth knew that it was coming from the Temple. He rose from his bed, not even bothering to dress. Wearing only a loincloth, Ranth went by the most direct route, over the wall of his private courtyard, alone in the middle of the night to answer the call. He found the High Priestess, Honia sul Urla, waiting for him and her mood was not pleasant.

"What has taken you so long to heed the voice of one who

calls?'' her voice thundered at him, sending echoes off into the chambers of the Temple.

He bowed deeply from the waist and said, ''Until tonight I thought the voice was merely a dream.'' What he did not say to Honia troubled him greatly. He suspected Septia was behind this in some way and he meant to know how.

''Come,'' she said scornfully to him. Honia turned on her heel, swirling her cloak around her as she entered the Temple.

He followed, feeling like a servant. He was trembling and felt queasy, but thought it was because he was so angry at Septia, never thinking he could be suffering withdrawal from a drug.

When the High Priestess turned to look at him she immediately knew something was wrong. She stopped and beckoned him closer. She felt his head and it was cold and clammy. As her awareness played along at the edges of his strong mental barriers, he reluctantly opened his mind to her in increments. Her touch was gentle and he was aware that she was not looking for images from his memory, but signs of illness. As the voice called to him again, Ranth gasped and opened himself to her in a tremendous rush of emotion. Honia not only heard it this time but also clearly felt the deep longing it produced in Ranth. She very gently withdrew her touch.

His teeth had begun chattering in the last few minutes. She clapped her hands loudly and a young priestess stepped from behind a column.

''Bring a cloak for him, and a chair. Hurry.'' The young woman bowed, turned and ran to do as she had been told. In an instant she returned with a long cloak and a folding stool. She opened the stool and Ranth sat down on it so hard his jaw clacked together. She put the cloak around him and his shaking grew for several seconds, then slowly subsided.

''Ranth, I beg forgiveness for such harsh words to you as you entered the sanctuary this evening. I was unaware of your condition. Tell me, how long have you been drinking the juice of the desert poppy?''

He looked at her completely puzzled. ''What? I do not take the juice of the poppy. Septia has gotten me used to a cup of wine each evening. She says it relaxes me after a hard day.''

''Relaxes you, does it? Well, we shall see about that another time. For now you are in no condition to meet with your Lifestone. I'm frightened to think of what might happen to you in such a weakened state.''

Though he heard Honia say the words, Ranth did not believe he had heard her correctly. He asked, "Did you mention something about a Lifestone?''

Before Honia could answer him there was a commotion behind her. Several priestesses were walking toward her as fast as they could without running, trying to maintain some sense of propriety.

"Honorable Mistress, you must come to see this. Please hurry,'' one of them said out of breath.

Honia turned from Ranth and was gone without another word. When she reached the chamber wherein lay the Lifestones, several other young women who were crowded around the entrance moved to make way for her. Peering inside, Honia could see a light pulsing from one of the crystals with such brightness that it seemed to be shaking the floor of the chamber. Already several crystals had fallen over and were bouncing on the dirt floor with each pulse of light.

All but forgotten, Ranth waited for Honia to return. Confused and tired, he felt a great anger welling up inside him. *Why would Septia give me a drug?* he asked himself, holding his head in his hands. Then he began to hear the voice calling out to him again, the same voice he had heard nightly in his dreams and his head snapped up. Ears straining to hear, Ranth could feel a new vitality seeping into him. Each time the voice called his name, the desire to unite with whomever was calling began to grow stronger. Finally he was unable to wait and he followed the route Honia had taken down the corridor.

When he arrived at the entrance to the Cave of the Lifestones his skin began to feel hot. He let the cloak drop to the ground as he passed Honia and the other priestesses and stepped through the doorway. Once he crossed the threshold, the voice became almost frantic with elation. Ranth spied a large stone that was bright topaz with striations of gold crisscrossing through it, and he bent down to pick it up.

Concerned only for his safety, Honia reached to stop him, and was rewarded with an arc of light that touched the back of her hand, similar to a slap. Shocked into submission she could only watch as Ranth picked up his Lifestone. It had claimed him. Together he and the stone were enveloped in a blinding flash of white light that just as quickly dissipated, a sign that he had been fully accepted.

Clutching the Lifestone in both of his hands, Ranth turned to leave the room, oblivious to those who had observed what had taken place. Honia and the priestesses bowed low to him. He returned the bow, though not as low, then walked out the door to return to his rooms in the palace. He held the stone, which was glowing brightly, and seemed to be having a conversation with it.

"Never have I seen anything take place like that. Surely they are a matched pair," whispered the High Priestess to the other women. When she looked at the back of her hand there was a small burn mark in the shape of the rune for Ranth: Changeling in Old Tongue.

"Now, go and bring Septia to me," she ordered the women who surrounded her. Her mood had darkened, and the look on her face was unpleasant. Two women bowed and left silently to do her bidding.

Minutes later Septia arrived. Knowing that she must protect herself against Honia in such a way that her use of the secret protection spell would go unnoticed, Septia began to weep.

"Honia, tell me what is wrong that you would summon me in the middle of the night? Has something befallen you or one of my family?"

Honia's face remained a mask as she reached for Septia. Without her permission she touched Septia's shoulder and began to question her mind-to-mind. Under questioning, Septia maintained that she was innocent and she denied that anything had been administered to Ranth. Honia tested her and came up with nothing that could incriminate her.

Hours later, exhausted nearly to the point of breaking down, Septia returned to the palace. She rid her chambers of any evidence of the poppy flower tincture that she had been administering to her husband, thankful that Honia had not pressed her further, grateful that Honia had not asked any questions about Zeraya and the herbs she administered to her.

But her mood was foul. Ranth now had a Lifestone and she had yet to be called. Yes, she could hear vague whisperings, but Ranth had been chosen, not her and not Korab. Suddenly, she became afraid. There would be no way to keep the news of Ranth and his Lifestone from Korab. Septia shivered for a long time before she fell asleep.

TWENTY-SIX

SEVERAL MONTHS HAD PASSED SINCE RANTH AND his father had returned from the initiation hunt. Benyar's wound was nearly healed and he hardly walked with a limp. Ranth was becoming more accustomed each day to his Lifestone. In fact, he had taken over the task of healing his father's wound and administering daily to Zeraya. His mother, too, seemed to be thriving under his care.

The only person who seemed to be difficult and withdrawn was Septia. She spent most of her time alone or with her serving women, using as her excuse fatigue due to the fact that she would soon be giving birth. Part truth and part lie, Septia had been avoiding Ranth ever since he had gotten his Lifestone and she had undergone Honia's terrible interrogation. It had sapped her strength more than she wanted to admit. Fearful now that she knew Ranth suspected her of drugging him, she avoided being alone with him as much as possible, constantly surrounding herself with a group of chattering women.

Ranth seemed not to notice, so busy was he with his parents and learning the art of war. The dead assassins he and Benyar had brought back with them from the desert were discovered to be from Tonnerling, and the border raids had escalated into full war. Learning that a band of traders with goods from Tonnerling had visited Kalaven the day they left on Ranth's hunt, it was obvious that the assassins had traveled with the caravan. It would be a long time before any merchandise from the People of the Water Caves, as Tonnerlingans were called, would again be welcome in Kalaven.

Septia had gone to the marketplace on the day the caravan arrived and purchased several songbirds from one of the traders. One of them was a small black bird in a large cage, and its song was a most mournful, sad little trill. The first time the bird saw Ranth, it began to sing. From that day on, every time he entered the room the small bird became very animated and seemed to be vying for his attention. At first Septia paid it no mind, but she soon noticed how the bird reacted to him, and so she gave it to him as a gift.

The bird and its elaborate cage were moved into his suite. Each night when he entered the room, it welcomed him with its song. Ranth was soon captivated by the sad trilling. One day when he reached into the cage to see if the bird would hop onto his finger, it did and he was touched by the awareness of a person he hadn't felt for the better part of a year.

The unmistakable trace of Bimily the Shapechanger was transferred to his mind instantly. He could see her face and hear her sighing, but the touch was so exquisitely light he was sure it was merely a memory. He thought it strange to even think of Bimily after all this time and when he put the bird back, the memory faded, leaving him feeling very unsettled.

Bimily had been a close friend of Shunlar's, after all, and he had still never gotten a reply from Shunlar in all the months since they parted. The bird watched Ranth when he left the room and stopped singing as soon as he was gone from sight.

Later that day when Ranth returned to his quarters, he was surprised when he wasn't greeted by the song he had gotten accustomed to in so short a time. When Ranth approached the cage, to his complete amazement, the bird was a different color. It was no longer black, but red and it was larger. For a minute he thought Septia or another might be playing a trick on him but he hesitated before calling a servant.

Instead, Ranth reached his hand into the cage and after several seconds of hesitation, the bird perched on his hand. He was flooded with images of Bimily. Again, there was the distinct feeling of Bimily's awareness touching him so very softly. He decided this time that it was not a memory and that he must tell only Benyar and no one else. Quickly covering the cage, Ranth left the room in search of his father.

Though Bimily had sworn him to secrecy, Ranth now told Benyar about her ability to shapeshift. He told his father how the bird in the cage had changed from a small black one to a red bird twice the size, and how both times it touched his hand, the sight of Bimily had flooded his senses.

Together both men returned to Ranth's quarters. Ranth uncovered the cage and the bird was still red, and still larger than the original one. Approaching the cage slowly Benyar began to talk to it and cajoled it to perch on his hand. He, too, saw the image of Bimily as soon as the bird touched him. Softly Benyar called out Bimily's name and the bird instantly was surrounded by an odd blue light. Startled, it flew from his hand and began to circle the room. When it landed on top of its cage, more blue color shimmered around it.

They spent several frustrating minutes trying to get the bird to perch on their hands, but it refused to, flying away each time one of them got too close. Finally, Benyar reached out to Bimily mind-to-mind. The bird flew to him immediately, perched on his shoulder, and he spoke to her in Old Tongue. It took some time, but he finally managed to convince Bimily that she was not really a bird at all, but a woman. Bimily seemed to understand and tried to shapeshift to human form.

But it wasn't working. The red bird remained a red bird. The effort was draining her as each attempt failed. Realizing that her strength was waning, Benyar asked Ranth for his help. With the bird on the floor between them, Benyar and Ranth linked minds. Concentrating on the human shape of Bimily, they projected her image onto the bird standing between them. The air sparkled again with blue light and Bimily once again became a startlingly lovely copper-haired woman.

She lay on the floor, stunned. She could hardly speak, and was very thin. When she tried to walk, Bimily had a pronounced limp. Ranth helped Bimily to a chair and she asked for water. With her thirst quenched, she began to take in her surroundings. She recognized Ranth and Benyar. Then she remembered what had happened to her mate. Her eyes brimming with tears, Bimily told them the story of how he was killed by the fishermen and how she took an arrow in the leg. When she was wounded, her shape-changing abilities were altered and the small animal brain took over, making her forget she was human.

They decided it was best to hide Bimily and tell only Zeraya about her. Benyar left Ranth's quarters and gave the guards at the door explicit instructions that no one but himself or Zeraya be allowed to pass through the doors into Ranth's room. He hurriedly returned to his quarters. Zeraya's advice was to deliver Bimily in secret to Honia at the Temple that evening, for if they wanted no one else to find out that she existed, then she must be taken away from the servants'— and Septia's—everpresent eyes. Ranth's instincts warned him not to tell Septia about Bimily.

Late that evening, when darkness had fallen, Benyar returned to Ranth's suite. Bimily was lying on the bed wrapped in a blanket. Ranth sat beside her and they were engaged in quiet conversation. Bimily looked confused, and Benyar could tell she was overcome with exhaustion.

"Lady Bimily, it is time to go. Whatever you and my son have to discuss must wait until you have recovered your strength." Benyar gave Ranth a nod and they both helped Bimily stand. She swooned for a moment, then seemed to recover her balance.

"Thank you, Benyar," she said with a tired smile. Benyar bowed a small bow to her.

He covered himself and Bimily with a strong illusion and then put the guards at the door into a deep sleep. When all was quiet, Ranth opened the door and what appeared to be two servants could be seen leaving Ranth's room. Benyar then delivered Bimily to Honia. Under strict orders from Zeraya and Benyar, Honia hid her and secretly administered to her daily, allowing no one else to know she was there under her protection.

No sooner had Benyar delivered Bimily safely into Honia's hands than Septia went into labor. It was the middle of winter and the child, a girl, was born within twelve hours. Septia was overjoyed when she learned it was a girl and she named her immediately, choosing the name Iola. Ranth seemed content enough but he soon left his wife's bedside. Overcome

with a strange sadness, Septia called for him to return. When
he would not, she sent word to Korab.

Bimily's recovery was slow, but eventually, she remembered all that had happened to her. One afternoon she told
Zeraya, Benyar, and Ranth her strange tale of traveling to
Kalaven with a band of people from Tonnerling and several
men of the Feralmon. She could not say who they were, nor
was she sure of what was said because they spoke the tongue
of the Cave People, but one thing did stand out in her mind.
She was certain someone spoke the word *korab* many times.

"Please my whims, but what is a korab?" she asked in-
nocently in Old Tongue.

"Not what, but who? Korab is not a thing, mistress Bimily.
He is my nephew," answered Benyar with the blackest of
looks.

Zeraya's eyes as well were terrible to see. She asked with
a worried voice, "Bimily, do you remember anything about
any of the times the name was spoken?" Ranth and Benyar
waited for her answer, their lips tight.

"There is one particular night that I recall when the name
was mentioned several times, and with a lot of anger. Unfortunately I could not see any of the men who argued, I am
sorry to say. I wish there were more to tell."

"What you have told us is already enough to cause Korab
to be banished. Do any other words come to mind?"

"Not that I can say. Because I don't speak the language, I
cannot be sure what I heard. Also, I was cargo and was not
considered to be the most valuable commodity. Most of the
time the cage I was in was covered so sounds were muffled.
If you would like, I could show you with a mind-touch so
that you may hear the conversation as I did."

"Yes, I believe we would all like that opportunity," answered Benyar. The others nodded.

Everyone was quiet for a moment as Bimily sent her memories of that particular night directly to them. When she was
finished, Benyar quietly announced, "Korab must be questioned tonight, for I fear I won't be able to hide my anger if
I wait any longer." His voice was nearly a whisper.

Bimily nodded her head. "Then tonight it must be. I will
help you in any way I can, Benyar. You and Ranth rescued

me and I am deeply indebted to you and your son. Had fortune not smiled upon me, I might very well be dead now. The body I had spent so many months in was nearing the end of its small life. My strength is nearly back to normal, thanks to the care Honia has given me. I will be present if you need me to be," she answered quietly.

"That will not be necessary. Ranth and I will handle this. Thank you again, Lady Bimily." Benyar bowed to her and she returned the gesture. Then he motioned for Ranth to join him and the two men left the room, a feeling of doom in their wake.

The men of Benyar's clan were summoned to a special audience that evening in their pavilion. Benyar and Ranth had arrived first and they were seated together, waiting as each man entered and took his place in the circle.

As if aware that something was about to happen, Korab chose to sit far on the other side of the circle, with his oath-brothers clustered around him. Though their faces were all set in careful, innocent masks, exactly like Korab's, their eyes shifted nervously as they waited for the rest of the men to assemble.

When the last man entered, Benyar signaled to the guards to close the doors. An uncomfortable murmur traveled around the room, quieting at once when Benyar raised his hand. With the fire lit and the torches extinguished, Benyar drank from the wineskin and passed it on to Ketherey who sat next to him. Then he began to clap a slow rhythm and was soon joined by Ketherey and others, all in accordance with their rank.

Once the wineskin had passed around the circle, Benyar and Ketherey stood, shed their robes and began the ritual sparring. Evenly matched, the brothers skillfully avoided physical contact with each pass. Others joined them, pairing off by size and skill. Ranth had by now become accustomed to the ritual and when he stood to join the "dance" with a much younger man, he did so warily. Though Ranth was older, the adolescent was quite skilled. Ranth came away with several new marks, grateful that he was able to inflict his mark at least once on his partner.

As the ritual wound down to its natural end, Benyar stood again, only this time he stood before Korab. Reluctantly the younger man accepted his uncle's invitation and soon they were the only pair in the middle. A strange quiet had settled over the men. Tentatively, slowly, Ketherey began to clap a rhythm and was joined by others as his son and brother circled one another before him.

As Benyar struck at Korab with a sideways kick, he simultaneously projected a strong mind probe at his nephew. Korab felt it and responded by sending one of his own that nearly matched it in strength. When Benyar felt the potency of Korab's retaliation, he responded faster and harder, provoking Korab to react with more strength. It was the response Benyar had hoped for. Because he suspected his nephew of treachery, he tested him unmercifully. With each kick or sweep of his foot, Benyar also sent a jolt of mind-probe that Korab reacted to instantly.

Soon Korab retaliated without thinking, trying to pummel Benyar with not only his blows, but with his mind as well, all to no avail. As fast as it began, Benyar ended it. He had all the information he needed. Korab had learned far more than his rank within the society allowed. His danger had only been suspected and now, in this moment, he revealed talents a man of his age and station, by law, should not possess. Always too sure of himself, Korab had by his actions directly challenged Benyar's right to rule. It did not go unnoticed by the older men.

Benyar raised his hands, loudly calling a halt to their sparring. Korab, panting as he bowed to his uncle, returned to his place in the circle. As he sat down, he realized that Benyar had not taken his eyes from him and only then did he begin to feel uneasy.

"Korab sul Fanon, how is it you have knowledge of techniques one of your rank should not?" Benyar asked suddenly. All heads turned to Korab.

"I do not know what you mean, Benyar sul Jemapree," Korab answered louder than he wanted to. Strangely, his voice sounded fearful.

"Korab sul Fanon, have you or any of your oath-brothers

ever had dealings with men from Tonnerling that in any way would jeopardize our people?'' Benyar asked.

"I have not, Benyar sul Jemapree, but I cannot answer for my oath-brothers.'' His voice had regained its usual arrogant tone.

"My son, join me now and do as I do,'' Benyar ordered Ranth. Ranth obeyed and removed his Lifestone from the pouch around his neck as Benyar had done. "Stand on the other side of Korab,'' Benyar instructed. Holding his Lifestone in his hand, Benyar pointed it at Korab and Ranth followed his lead.

Korab was instantly covered in an aura of amber-colored light, unable to move or speak. Benyar reached out to the men of the circle with a mind-touch that directly conveyed the conversations Bimily had remembered of the Tonnerling and Feralmon men meeting. As when Benyar and Ranth had first heard the strangers speaking, only one word could be understood by the men: Korab.

Emotions flared brightly as the men of the clan bombarded Korab with feelings of disbelief, distrust and a deep sense of betrayal. He was doing his best to keep his mind closed behind tight barriers, but sweat dripped down his face and his brow was furrowed from the strain.

Ketherey alone dared ask, "My lord Benyar, what is the source of your information?'' with such profound sadness in his voice that Benyar nearly hesitated. Could he himself bear the pain and guilt he was sure his brother was feeling if Ranth was the one being accused as Korab now was? Slowly Benyar turned his attention fully on his nephew.

"Korab sul Fanon,'' Benyar's voice demanded. "I ask again, have you had any dealings with men from Tonnerling?''

Imprisoned as he was within the light of the Lifestones, Korab could only answer the truth. "Yes,'' was his answer in a voice void of emotion.

"Tell us when and what transpired,'' ordered Benyar, calmly this time.

"During the time that I was silenced, I left Kalaven to seek the men of Tonnerling. My object was revenge for the punishment that had been set upon me.'' Korab's voice had begun to quiver, yet he continued speaking. He told them how he intended to rule in Kalaven and that he had offered gold and women as an enticement to the Tonnerlingans. Then his voice faltered and Korab's face became red as he glared with hatred at Benyar, his lips pressed firmly together.

"And did you promise them anything else?" Benyar insisted, aware that Korab was losing the fight against the force of the Lifestones.

"Lifestones," finally squeezed from his lips. He panted from the strain but refused to speak further.

"Tell us why you would betray your people, your clan, your blood!" shouted Benyar.

A terrible silence followed. Though he tried to remain silent, Korab did not succeed. His body shook and his nose started to bleed. Suddenly he slumped forward and pounded the ground with his fists. Leaning wearily on his elbows, Korab raised his head to look at Ranth.

"This one was called by a Lifestone," Korab pointed at his cousin. "I studied the texts. I tried to make myself ready for months to be called, but instead, *this one* was called, not me. Ever since you returned my life has been handed over to you. Even the woman was given to you." Physically spent, Korab collapsed, falling onto his side.

Benyar lowered his Lifestone and motioned for Ranth to do the same. Now that Korab had confessed, he was released from the beam of light.

As realization settled upon them, one by one, the men of the circle stood and faced Korab. Finally he struggled to his feet, knowing that he must now face the judgment of the men of his clan. One by one, they removed their daggers from their belts and placed them on the ground, the points toward Korab. Down to the last man they asked for his death. Many of them had lost a relative or a friend to the war already. But Ketherey could not move. He stared at his son for the longest time, then ever so slowly turned his back on him.

When it was Ranth's turn, he was sure about one thing, Korab was responsible for the ambush on himself and his father. Ranth placed his dagger down, never taking his eyes from his cousin.

Benyar was last to place his dagger of judgment down. He

never hesitated, but placed the dagger down slowly and deliberately, the point facing Korab.

"His actions have betrayed us all. There is no greater evil than selling out your own people to the enemy. Take him from this place, guard him day and night. We will decide when to carry out the sentence." Benyar's voice was hard. The men obeyed without question. As one of them approached Korab from behind and bound his arms behind his back, two others took hold of an arm and led him from the pavilion.

Defiant to the last, Korab spat at Ranth as he passed him. With spittle running down his cheek, for an instant Ranth's memory was sparked and he saw his wife, Septia, in Korab's arms. He suddenly remembered seeing that scene many times, always thinking it was a nightmare. This time when he saw it, he believed his worst fear.

"Stop!" Ranth called out loudly. The men obeyed. Ranth approached Korab, grabbed him by his hair and roughly pulled his head back.

What of the child? Ranth demanded of his cousin, in full rapport with his mind.

Mine, was Korab's answer inside his mind. With a grin Korab laughed and pulled his head free. "Mine," he said aloud with a sneer. The men roughly dragged him from the pavilion.

Ranth took a few moments to compose himself and then left in search of Septia, ignoring Benyar's call. The two brothers were left alone as the last of the clan filed out. Benyar turned to Ketherey and put his arms around his brother as Ketherey began to sob.

When the time came to declare Korab's sentence, most of the inhabitants of Kalaven had gathered before the Temple. Zeraya and Benyar stood on either side of Honia sul Urla. The High Priestess looked down upon Korab, who knelt before them with Septia at his side. Both had their arms bound behind them.

"You will be taken from here and ridden far into the desert. There you will be released with no weapon, no water, and no food. You have done much to deserve even worse. Because of your station and the nature of your crimes, you will meet death slowly, with much suffering.

"Septia sul Prakur. Your name will be erased from the record of the Temple and you are stripped of your rank as consort to Ranth sul Zeraya. Your child is taken from you and will be raised by another."

"No, please," Septia suddenly begged. She had not uttered any words until now, but upon hearing that her child, Iola sul Septia, would not have her name, she broke down. "At least leave her my name. I know I will be cursed forever as an oath-breaker, but leave something of me behind, I beg you."

"It is done. She has another name," was Honia's grim answer. Septia bowed her head; sobbing, she leaned heavily against Korab.

"Korab sul Fanon. Your name will be erased from the record of the Temple and you are stripped of your rank and entitlements within the clan. Your folly has caused the death of many of our people. May you meet death slowly and painfully."

Korab said nothing as he and Septia were pronounced banished. For once he seemed subdued. He kept his eyes on the ground, even when he was led away. They were both to be taken on horseback three days' fast ride into the deep of the desert and left with nothing but the clothes on their backs.

To make it even more shameful, Korab's relatives, his mother among them as well as Septia's, came along. None spoke to them and they were given only water to drink while they rode.

When the time came for them to be left, Septia ran to Ranth, fell on her face before him in the sand, and grabbed hold of his leg. *My daughter. Tell her of me, I beg you,* her words echoed in his head.

The entire party remained silent, watching and waiting. While she touched Ranth, they knew she was communicating a very private message.

Why, Septia? We could have had a long, happy life together. I loved you! Why all the deception? Have you no words for me? She remained silent, only raising her face to meet Ranth's eyes.

Minutes passed until finally he bent over to disengage Septia's hands from his leg. She struggled out of his grasp, grabbed hold of the pouch containing his Lifestone with one hand and pulled his dagger from his belt, with the other, slashing out at him. Ranth reacted instantly, backhanding Septia, who fell with a thud into the sand. She shook her head, got up and ran to Korab's side. Together they turned and walked away into the desert, a small dagger their only weapon.

"It is done," announced Ketherey. No one tried to retrieve Ranth's dagger. For several minutes the party watched as two people began a long climb across a sand dune. Then they turned their horses and rode away slowly, none looking back.

TWENTY-SEVEN

SHORTLY AFTER RANLA'S DEATH, LOFF LEFT THE Valley in the company of several of his friends. Young people were never discouraged from leaving the Valley of Great Trees to explore the world. Most returned when they had their fill.

After many months of wandering, Loff found himself once again in Vensunor. He wasn't sure if it was a perverse way of being near Ranla, as the city was where she had lived her short life before joining him in the Valley of Great Trees. Whatever the reason, he seemed to be drawn there.

Because of its location the city had been caught in the middle of the war between Tonnerling and Kalaven. Loff sent word to Shunlar that fighters were needed to defend Vensunor and that he had joined them. Receiving that news helped Shunlar make up her mind. She decided to follow her half-brother and enlist in the protection of Vensunor.

Four months had passed since Shunlar had given birth. She quickly found out that motherhood was something she was very ill-suited for. Thankfully, her mother Marleah agreed to raise the boy until Shunlar returned from fighting the war. The child had yet to be named, and Shunlar stubbornly refused to give him one. She had decided he would choose his own name when the time came, as she and Ranth had done.

One month later, Shunlar had found Loff and they had both enlisted with a band of warriors from Vensunor, made up mostly of mercenaries, some of whom were her old acquaintances. Her back and bottom once again had adapted to spending long hours in the saddle on patrol. The ground no longer seemed as hard as it had the first few weeks, accustomed as she was to sleeping on a real bed, but she was beginning to tire of sleeping in the chill night air. Several days they had woken to snow. Winter had arrived.

Vensunor had no army to speak of. The wealthy merchants who could afford to hired private guards. A small garrison paid for by city taxes was also maintained. Thus mercenaries were hired to watch over the outlying farmlands that surrounded the city. The pay was generous, which enticed many a bored young potential farmer to turn in his or her scythe for a staff or a bow or whichever weapon he or she wielded with most skill.

So far there had been one or two small skirmishes near Vensunor, but nothing that overtly threatened the population. Shunlar had found Loff within the first week of coming to the camp and they became campmates. Loff made a perfect companion for Shunlar's taciturn mood. He was still recovering from the loss of Ranla; only time would make him pleasant company, something that Loff was well aware of. Sharing a wineskin or two over the fire and telling stories of the battles they had fought brought them closer together than they had ever been. The bond of the warrior went deeper than the bond of the blood they shared. But it would take more than tales of heroic deeds for Loff to feel at ease around others. Most nights they shared a meal and spent the rest of the evening repairing, oiling, or polishing some part of their gear in silence around the fire.

One night a large group of riders came into the camp just after dark. Three among them were distinctly different in dress and mannerisms, and Shunlar immediately recognized them as Feralmon. It was still fairly uncommon to see someone from Kalaven, as they tended to keep to themselves and not much was known about them. All that would change, however, as the war came closer to Vensunor. And if these three traveled here now, could a larger force be close on their heels?

Shunlar and Loff had finished their supper and were hard at work oiling yet another piece of equipment when two men and a woman walked into the light cast by the fire.

"May we share your fire?" the younger of the two men asked, holding up the carcasses of several large rabbits as possible enticement. His accent was thick.

Shunlar looked first at the offering and then at Loff, who was still busy working oil into a newly mended harness. "What say you, brother?" She refused to let her curiosity show in the tone of her voice.

"I would welcome a man who can hunt and offers us fresh meat. Sit, warm yourselves," Loff offered, still engrossed in the harness on his lap. When he raised his head to watch his new companions settle in, he held his breath for several careful seconds before exhaling.

The two men dusted themselves off and coughed as they thumped and shook their cloaks, sitting down at last, wearily. The woman, however, was silent. She appeared not to have ridden as hard or as long as the men and she made no sound. The cut of their clothing and the way they moved reminded Loff of someone; he could not remember who just yet, but it would come to him, he was sure.

As the hairs on the back of Shunlar's neck rose, her eyes darted up first, closely followed by her head raising in a calculated way. Since giving birth, her familiar trap warning signal had returned, along with her ability to see the heat trace left on the air by others. She meticulously made note of the trio who were busy arranging themselves around her fire before she gave approval.

The older man was muscularly thin and wiry with dark skin and a warrior's braid heavily peppered with gray hair that was plaited desert-fashion, with beads woven into the many braids that became one. He wore a sword that looked to be well used and meticulously clean by the sheen of the polished leather of the scabbard. He had several daggers hidden in the seams of his clothing, she was sure, and she saw the slight bulge of an outline of another at the top of his left boot.

The younger man was dark also. His shoulders and chest were broad and well muscled, as were his legs. Shunlar looked him over, knowing it was definitely the woman who made her uneasy. She knew she would sleep with her dagger in hand with this woman close by. The woman moved too quietly, something which gave her away as far as Shunlar was concerned. Short in stature, her arms were scarred and the muscles corded. She kept her head covered, though Shunlar was certain she wore a braid as well.

"Warm yourselves," was all Shunlar answered as she bent over her mending and busied herself again. Without picking up her head, she glanced from the corner of her eye to scrutinize the woman, who was sitting very still, staring at her. Suddenly Shunlar felt an intense burst of mind-probe projected at her.

"But," Shunlar added just loud enough to be heard, "I would caution you not to try that again with me, or my brother. We have not exchanged names and now I find I do not wish to." She fixed a stare at the newcomer, whose face held a look of disbelief that once seen, vanished and was quickly replaced by one of innocence. "Because the hour is late, you are welcome tonight, but only tonight can the woman stay. Tomorrow she finds another fire to warm her."

The woman and the older man shifted uneasily. The younger man eyed his companions suspiciously and set such a look of malice on them that Loff put aside the harness he was mending in case a fight broke out. After several tense minutes, the younger man picked up a rabbit and began cleaning it, his stomach grumbling as he worked. It was clear they had not eaten yet. Shunlar picked up a wineskin and tossed it to him after he had the first animal spitted over the flames. The man and woman set to work cleaning the remaining rabbits as he laid back against his saddle and took a long pull of the wine.

When he raised his arm to cover his eyes, Shunlar took the opportunity to study him closer, having given him only a cursory glance at first. Now she noticed the thick mass of dark braids that were pulled back into one braid at the nape of his neck. His skin was dark, from what little she could see of his arm and face, and the muscles of his shoulders told her that he had a strong sword arm. Though he was reclining and she had never stood next to him, she could tell he was taller than her by at least a head. But his profile in the firelight unnerved her. He reminded her of Ranth as no one else had in all this time. When he uncovered his eyes to take another pull from the wineskin, he saw how she watched him and he quickly sat up to check on his roasting rabbit.

Shunlar returned to her work. Later that night when she rolled herself up in her blankets to sleep, she couldn't tell if the eyes that she felt staring at her over the dying embers of the fire were his or the woman's. In the morning just the younger man remained. The woman and the older man—possibly her partner—had left, their impressions in the ground the only evidence that they had been there at all.

The lone Feralmon became their constant companion. He proved to be an excellent hunter, and Loff took an instant liking to him. The first nights were spent passing the wineskin back and forth, telling hunting stories. He seemed to be naturally comfortable in Loff's presence.

Shunlar remained wary and held back joining in on their conversations. Always, however, she was aware of his eyes on her. It was to stay this way for weeks. Several times they fought bands of men who marched from Tonnerling toward Kalaven, looking to ravage a farm for easy food as they marched. The Feralmon proved to be an excellent man to have on one's side in a fight. As she had suspected, he was better than most with his sword.

The third night he finally told them his name, only after Loff had offered his and asked him where he was from. "I am Avek sul Zara and I come from the Desert of Kalaven. My people were nomads for hundreds of years but, as was foretold by the high priestess, a young couple found a cave that contained a spring in the desert. Upon that site was built a temple and then a city was built around it. That was twenty-some years ago and we have been city dwellers there ever since.

"The woman of that couple, Zeraya sul Karnavt, became our queen. She and my foster mother, Zara sul Karnavt, are sisters, though I can claim no blood relation."

"And the man of this couple, what is his name?" asked Loff suddenly very curious.

"Benyar sul Jemapree."

"Benyar you say? But, we know him and his son, Ranth, though we have not seen them or heard from them for more than a year. What news do you have of them?" Loff asked suddenly, more animated than he had been in months.

"Benyar and Zeraya have been reunited and she is recovering from the wounds she suffered so many years ago. Ranth, as you must know is their heir and he has probably married by now. I left just after the news of their betrothal." This last sentence he mumbled to himself, suddenly becoming very quiet.

Hearing this information, a stricken look crossed Shunlar's face after which she rose stiffly and left the campsite. Loff and Avek watched her leave, saying nothing. Avek could sense something was wrong, but he was too polite to ask. After several minutes, Loff excused himself and went to find her.

"Shunlar," Loff called out quietly to her in the darkness. Hearing a scraping noise he turned and could just make out her silhouette leaning against a tree. "I know hearing this about Ranth is upsetting." Loff tried to console her with his words and softly placed his hand on her shoulder.

She shrugged his hand away saying, "Promise me you will not say a word to Avek of my involvement with Ranth or the child. I want no one to know." Her voice was strangely flat and hard.

"Aye. He will learn nothing from me."

After several minutes of awkward silence, Shunlar pushed herself from the tree and walked away. Loff returned to their camp to continue his conversation with Avek.

The next weeks were hard for Shunlar. She tried to avoid Avek as best she could, but he seemed to always be underfoot and watching her. At first it made her uncomfortable, but then something in her changed. She secretly enjoyed the attention and began to relax around Avek. One day she found what appeared to be a gift of several strips of finely tanned leather laying across her bedroll; they would come in handy for repairing harness or saddle. When she thanked Loff, he looked at her blankly and denied knowing anything about them. Avek seemed to become very interested in his boots.

Two days later there appeared a pendant of finely carved bone in the shape of a cat's head, attached to a thin leather thong. Loff, again, denied presenting her with such a gift. Shunlar knew then that it was Avek. Holding the pendant up

so he could see it, she put it on and turned to show Avek that
she accepted his gift. When she thanked him he blushed, nodded his head and walked away without speaking to her. His
behavior was odd and left her standing with her mouth open
and a confused look on her face. Had she done something
wrong, she wondered?

"This is ridiculous," she mumbled to herself. "Avek," she
called after him. When he stopped and turned she caught up
to him. "Mind if I walk with you?"

"No," he blushed. Looking at his boots again, they started
walking through the camp.

"Tell me, have I done something to offend you? Was I not
supposed to put this token around my neck?"

"Shunlar," he cleared his throat. "Are you aware that in
my culture single women and men are not permitted to speak
to one another, unless a relative of one of the parties is present?" With Loff in the camp, speaking to Shunlar was not a
breach of etiquette. Though Avek was no longer under the
scrutiny of his culture, old habits died hard.

"I know nothing about your people. Tell me more, for
though I believe it to be a very strange custom, I am interested
if it will explain your strange behavior."

Taking a deep breath, Avek began. "You see, I broke that
rule." Avek looked at Shunlar rather sheepishly.

Several awkward silent minutes went by before he continued. "I had fallen in love with a young woman and I was
desperate to tell her. Finding out that she was to become
Ranth's wife made me foolish. I approached her and declared
my undying love to her. I was caught in the act by Honia,
the High Priestess. There being nothing I could say to defend
myself, I threw myself on her mercy. Honia took pity on me,
for what young man wouldn't desire her protégée, Septia?"
This last statement came out very sarcastically.

Shunlar cast him a sideways glance, first to see if he had
seen her flinch at the mention of Ranth's name—he hadn't—
and second to see if she could tell the reason for his sar-
casm—she couldn't, unless she asked. She decided against it
as he continued speaking.

"Nevertheless, having broken one of the most stringent of
our laws I was punished. I am an outcast, having been cast

out for the period of two years, after which I may return and resume my place within Feralmon society. I had not disclosed being banished to Loff or you, as it embarrasses me greatly."

What Avek did not tell Shunlar however, was that while he was waiting for his sentence to be delivered, one of his oath-brothers, Emun sul Setta, visited him with the most startling tale to tell. Emun, it seemed, had been drinking with a group of friends, all of them commiserating over Avek's having been found with Septia. He was quite drunk and was stumbling home very late in the evening. It was a night when sound traveled far and he overheard two people arguing. Snickering to himself, Emun decided to eavesdrop and found himself a hiding place behind a pillar.

As the argument continued the woman kept trying her best to quiet the man, to no avail. Though fully in his cups, Emun recognized Korab's voice, and the next thing he knew Septia ran past his hiding place into the night. Korab followed her; it was not until after their footsteps had faded that Emun had the courage to leave his hiding place and hurry home. He was afraid of what might happen to him if Korab knew he had seen him with Septia.

Avek's sentence of banishment for two years delivered, he left the Feralmon, humiliated and heartbroken, suspecting that Honia had exiled him in order to protect Septia, but nothing could have been further from the truth. And there was no one among his peers who was willing to question Korab about his involvement with Septia.

"In a small town near the desert I met Deeka and Orem. Being a warrior, I naturally want to protect my people so when they told me about the impending war, I came with them to hire on in Vensunor to fight the Tonnerlingans as they march on their way to Kalaven."

"But that still doesn't answer my question. What did I do to make you just get up and leave?"

"You accepted my gifts. Giving you the gifts and remaining anonymous as I had were one thing. To see you accepting the cat, which in turn I hoped would mean that you would accept my affection, reminded me of all that I have lost since leaving home."

"Oh," Shunlar answered quietly. But she did not return the pendant.

Later that afternoon Shunlar and Avek tried to convince Loff to go into Vensunor with them and a group of their friends for a night of tavern crawling. They'd been living and fighting hard for weeks without a break, and they desperately needed some diversion. But Loff declined on the pretense of being too tired. He had seen the way Avek watched Shunlar when she was occupied with something else. He had also seen how this mysterious half-sister of his watched Avek, all the while pretending not to. Since nothing short of a raging storm could convince Loff to leave his bedroll once he made up his mind, Shunlar and Avek finally gave up and rode away with several others of their band who were looking for a night of drinking or pleasure or both.

They began the evening by consuming a large meal at the first inn they came to. It proved to be a good choice. The food was excellent: crispy-skinned fowl with plenty of garlic and pepper, a thick stew of vegetables and goat that had been simmered with a generous portion of wine and herbs, and crusty loaves of brown bread to soak up the gravy. The wine was of a superior quality and soon the men and women that had become Shunlar's close companions these last months were happily singing along with the minstrel who played for them, so long as they kept pouring and throwing coins his way.

The next inn the group moved on to was not so friendly. Many of the locals gathered there preferred their own company. After only one pitcher of watered down wine the happy group left, glad to be quit of the sour company as well.

Having spent no time in Vensunor for over a year, Shunlar was surprised when they turned a corner and came upon the Dragon's Breath Inn. She remembered the place well and hoped Bente was still the proprietoress. As the aroma of food invaded her nostrils, Shunlar realized she was hungry again. All the drinking had whetted her appetite. Since giving birth, she had returned to her human form. No trace of smoke exuded from her nostrils nor were there scales to be seen anywhere on her body, but her appetite had not returned to that of a woman of small stature.

"Come on," she called out to her companions happily. "I know this place and if the innkeeper is the same, we shall dine and drink well." Shunlar's mood dropped several notches as they approached the Dragon's Breath Inn, however, for hovering on the air were the unwelcome heat traces of the two who had been Avek's traveling companions from Kalaven.

Only Avek seemed pleased to see them; he took a seat with them near the back of the room talking in quiet tones with the man and woman he had ridden in with mere weeks ago. To find them in this tavern was somewhat of a surprise. They had been gone from the camp and most people had assumed they had returned to Kalaven or moved on.

Shunlar had learned that the woman was called Deeka sul Bareth, and the man went only by the name Orem. Though Avek partook heartily of their wine as he talked to them, neither Deeka nor Orem drank, something that Shunlar did not miss. Her neck hairs still rose whenever she came within close proximity to Deeka, so she never let her guard down for a moment when the woman was around. She moved too well not to be taken seriously.

Ravenous, Shunlar ordered more food. Here she knew she would find the cactus alcohol she and her father Alglooth and foster-mother Cloonth were so fond of. She ordered two bottles for her friends and sat down to pour herself a goblet. Closing her eyes she let the first sip of the clear greenish-gold liquid send a film of liquid fire down her throat. When Shunlar opened them Avek was sitting next to her on the bench, quietly sipping his drink.

"This is good, but the most refined *taloz* is not exported for trade by my people. And, sadly, I have only a small amount with me. Perhaps you would like a taste of it?" his deep, accented voice offered. His smile was a bit crooked, something that appealed to her. His teeth were straight and white, in contrast to the darkness of his skin and the blackness of his eyes. Close up he looked nothing like Ranth; only his profile reminded her of the man who was the father of her child.

"I *would* like to try it, Avek. Perhaps you will share a cup with me some time." Her tone was guarded and she tried not to look at him. Backlit as he was by the tavern's fire, his resemblance to Ranth put a lump in her throat.

"Perhaps sometime is right now." He reached under his belt and brought out a flask that looked to be hand-beaten silver, shaped to lay against one's hip. Pulling out the stopper, he handed the flask to her. She put it to her lips and tilted her head back, taking a larger mouthful than she intended to. The faint taste of a smoky-spice was pronounced, but there was no bite to the liquor. No fire went down her throat, just a pleasant warmth that trickled all the way to her stomach, bringing a smile to her lips.

"The evening gets better," her throaty voice proclaimed. Shunlar had been drinking the better part of the night. Avek smiled, saluted her with the flask, took another swallow, and handed it back to her. Another swallow and Shunlar realized a most delicious hum was moving through her limbs. Avek's presence was drawing her closer and she flashed him a smile not quite knowing why.

On impulse Avek asked, "Would you walk with me? The room feels too close." She nodded, rose, and followed him outside. She was tipsy and smiled to herself as she tried very hard not to weave as she walked.

It was the time of night when no breezes stirred, yet she was aware of the scent of the man next to her. He smelled of sweat that was mingled with the scent of horse and leather. They pulled their cloaks closer against the chill of the night air and for a time they walked in silence, side by side, until they came to a square with a large fountain in the middle. During the day, this square teemed with people shopping and gossiping and washing laundry. At this hour, all was still and quiet. Sidling closer to her, Avek put his arm around Shunlar's shoulder. She drew a quick breath, noticing that in the last several seconds her pulse had increased and she was aware of how it seemed to thunder loudly in her ears.

Shunlar welcomed his embrace and returned it. Putting her arms around his waist, she had to stand on her toes to reach his mouth. Kissing tentatively at first, they parted once to search each other's eyes. A second kiss began to melt any reluctance Shunlar might have had. This man—who was not Ranth, yet reminded her so much of him—was here, standing before her as Ranth was not. She shuddered as a wave of deep passion washed over her. Avek was offering her comfort for the night of the kind she had not been interested in from any man since she had met Ranth.

She stepped back from him and took his hand. Hand in hand they retraced their steps back to the Dragon's Breath Inn. Shunlar approached Bente, gave her several coins and whispered to her discreetly. The blonde woman simply nodded, handed Shunlar a lit candle, and Avek followed her up the stairs to a room. Shunlar was aware that two pair of eyes watched them from the back of the tavern but she ignored them.

Once they were inside the room, Avek barred the door. Shunlar set the single candle in the holder on the table next to the bed and blew it out. In the dark he came to her side and encircled her in his arms. Touching her put him in direct contact with her mind and she began to show him just how much she longed for his touch. He responded to her, slowly at first, then more confidently. Knowing that her thoughts were showing him exactly what to do, she opened up her mind to him.

Avek gasped as she seemed to melt into and blend with his thoughts, but he didn't stop her. She hesitated and stopped when he gasped again, and she could sense his fear at what was happening. The Feralmon were very used to mind-touching each other, having been trained since birth. Avek had never expected Shunlar to have such strength in her touch.

She parted her lips to speak but he put one finger up to them and when she waited silently for him, he kissed her slowly, his fingers trailing down the sides of her face. She reached down with her awareness into his hands, from inside of him, and guided his fingers. Aware of what she was doing, Avek trembled but he didn't try to stop her.

He moved slowly, the way her desire showed him to, building, then pausing, then building again. The merest thought of fear crept into her for only a second and Avek was there absorbing the fear, replacing it with passion so deep she could scarcely breathe.

He listened to every nuance of her wishes, and when she

thought she had shown him all he could do to satisfy her, he began. A minute part of his mind opened at first, then incrementally larger sections opened, until he was sharing his physical feelings with her. Every caress of her hand, every touch of her lips, every turn of her hips against his was transferred to her body. She could feel him from the inside out. They seemed to exchange bodies. A slow pulse that increased with each second began moving within them, bubbling up from inside, as bursts of color exploded behind their closed eyelids.

Later, when they had quieted, she turned her head to look at the man beside her. Feeling her move, he propped himself onto one elbow and turned his body toward hers, tracing the outline of her face with one finger. Shunlar reached for his hand and their fingers and bodies entwined, they slept.

In the morning she awoke before him. Avek's profile in the dawn light brought a reminder of Ranth and a lump to her throat. She tried to rise without waking him but he was much too light a sleeper not to notice the movement. He reached for her and only brushed her back with his fingertips as she stepped away from the bed.

"I must go back to the camp. Alone," was all she said, her voice thick with emotion, her back to him. Avek nodded his acceptance as he laid back down, covering his eyes with his arm, listening to the sounds she made as she washed and dressed. When he heard the door open and close, he got up and did the same, then went down to the tavern, the smell of fresh bread making his stomach growl.

Avek sat at a corner table waiting for Bente's large, aproned form to amble over to him.

"How do griddlecakes with honey and cinnamon sound?"

"Like food from the goddess," he smiled at her. "Is there sausage too?" he asked hopefully.

"If yew like, young man," was Bente's reply over her shoulder as she walked away. "But only tea is served with breakfast in this establishment," she finished.

"Fine, bring pots of it, if you please." Avek smiled as he thought of Shunlar. *I am beginning to enjoy this city of Vensunor more each day.*

Once he had finished he went after his horse, which had

been boarded at the first tavern they had stopped at the previous night. Mounts that belonged to several of their companions were still stabled there, and Avek tried to imagine which of them had coupled and which of them had drunk too much to make it back to the camp.

Shunlar's horse was gone, as he expected it would be. When he did not find her in the camp with Loff eating breakfast, he still did not think anything was amiss. Later, however, as darkness fell, he began to feel uneasy and suspicious. It was not like Shunlar to be gone an entire day. Loff agreed and they decided to look for her.

TWENTY-EIGHT

THOUGH THEY HID IT WELL, DEEKA AND OREM were elated when Avek and Shunlar walked into the inn. Little of the two Feralmon had been seen around the camp. In the few skirmishes they fought in, they fought well, but soon they disappeared from the camp altogether. Avek had been surprised to find Deeka and Orem at the Dragon's Breath Inn. He sat and talked to them for a short time, then joined Shunlar and the others, quickly forgetting his old companions.

They, however, did not forget him or Shunlar. Deeka watched vigilantly from the shadows as they sat beside one another. She could sense something in Shunlar, something like reluctance or sadness. It sparked her curiosity and she watched Shunlar closely as she drank the *taloz* from Avek's flask. Deeka waited patiently for Shunlar to take another drink and when she touched her lips to the flask, Deeka touched Shunlar with a mind probe that filled her with a warming sensation, making it feel like the effects of the alcohol. In that moment Deeka was able to see Ranth in Shunlar's mind and she knew without a doubt who Shunlar was. She was the prey, the woman Orem had contracted to find and kill. But where was the child?

In his foolishness, Orem had agreed to share the gold with Deeka, if she helped him. He couldn't remember how he had come to make a bargain with her, but no matter, Deeka had become more than a business partner.

"It *is* her," Deeka hissed at Orem.

He blinked and swallowed hard, eyes going wide. "That one? But I thought the woman we sought came from a wealthy family; a soft woman. One such as her will be harder to kill."

As Shunlar and Avek rose to walk outside, Deeka answered, "Harder, I agree, but all the more enjoyable."

Deeka's talent lay in placing a touch upon someone's mind that enabled her to read their thoughts in seconds. With most of her victims it was enough. Upon touching the person she would implant sensuous desire in them so strongly it confused them long enough for her to read their thoughts and not realize what happened. That was how she managed to strike up this strange partnership with Orem. Orem did not suspect that when they had killed Shunlar and her child, Deeka would kill him.

The first night in the camp Deeka had tried to touch Shunlar in her special way. Unfortunately Shunlar had felt the attempt and stopped her, making it impossible for Deeka to try again. Tonight she had succeeded because Shunlar had been drinking for hours with Avek. Deeka had also succeeded in planting strong desire in both of them before they left the tavern.

When Shunlar and Avek returned to the inn and climbed the stairs together, Deeka knew her trap was indeed in motion. Her smile unnerved Orem as he watched her observing the young couple on their way to their room for the night.

"Let us also find our way to bed. We need to be fresh in the morning when our young prey leaves here." Deeka rose and Orem followed her, the corners of his mouth twitching in an odd manner. Since traveling with her, he looked forward to her strange moods, though he never entirely trusted her. Sharing her bed had been one of the unexpected pleasures of their uncomfortable partnership, and he had never been a man to turn away from pleasure.

Hours later Orem woke in the tangle of bedclothes to Deeka's insistent shaking of his shoulder. It was still dark and he yawned hard and stretched. His thighs ached, as did his arms, but he dressed as fast as he could and together they left the room. Walking down the hall behind Deeka's small form, he tried as best he could to mimic her silent way of moving.

Once outside, they set off at a brisk trot to retrieve their
horses and Shunlar's as well. Avek had told them easily
enough where their horses had been stabled for the night.
Deeka had merely asked where the cheapest stable might be
found, an innocent enough question. They hid the horses in
an alleyway nearby and then carefully chose a hiding place
for themselves in which to wait for Shunlar. About forty-five
minutes later, Shunlar left the Dragon's Breath Inn, heading
for the stable and her horse.

Shunlar was in turmoil this morning and gave no thought
to her safety. The night she had just spent with Avek had
confused her beyond reason. If she was still in love with
Ranth—and she had in fact been determined not to take another lover until she solved the mystery of why Ranth had
never replied to any of her letters—why had she just spent
the night in another's arms? And why was she so damned
emotional? Her head spun with questions and self-doubt. She
began crying as she walked to the stable on the other side of
Vensunor. In her confusion, she forgot that tears would im-
pede her ability to see another's heat trace in the air.

Her neck hairs rose as she passed an alleyway and she
peered into it, blinking hard, wiping her eyes with the back
of her hand, desperately trying to focus the heat trace pattern.
Blinded by tears, she never saw who it was that jumped her.
One assailant put a sack over her head. As the other one hit
her head with a loud thwack, her knees buckled.

Before she hit the ground, Orem scooped her up and
roughly threw her over the saddle of her horse, belly down.
He quickly threw a blanket over her, to hide her identity
should anyone take notice of them, although in these times
of war a body on a horse was not an unusual sight. He looped
a rope over her body as one did to secure a corpse and tied
it around her. Likely if they were seen people would believe
it to be another fallen warrior that the healers could not save.

When Shunlar awoke her head ached, and her arms were
bound so tightly behind her back that her fingers could touch
her elbows. She was cold, and realized her boots were gone
and the laces of her clothing were undone. Her chest and belly
were exposed, as if someone had examined her body. Her

mouth had the most horrible taste, and her tongue felt swollen and sticky. The dusty cloth bag covering her head made her sneeze and cough. She called out loudly several times until a fit of coughing silenced her, but no one responded to her. She lay on the floor straining to hear something, anything.

She stiffened as she inhaled, suddenly realizing that the cloth tied over her head had been dusted with whiteflower root. Soon, she knew, she would be unable to stay awake or control her bodily functions. The insidious thing about white-flower root was that although it made you helpless, it did not relieve pain. Knowing she must maintain control of her mind, Shunlar tried to stay awake as the drug-induced sleepiness began to pull her down.

What seemed like hours later, Shunlar heard the door open and felt her neck hairs rise and tingle. She sat up as best she could, without the use of her arms. Straining to recognize the footsteps of the person who approached her, another blow to the head knocked her over. Just as she began to lose consciousness, she felt someone trying to pry into her thoughts. She slammed down the barriers to her mind and was rewarded with a hard kick to the ribs as darkness pulled her down.

When Shunlar awoke the next time, she couldn't tell which hurt worse, her head or her ribs. Her left temple throbbed so hard she was nauseous. Her arms were numb from her shoulders to her fingertips from being bound so tightly. Very slowly she opened her eyes, hoping, praying, that the sack had been removed. It hadn't been. She swore under her breath. Her trap warning mechanism, her neck hairs, were standing firmly on end. Someone was there, but who it was, or where in the room the person was, she couldn't tell.

Just when Shunlar was about to move, the same quiet footsteps she had heard before, when her ribs had been kicked so soundly, approached her from the side. She braced herself and held her breath as she waited for the blow that never fell. A soft chuckle came from near her head and when she jumped at the sound of the voice, she was rewarded with another kick, this time to the stomach. It took the wind out of her; as she gasped for breath, the dusty bag sent her into another coughing fit. The muscles of her stomach now ached as much as her ribs and her head. When she finally could draw a breath without gagging, her tongue became numb, and sticky saliva drooled from her mouth.

Her ears began to buzz, further muffling any sound. She thought she heard footsteps walking away from beside her and then a door closing. When Shunlar sat up she grunted from the effort and the pain. She started to shiver from panic, exhaustion, and shock. It took a lot of effort to control her trembling. Somehow she finally managed to quiet herself down, only to begin crying. *Where am I? Who has captured me and why do they want me? Do they mean to kill me?* The questions tumbled around in her mind.

Suddenly she knew she was not as alone in the room as she first thought. A sound made her instinctively fall over onto her side, as she heard a metallic thud of something hit the wall where she had been sitting. She pushed herself up into a sitting position again, sliding against the wall for support, the cold, damp, wooden walls leaving splinters in her elbows as she fought to regain her balance. Her head was spinning and her breath came hard. She ducked again and a small knife thudded—very firmly impaled in the place where her head had just been.

Whoever played this cruel game meant to keep her confused and off-balance. In this state it was impossible for Shunlar to concentrate on anything but surviving. If she were left alone long enough and able to focus, Shunlar could bring back the fire breath and the wings that had grown when she was pregnant, and fight back. As it was, her captors—who had now become her torturers—were keeping her drugged or unconscious. If her strength continued to be depleted she would never be able to retaliate.

But she would die trying, and with that vow on her lips, Shunlar again succumbed to the effects of the whiteflower root, falling into a deep, uneasy sleep. During the hours that passed a voice whispered incessantly in her ear, "Where is the child?"

Every time the question was the same. Shunlar buried thoughts of her son, driving the whispering voice away with visions of herself brandishing her sword. Although Shunlar never knew how much time had passed, she knew it was hours. Whoever questioned her thought they would wear her down, and it very nearly worked.

A woman's voice was the next sound she remembered. Someone whispered, "Don't pretend you don't know what I am asking you. I can tell from checking your body that you have recently had a child."

Her eyes popped open and Shunlar discovered she was still a captive and still could not see. Though her thoughts were muddled, these last words from the woman had made her alert enough to remember that she had been drugged. Her arms and hands were numb, her head hurt, and she realized she was drooling uncontrollably. Another blow from an unseen assailant knocked the wind from her and she lost consciousness yet again.

Waking to pain, Shunlar was vaguely aware of a voice prying into her awareness. It asked, in a kind, nearly gentle way, about her baby. *Where is he?* the voice soothingly crooned. *Just tell me and I will set you free. Show me where you have hidden him.*

None of this made sense. *Why imprison me and torture me? And how does she know I have a son?* Trying to clear her head of the effects of the whiteflower root, concentrating harder, some feeling of control began to return to her and she realized that she had to relieve herself, urgently. "I need a chamber pot," she mumbled, cursing under her breath. When no one responded to her, she tried to sit up, but rolling onto her arms sent such intense pain into them that it cleared her thoughts further.

"Please, untie my arms and bring me a chamber pot," she gasped.

"Or what?" a familiar voice spat. "You'll wet yourself? You've already done that, you stupid cow. Tell me where your son is and I'll consider your request."

Startled to hear someone reply to her out loud, Shunlar could only try to figure out whose voice it was she had heard through the cloth that was still over her head. Where had she heard that voice before? Slowly the anger begin to boil up inside. Her mouth remained sticky and she was still unable to see anything because of the damned rag over her head. Sitting up, she bent forward, put her head between her knees and grabbed the cloth, to pull the rag off. A hard boot in her side only made her more determined until she finally succeeded, only to see a candle wink out as soon as her head was free. Blinking her eyes, she could barely make out the shape of someone standing near the door.

"I know it's you, Deeka. Is Orem here too, or do you work alone?"

No one answered her, and for several breaths there was only silence. Then a small shrouded figure opened the door onto a dim hallway and slipped out of the room. Shunlar was positive once she saw the way the person moved that it was Deeka.

Now that her head was uncovered Shunlar wrinkled her nose when she got a whiff of her prison. The sour smell of sweat and urine, hers, tainted the room, along with another faintly metallic odor that matched the taste in her mouth. Her breeches were soiled beyond washing; obviously the white-flower root had worked. Anger fed her need, giving her strength and she tugged at the leather that bound her arms until her skin grew slick with sweat from exertion. With her arms tied behind her back, any movement proved to be both awkward and difficult. Tiring easily, she stopped to rest. When she began again, the leather bindings, which had gotten damp from her sweat, seemed to give a bit, but she wasn't sure she had the energy to continue pulling and tugging.

Wet leather would stretch, but it needed to be soaked thoroughly and there was only one way to do that in this room with no water available. *Ach, only to save my life would I think of this. At this point it doesn't matter, I already smell worse than a gods-forsaken goat. I vow, Deeka will pay for this.*

Shunlar relieved herself, on purpose this time. She slid on the floor to the puddle and lay her arms in the warm liquid, soaking the thongs and pulling at them with all the strength she could muster. Finally, her arms and hands could move a bit. However, when the blood began to pump into the veins and capillaries, after having been squeezed out for so long, she very nearly screamed from the pain.

Biting her lip to keep from crying out, Shunlar swallowed blood, choking back small cries. Twisting onto her side she felt the leather giving a little more, and Shunlar kept at the bindings until her arms were free. At first she lay on the floor and cried, her arms being no use to help her sit up. Her shoulders burned as circulation returned to the strained joints. Every minute movement brought another sharp stab of pain. When she was able to sit up, the effort made her dizzy. There was no light to see what damage had been done to her arms. Her hands lay limply in her lap, throbbing. Before long the pain became duller and she fell into an exhausted sleep.

The sound of a scuffle on the other side of the door woke her with such a jolt that she banged her head against the wall. Every bone in her body ached and when she tried to stand, the pain in her side made her suspect she had more than bruised ribs. Once on her feet she took a breath that was too deep and the pain in her side nearly brought her to her knees. More loud noises on the other side of the door, this time that of swords meeting, got her hopes up as she slowly crossed the room.

Just as she reached the door someone screamed and she heard what could only be the sound of a body slamming against it. Scuffling sounds of a body being dragged away could be heard and then the door opened, the light blinding her. From the doorway the silhouette of a man with a weapon in his hand was coming toward her and she went into a defensive crouch. Instinctively she fumbled for one of her hidden daggers, only to find it gone. The man took another step and she stumbled back.

"Shunlar," he called. It was Avek, and Loff was right behind him. Both men rushed to grab her as her knees buckled. All she remembered was the smell of fresh air as they half-carried, half-dragged her from the room. On the other side of the door lay two still bodies, but they got her out so fast she never got a chance to see who they were.

The excited voices of people she knew—fellow mercenaries who had helped Avek and Loff rescue her—as well as her pride made her struggle free to stand on her own. She stumbled into the alleyway, pressing her hand against her ribs.

"Did I see right? Were there two corpses?"

"Aye, there were two of them. They can't bother anyone now," Loff answered.

"Can you ride?" asked Avek in a worried voice.

"Riding won't be the problem. It's standing I'm having trouble with," she answered sarcastically.

"Aye, perhaps it would be better if I sat you on my horse with me?" he offered.

Shunlar grinned menacingly. "Bring me my horse. Take me somewhere where I can get a bath and new clothes. And take care not to ride downwind of me when we leave. Any who does will regret it." She weaved where she stood, on the verge of collapse from her ordeal.

Several of their companions shook their heads in agreement, avoiding her gaze as she shakily accepted help mounting up. They rode out of Vensunor, taking her to the safety of their camp where she collected her belongings and immediately left again with Avek and Loff. At the Thrale River, she dismounted and began to strip, though very slowly.

"What are you doing? There's snow on the ground. At least wait until we have a fire going so you don't turn completely blue," Avek advised as he inspected the bruises that covered most of her.

"I'd say you'd better hurry with that fire," was her reply. Throwing her clothes into the current she plunged into the icy water with a scream.

Loff had a fire started and Avek was busy lashing a blanket between two poles for a wind-break as she stumbled from the water. Teeth chattering, she quickly pulled on clean, dry clothes. In the daylight she could see the bruises that covered her from her elbows to her fingertips.

"The clothes were ruined and my boots and weapons are gone," she explained as she dried herself.

"Well, not exactly gone," Avek said slowly. He held up her boots and shook them.

She could hear the jingle of metal; the sound of the three daggers she carried hidden in the seams of her shirts. Slowly a wry smile turned up one side of her mouth.

"If I were not so injured I would throw my arms around your neck and kiss you."

"That would be very welcome, but I'm afraid it would only be misplaced gratefulness. It was Loff who found your boots and daggers," Avek grinned.

"Is that so? And who was it that found me?"

"I can't take all the credit, although I'd like to," answered Loff with a laugh. "I may have rescued your boots, but Avek found you."

Shunlar nodded thanks to them and reached for her boots, something she wished wholeheartedly she hadn't done. Her knees did buckle then, and Avek was at her side to help her. This time she didn't push him away as he helped her lie on a blanket beside the fire.

"It's my ribs. Deeka got in several good kicks and probably broke one or two. I may be hard-headed, but my ribs seem to be soft."

"Hold still so I can examine them." Avek put his hand under her tunic and gently prodded. "Not too bad. Several seem to be cracked though. Take off the tunic and I'll bind them for you."

Shunlar looked at Loff. He cleared his throat and said, "I'll just go back to camp while you take care of this. Think you can manage alone?" Avek smiled and nodded.

But before he could go, Shunlar reached for his hand. *Thank you,* her voice whispered directly in his mind. Loff bent down and gently kissed her cheek.

"Brother, if Avek will accompany me, I have a place not far from here and I need to go away for a time. Avek will look after me, so don't worry. We should be back within two or three weeks." He nodded, clapped Avek soundly on the arm, and left him to bandaging her ribs.

"Did I hear you say it was Deeka who kicked you?" Avek asked as he wound a soft cloth tightly around Shunlar's ribs.

"Yes. She and Orem were my captors. But now that they're dead, I'll not be able to return the favor of broken ribs."

"You're mistaken, Shunlar. There were two others in the room guarding you, and it was their bodies you saw on the floor when we freed you."

"No. I tell you it was Deeka. I recognized her voice and I know that she and Orem are never too far apart. They're like a pair of snakes, slithering in and out from under rocks." Shunlar found she was breathing very fast and had started sweating. She felt panicky and couldn't seem to figure out why.

"Shunlar, why would Deeka and Orem want to capture and torture you? I know to you they seem like strange people, but aside from me, you have only met one other person from Kalaven, and he spent most of his life traveling in disguise, living within other cultures. When first I met Benyar, I was surprised at how different he seemed to me. There was a sense of 'other' that I had no knowledge of. Every three or four years, when Benyar returned to Kalaven, he was again changed, but because I knew to look for the differences, I grew to accept them." Avek spoke as he worked.

Shunlar didn't have much to say as Avek bandaged her ribs. Several times she winced from the pain. Having never told Avek that she and Ranth had a child, she couldn't find the words to explain it to him now. Could Avek be right? Was it really someone else and not Deeka or Orem who had captured her? She doubted herself and found that she suddenly didn't want to think about it anymore.

When she finally spoke, it was only to say thank you. After she was warmed through, Avek broke down the camp and then helped her onto her horse. Together they rode through the trees to her small cabin in the woods. She chose not to speak as they rode, her face closed.

Entering her cabin after being gone so long, she remembered who she had spent the last night with under this roof. Avek was busy placing wood in the fireplace, so he did not see how she watched his profile in the dim light. Once he had set a spark to the wood he turned to see her wiping her cheeks with the back of her hand.

"It's cold and musty in here, but the fire should dry things out soon enough. I will tend to the horses and bring in our bags and the bedrolls. Lie back and rest," he said, gently touching her cheek. She merely nodded, watching the fire burn.

Her arms ached and there were great purple welts where they had been tightly tied behind her back—for how long, she didn't even know. Lying on her own bed, in familiar surroundings, tears came, and a feeling of such fear washed over her that she began to shake violently. She knew she was finally succumbing to shock.

Avek entered with their belongings as the tremors were washing over her. He recognized her state and dropped everything, rushing to her side with a blanket.

"I will make you some hot broth. Soon you will be warm. In the meantime, drink some of this." He thrust a wineskin toward her, but her hands were shaking so that she could not pull the plug. Avek took it back, opened the spout and pointed it at her mouth. She felt like a bird, but she shook and drank, not minding that some of the wine ran down her chin.

"Bring another blanket. Please," she asked, still shaking.

He unfurled the bedroll over her and then began to undress. "My body heat will help warm you faster than a cold blanket," he grinned.

By the light of the fire she watched as Avek pulled the shirt over his head. His chest and shoulders were marked with a strange circular pattern of scars that scattered down across his ribs. Her eyes widened as she took it in. The only time she had been this close to Avek was the one night they spent in the Dragon's Breath Inn, and she had not seen his body in the dark room. He was right though. His body heat did warm her and stop her shaking, but nothing he did could stop her tears. He held her close and stroked her hair as she sobbed. Finally, out of tears and exhausted from her ordeal as a captive, Shunlar slept.

TWENTY-NINE

THERE WERE DAYS AND THEN THERE WERE DAYS. Winter was nearly over and the moons seemed to smile on them and grant them a sunny day. Following the path that led to the natural sulfur spring, Shunlar left her clothes on the rocks and eased herself into the steaming water. Lazing in the late afternoon sun, she chewed on a blade of grass, twisting another, worrying and remembering. When the memories were too painful, she closed them off.

She had spent three weeks recuperating at her haven in the woods. The hot springs that bubbled up in the bend of the river had done much to repair the bruises and sore muscles. And Avek had done much to make her remember she was a woman. But she still could not shake the feeling that gnawed relentlessly at the back of her mind.

She knew as sure as she breathed that she was avoiding the confrontation she must have with Ranth. When she thought of him these days it was with a deep and sorrowful anger. She had changed from the young, naive woman she had been when they first met. No, she had a child now, one that she missed so much these days, it was painful to think of him. She knew he was safe and secure, being raised by her mother. He had an immeasurable amount of love being given him each day. Also, her father and stepmother were there, surely caring for him, along with six half-sisters and brothers. Knowing what she must do, Shunlar decided it was time to quit this charade and go to meet with Ranth.

First, however, she must figure out how to tell Avek about

Ranth and their son. Would Avek even agree to take her to Ranth once he knew? Avek had confided in her that he had been sent into exile for two years. If he returned in the course of that time, he could suffer serious punishment, or his time of banishment could be doubled. And, he had another year yet to go before he had fulfilled his sentence. Could she in good conscience ask him to take a risk that could cause him to suffer more?

Shunlar knew now that Avek truly loved her. She was not so sure how deep her feelings were toward him, not until she could bare her soul to him, and tell him everything about Ranth and the son they had. Today would be as good a day as any, she decided. When he returned from hunting, she decided to tell him. She only hoped he wouldn't take it too badly.

The sound of footsteps let her know that Avek had returned, probably with several large birds and rabbits. He had proved to be an excellent hunter—and more than that, a caring and tender lover. Should she risk hurting him, or worse, losing him when they had just begun this tentative but highly satisfying partnership? Perhaps he could just give her instructions on how to find Kalaven.

She watched him undress and ease himself into the water beside her.

"Avek," she began, "while you were hunting I made some decisions. I must tell you my plans and leave it up to you to decide whether you will join me or return to the camp and the fighting in Vensunor."

He suddenly took her face between both of his hands, kissed her fiercely and then let her go. "I will go with you. There is no other choice for me. You have my heart and I have given it freely. What more can I do that will convince you of my devotion?" He gave her such a determined look that it made her stop and reconsider for a moment.

There was no way to tell if Ranth would even be interested in her and their child. After all, he had married and this wife of his had probably had a child by now. It seemed all too clear to her that Avek was the man to trust if she were to ever reach Ranth in the Desert of Kalaven. But would he agree to be the one to take her there once he knew?

Taking a deep breath, she began. "One night in the camp, the night that Loff asked you to tell us of yourself and your people, you mentioned a man named Ranth sul Zeraya. I never knew how to tell you this, but Ranth and I met right before his reunion with his father, Benyar, and their return to Kalaven." Shunlar watched Avek's face turn quiet, then sad, then become an unreadable mask. He sat straighter and looked off into the distance, listening.

"Should I continue?" Shunlar asked. Avek nodded once, very slowly. With a sigh, she said, "Ranth and I have a son. But I don't know if he has ever gotten my letters in all this time, so I can't be sure if he even knows that much. He has never sent a word to me since we parted and it is over a year now."

Avek's face hadn't changed but she could feel the sadness radiating from him. "What do you want me to do with this information?" was all he said.

"I don't know yet. All I can say is, you and I have known each other longer and in different ways than Ranth and I ever did. All he and I had was a total of three weeks together. It was long enough to create a child, but apparently not long enough to make him wait for me as we promised one another. The news that he had married another did not endear him to me. It made me question myself and my pledge to him as well."

"What of this plan you mentioned? Am I part of it?" He almost sounded hopeful as he asked.

Shunlar looked deep into his eyes before she answered him. "If you were willing, could I persuade you to take me and my son to Kalaven to meet Ranth?"

"Why must you seek one who has abandoned you for another? I am here and I would gladly raise this boy as mine. Perhaps we could even have children of our own," he answered.

"You don't know what you ask, Avek. There are things about me that you should know before we go further or deeper here. I am not just this woman you see before you. I am capable of looking like something from a nightmare, not for the weak of heart," she said with honesty.

He laughed at her openly now. "You who I have taken in

my arms each night, you tell me you can become another person, something to frighten me? This is hard to believe." He laughed again.

But she stood up and climbed out of the water. "Watch then," she whispered. Closing her eyes Shunlar breathed and saw in her mind's eye the wings, the white hair, the scaled arms and legs and began to change, growing taller as his eyes grew wider.

He jumped to his feet and clambered from the water, watching in amazement as Shunlar continued to grow. Then she exhaled a stream of fire over his head with a scream that made him duck and cover his ears. He looked up at her and after checking himself for burns, laughed out loud.

"You truly are a goddess, or a demon. But with you around I would never want for the warmth of a fire." Now Shunlar laughed. She leaped toward him, put her arms around him and planted a big kiss on his lips while she picked him up and began turning around in a spiral that soon took them above the treetops.

Several minutes later, shivering from the cold, they landed and dressed. Avek picked up the game he had killed and they returned to the cabin and the fire, discussing their plans as they ate. Finished with their dinner, they checked on the horses, seeing to it that they would be safe and fed for the one day that they would be away.

Shunlar knew their flight would be a cold one, so she advised Avek to dress warmly and to secure his cloak around his body with leather thongs. One small bag over his shoulder and their cloaks tied tightly around them, Shunlar and Avek were ready.

"Don't look down," she warned as she embraced him and they were off, flying in the direction of the Valley of Great Trees. He wrapped himself around her and they soared higher and northwesterly, his heart pounding against her chest until she had to rest. Sometime after sundown they arrived in the Valley, where Marleah welcomed them heartily. "Meet my mother, Marleah. She agreed to raise my son until I came for him."

Marleah, though happy to meet Avek, naturally had many questions to ask. Unfortunately he wouldn't leave Shunlar's side long enough for her to be alone with her daughter to do so. Marleah had to be content to just accept the situation.

Gwernz and Klarissa were delighted to see Shunlar after so long. Gwernz had taken his place as spiritual leader of the Valley, finally giving Arlass a long deserved rest. The mantle of office rested gracefully upon Gwernz's shoulders. Upon greeting Shunlar and Avek, he immediately began to speak a message from the Trees.

"The Great Trees have told me that you and Ranth will see the child named at last. His naming will be cause for great celebration. I have also been told there is a man at your side who is devoted to you." With that he bowed to Avek and embraced him as he would a kinsman. Avek was deeply touched.

But the boy was happiest to see his mother. He was a good-natured child who, Marleah reported, cried rarely, if at all. Seeing his mother for the first time in months, he wouldn't let her go. He clearly knew she was his mother. She couldn't put him down even to sleep. He'd wake and whimper so she carried him around in a sling so he could nap. And he accepted Avek immediately. That night they slept with the child between them.

The next morning they went to pay their respects to Cloonth, Alglooth, and the children. Shunlar thought to prepare Avek on the way, but no words could truly do justice to describe her family. "We're going to meet my father now, and my foster-mother and their children," was all she gave in the way of explanation. Face to face, he looked from them to Shunlar and understood. Soon he had four children crawling across his lap and two fluttering around his head.

Alglooth asked Shunlar in Old Tongue "Please my whims, daughter, what do you plan now that Avek is here? I don't believe he's just a good friend, or are my perceptions off?"

"Avek has agreed to help me journey to Kalaven so that I can introduce Ranth to his son. He informed me that Ranth has married. I found that to be quite interesting and thought that he should meet his firstborn before too long."

Alglooth had a worried look. "Caution, Shunlar. Revenge is a dish best served cold. Search your soul before you do anything that would endanger you or this child. You have no way of knowing what has transpired with Ranth in all this time. Perhaps he was pressured into a marriage by his parents or by the fact that his is a family and culture that is bound by honor and many different customs. I can only ask you to remember my situation and the circumstances surrounding your birth and upbringing.'' He gave his daughter a long, meaningful stare. Finally she shook her head in the affirmative and gave him a quick hug.

''I will never let harm come to my son. I may not be made of motherly material like Cloonth or Marleah, but he is my child and I will give my life before any harm touches him.'' Hearing those words seemed to make Alglooth feel better.

''We have come to say hello and then farewell. I am anxious to begin our journey while the good weather holds out.''

Departing with everyone's good wishes and copious tears from Marleah, they flew over the valley, retracing the route they had come the day before, with the boy tucked safely between them. They stopped and spent the night at Shunlar's cottage by the river to collect their horses and pack their gear.

Happier than she remembered feeling in a long time, the prospect of seeing Ranth filled her with hope rather than anxiety. That evening as she and Avek ate their meal they discussed the travel route. Their first stop would be the mercenary camp for the latest reports on the whereabouts of the soldiers from Tonnerling. With the weather changing, it was likely the fighting would resume soon. Reinforcements would be on their way now that the spring thaw was underway and the passes would soon be open.

The next morning they rode into camp and found Loff huddled around his fire eating breakfast. As soon as he saw his nephew's tiny face peeking from beneath Shunlar's cloak, he knew they would not be staying. He chose to accompany them, leaving behind the mercenary camp.

While winter had been in full force and the snows around Vensunor kept the fighting down to an occasional skirmish, Loff had been restless. Over the last three weeks he had gone on several scouting expeditions, mapping the location of towns or oases where soldiers from Tonnerling camped for the winter, something that would prove invaluable to them.

And so the four struck out for Kalaven, Avek leading the

way, the baby cradled to Shunlar's breast, Loff bringing up the rear. Without incident, ten days later, the snows of Vensunor far behind them, they reached the small city of Obboda, the place Avek had spent most of a year when he was first banished. In Obboda, Avek and Loff would wait for Shunlar's return or a message from her. Avek, still unwelcome in Kalaven, gave Shunlar the name of his most trusted oath-brother, Emun sul Setta, if she should need to get a message to him, or required other aid. Besides, she insisted on traveling alone from there.

Thirty

A LONE HORSE AND RIDER WAS SLOWLY PICKING ITS way toward the rocky entrance to Kalaven. As Ranth studied the person who advanced from his observation point atop one of the pinnacles, a shudder of recognition passed through him. He signaled his nearest companion, who in turn sent a message to hers. Soon they were making their way down to the sandy floor of the portal, something that the rider did not miss.

The horse snorted and stamped, but the rider kept a taut grip on the reins to prevent it from bolting. With its flanks quivering, the tired animal, now wide-eyed and alert, kept its steady uphill pace.

As horse and rider neared, Ranth made his way down the slope where he had been hidden in the rocks to stand with the other sentries who guarded this entrance. He and the others wore clothing that blended well with the surrounding rock. Their faces were covered with masks to keep out the constantly blowing sand. None had weapons drawn as the rider came into their midst, yet they took note of the slender hand that gripped the pommel of a sword while the other controlled the animal.

"I come for Ranth sul Zeraya," a familiar voice echoed loudly off the surrounding cliffs.

"Who asks for him?" Ranth demanded back.

"When he sees me, he will know. I refuse to give my name to any but him," the woman answered defiantly. "He gave me this for safe passage within your city." From beneath her tunic she pulled a thick chain with a gold medallion on it up for everyone to see.

"Shunlar?" whispered Ranth in disbelief as he unfastened his mask.

For several minutes they stared at one another. Then she pushed back her hood and opened her cloak which enabled everyone to see the small face that peered out from the bundle she carried against her chest. The air became still suddenly as Ranth looked at the child. He was small and dark with a head of curly, black hair, and he looked boldly at Ranth. One small chubby hand came up and he pointed at Ranth and smiled, then hid his face within his mother's bosom, shyly.

"I have brought you your son," she answered him quietly.

AVON EOS

RISING STARS

Meet great new talents
in hardcover at a special price!

$14.00 U.S./$19.00 Can.

Hand of Prophecy
by Severna Park
0-380-97639-0

Child of the River: The First Book of Confluence
by Paul J. McAuley
0-380-97515-7

AVON EOS PRESENTS
MASTERS OF FANTASY AND ADVENTURE

THE ROYAL FOUR
by Amy Stout
79190-0/$5.99 US/$7.99 CAN

RAGE OF A DEMON KING
by Raymond E. Feist
72088-4/$6.99 US/$8.99 CAN

THE DARK SHORE: BOOK ONE OF THE DOMINIONS OF IRTH
by Adam Lee
79617-1/$5.99 US/$7.99 CAN

DRY WATER
by Eric S. Nylund
79614-7/$3.99 US/$3.99 CAN

THE ARM OF THE STONE
by Victoria Strauss
79751-8/$5.99 US/$7.99 CAN